Little G

CW00326587

Piara Strainge

Dear Craig,
Lekker you're supporting me,
I really appreciate it!
Hope you enjoy the first of
The Dalton Trilogy.
          Best wishes
              Piara
                xx

chipmunkapublishing
the mental health publisher

Published by
Chipmunkapublishing
PO Box 6872
Brentwood
Essex CM13 1ZT
United Kingdom

http://www.chipmunkapublishing.com

Chipmunkapublishing gratefully acknowledge the support of Arts Council England.

Author Biography

Piara Strainge was born in Bath on the 6th November, 1982 and educated at Warmley Church of England and at the Sir Bernard Lovell School in Oldland, Bristol. Leaving home at 17, she moved to Fleet in Hampshire where she has been living ever since. The last 11 years have been spent travelling all over the world as Piara works for an Adventure tour operator in Farnborough. Writing is her first passion, closely followed by travel. It took 10 years to plan her debut novel *Little Child* and finally, in September 2009, she sat down and wrote the story during a 6-month break.

Little Child deals with different types of abuse and touches it on all levels. On a personal level, Piara has experienced and witnessed emotional and mental abuse and it weaves itself through her family, passed on from one generation to the next. The different forms of abuse are widely acknowledged in the family and her generation is working hard to stop the cycle as they create a new generation - primarily by being aware of it. Piara accepts they won't all be successful because traits are ingrained, but at least the acknowledgement is there. Mental abuse fascinates her the most as it is so subtle.

Visit Piara's website at www.piarastrainge.com

Piara Strainge

CHAPTER 1
Coming Of Age

Two people were meeting today for the first time. It was an unusual collaboration. One was young, fresh and ambitious. The other was older, wiser, knowing. Both were interested to see what each could offer and both had only one goal in mind – to take as much from the other as they could. Their lifestyles and principles were very similar. Neither of them lived by the saying *Indifference to chance is a vanity in any game*. Instead they preferred to play by their own rules and take whatever chances they had to, to get what they desired. They were wealthy but only because they strived for the best. They had the best but only because they were dishonest. Every move carefully calculated.

It was an addiction; every morning they woke up, popped the pill of success and carried on triumphing. They did deals, shook hands, sweet talked clients and money oozed from their bank balances. Neither of them realised how powerful the other could be; that was part of the reason for meeting. There was still some mystery about who would gain more from this partnership, but the speculation was all theirs as no-one knew it was even taking place. It was a secret collusion shrouded in deceit, corruption and fraudulent deals, and would be kept that way until one of them decided it was time to make waves. The object of the game was simple - to survive. It was a dangerous game, one not many people would dare to participate in.
You had to be of a certain calibre.
Unyielding.
No remorse.
Without fear...yet for the players, it was that very thrill which drove them on. They had to play. They had to be the best. And these two were just like that.
They were ready to roll the dice and start playing.

*

Maggie Dalton, the guest of honour, glided up to the podium with grace, her long red dress moving silently over the thick carpet as each step took her closer and closer. Off the shoulder, it hugged her petite frame, yet what she lacked in height, she made up for in poise. Striking and assured, she was the most beautiful woman in the room; laced with diamonds and wearing the finest silk money could buy. Her chestnut hair was elegantly piled on top of her head showing off her long slender neck. Nobody could take their eyes off her. She was magnetic. Flawless. This was her coming of age party, but at the last minute she had honourably decided to present the event as a charity ball in memory of her late father, Richard Dalton. He had been a brilliant businessman and kind and generous in the local community. He had been her idol until his tragic death seven years ago. His reputation had been immaculate, and now his legacy was strong. People had thronged to the occasion which pleased Maggie. She didn't want people to forget what her father had done for them. Her father had seen to it that she, and them, had never wanted for anything. So, when she spoke her carefully rehearsed speech to the refined audience below her, she was not asking for their cheques or for their acceptance, she was simply asking them never to forget. She understood their loyalty was more important than their money at this stage. Money could come later once she had made her definable mark. It had taken three long years to get this far and now she was here, on the eve of a glorious new beginning. The applause rang out and echoed around the room. It made her feel lightheaded as she bathed in their adoration. And then it was over and she was drinking and laughing, celebrating and dancing with her many friends, admirers and lovers, the quickstep swirling her around the ballroom, her feet tapping out a faultless rhythm. Guests clapped and cheered as she closed her eyes and let the music take her. The beautiful, sophisticated, twenty one year old with her whole life stretching out in front of her. Gone were the abusive moments with her mother, the orphanages and the foster homes. It had only been four years before she was rescued by her father's constitution at the age of eighteen, but it had felt like forever. The struggling and the unknown had ripped her soul bare. She was finally back where she belonged, with her father.

And this was her night. She was going to enjoy every second of it.

Little Child

The shot rang out and reverberated around the room, dulling the music in its wake and silencing the buzz of chatter and laughter. Maggie's dance partner slumped forward in her arms and, for a split second, she froze, holding his weight and watching the blood seep through his tux. She felt herself being thrown to the ground as chaos erupted around her. The body thudded to the floor, the ashen face adjacent to her own, as she stared into the expressionless eyes of a dead man. One of her bodyguards had dived to cover her and now he was pulling her to her feet and dragging her out of the room. She was screaming, she knew it but she couldn't stop, and he was shouting at people to get out of their way. She had two on each arm now hustling her through the throngs of confused, frightened people. Suddenly they were outside, the cold night air filling her lungs. She started to shiver uncontrollably. A heavy overcoat was wrapped around her before she was bundled into a limousine and one of the men got in with her as it sped away.

"Miss Dalton, are you alright?"

She looked at him and was relieved when she recognised who it was. She leant back against the headrest. Pulling the coat closer around her shoulders, she closed her eyes and let the emotion rush over her.

"Johnny…that man…is he dead?" She already knew the answer.

"Yes, Miss Dalton," Johnny answered quietly, "I don't mean to scare you Miss, but somebody was trying to take a pop at you back there."

Her eyes snapped open. The thought hadn't even occurred to her. Her hand flew to her mouth as she gasped.

"I thought…I thought it was…" Faltering, she didn't actually know what she was trying to say, or what she thought.

"Don't try and talk Miss Dalton, we'll get you back safe and sound." Johnny patted her arm and for some reason she started to cry.

"Johnny…please hold me," she sobbed, reaching for him, "I feel so terribly alone."

He moved closer and put his arms around her. She held on tight.

"Just get me home Johnny, please, just get me home."

*

Maggie was startled when there was a knock on her bedroom door and her maid came rushing in.

"Miss Dalton, they're waiting for you!" she announced, coming over and giving Maggie a shake.

Maggie rolled over and blinked her eyes several times trying to wake up. She couldn't remember getting into bed last night, yet here she was. What time was it?

"Who's waiting?" she croaked, reaching for the glass of water on the bedside.

"Mrs Peters. She has your clothes laid out in the next room. She has to get you ready for a meeting with your father's people after what happened last night. You must hurry!" She began making the bed around Maggie.

"Jesus Lucia, can't you see I'm still waking up?" Then it dawned on her. "Lucia…it was real, wasn't it?"

The maid stopped fussing to look at Maggie. "Yes, 'fraid so Miss. Someone took a shot at you. Your father's people want you present to discuss the incident. There's been a big commotion outside, lots of Press. The papers are full of it. Now you must hurry. Mrs Peters has been waiting, and they in turn are waiting for you. Come on now." She was only slightly younger than Maggie, but she commanded her about as if she were older. Maggie always assumed it was because of the wrath of Mrs Peters. She was a battle-axe and Maggie, like the junior staff, was also wary of her.

"Come, let me bathe you Miss. You were in quite a state last night."

"I don't remember any of it Lucia, only the blood on that man's tux. I can't even remember who I was dancing with." Maggie shuddered, as she let Lucia wash her face.

"Mrs Peters was concerned so she gave you a sedative to help you sleep. Mister Johnny stayed outside your balcony the whole night. They want you to have round the clock protection from now on."

"They they they…who's *they* Lucia?" Maggie was intrigued.

"Why, Mister Anderson and Mister Coombes of course!"

Maggie rolled her eyes. Thomas and Alex were impossible.

"Mister Hamilton doesn't think it's necessary and they've been arguing this morning. That's the latest gossip from Cook."

Little Child

"Well, at least I know one person is on my side," Maggie remarked.

Lucia's hand flew to her mouth. "Oh, I'm sorry Miss, I got carried away just then!" she exclaimed.

Maggie smiled to reassure her. "Don't worry Lucia, everything you tell me I keep in the strictest confidence. You know that."

Lucia smiled back and without another word carried on with her duties.

*

"Come along Margaret!" Mrs Peters ushered Maggie into the room and sat her down at the dressing table. "I've been waiting a long time for you. Have you and Lucia been gossiping again?"

Maggie did as she was told, letting Mrs Peters fuss over her. It was sad, but she was the nearest thing she had to a mother.

"I'm sorry about what happened last night Carmen. I feel like I've let everybody down."

Mrs Peters patted her arm. "Dear dear, it was a terrible thing."

"Are all the guests accounted for? Have they been told?" Maggie knew it was safe to ask Mrs Peters as she was pretty sure Thomas or Alex would already have briefed her housekeeper.

"Yes, your father's people took care of that and nobody else was hurt. We've organised flowers for the Lewis family. It was young Bradley you were dancing with."

Maggie felt some pieces of the jigsaw fitting into place. Up until that point, she couldn't remember whom she'd been dancing with. "I'm sorry," she murmured. The dead face came into her mind again, and she shivered.

"Are you alright Margaret?" They stared at each other in the mirror. Maggie sighed and then nodded her head slowly, avoiding her housekeeper's eyes. She couldn't speak, suddenly her heart felt very heavy indeed.

They were silent for a while whilst Mrs Peters finished Maggie's make up and hair and helped her into her business suit.

"You must attend the funeral of course, once it's settled, and the press conference later today."

"I do know my duties Carmen. Must I wear this?" Maggie protested, but one look from Mrs Peters and she knew she must. Then, "Was that shot really meant for me Carmen? Please tell me the truth. You're the nearest thing I've got to a...well a...you know...someone I can trust. Please tell me."

Mrs Peters looked at the beautiful girl standing in front of her and her heart went out to her. She had so much weight on her young shoulders; it was unimaginable that she could take anymore.

"Margaret...Maggie...sit down here." She patted the chair and waited for Maggie to finish with her blouse, before carrying on, "We didn't know the Dalton business had any enemies up until yesterday. This has come completely out of the blue. I'm not going to pretend we're not worried...because we are. But you have a good team around you here and they'll find who's responsible, I'm sure of it."

"But why me Carmen?"

Mrs Peters shook her head. "Maggie, do you really not know the answer to that question? Look at you! You've come of age and now own your father's business empire. You are your father. We all work for you!"

"Such a huge responsibility Carmen. What if I can't do it?" For the first time, Mrs Peters heard an edge to her voice. She had never seen Maggie Dalton so unnerved as she was now. Even when they'd tracked her down and rescued her from that terrible foster home, she'd always had defiance about her and a strong, unstoppable spirit. Her housekeeper snapped into action. There was no room for this kind of self-pitying discussion. "You have to be strong," she said simply, "You are the boss Margaret and we will all guide you as best we can. Do you understand? Now where is that list of today's engagements? We must run through it before your first meeting."

Maggie watched on, understanding perfectly. She had to toughen up.

*

Little Child

The argument was going round and round in circles and Maggie was getting bored. She was sitting at a long table in her father's office with her father's people listening to them debating her safety and discussing the press conference. She was waiting for the right moment to interrupt. Sooner or later they would realise she was there, that she was actually their boss, and it would be up to her to decide on the best course of action for herself.

"I don't want Miss Dalton to leave here for anything without Johnny." Thomas was adamant. Alex nodded in agreement. She knew perhaps half of the men here reasonably well, mostly the younger ones, and the other half were all new to her. They were all Directors of her father's business but with varying degrees of power. She caught Sean Hamilton's eye and he winked at her. She was bemused by his flirtatious behaviour.

"Why don't we let the lady decide what she would like for herself? After all, she is the new boss around here." Sean spoke loudly as he leaned back in his chair, completely at ease, and folded his arms across his chest waiting for Maggie to speak. Maggie took the impromptu cue, rose from her seat and crossed to the head of the table, where she stood and surveyed the dozen or so men in the room. Her simple movement had focused their attention. She knew she had the perfect tempting figure and they couldn't take their eyes off her. She rested her hands on the desk leaning forward slightly to expose her cleavage, and looked every man in the eye one by one as she spoke.

"Now that I have your attention gentleman," she smiled wryly, "thank you all for reacting so quickly to last night's events. From now on I would like to be briefed on any new developments and..."

"I don't think this is necessary Miss Dalton. We have a very good team taking care of it," Thomas interrupted her. He wasn't standing for any childish nonsense even if she had come of age overnight. She might have the Dalton Empire in her hands, but she certainly didn't have the years of experience.

"What the lady wants, the lady gets," Sean intervened.

"Don't be a fool Sean," Alex chipped in, "I'm on Tom's side here." Others around the table nodded their heads, agreeing.

Maggie glared at Thomas. "If you would let me finish Mr Anderson, thank you. With all due respect, somebody tried to kill me last night, and now this matter is personal. I run this company," there was muffled laughter around the room and Maggie was starting to get irritated, "I run this company," she repeated louder this time, piercing each of them with her bright steely blue eyes, "maybe not in years, but certainly on paper, and I will not tolerate insubordination from any of you!"

There followed stunned silence, and out of the corner of her eye she could see Sean grinning at her.

"With all due respect," Thomas was on his feet now coming towards her. He had to put a stop to this outrageous behaviour, "Miss Dalton you are inexperienced in this business. Your father hired us so we could protect him, protect you and protect his interests. We know what is best and you have to trust us."

Maggie looked at him coolly. "Don't patronise me Mr Anderson. I know you don't have a clue what's going on because this company has no known enemies." Turning to address the room, she said, "This meeting is over. Please continue with whatever you people do, and will somebody please get rid of the Press. It was a nightmare being driven from the house to the office earlier. Damn Paparazzi everywhere!"

Everyone began gathering up their papers preparing to leave, but Thomas remained where he was.

"Come to my office in an hour or so Mr Anderson, so we can discuss this press conference."

He started to protest, but she turned on her heel and left the room with the others.

*

"Quite the fireball, aren't you." Maggie looked up to see Sean standing in the doorway of her office. "Your father was always so mild tempered. Perhaps you must take after your mother."

"I don't like where this conversation is going." She carried on typing. Any reference to her mother was blocked out immediately. She couldn't go back there. "Did you want something, Mr Hamilton? Because I'm a very busy woman..."

"Please call me Sean." He came in and sat down.

She stopped typing and looked at him. "That's funny, I don't remember inviting you in."

"Hmmm, quite the fireball indeed," Sean mused out loud, "Actually I have a proposition for you."

"And what may that be?" She was wary of this man and not in the least bit interested in him or his proposition.

"You want to make your mark don't you?" He was taking her all in, the long chestnut hair falling effortlessly over her shoulders, the perfect cheekbones, and those soft red lips. Such a delight, if he could only get to her.

She shifted in her seat nervously. "Of course," she replied.

"Then come with me to dinner tonight." He leaned forward and put his hand over hers. She immediately withdrew as her phone buzzed loudly. She was tempted to pick it up, but didn't, not right away.

"That won't be possible Mr Hamilton." She didn't offer any explanation. Their eyes met and Sean knew he must have her. The phone was still buzzing. "I must get that."

"I'll wait," Sean said quietly, getting up, "There's plenty of time."

She watched him leave, all the while wondering what he could offer her, despite her reservations. He was persuasive, audacious and enterprising. A real live wire. She would never admit it to him, but she was starting to like that. Distracted, she picked up the phone.

"Yes?"

"Mr Anderson to see you Miss Dalton."

"Ok, send him through."

*

"Whatever you're doing Miss Dalton, I don't advise it." Thomas was pacing up and down her office. They had run through the press conference and now the conversation had turned back to the meeting earlier today. Thomas was still angry at her interference.

"Call me Maggie, Tom." She lazed back in her sumptuous leather chair letting it engulf her. "Would you like a drink?"

He stopped to face her, incredulous. "You are quite something Miss Dalton. This isn't a game. You can't simply come of age and expect everything to fall into place. You don't even know what your Board of Directors does!"

"So teach me Tom, I'm a very quick learner." She was playing with him and he didn't like it. Of all of them, he was the one she wanted most of all. Strong, muscular, handsome, and only twelve years her senior, she had fallen in love with him almost immediately. But he treated her like a child and at first she resented it, desperately tried not to be in love with him, yet it was impossible. Three years she had watched him, every calculated move, every business decision, every deal he clinched, and she had learnt all she needed to know. It was like watching her father all over again, and just like with her father, she adored Thomas Anderson - despite the way he treated her.

"This is ridiculous," he murmured, hands on hips, looking skywards for some inspiration, "You can't speak to the Board like that!"

Maggie was unperturbed. "It's the dawn of a new era Tom. I can do what the hell I like."

He stared at her in disbelief. First real proper day on the job and she was already a nightmare. He hadn't been prepared for this side of her. He knew, of course, that she was a handful, Mrs Peters had given him the low-down there, but the way she was acting today was something else.

"Miss Dalton, Maggie," he said, mustering some patience from somewhere and sitting down opposite her, "Your father, god rest his soul, had the greatest reputation a man could ever wish for, but somebody wants you dead. This is serious. It doesn't make any sense."

"Tom, can I call you Tom? I would feel more comfortable if I did." She reached for his hand and strangely he didn't pull away. "Don't underestimate me. I am ready for this. You know I'm ready for this. Let's not fight."

She was so irresistible. He didn't want to be seduced; yet he couldn't stop himself. Everything about her was screaming pleasure.

"Last night I saw you Tom, I saw you watching me."

What was she trying to do to him! "Maggie, we can't do this! I am responsible for you!" He pulled away from her and ran his hand through his thick black hair. "You *are* impossible."

Little Child

There was an uncomfortable silence, then, suddenly he laughed. The tousled hair and the laughter momentarily fazed her. She wanted him so much. He was always serious. She couldn't remember him ever laughing before.

"Ok, if you want to play with the big boys, let's do it," he conceded. He had to get her on side so she would play the game his way.

"Really?" She sat on the edge of her chair, eager.

"Yes, but let's get one thing straight. I'm in charge, make no mistake about that."

She pulled a face. "But this is my company!"

He stood up and gave her a knowing look. "There's a reason why we're here Maggie. Now come on, the press conference is about to start. Let's straighten out those rumours."

He picked up his briefcase and snapped it shut.

"Just one more thing Tom." She moved around the desk to be near him.

"What's that?"

She pressed up close to him. "Take me to dinner tonight."

He shook his head and the hint of a smile danced across his lips. "Ok Miss Dalton, ok."

*

James Bridges was thinking about her. And right now he was painting her. That stunning girl he'd fallen in love with three years ago who had been taken from him. It had been impossible to believe that what they'd shared had ended so suddenly. He knew deep down he still hadn't properly recovered from their separation. Why would he be painting her if that were the case? Why would he be concentrating so hard trying to remember the exact shade of those bright blue eyes, and the exact tone of those full red lips that he had kissed so often...? He was still so much in love with her. It was criminal the way they had been ripped from each other. He had seen her crying one day after school and he had gone to her straight away. Comforting her, they'd walked home together. She lived in a foster home the other side of town but he hadn't minded walking that extra few miles for her. She didn't want to go home but she wouldn't explain. He was nervous around her, and she with him, but over the coming days, weeks, months, they got closer. She didn't have any real friends. He thought it must be tough for her but made sure to steer clear of the subject even though he desperately wanted to know what was troubling this beautiful lost soul. He remembered endless summer days sitting in the park, reading to each other, or messing around, or sometimes just being quiet. And then the relationship became physical and it was so, so tender. It was like nothing he had ever experienced before. But she was always frightened. She trembled when he made love to her. He never understood why. Two days before she said she loved him, they'd quarrelled, and two days after she'd said those magic words, she was gone. Vanished. Taken from him. And then the story unfolded through the newspapers that Margaret Dalton had been found, rescued from awful foster care and brought back to her family home. And James began to piece everything together and suddenly it all made sense.

But he couldn't give her up.

He could never give her up.

The television was on in the background. He was getting irritated with the noise. This was his special time to be alone with the only girl he had ever wanted, and he needed some peace. Like all artists, he had his temperamental moments. He was about to switch off the set when he saw her. But no, surely it couldn't be. He hadn't heard or read anything about her for ages. The Paparazzi were kept at a distance and it was rare for them to get any photos. She was so heavily protected after being found. But was it actually her? He got up close and pressed impatiently at the volume button. He couldn't believe it. It was! It was Maggie! She was doing a press conference and offering her condolences to the family of someone who had been shot last night at her charity ball. Then the man next to her was speaking indicating they would find whoever tried to shoot Maggie. What?! James couldn't believe what he was hearing. Somebody tried to shoot Maggie? That was insane! He was thinking quickly, running through the plan in his head. He had to do something. He needed to see her. He picked up his mobile and dialled the number of his private investigator who his parents had hired for him once before.

Little Child

*

Thomas and Maggie had finished eating. Thomas was surprised at how completely at ease he felt with her, despite being warned she was capricious. Tonight he had touched on a side of her he liked very much. They were sipping their wine. Most of the evening had been spent talking business, but now the conversation was turning intimate.

"Maggie...I took the liberty of speaking to Johnny last night."

She didn't flinch; she knew he was watching her closely for signs of vulnerability. She carried on drinking with no intention of letting down her guard.

"He said you were very shaken which is understandable given the circumstances."

She felt his leg press up against hers and then he put his glass down to take her free hand in both of his. She loved his touch, tender yet strong.

"Maggie, it's alright to be afraid," he whispered, "What happened was terrible. Johnny told me you were lonely."

She took another sip, then, looking straight at him, "Maybe I'm alone Tom, but I'm never lonely."

"And there's a difference?" he asked, watching her intently.

She waited a moment before replying, "Oh yes, there's a difference." He saw the devilish twinkle in her eye. She swished the wine in her glass before finishing it off.

"Would you like me to pour you some more?"

She nodded, withdrawing her hand. He could sense she had something else on her mind, something else that was going to take precedent over explaining the difference between being alone and being lonely. He would come back to that later. He knew he had to push her to see how far she could go. She needed to be aware of what she'd been born into, of what she'd inherited.

"Tell me Tom, is my mother still alive?"

Thomas was taken aback by the question, but he carried on pouring, showing no signs of his surprise.

"I wondered why you were subdued tonight." He placed the bottle back down on the table and offered her the newly filled glass.

She ignored his goad and took the glass. "Will you answer me, or do you not know?"

There was a moment's silence.

"We don't know." He felt uncomfortable lying to her but it was better this way. He already knew Maggie's mother wasn't alive. He'd been the one to order the hit. It had had to be done. But maybe he'd been too hasty in his decision. Was this latest pop at Maggie somebody taking umbrage? Had he only served to open a can of worms rather than contain the situation? He wasn't proud to admit it and had tried and tried to wash his hands clean of the deed. And rid his mind. The late Richard Dalton wouldn't have approved. He had been clean and honest and upfront. It made Thomas feel dirty. He shivered. Only two people knew his guilty secret and he didn't want it to become any more.

"I thought you people had your finger on the pulse?" It was her turn to goad.

Thomas looked philosophical. "On most things, yes, but not on that. Your mother is pretty illusive." More lies. One day he would have to tell her, but for now...

"In other words, always one step ahead of you."

Thomas cleared his throat. "I wouldn't put it like that."

"Would she want me dead?" Maggie heard herself saying the words, but she wouldn't allow them to register. It was painful. She knew with time it would get easier, but for now parts of the past were still raw and cut and clawed at her very being. Time was a healer, and she knew she had time.

Thomas didn't speak. *Probably, but there was no chance of that now.*

"Tell me what you know Tom?" She searched his face, but it was impossible to read what he was thinking. Years of training from her father had taught him to never give anything away with facial expressions or body language, unless it was intended.

"Tell me," she persisted.

Thomas took a long time to reply. "I can't answer you," he finally admitted.

"But you have your suspicions?"

"Perhaps. We'll investigate anything we feel needs investigating," he assured her.

"I'm not afraid Tom," she paused, taking a long drink from her glass and building herself up, "I'm not afraid of her, I'm not afraid of whatever's out there waiting for me. I've been through things Tom, unimaginable things that I can barely speak about. Things that I block from my mind because it's too distressing to remember. But it's made me stronger Tom, and I am ready. If it is her, I will be ready."

"And if it's not?" He could sense she was a little drunk. Marginally. But it was enough. He didn't believe she would be confessing these things if she wasn't slightly inebriated. It wasn't Maggie's style. Just as she had been observing his every move over the last three years, he had been doing likewise.

She shook her head defiantly. "I'll still be ready."

He wasn't so sure. He got up from the table, a part of him not wanting to see her make a fool of herself, but another part of him wanting her to continue to see where it would lead. To see if she would slip up. But no, he would wait. There was plenty of time yet to test her.

"Come, let me take you home. It's late and you must rest."

He held her firmly by the arm and steered her towards the entrance. She was trying desperately to compose herself as she let him lead her out of the restaurant. Their limousine was waiting outside the door. Johnny got out of the driver's seat and opened the door for her. Thomas helped her in.

"She's a little tipsy Johnny. Make sure she goes careful and please see her to her room."

Johnny nodded shutting the car door. "Yes Sir," he replied, tipping his cap and climbing back into the driver's seat.

Maggie relaxed back on the sofa and tried to remember what she had said, but her mind was confused and she could only picture her mother's face.

Thomas watched the car pull away and went back into the bar for a nightcap, alone.

*

She sobered up as they reached the estate. They went through security and snaked up the driveway. Halfway to the house, Maggie decided she wanted some fresh air.

She picked up the phone. "Stop the car Johnny."

"What's that ma'am?" he replied.

"Stop the car. I fancy walking the rest of the way." She placed the receiver back and waited for the car to stop so she could get out.

Johnny came down and opened the door.

"But Miss Dalton, I was under strict instructions to see you to your room."

She swung her legs outside and Johnny offered his hand so she could pull herself out.

"Johnny, I'll be absolutely fine. I just fancy a walk, that's all. If I'm not back in my room in fifteen minutes, send out the search party, ok." She was joking with him, but he looked at her gravely.

"Miss Dalton, I don't want to get either of us into any bother."

"Well, you won't," she said brightly, "because you're my chauffeur and bodyguard and I asked you to let me walk."

"Well, take this." He offered her his jacket and she put it over her shoulders. "I'll be close by then Miss."

She nodded and waited for him to continue driving up to the house. Then she made her own way on the gravel. She stopped at the fountain and watched it for a few minutes, completely absorbed with the rhythmic sound of the water, until something caught her eye under the shadows of the nearby oaks.

"Hello?" she called out, "Hello, who's there?" She began walking slowly towards where she'd seen the movement, but she didn't know what she was doing. If only she carried a gun, then she wouldn't feel afraid at all. She made a mental note to press Thomas about that. If she could fire a gun, she could protect herself. Right this moment, she figured if someone was going to take a shot at her, then they would have done it by now considering she'd been a sitting target for all of five minutes standing at the fountain.

"Hello?" she called again, getting closer to the trees.

A figure crept slowly out of the shadows and she gasped unable to stop herself. Her hand went straight to her mouth as he put his finger to his lips. By now she was only a few feet away from the edge of the oaks.

"Hello Maggie, how are you?"

CHAPTER 2
Coming Of Age

She gasped again. "James! Oh my god, James! Is it really you?" She couldn't quite believe what she was seeing.

Time stood still as they gazed at each other, paralysed, hearts pounding with the shock and excitement. Two ghosts, haunting one another for so long. James was grinning from ear to ear. She remembered that grin so vividly. Then, she also remembered Johnny was up at the house waiting for her. Thinking quickly, she frantically beckoned to him. "Come out of there and walk with me to the house. I can't explain right now, just come. Hurry!"

"Oh god Maggie, it's so good to see you again." He wanted to take her in his arms and kiss her all over.

"Sshhh, just follow my lead. My bodyguard is up at the house waiting for me. How I'm going to explain about you, I don't know." She started to smile. "Put your arm around me."

"Why?"

"Just do it!"

James did as he was told and they sauntered up to the porch. Johnny had taken the car to the garage and was standing outside as promised. He raised an eyebrow when he saw James.

"And who is this young man?"

"Johnny, that's no way to treat a dear, dear old friend of mine."

"Miss Dalton..." he began, but she waved him away.

"Johnny, please. This is James. We knew each other once, for a while, and at this moment we would appreciate some privacy. Please? It's ok."

Johnny was thinking about it. "I never say no to you Miss Dalton, so if you let me search him, I promise I won't say another word on the matter."

"And this stays between you and me?" she inquired.

He nodded. "Yes, just between you and me."

"Good." She turned to James. "James darling, I hope you don't mind. It's just a formality." She looked up at him and the light from the high stone porch ceiling danced across her hair. A few loose strands now breezed across her face. So many things he remembered about her.

He held out his arms and Johnny patted him down. Once he was satisfied, he tipped his cap and moved aside so they could enter the house.

"Have a good evening Miss."

*

James had been intimidated by the appearance of the grand house - its imposing structure and huge columns, the giant bay windows and extravagant brickwork...but inside was something else altogether. It simply took his breath away. They ran from one chandelier lit room to another, through oak panelled passageways and arched hallways, up deep carpeted winding stairs, then through more chandelier lit rooms and even more oak panelled passageways until finally she opened a door and they stumbled into her private sitting room, laughing.

"Have a good evening Miss," he mimicked Johnny, tipping his pretend cap.

Maggie whacked him with her bag. "Sshhh, you'll wake Mrs Peters and Lucia!" she hissed, stifling her giggling. She suddenly felt like a love struck teenager again heady with the prospect of what could follow, should she let it...

"Who the heck are Mrs Peters and Lucia?"

"My staff! Now shut up and come here." She pulled him close and kissed him without warning. He wrapped his arms around her and kissed her back, tenderly at first and then with all the hidden passion he'd restrained within himself for so long.

"Oh my God, you are as beautiful as I remember Maggie," he whispered.

"Let me take a look at you." She pulled free and held him at arms length, appraising him slowly and deliberately, allowing herself to feel everything she had once felt. All of that love, all of that passion, all of those feelings she'd locked away until now.

"I waited for you," he said quietly.

She bit her lip. "I know, but it was complicated James. You'll understand when I explain."

Their eyes locked and he studied her face, wondering if he was ever destined to find out what was going on inside her head.

She quickly changed the subject before he could press her further. "I assume you didn't get in using conventional methods!" She walked up the steps into another room, sat down at her dressing table and shook out her hair. James followed, mesmerised, and his eyes never left her as she began brushing.

"No, I had some help. Let's just say a diversion of sorts."

"How did you find me?"

"Like I said, I had some help."

"You're very lucky I found you in one piece considering somebody is trying to kill me. You could have been killed yourself! Everyone is on red alert."

She always did have a matter-of-fact way about her. Like everything was a done deal.

"You seem very blasé about the whole affair."

She stopped brushing and looked up at him. "It's part of who I am now James," she sighed.

"And who is that Maggie? Do I still know her?"

She put her brush down and got up very slowly. "I hope so," she whispered, coming towards him, "Do you want to start again?"

James swallowed. He couldn't help wanting her. It had been too long. God, she was beautiful. He pulled her to him and gently stroked her hair. All of the years melted away.

"Yes," he murmured.

She silently took his hand and led him into the bedroom.

*

There were three people in the room. The man bound and gagged to a chair was whimpering quietly and bleeding from a head wound and a punched nose. His immaculate, expensive suit was crumpled and dusty from being kicked and beaten to the floor, then dragged and forced into the chair. His once crisp, white shirt was now bloodstained and dirty. His shoes were scuffed. He was pulling on the ropes trying to loosen them, but they held him tightly in place. One of the others was pointing a gun at his head.

The third person known as the Chief stood in the shadows, smoking a cigarette. The Chief was in charge of the operation. "This is what happens when you don't finish a job properly." The words were spoken harshly and quietly. Smoke drifted out and laced the stuffy room.

The man in the chair kept whimpering into his gag, fighting his bonds.

"You've let us down Carlo. You didn't do what we wanted. There's always a price to pay when you don't do what *we* want." Finishing the cigarette and stepping forwards, there was complete silence in the room until Carlo's stifled yelp pierced the air as it was stubbed out on his hand.

Nodding to the Contract pointing the gun, the trigger jerked back and a bullet escaped. Carlo stopped moving. The two of them watched it blow his head apart.

The Chief nodded again to the killer and said, "Dispose of him." Then walked back to the car and dialled a number on the phone.

"It's done."

"Good," came the reply, "don't mess up again."

*

James was propped up on one elbow, watching her sleeping. For him, after waiting so long to see her again, it had been an unforgettable night. He traced her cheek with the back of his finger remembering every little detail of their lovemaking. She didn't stir; just lay there serenely, looking beautiful and unfazed in the half-light.

He couldn't lose her again. He mustn't lose her again. For some reason, there was uneasiness in the pit of his stomach and for the last little while he had been trying desperately to dissect the feeling, so he could move on and enjoy this special moment with Maggie without worry, and without fear. He racked his brains. He had to understand what was burdening him. Apprehension about where this relationship could go? Insecurity because he couldn't offer her anything she didn't already have? No, it was something more than that. He lay back down on the pillow and closed his eyes, letting his emotions take over…and slowly it came to him and he began to piece the feeling together in his mind. It was part of their conversation last night. The resigned tone she'd taken with him when they'd briefly discussed the shooting. *It's part of who I am now James.* How could she be unconcerned?

Where was her fight? Maybe she *was* anxious, but time had taught her to bury her fear. He didn't know, but he must find out.

He pulled himself up again and looked around the bedroom for the first time. He hadn't noticed how luxurious it was; the four poster bed that enveloped them, the pure silk curtains shimmering in the early morning sun, the thick cream carpet, the antique furniture. It was a million miles from what he knew. Sure, his parents were reasonably well off, but certainly nothing like this. This was a different league altogether. He suddenly felt humbled. Everything was so pristine, so elegant; it awakened a nervousness in him. Maggie had really landed on her feet.

She stirred and he felt her watching him. He turned to face her.

"Don't be in awe James," she murmured, stroking his face as he slid back down next to her. The air in the room was warm and musky. He lay on top of her and rested his head on her breast. She continued to stroke his hair.

"Why did you really come back James?" she asked.

He listened to her heart beating and fell in rhythm with her breathing. Their world was standing still and he wanted to savour this moment forever.

"To save you," he whispered.

He felt her body tense, then relax, and then she started shaking and it was a second or two before he realised she was laughing.

He jumped up offended, slid out of the bed and pulled on his boxers. She was still laughing.

"Stop it!" he shouted, "Stop laughing at me!"

"Oh god James," she protested, unable to control herself, "you are too funny!"

She was hurting his pride and she knew it, but that didn't make her stop.

The phone rang next to the bed. She cleared her throat several times before answering, and then picked up the receiver.

"Hello?" There was still a smile playing across her lips.

"Miss Dalton, will you be wanting breakfast?" It was Saturday morning and Lucia never barged in on her mistress at the weekends. Maggie often had company.

"Yes Lucia, for two, and hurry, we're starving." She placed the receiver back in its cradle and turned round to find James. He was standing at the window looking out across the vast gardens, a blank expression on his face.

"James, darling, I'm sorry," she apologised, "but save me, honestly…" She faltered, unable to finish her sentence. To her it was too ridiculous to even comprehend.

James composed himself. He had a big speech to make and he wanted to get through it without her laughing hysterically again. He exhaled loudly; aware she was staring at him waiting for him to do something. When they made love it was like they had never been apart, those three years melting away into nothingness, but now, she almost felt alien to him. She had never mocked him before. It had hurt. Who was she? Was she still the person he remembered, or had things changed? He was confused and he wanted answers.

"James, darling darling James, I am so sorry."

He looked away from the window and let his gaze rest on her. She was sitting up in bed, naked. He took it all in, every single little detail because he never knew when he might see her again. He would paint her. In this pose. Naked. Beautiful. Flawless. Perfection in every way and unblemished in his eyes.

"Come to me," she said softly.

That was the invitation he was waiting for, but he held back for a moment.

"Come…please…" she said again.

Another moment's pause, then, "Maggie I can save you! I can take you away from all of this. Well, not this," he gestured around the room, "but from the uncertainty. We can hide out! No-one will ever find you." He was beside her now holding her face in his hands, imploring her to at least think about it. He half expected her to laugh again, but she didn't.

"Oh James," she said, looking up at him with those striking blue eyes, "Oh James, if only that were true."

He was still just a boy, the boy she had fallen in love with. Their worlds, once so close, were now in different orbits. She realised she had grown up quicker than him, been forced to in many respects. He had always taken care of her, but really she had dictated the relationship. When she was happy, he was happy. When she was sad, he was too. He mirrored her, but he didn't own her. In his perfect, easy world everything slotted into place neatly and there were no kinks to iron out. It was all smooth and simple. He had a problem; he fixed it. Just like that. Nobody demanded his attention. Nobody expected anything of him. Nobody wanted him dead. *Dead.* The word started alarm bells ringing in her head. That was what this was all about, but he couldn't protect her. No one could.

"It would work Maggie, it really would!" He was nodding excitedly, mistaking her silence for consideration, "We could take your staff and your bodyguard with us and buy a place out in the country, well, much further out than this. And nobody would know... What's wrong?"

She was shaking her head.

"Maggie, please, think about it. We can do anything if we really want it. Remember, that's what we said, way back when? If we want something, we'll get it. Dreams Maggie, dreams, we can make them come true."

She pushed him away. "James, this is stupid talk," she said finally, "and what would we have in this house far, far away hidden in the country? Chickens, pigs, some children perhaps..."

"Yes, we could, we really could! I can see it now. It would be so perfect Maggie. It would be perfect. Just you and me, and our chickens and pigs."

She laughed, and he laughed too.

She sighed. "It can't happen, darling."

"But why Maggie? This is the perfect opportunity. I would protect you. I don't know why you won't consider it!"

She was getting impatient with him, even though she'd been humouring him only moments before. Why couldn't he see it for himself? Why did she have to spell the obvious out to him?

"I'm Margaret Dalton for Christ sake!" she snapped.

There was silence. She got up from the bed, pulled her chemise over her head and wrapped herself in her satin robe, and walked to the door.

"Lucia will be bringing breakfast any minute now. Come, let's talk about all of this while we eat."

He rose from the bed and threw on a gown Maggie had draped over the chair for him. He followed her down the steps into the dressing room, then through the sitting room into a dining area. There was a large oak table and chairs, and a bar in the corner. The room led out onto a balcony.

"Is this all of yours?" he asked, amazed at the size of everything.

"What do you mean?"

"Well, all of these rooms, are they your private residence?"

"Oh, yes," she said smiling, "Here, let's eat outside." She unhooked the latch on the door and slid it across. The sun was fully up in the sky now, shining down on them. It wasn't too hot. Beautiful, late, August sunshine.

She sat down and watched James peer out over the balcony. More pristinely manicured garden stretching out as far as the eye could see.

"What floor are we on?"

"The third. There are four altogether. I'll give you a tour later if you like."

He turned and came and sat down opposite her. "I would like that."

They heard someone fussing in the sitting room.

"Lucia, we're out here," Maggie called.

Lucia and another maid came bustling in with their breakfast things and between them they laid everything out neatly on the table. There were eggs and bacon and toast, jam, butter, orange juice. James was suddenly very hungry.

"Don't you catch cold Miss," Lucia said, as she poured coffee for them both.

Maggie just smiled. "Don't fuss Lucia. I don't have any engagements this morning do I?"

"No Miss, the weekend is completely free for you to enjoy with your friend." She smiled at James, a knowing smile he thought.

The other maid retreated back into the house.

"Is Johnny still around the front?"

"Yes."

"Keep him there. I don't want him eavesdropping on our conversation."

"But Miss…"

"No *But Miss* anything Lucia. Do as you're told. Keep him occupied. James and I have a lot to discuss and I don't want to be interrupted by *anyone*."

Lucia nodded and hurried off with the empty tray.

"Said with such authority," James smirked, helping himself to toast.

"Trust me, it gets quite tiring," Maggie said, sipping her coffee. "But you wouldn't have it any other way."

"Perhaps. I've got used to it I suppose."

She put her cup back in its saucer and was quiet for a spell, thinking. "Listen James, about earlier. There are things you should know." She wondered how far back she needed to go. "James, I don't know where to start," she confessed.

He was listening to her. He noticed the edge to her voice, maybe even a hint of despair. She suddenly looked small and lost. That air of surety had temporarily deserted her.

He helped himself to another slice of toast. "Why did they take you? Start from there. It'll be ok Maggie, go on."

She nodded. "My father died when I was fourteen and he left everything to me; the family estate, the business, the staff, everything. My father's associates had to find me before I turned eighteen so they could set me up in the business. That was my father's wish you see to take over from him when I was eighteen. There were other legalities as well, but I won't bore you with the details. I wasn't allowed to be on the Board until I turned twenty one, but I had a lot to learn before then."

"And your mother? Where was she?"

Maggie's face went dark. "She left when my father died." There was finality in her voice and James picked up on it. "I was...I was fostered around." She could barely say the word. *Fostered.* It felt cheap and dirty. She shivered and hugged herself tightly, forcing the memory away.

"So, it's been an endless round of business lunches and dinner parties and charity balls for you then?" he joked, munching on his toast and taking a swig of orange juice, trying to steer the conversation back, "I must say it was hard to find anything on you. The Press have certainly been kept on a tight leash."

"Don't make fun James; it hasn't been as easy as you think, and as for keeping the Paparazzi at bay, that's all about to change."

He looked apologetic. "Sorry Maggie, I shouldn't have said that."

"Now I've officially 'come of age' I have obligations to the Press. We promised them they would have more access, but in hindsight, this was a terrible mistake especially now that someone is trying to…well…you know…" She couldn't bring herself to say *kill me*.

James understood. They ate in silence for a while. Finally, he couldn't stand it any longer. He knew she was vulnerable; he just had to tap into it. Provoke her, maybe. That was the only way of breaking down her defence. She had never spoken about her past, and was never likely to. She kept everything so close to her chest and he knew it would destroy her if he didn't get to her first.

"I'm offering you a way out Maggie. All you have to do is say *yes* and we could be away from here."

She looked across at him hopelessly. "It's not as simple as that James. I've told you. I have responsibilities now, big responsibilities."

"So hand them over! Hand it all over! I know you Maggie and I know this is not what you really want. You might want the lifestyle but I know you don't want the pressure. This is not you!"

"James!"

"Answer me this Maggie, do you enjoy this life, honestly? Do you thrive on the fact that somebody somewhere wants to get rid of you? Does it make you feel you're *somebody* at long last?"

She pushed her chair back sharply, picked up her cup and threw it at him. He ducked just in time and it smashed against the balcony railings. "How dare you, you sick bastard!" she screamed, storming back into the house. She went straight to the bar and hands shaking poured herself a large Scotch. She drank it down and then refilled. James waited a moment and then went in after her. They stood glaring at each other until Mrs Peters, closely followed by Lucia, came rushing in, interrupting the silence.

"What's going on?" Mrs Peters demanded.

Maggie stared at her blankly.

"What's going on?" she asked again.

Lucia hurried outside to clear up the mess. James felt awkward in the silence. He cleared his throat, but before he could say anything, Maggie spoke quietly.

"Please leave Carmen."

Mrs Peters didn't move.

"Carmen, please. Take Lucia and leave us be." Her voice trembled as she finished the sentence.

"Are you sure you're ok?" She was watching Maggie closely. Maggie nodded.

"As you wish Margaret." She turned to leave. "Lucia, come!"

They left the room, but Mrs Peters made a point of glaring at James as she brushed past him. She clearly disapproved of his involvement with Maggie.

When Maggie was certain they had gone, she finished her drink and placed the glass very carefully back on the bar top. This time when she spoke, there was no tremor in her voice.

"Ok James, you win. Talk me through the plan."

*

It was Monday morning. Thomas stood with his hands on his hips, his back to her, looking out of the window and looking about ready to burst as she entered his office and casually sat down.

"Who is he Maggie?" He didn't turn around.

"How do you know?" There was no point denying it, but she was curious to know how he had found out. Probably from Mrs Peters.

"Who is he?" he asked again.

She could see he was angry. His body was tense, shoulders hunched, tone sharp. Was he jealous?

"A harmless old friend," she replied.

"A harmless old friend you fight with?" Maggie almost winced at the fury in his voice. She said nothing.

"Did you sleep together?"

She didn't answer, but waited for him to turn around because sooner or later she knew he would. His hands came off the hips and curled into tight balls, then released, then curled, then released. Any minute now...

"Well?" he demanded, swinging round and thumping his hands down hard on the desk.

She remained composed. This was none of his business.

Shrugging, she said, "We had something once."

"How did he get in?"

"Well, quite frankly Tom, security must be poor. I should look into it if I were you." She couldn't help provoke him further.

"How did he get in?" He banged his hands down on the desk again.

"I don't know!"

"I'll fire Johnny's god damn ass. In case you've forgotten, you're in grave danger! So how do you deal with it? You sleep around like some whore!" He spat the words in her direction.

"What is wrong with you Thomas? Are you jealous?"

He glared at her.

"Are you?"

He said nothing.

"Because a woman has needs Tom!" As soon as the words escaped her lips, she regretted them, but it was too late. She quickly changed tact. "Don't fire Johnny, it wasn't his fault."

He looked at her for a long time before speaking again. "You can't mess around Maggie, not now. You aren't a child anymore. The business comes first, your business. You screw up, and it'll finish you as quickly as that," he clicked his fingers together, "You want loyalty, you earn it. You want respect, you earn it. You want to pull off big deals, you earn it. It's not your right just because your father is dead. We may all work for you, but you also work for us."

He walked to the door holding it open for her.

"You'll spend the week with Mrs Peters."

She swivelled round in her seat and glared at him. "What?"

"You'll spend the week with Mrs Peters," he repeated patiently.

She wanted to argue, but something told her not too. She knew when she was in enough trouble. She got up and stormed out of the room.

"And remember Maggie," Thomas called after her, "I have eyes everywhere."

He had all the information he could want on James Bridges. Alex had run checks on him first thing and there was no threat. He was some childhood sweetheart, now running an art gallery in the town they'd found Maggie three years ago. As she'd said – harmless. They could easily run him off the scene if needs be, or use him, if needs be. There were certainly possibilities.

Sending Maggie to Mrs Peters had been the last resort, but he hoped absolving her responsibilities for a week would settle her down. Thomas had predicted to the Board that the power would go straight to her head, and he was right after the catastrophic meeting on Friday. She was screwing up all over the place. But it was ok. She would learn. Now that he had briefed the other Directors and had them on side, he was sure of it.

*

Sean had been elected to talk to Maggie. She hadn't seemed that interested to begin with, but since the rebuff, she might be more willing to listen to him now. He was going to make this so slick, he knew she wouldn't be able to resist.

She was finishing up for the day when he caught her. She looked up when he walked into the room unannounced and pulled up a seat.

"What do you want?" She was still in a foul mood even though her reprimand had been almost a week ago. Thomas was ignoring her and she couldn't get any assistance out of the rest of them. It was like the Board were shunning her, and she was deeply aggrieved by it all. Who did they think they were anyway?

"You're not very friendly," Sean commented, getting up and helping himself to a drink, "Everything ok?"

"No!" she snapped, "It most certainly isn't!"

Sean decided to plunge straight in before she took off and he lost another opportunity. "I can help you." He sat back down in the same chair and took a long swig from his glass.

"How?" She was barely listening as she packed up her things. Sean was hardly the Director holding all the power, so why should she give him the time of day?

"I can get you back in favour." He watched her pause and consider the possibility. This time she stopped what she was doing and looked at him carefully.

"How?" she repeated.

"There's a meeting coming up, an important meeting. Thomas says you can go if you think you're up to it." He knew he had her attention now.

She continued to look at him, a part of her wanting to retort and send him packing, but the other half of her intrigued and ready for the challenge. She wanted to show them what she was capable of.

"Will I be briefed?"

Sean took another long swig. "Of course."

"And just how important is it?"

"Enough to get you back in favour," he winked at her, "if you pull it off."

Maggie felt that cautious yet excitable churning building inside of her. Did she trust him? Did it matter? Right this moment she certainly felt like she had nothing to lose.

"Ok," she said slowly, "what do I have to do?"

Sean finished his drink before replying. "There'll be a file on your desk in the morning. Read it, memorise it, then bring it back to me. Understood?"

"Yes, understood," she paused, "And that's it?"

"That's it." Sean's eyes glinted as he got up to leave, handing the glass back to her. "You won't regret this Maggie."

*

Maggie was sitting at her desk. She had read the file. It was not even 11 o'clock and she was drinking. She'd locked the door to her office and told her secretary she didn't want to be disturbed. She had come to a junction and she didn't know which road to take. She was so confused, so terribly confused. She took another swig. It was maybe her fourth or fifth shot, she couldn't really remember. Here an opportunity had presented itself so she could prove to them all that she wasn't just Richard Dalton's daughter, the waif and stray they'd rescued three years ago who was failing miserably to live up to their expectations. One mistake. That's all she'd made. But it had been enough. She'd wanted their loyalty, now all she had was their pity. Yet she could show them. There was still time. The file in front of her would be the turning point, if she let it.

But then there was James. Dear, dear, darling James who knew her better than she knew herself. She wanted to be with him more than she dared admit to herself, but it was too complicated. Could it really work, or was it only ever going to be a very sweet dream? She hadn't stopped asking herself that question since she'd said goodbye to him in the early hours of that sweet Sunday morning and promised to be in touch.

Little Child

She had to make a choice, and in her heart she already knew which one it had to be.

CHAPTER 3
Coming Of Age

"Have you considered delaying tactics?" The Chief was being very bold, pushing luck over the edge. Pushing all boundaries. The other person, known simply as Kite and considered the boss, could have the Chief killed in an instant. But the Chief wasn't concerned or afraid. The Chief didn't feel fear. Once an assassin and now in collaboration, the transformation hadn't taken long. Quickly moving through the ranks becoming second in command in just under a year, there was no doubt about it; the Chief's position had definitely helped.

Understated and underestimated; the circumstances were perfect for both of them, and an alliance formed straight away. There was silence at the other end of the phone.

"I have something going that may interest you. We can take this whole operation to another level."

Still silence.

"Will you consider?" The Chief was keeping his excitement controlled, his level voice giving nothing away.

Kite was thinking about it. The Chief could hear soft breathing punctuated by long draws on a cigarette.

"Come in and let's discuss," Kite said finally, "There's been a change of plan this end as well."

They each knew the other was driven by the same things – money and power – in that order. The prospect to gain more was enticing them both. A smile crept across Kite's lips as the phone hung up and the smoke from the cigarette continued to swirl. The Chief too was smiling as he placed his phone in his top pocket and turned the key in the ignition. So sure was he that the boss would accept his proposal, he'd been ready and waiting in his car.

*

Maggie was marching down the hall to Sean's office, clutching the file tightly against her chest. Her textbook persona was masking the mixed emotions she was desperately trying to suppress. Inside she felt dishevelled and dirty. She had drunk too much and it was screwing her up.

She could barely think straight. She had splashed so much water over her face, her collar was wet and her hair a little damp. Shaking, she'd re-applied her make up. Considered calling Lucia but didn't want to raise suspicion. This was her battle, her fight, and she must do it alone, like so many times before. She got to his door and knocked, before opening it to peer inside. He was humming to himself looking very happy. His fingers tapped a rhythm as he typed on his laptop. She took a moment to steady herself, straightening her skirt and tucking some loose strands behind her ear.

"Maggie," he said, gesturing for her to sit down, "how nice to see you."

She looked at him warily. What was he so happy about?

"Did you read the file?" He finished up on his laptop and shut the lid.

She nodded. "You're not asking much are you? He dislikes women. Can't even bear their perfume!" She handed it back to him keeping her arm steady. She was concentrating so hard on making this a faultless performance; it hurt every fibre of her being.

"So if anyone can charm him and get him to sign away this deal, it'll be you. If I may say so myself, you are not the average woman." Sean was grinning from ear to ear as he placed the file back in his top drawer and locked it. She really had little respect for him, but he was holding her future credibility in the palm of his hand courtesy of Thomas and the Board and she had no choice but to run with it. This was the way it had to be if she wanted even a hint of her standing back. For a minute she considered seducing him, but she felt the bile rise in her throat and knew she couldn't do it. Maybe that was the result of all the alcohol she'd consumed, yet his charm fell flat on her and dampened any feelings of romancing.

"And that's really it? I go in there, woo him, get the papers signed, and the slate is clear?"

Sean nodded.

"So why don't one of you do it? If the deal is so important to us, surely I'm putting you all at risk?"

Sean nodded again, the grin turning quickly to a smirk, which spread across his face and stayed there. And suddenly she understood. That was the whole point. They were playing her. That was the test.

"And Thomas agreed to this?" She couldn't believe he would do something so reckless.

"He briefed us. It was completely his idea and we added our input." He wanted to add *to spice it up a little* but that would surely give the game away.

She stared at him for a long moment.

"Ok," she said quietly, "what happens next?"

"We go and do business."

"We?"

"I will be escorting you, yes."

She considered arguing, even opened her mouth to say something, but then clamped it shut again.

"In case anything should happen..." He was teasing her.

She tried not to bite.

He decided to be serious. "I'll be watching your back, that's all. I promised Thomas."

She said nothing.

"You know Maggie, you still haven't let me take you to dinner. I think it's rather important now that we're partners. Don't you?"

She swallowed hard. Too many sacrifices. Too many forfeits. She was going to explode before *too* long.

"Let me sleep on it," was all she could manage.

"You do that. Meanwhile I'll call him, set up something in a couple of weeks. I won't mention you. I think the element of surprise could work well in your favour."

She nodded weakly. She needed to get out of here.

"Prepare well and this will be a piece of cake."

She nodded again and left his office.

*

"Johnny, I must see James. Here's the address. Take me there now." She slid quickly into the car and handed Johnny the piece of paper.

"Are you sure this is a good idea Miss Dalton?"

"We won't be long. No one need know."

They were using a different limousine so Security wouldn't recognise Maggie leaving the estate. She had coerced

Johnny into driving her. She had a scarf pulled down covering most of her face so should anyone peer inside; they wouldn't know it was her. She knew she was taking a gamble less than a month from the shooting, taking unauthorised trips without back up. Thomas would be furious. But this had to be done. She had to see James. Any Paps would only get shots of the car; they wouldn't know who was inside. Like her own, the limousine they were using was a Rolls and had blackened windows, but this one was a deep blue, whereas hers was the signatory black. She had considered ditching the limousines altogether and using one of the Discoverys or Bentleys, but that would be sure to arouse suspicion. Limousines came and went from the estate every day of the week so it was important to blend in and just be *another* limousine.

They got through Security without a hitch and headed for Farnham and James' art studio. He was renting an apartment above it.

"Drive quickly!" she urged.

She was sitting in the front compartment so she could talk through the window issuing the odd instruction to Johnny as he drove. She was running through the conversation with James in her head, what she should say. Johnny interrupted her thoughts.

"Miss, Farnham is a small town. This limousine will cause a stir if I drive through the high street. Should I drop you down a side street and you walk in?"

Maggie thought for a second. "Yes, I'll keep my face covered. It'll be ok," she assured him.

Her heart was thumping in her chest. She knew she had to see this through but it would be difficult. James would be difficult. And then there were the other emotions raging inside of her. The ones she didn't let surface because she didn't know how to deal with them. She hadn't been back to Farnham since leaving it seven years ago; she purposely had done everything she could to avoid coming back. If clients wanted to meet her here, she politely rescheduled. If there was a social gathering being held, she politely declined. Someone would always attend on her behalf. There was no resistance from Mrs Peters or Thomas or Alex. They understood.

They were approaching Farnham inside of thirty minutes. Johnny had sped down the motorway.

"Drop me here Johnny." She pointed to a small close where he could tuck the car away. "This won't take long. I'll be twenty minutes max." She didn't wait for him to answer, or even to open the door for her. Time was of the essence and she wanted to get this over and done with and back to Virginia Water as quickly as possible.

Johnny watched Maggie hurry down the street towards the centre of the town, and then he got out of the car, flung his cap onto the driver's seat before locking up and following at a safe distance. Without the cap, he was just another businessman in a suit. Expert at keeping a low profile, he'd turned his profession into an art form.

She found the studio relatively easy. It was right on the main street. Tempted to enter from the front, she decided against it as there were customers musing inside, so she walked down the alley to get to the back of the property. She tried the door but it was locked. Rang the bell and waited to see if anyone would answer. Maybe she would have to walk into the studio after all. She made to leave, when suddenly the door opened.

"Thought I heard the bell." She turned to see a thirty-something woman standing in the doorway.

Maggie pulled the scarf closer around her face. "Oh hello, I was looking for James." The woman seemed familiar, but she daren't let down her guard.

"Well, come in. I'll call him. He's just dealing with a client. I came up to make us a pot of tea. Would you like some tea?" she offered.

Maggie stepped forwards and followed the woman inside. "No...no thank you," she murmured, "I won't be long with James, just something I have to tell him."

The older woman led Maggie into the kitchenette, James's she presumed, and busied herself with making the tea.

"Sorry, where are my manners. I'm Laura by the way. His older sister." She flipped the switch on the kettle and extended her hand. Maggie shook it. "Don't worry, I know who you are," she whispered mischievously, "James told me you were back in touch with each other. Delighted to see you again Maggie."

Maggie withdrew her hand. "Laura!" she exclaimed. She wanted to throw her arms around the older woman, but it didn't feel appropriate somehow. She'd been a small part of their lives during the time Maggie had dated James, but university and gap years had kept her on the move for most of it. Maggie only recalled seeing her at Bridges' family gatherings, special occasions and the odd party, and even then it was usually short and sweet.

"I won't be needing this then." She took the scarf off and stuffed it in her coat pocket. "Do you work with James?" He hadn't mentioned her and she hadn't asked. Their whirlwind weekend had been just about the two of them, rekindling their lost love.

Laura was filling the mugs. "Yes, but only temporarily. He's hoping to set up his own gallery out in the sticks at some stage." She smiled. "James and his dreams. I bet I'll still be working here in a year's time despite what he says!"

Maggie nodded, pretending not to know anything about James' plans. He had already told her as much.

"We really have a great portfolio of clientele now. James would make a super job of it, I'm sure." Laura continued, but Maggie had tuned out. She heard footsteps on the stairs.

"Sis, hurry up with that tea will you!" She recognised James's voice. He wandered into the kitchen and stopped short when his eyes rested on Maggie.

Laura, sensing the tension, made her excuses and left. She knew a bit about their history together. She also knew James had never got over Maggie. They heard her walk back downstairs to the studio. Neither spoke. James sipped at his tea.

"What's up?" he asked finally. He could also sense the urgency in Maggie's demeanour.

Maggie decided to plunge straight in. She checked her watch. She was running out of time.

"I can't do this James," she whispered, looking straight at him.

"What do you mean?"

"I can't do it!"

He started to shake his head. "No Maggie, you can't back out now, you can't leave me stranded. This is not what you want and you know it."

She was shaking her head too.

"No, Maggie!" He was pleading with her and she was crying. She couldn't stop the tears.

"Don't make a scene James darling, don't make this harder than it already is. Please don't."

They were holding each other, rocking backwards and forwards. James didn't want to let her go. This would be it. This would be the end. And he couldn't bear it.

"You can't go back." He was begging her. "You can't go back Maggie." She had reduced him to a terrified little boy. He clung to her desperately.

She waited a minute longer, timed it subconsciously in her head, and then pulled away.

"I can't do this," she repeated, "It's over James." She wiped the tears off her face and pulled the scarf back on. Before he could protest anymore, she walked quickly down the hall and out of the door, not looking back once.

Back inside James crumpled into a heap on the floor and wept silent tears.

*

Kaiser was talking into his phone again. That's what Kite had nicknamed him. When the boss wanted, the boss pulled a sense of humour from somewhere. The meeting had gone well. He had broken the deal down into its simplest form and Kite had given the seal of approval. The split was 51/49 in Kite's favour but Kaiser knew that would balance out in time. He would just bide it, and wait.

"How quickly can you make the arrangements?"

"How quickly do you want it Chief?"

"You have two days. Then we start dealing."

*

Maggie had spent almost all of the two weeks allotted to her on her preparation, not so much because Sean had instructed her to, but because this was big and deep down she knew it was her duty to protect her father's good name. There was also a certain arrogance in her thinking. She wanted to show the Board who was boss around here and she wanted Dominic Clayton to appreciate just whom he was liaising with now. She would bring him down bit by bit if he made trouble for her. She clung to the thought of white-hot revenge should anything go wrong tonight. She was feeling confident now that she'd made her choice and ditched James and her personal life. No one had found out and Johnny was sworn to secrecy.

She felt fresh and alive again, not even daring to take a shot of whisky beforehand lest it should cloud her judgement. She would stay well away from alcohol tonight, even if offered any. There was nervous excitement building up inside of her. She snapped her briefcase shut and waited for Sean to fetch her. They were meeting Mr Clayton on his yacht on the Thames for drinks. Sean would accompany her as far as the mooring and then she was on her own.

When Sean came by, he appraised her carefully and smiled. He had forced her to have dinner with him last night and then he'd accompanied her back to her private residence where Mrs Peters was waiting to give Sean a dress rehearsal of Maggie's outfit. She had protested, but Mrs Peters was under strict orders and followed them through to the letter. As always, Sean got exactly what he wanted. Maggie had been repulsed the whole evening and made it known that she was not happy being this closely scrutinised. Sean had just given her a look to say *take it or leave it*, which had aggravated her still further.

But right now, she'd put all of that behind her and waited patiently for Sean to finish looking her up and down. The outfit was critical to making this work since Mr Clayton did not appear to respect or even like women anywhere near him. She had to be tempting, but not sluttish. She knew Sean couldn't resist the tight black low cut cocktail dress that curled over her bottom and finished at the very tops of her thighs, the four inch heels that made her slender legs look like they were going on forever, and her flawless, understated make up highlighting all of her facial features spectacularly. Her carefully selected diamonds dripped all over her body powering the adornment. She shook out her hair and said with all the seductiveness she could muster, "How do I look?"

He licked his lips. "Delicious. If Clayton doesn't fall for you, he needs his eyes tested."

He placed her fur coat around her shoulders and leant into her neck to inhale. "Good, no perfume," he whispered, "You remembered."

She resisted the urge to shiver as his breath tingled the hairs on the back of her neck. "Let's go," she ordered, immediately commanding the situation. It was the first time she'd been brave enough to do that since the Board's rebuff. But this was different. A whole new level. And tonight was going to be her night. She could feel it.

*

The limousine drove them right up to the embankment. A small motorboat was waiting to take Maggie across. Sean helped her in and wished her luck.

Then he sat back in the car and waited for the phone call because he *knew* it was coming.

Maggie was met with surprise from the hired boatmen, but she ignored it. She had to save all of her retorts for Dominic because he would be the one most surprised of all.

One of Clayton's men was waiting for her when she stepped from the motorboat and onto the yacht.

"Who are you?" he demanded. His accent was thick and foreign.

"Miss Dalton," she replied, keeping her voice steady. The first bit of resistance.

The man frowned at her and nodded to his smaller colleague. He walked quickly ahead and went around the corner and out of sight.

"We were expecting a man."

"Well, I'm here instead, so take me to Mr Clayton please." She played it calm. The other men lurking were appreciating her, but this one was not. He looked harassed, like he didn't need this tonight.

The smaller man came back and breathlessly relayed a message out of earshot of Maggie. She waited patiently, ready to make her next move should they decide to kick her off of the boat.

"He will see you. You are very lucky. This is not normal practice, but he has had a good day."

Maggie nodded and followed the man. She, in turn, was followed by two other men who kept pace behind her.

He led her off the deck and up some steps, down a long corridor and up some more steps. Back in the car, Sean mapped her movements in his head. Dominic had just blasted his ear. Why had they sent a woman, a young woman at that? Where was *he*? Why had the arrangement changed at the last minute? He didn't appreciate surprises. That sort of thing. Sean had played it especially cool. He was used to this kind of backlash. It was his metier. He had appealed to Clayton's requirements and had him eating out of the palm of his hand before the conversation was over. Sean knew nothing could go wrong tonight. His life was at stake as well as Maggie's. It was in his interests to keep the situation under control. And control was his middle name.

They came to a door and the man knocked.

"Enter." A voice boomed.

He searched her before opening the door and then cautiously let her through and announced her arrival.

Mr Clayton sat with his back to the door and didn't turn around immediately. A fire was burning in the grate and Maggie, having a quick look around, saw this must be his sitting room.

The two men waited outside and the one who had greeted her unceremoniously on the yacht stood waiting by the door. She noticed the smaller man standing at the other end of the room. *All exits blocked and being watched* she thought.

"Why are you here?" he hissed. He was puffing on a long Cuban cigar. The aroma filled the room.

"To do business with you Sir."

A long pause, then, "I don't do business with women. Not unless they're intelligent women. And there are not much of those types left in this world. All my life I have been surrounded by bimbos. I am tired of bimbos." He snorted and chose that exact moment to spin around on his seat and face her.

They each took a moment to sum the other up. His eyes were ruthless and cold. She concentrated hard on piercing him back with hers.

"You think just because you're Richard Dalton's daughter, this is ok?"

She assumed by *this* he meant sending a woman instead of a man to do business.

She said nothing.

"I don't like being tricked. My instinct is saying to throw you overboard."

Still she said nothing.

"I hold all the cards."

That was the cue she was waiting for. She boldly stepped forwards. "That's where you're wrong Mr Clayton. It's now me holding all of the cards." She was bluffing. She really couldn't afford to walk away now, but he didn't know this. For all he knew, she had investors coming out of her ears. One refusal was not going to make any difference to her. Or so she hoped he might think.

"Hmmm, so the madam likes to bargain." He wasn't going to admit it, but he liked what he saw. He actually had never done business with her father, but he respected a man whose reputation preceded him, even if their real line of work was far removed from anything Richard Dalton would ever dabble in.

"Sit," he commanded.

The man behind her took her coat and she sat down on the chaise. Placed the briefcase next to her feet and waited. The less she had to speak, the better.

He puffed away on his cigar forming smoke rings around her. "You going to show me what's in that case or what?" He signalled to the smaller man. "Get me a drink, and get the lady one too." He turned back to her. "Scotch?"

She nodded, despite her earlier resolution. It would be a bad move to refuse now. She waited for their drinks, took a sip of hers and then opened her briefcase.

"These are the papers."

"Read them," he ordered the smaller man.

Sean counted down the minutes in his head. Any time now and they would be here. He sat back in the car and waited for the signal.

"Everything is in order Sir." The smaller man handed the papers to Mr Clayton and produced a pen. "Sign here."

Maggie waited. This was much easier than she'd anticipated. She was completely unaware that Sean was pulling all the strings and smoothing over the pathway for her.

Sean checked his watch. Any second now…

Mr Clayton handed the papers back to her and she put them in the briefcase. Five more minutes and she could be off this yacht and away from here. She finished her Scotch and got up to leave.

"Where are you going?"

The colour drained out of her face. She thought she was home and dry.

"What about my package?" There was a threatening undertone to Clayton's voice. The other two men in the room moved a fraction closer in her direction. She stood firm, clutching her briefcase.

Package? Package? What package? Had she been set up? Had she missed something? What damn package?

She was thinking frantically.

Shit, where was Sean?

"Where are you hiding it?" He had stopped puffing and was staring at her, his cold eyes narrowing by the second.

Shit, what package?

The two men moved in closer.

She started to panic. It was like a tidal wave rushing through her. *What was the package? Where the hell was Sean?*

"You don't have it do you!" Before she could reply, the man behind her knocked the briefcase from her hand and had her arms twisted up behind her back where he held her whilst she struggled. She groaned as the dress ripped under her arms, and dared to look up to see the smaller man pointing a gun barrel to her head.

Shit!

Sean watched a different motorboat roll up to the embankment and he got out of the car and stepped aboard.

"You're late," he growled, "she could be dead."

The other man shrugged and manoeuvred the boat towards the yacht.

"If she's dead, you're dead." Sean threatened. He pulled out his shiny revolver and flicked off the safety catch anticipating trouble. Three minutes behind schedule could make all the difference.

Maggie heard the motorboat and instinctively knew it must be Sean. The other men in the room heard it too.

Clayton slammed his glass down and got up from his chair. "This better be it bitch!" He slapped her hard across the face.

"No more games." There was silence in the room. The smaller man was trigger-happy pulling back on it bit by bit to scare her. She knew it could go off at any second and that made her feel sick to her stomach. Clayton went to the door and ordered one of the men outside to find out. Then he stood in the doorway and waited.

Sean barged his way on board pointing the gun at anyone who stood in his way. There wasn't much resistance. The messenger had cleared the path for him. The package bounced around in his jacket pocket as he ran to the room, the layout of the boat firmly etched on his brain, and entered without waiting to be announced. He appraised the situation within a matter of seconds. He was a professional, after all.

"Lower your weapon." Clayton demanded. He had moved to the middle of the room and was pointing a gun at Sean.

Sean didn't move. "Give me the girl. I have your package."

"I could kill you here and now, and the girl."

"But you won't. Give me the girl in exchange for the package. We don't want a scene, not here on the Thames."

Maggie couldn't believe what she was hearing. Sean had set her up! Panic and fear quickly turned to rage. She watched him reach into his jacket pocket and pull out the package. He tossed it at Clayton's feet. They still had their guns raised.

"Now give me the girl."

Clayton nodded to the man holding Maggie and he released her. The smaller man moved away lowering his gun. She grabbed her briefcase and coat and ran to Sean's side.

Finally Clayton and Sean lowered their weapons too. Clayton bent down to check the package. He ripped it open. Maggie thought the tension in the room was going to suffocate her. She saw the packets of white powder tumble to the floor.

"The purest you could wish for."

Clayton looked pleased.

"And there's more?"

"Oh yes, this is just a sample. I'll be in touch." Sean flipped the safety catch on his gun and tucked it back in his waistband. The drama was over.

"Payment will be in your bank account tonight."

Sean nodded, and then grabbed Maggie by the arm as they were escorted off the yacht and into the small motorboat within seconds. The different emotions she'd been taken through tonight suddenly all came to a head and she flipped on the ride back to the bank. She was cursing him and hitting out in anger and frustration, and it took all his strength to restrain her. She was calling him a bastard over and over again. Sean had made sure Johnny was not on this job and had chosen his own men to accompany them instead. He looked around as he dragged her up the embankment. Luckily there was no one around to hear her screaming. He tried to wrestle her into an arm lock and put his hand over her mouth, but she was fighting him all the way, hysterical and biting at his fingers. The driver got out of the car along with his bodyguard and they took Maggie off of him and forced her down onto the back seat.

"Give her a jab of Versed, strong dose, and make sure Mrs Peters puts her straight to bed. She won't remember any of this in the morning. She'll only remember what an amazing job she's just done."

And Sean was right. When she awoke the next morning, still somewhat dazed and confused, it was only the memory of the signed papers tucked away safely in her briefcase that filled her head. And then she suddenly felt more alive than she'd ever felt before. She lay back in her bed and pulled the covers around her, shivering with excitement, feeling heady, and letting every part of herself indulge in this glorious feeling of accomplishment and triumph. She slid down into the pillows and couldn't wipe the smug grin off her face for a very long time. Even when she opened up the briefcase and looked through the papers, and all through the meeting with the Board, she maintained the same conceited look about her, but subtly done so she didn't piss anybody off. That was not the intention, at least not for now. She listened to their praise with gratification and absorbed as much of it as she could, so she would savour every moment for later when she was once again alone. Finally, Thomas came up to her. He waited until the others had left the room. He had been smiling at her throughout the meeting, as had Sean, but he was saving his congratulations for the right moment, and the right moment was now.

"You did a tremendous job last night."

"I'm glad I could live up to your expectations."

"I know you've already heard it a dozen times, but your father really would be very proud of you today."

She wanted to ask him why her father would ever deal with a man like Dominic Clayton, but she couldn't do it. She had just pulled off the biggest deal of her life and been catapulted once again to the very top alongside him. She didn't want to risk losing that momentous standing by asking dumb, insignificant questions. What the heck anyway, she'd done it hadn't she!

"There were no problems?"

"Nothing I couldn't handle," she lied. She vaguely remembered a struggle, but her mind was hazy. She didn't know it, but the needle Sean had given her was a sedative called Midazolam used before surgery to calm a patient down. It also caused short-term memory loss.

"Good." He held out his hand.

She shook it, smiling. And in that split second she doubled over and the smile turned to a grimace.

"What's wrong Maggie? What's going on?"

"I feel terribly sick."

"Did you eat anything on Clayton's boat?" That was his first suspicion. Poison.

She groaned as Thomas helped her to her feet. "No, I didn't eat anything." She tried to laugh. "I was too nervous." She groaned again. "I just need to get to the bathroom."

"I'll call Mrs Peters or Lucia." He reached for the Boardroom phone, but she pushed it away.

"No, I'm fine. Leave it. I'll see you later." She shuffled out of the room clutching her stomach. Thomas tried for the housekeeper anyway, but there was no answer. He tried twice more hoping one of the two might pick up, but still no answer. He made a mental note to check up on Maggie later that day, but when he tried to get hold of her, she was nowhere to be seen and Mrs Peters and Lucia hadn't seen her all day either. Sean was also missing and so was Johnny. He concluded that she'd probably gone out to celebrate with one of them, or both, and didn't think anymore of it.

*

"You took a risk."

"But it paid off."

Kaiser was talking to the boss, giving Kite an update on the first shipment and subsequent trading.

There was silence at the other end, then, "Don't take risks. You put me in danger again and I *will* kill you."

He smiled down the phone. "Not if I kill you first." And hung up.

*

Maggie sat on her bathroom floor staring at the pregnancy test in disbelief. Fate...that's what it was...but she couldn't accept it. Not now. Not when she'd just made it. Finally. Into the Business world her father had once controlled. What was Fate doing to her? Tearing her apart! Making the road twist and turn so she didn't know whether she was coming or going. So much turmoil inside of her, so much confusion. God it hurt. Another decision she didn't know how to make. She felt wretched. This was going to slowly drive her insane. She rocked herself on the floor trying to comfort her galloping mind. She was shaking and sobbing into her knees praying for this to go away. But it wasn't going to. She was carrying a baby inside of her and she couldn't abort it. No matter how much she tried to reason it was the right thing to do to keep her career and the business on track, she couldn't kill their baby. She wasn't a monster. Not like her own mother. She was no monster.

*

It was all playing out like before except this time she hoped he would smile, that sweet sweet smile...and laugh...oh how she loved it when he laughed! Johnny had smuggled her out, drove fast, taking her back to Farnham, the second time in less than three weeks. Nothing but James would ever have brought her back to this place.

"Why are you here?" he demanded, "Have you come to stick the knife in some more? Is that it? Come to gloat?"

She was searching for the right words, but there was no other way to say it. Breaking the news gently, she said, "I'm pregnant James. With our baby."

CHAPTER 4

If I were scared, would you come to me?
If I were hurting, would you take my pain away?
I am frightened. I am so very frightened.
I ask questions. I ask a lot of questions. Up here in my head where no one can find them. No one can go there except me. I'm terrified of the answers. Can you answer me? Will you answer me?
Nothing I do for my mother is good enough.
When does it end?
When does the anger end?
When do all the beatings end?
She keeps drinking. She is drowning in drink. And she is so angry with me.
Why is she angry?
Is there purpose to my life? Am I worth something to somebody?
Why am I here?
I never meant to do anything wrong.
I've always been polite, well mannered, and respectful.
But this is not enough for her.
I have friends. I have my father who I love so much and who loves me in return. I have a home. I have food and clothing. I have lots of things just like everyone else.
I also have a mother who despises me.
Is this what makes me different?

I go to school sometimes and see happy, smiling faces. I smile too so I am the same as my friends, so I won't stand out. They don't see the pain I hide. I give nothing away.
I have a secret no one knows.
She beats me every day.
I won't tell anyone.
I wouldn't want to turn the smiles into tears, the laughter into sadness.
I can't tell them. I swore to myself that I wouldn't tell them.
Was I a mistake?
Maybe this is the answer I am frantically searching for.

Little Child

I sit here in the darkness, lost in my nightmare, lost in my questions, and terrified of the answers. Wondering what the next day will bring, wondering how much more I can bear.
I pray silently but I don't know who I'm praying to, or whether they will help me.

*

She slammed her into the dining room table and watched as she toppled over, her flailing arm taking a chair with her. Emily's screams pierced her anguished thoughts. She looked at the glass in her hand and then at her daughter, a crumpled heap on the floor. She tried to squeeze the glass. She wanted it to break. It was too much, it was all too much. The threats. The scandal. The suspense. Losing control, release, was the only thing she had left. She slumped down into the nearest chair and reached for the bottle of Scotch.
Emily watched silently as her mother poured yet another glass. This was the way it was, the drinking and the abuse, day in, day out. Emily felt the tears stinging her eyes as her mother got up and stumbled out of the room, the whisky bottle in one hand, the glass in the other. For a long time afterwards she didn't move. Her heart bled. Every ordeal leaving a deeper scar.

*

Maggie Dalton sifted through the hangers of designer clothes, admiring here, discarding there, as her eyes moved over each individual garment.
I love shopping, she thought to herself, fingering the beautiful items one by one.
A suede coat caught her eye and she pulled it out in anticipation, searching for any mishaps in the design.
Perfect, she mused.
The changing rooms were empty when she walked up to the assistant and was handed a ticket for one item of clothing only.
"Looks like you've picked the best time to shop," the assistant remarked, smiling pleasantly.

"I hate the crowds," she replied, "I find going shopping just before my daughter finishes school makes things a lot easier. Doing it this way, I can go straight from here to the school and pick her up. Kills two birds with one stone, if you see what I mean."

The assistant nodded approvingly, not realising the malicious pun that was intended.

"Is she in for a surprise today, your daughter?"

Maggie was caught off guard momentarily, "Oh no, no she isn't. I actually bought her some new clothes last weekend." She hadn't, but how was the shop assistant to know she was lying. "Well, I suppose I really should get a move on with seeing if this fits." *Subtle change of subject,* she thought cunningly, *I wonder if she suspects.* The conversation was beginning to make her feel uncomfortable.

"I'll be pleased to help if you need my advice." The assistant called after her, still smiling, unhurried, unknowing.

Once in the private changing room, she breathed a sigh of relief. It was always the same when she ventured into new stores - did they know, didn't they know. She could never tell. Sometimes she would see them whispering, other times they would simply address her calmly and respectfully. Settling the bill was always fun, especially if her PA had phoned ahead to set up a new account. Then they would realise who they were dealing with. Well, when you owned the largest Investment Corporation in the City, surely you were entitled to special treatment. Maggie smiled to herself. *Of course she was.* She liked the excitement of trying out new places but there was a danger in being too bold. Lately, there seemed to be good things and bad things printed about her on a daily basis, so she had to choose her moments carefully. First impressions were important to her because she didn't want the hassle or the scandal that might follow afterwards. People didn't ask her for autographs, they didn't dare. She had a reputation for being untouchable, even though she wandered the little town where she lived freely without bodyguards or chauffeur driven cars. Her advisers told her she was crazy, but it fell on deaf ears. If somebody wanted something from her, she assumed they would be big enough and brave enough to come and ask for it, otherwise they should stay well away. Ever since someone had attempted to murder her thirteen years ago, she had promised herself she was never going to shy away like a coward. If they wanted her, well here she was. It was a huge risk, but she thrived on it. It was the business aura that surrounded her and the rumours that she couldn't shrug off, they haunted her past but in many respects they were also her saviour. People knew she could be trouble so they revered her with a mixture of fear and respect, but nobody really knew if what they read in the business sections of the broadsheets was true. If they wanted to find out then they would have to get involved, and nobody dared do that. You didn't take an encounter with Maggie Dalton lightly.

She slipped out of her old coat that would still last another winter yet, and carefully put on the new one. She stood admiring herself in the full-length mirror, and then peered closer to look at her face. Something had caught her eye and was beginning to trouble her; was it the gradual build up of lines that were appearing around her eyes and mouth, or was it the slight sagging of her almost perfect cheekbones. She couldn't tell. *Maggie Dalton, don't you dare age,* she told herself sullenly. No sooner had the words escaped her lips, she realised it was inevitable. Her mind span back to her own mother scorning her every move and telling her how ugly she looked. As quickly as it appeared, the image was gone and her mind snapped back to reality. Such flashbacks never lasted long and weren't allowed to, although the irreversible impression was always there, lurking just beneath the surface.

More Botox would fix it, and now the coat was on her, looking fantastic.

"I'll have it," she said out loud, meaning for the shop assistant to hear her. She quickly changed back into her other coat and snatched up the rest of her shopping. A quick glance at her watch told her it was nearly time to leave, or the assistant might become suspicious.

"Any good?"

"Perfect, exactly what I was looking for," she answered, handing in her ticket, "Where do I pay?"

The assistant took it and motioned towards the cashier's counter.

"It's just over there," she said brightly, and then added, "You'd better hurry, doesn't school finish about now?"

"Oh yes," she replied, feeling annoyed at the nosy shop assistant but masking it well, "I'd better get moving, thanks."

"No problem," the assistant said, still cheery, still unknowing.

Maggie walked over to the counter and placed the coat carefully on its polished surface, waiting for the cashier to acknowledge her. *Would he know?*

He looked up and smiled. "Mrs Dalton, it's a pleasure to have you shop with us today."

She returned his smile. "I believe I have a new account with you." So cordial, this was impressing for her.

The cashier put her purchase carefully into a bag, noticing the look of irritation on her face when it caught slightly on the handle.

"We'll add it to the account ma'am."

More polite smiles and the exchange was nearly over; the receipt was being put in the bag.

"Thank you," she said, turning to leave.

"Goodbye Mrs Dalton."

She walked out feeling satisfied with her purchase. Shopping took the edge off her business troubles, and there had been a lot of them recently. *Too* many.

It was mid afternoon and the high street was suddenly packed with people. Another school day was over. It was times like this when she wished she had a chauffeur on stand by. Being hustled and bustled by ordinary folk was never a very pleasant experience. But a limousine would attract too much unwanted attention and when sober, she had a yearning for the quieter life these days. It was keeping up the pretence she found the most suffocating. That experience in the shop had almost killed her.

Why would anybody want a family? she silently asked, as she watched mothers and children go by, *It's unfortunate I have one now, but I never asked for it. This is my mother's curse, I'm sure.*

Her reasoning went unnoticed, as vicarious as it was. People kept on passing her by in worlds of their own, unknowing, uncaring, just like the shop assistant. To anyone looking in, she was just an ordinary wife and mother, living an ordinary life despite her business ventures, and going home to eat a meal with her family before being taken to bed by her husband. No-one would have ever suspected that the woman walking down the street towards her car, supposedly heading towards the school, was a cruel, heartless abuser, about to inflict pain on her own daughter, both physically and emotionally.

*

I wiped down the kitchen cabinets one final time and stood back to look over them. My mother would be home any time now to inspect what I'd done and I knew what the punishment would be if it didn't look up to scratch. These moments terrified me. I couldn't do anything to please her. She was never satisfied however hard I polished or scrubbed or cleaned. I could never do enough. I could never get it right. This was the way it was since as long as I could remember.

My father was working at his art studio in town. We lived off his wages. My mother was a multi millionaire but we never saw a penny of it. She didn't seem to do an awful lot, she was happy to let everybody else run her business affairs, hiding behind her study door and whisky bottle most of the time. She took it upon herself to see to the clients and this she did extremely well. We had never been a part of her real life; we never went up to the country estate to meet her close, personal advisers or any of the staff. I think this is how she wanted it. I think she wanted to keep us hidden away because we were an embarrassment to her and she was ashamed of us. We only came out for business dinner parties when it suited her. When it was convenient.

Well, we were ashamed of her too, except we were afraid to do anything about it.

I slaved for her all day, every day, rarely going to school, and she rewarded me with beatings for my work.

The door burst open and she came through loaded down with the latest designer labels, a flurry of Elizabeth Arden, Gucci, and Dolce and Gabbana bags, besides many others.

"Get out of my way you stupid girl!" she snorted, as she passed by to slip her shoes off. I scrambled to the other side of the room and carried on working. She was in a fool mood even though she'd been shopping to her hearts content.

Within a few minutes she came back into the kitchen and started to look around. I started to tremble, knowing what was coming. This was always the calm before the storm, yet I had no way of escaping.

She turned on me suddenly and I shrank back into the corner.

"I don't know why you bother," she scorned, "the place looks worse than when I left it this morning."

"But Mother…" I began to protest, but she cut me off.

"Shut up child! Shut up! I've had enough of you and your pathetic excuses. Go and get me some cigarettes."

I looked at her dumbly, words failing me.

"Did you hear what I said?" She was coming closer, fists raised.

"I can't," I whispered.

"You'll do as you're told!" I held my breath, waiting for the strike. It was then that I felt the impact knocking the wind out of me. I tried not to keel over, grabbing the nearest cabinet to steady myself.

"I can't buy them, I'm under age!" I managed to plead.

"Well, we'll soon solve that." She grabbed my arm and hauled me into the living room where her bags had been dumped. Pushing me into a chair, she delved into her handbag and pulled out a lipstick.

"Ah ha! Just the thing." She came over to where I sat and yanked my hair back forcing my face upwards and flipping off the lid, began to apply the colour to my lips.

"There that makes you look older." She seemed satisfied. "Now go and get my cigarettes!"

I did as I was told and left the house not stopping to bother to ask for any money. This would be out of my own pocket and I couldn't even afford it.

I hurried along the street still shaking. Every day was the same. I wondered whether it would ever get any better. I painfully watched people having a good time; I saw their smiles and heard their laughter. Yet if I shared my secret with them, it would change everything. Nobody likes to witness sadness and pain. People don't care unless it happens to them. I only had my father to confide in and he was subjected to the same fierce, relentless abuse.

I am alone in this world, waiting for my time, certain of my destiny.

Little Child

The clock ticks, but there isn't anyone who can change my fate.

I bought the cigarettes quickly and was about to cross the road leading back up to my house when I heard someone calling my name. I span around and watched the twins; two of my closest friends come running towards me. Quickly I wiped the lipstick off onto the back of my hand.

"Hiya," I said, trying to sound lively; this was the last thing I needed. Mother would punish me if I was away too long.

"Hi Em! How's it going?" Ali was the first to reach me.

"I'm ok, just taking a walk to get some fresh air," I lied.

"How are you feeling?" Jason asked, joining us.

"I've been better thanks." I didn't really know what to say, I wasn't in the mood for talking.

"How about coming to ours? Mum would love to see you." Ali linked my arm and we started to head in the direction of home. They only lived one street away from our big house, but it might as well have been another world. I just wanted to get home and finish the beatings for another day. This was more than I could take.

"We could have a catch up and watch a movie. Come on Em, it'll be fun. You look like you could do with some cheering up," Jase added, walking the other side of me.

"I'd love to but I'm very tired."

"More hospital stuff?" Ali inquired, looking concerned.

"No, just a bad day." I was unable to hide the dejection in my voice.

"So, all the more reason to come round!" Jason persisted.

I stopped. "I can't right now, I'm sorry but I'm really not up to it." The pressure was getting to me. My friends were great but they didn't know about the abuse I went through every single day, or the pain and humiliation I felt inside. It was too much for them to understand, and besides, they *wouldn't* understand.

"I have to go."

"We'll walk you to your door."

"Jason, please, I would prefer to be alone."

"Is there anything we can do?" Ali asked, while Jason stared at me. I knew I'd upset him.

"I'll be fine, the tablets make me like this. I hate it but there's nothing I can do. I'm sorry." More lies and I seemed to be forever apologising. What tablets? I didn't even have any medication! This long-term illness story was getting way out of hand.

"It's ok, we understand." Jason broke his silence and gave me that lopsided grin I adored.

Do you? I thought to myself.

"We just worry Em. We miss you at school," Ali added.

I nodded. "I know," I heard myself saying.

"We'll tell Mum we saw you." They started to walk away; I wanted so much to be with them, I almost ran to catch up.

"Bye!" I called, watching them disappear.

Ali turned to take one last look before they rounded the corner. "We'll see you soon Em!" She lifted up her hand and waved.

I waved back and then they were gone.

I hoped I hadn't offended them. Their mother was my Tutor and English teacher. I loved English. When I was in Mrs Cash's lessons, everything was ok and I felt so safe. If only I could have gone with them.

When I arrived home she was waiting for me sitting on one of the kitchen stools at the breakfast bar with a glass in her hand. The bottle of Scotch wasn't too far away.

"You better have a good excuse. You've been ages. Where are they?" she demanded, glaring at me.

I didn't dare answer back as I pulled the cigarettes from my pocket and handed them over.

She grabbed them and I watched in horror as a look of disgust crossed her face.

"Just as I thought," she said quietly, "you've brought the wrong ones."

I debated whether to lie telling her that that's all they had left, but what was the use, she'd probably drag me up there and make a scene and I would still receive a punishment anyway – double humiliation.

"You've brought the wrong ones!" she repeated, her voice rising, "You stupid, stupid little girl. I don't like Silkcut. This is what I smoke, this!" She shoved a Benson and Hedges packet in my face and I tried to back away.

"But I couldn't afford it!" I stammered, realising that my excuses would be pointless against her craziness.

"You couldn't afford it? Couldn't afford it! Well, tell that idiot father of yours to give you more pocket money." She was off the stool and slapped me hard across the face.

I reeled back and reached out for a cabinet to stop myself falling.

"Mother please don't hurt me…please!"

"Stop crying you baby, take your punishment." This time a punch caught me in the chest and I fell forwards. "You brought this upon yourself!"

She hauled me back up and slammed me into the cooker; I hunched over and felt the tears stinging my eyes.

"Mother!" I pleaded, "Don't, please don't!" But she wasn't listening, I had made her angry and now she was going to punish me. The cycle wouldn't be complete if the beatings didn't happen.

"You are so pathetic. Why do I even bother with you?" Another punch, another kick, more heartless words. "You make me hit you because you can't do as you're told. I don't want to waste my time punishing you but you bring it upon yourself, you stupid lazy little girl!" She was shouting at me and using her fists to make an impact.

I couldn't breathe; my whole body was racked with pain. It was a test of survival, a test of determination to see whether I could stay alive. I was screaming at her to stop but she overpowered me, nothing could hold her back from getting her retribution.

She was saying she hated me over and over again. I lay in a crumpled heap on the floor taking my discipline. I deserved this, she wouldn't be doing it if I didn't deserve it, and I shouldn't have infuriated her.

No, no, no! Why was I blaming myself? I couldn't please her; I would never be able to please her. My father said it wasn't my fault, he said she was an evil, bitter person who took her anger out on me because I was always there – an easy target. He told me I was a good person. That I should never change. So why did my mother hate me so much? Why was this happening to me?

"Don't ever disobey me again." The words were harsh, sinking deeper and deeper into my soul. "I won't forget this, I won't forget it!"

"Mother," I whispered, "why are you doing this to me?"

She didn't hear me; her own voice was far louder, far more powerful, drowning out my questions, drowning out my thoughts. I was sinking into a world beyond the hell I experienced here and yet I didn't want to leave it. Why was I holding on? Why was I trying to delay what could eventually be my freedom? I tried to imagine a better place where my father and I could live in peace away from this torture.

But there was no better place.

We were always running from our fear.

It was over and I couldn't move, my body ached yet my heart was numb. My father would be coming home soon and I knew how awful he'd feel if he saw me lying here, helpless, frightened, his little child all black and blue. 'Save me God,' I prayed, as I wept silently, 'save me from this anger and hatred, allow my mother to open up a place in her heart to love me, please God.'

This was the prayer I uttered every time I went through this ordeal of abuse. I didn't know whether I believed my mother could ever have a change of heart, I didn't even know whether I believed in God, but I prayed to him all the same.

*

James bounded through the door full of life and energy even though he too had to suffer the same treatment as Emily. He loved coming home to see his little girl after a concentrated day at the studio. She was everything to him; he lived and breathed for her, so when he saw her lying in a mess on the kitchen floor, his heart sank and he cried out in desperation. Immediately rushing to her side, he dropped to his knees and gently swept her up into his arms.

"Oh god! Oh dear, dear god! What has she done?"

Emily pointed to her ribs where it hurt the most. She could barely speak.

He hated Maggie for what she did to them. He hated her for losing control, and for dictating their lives, for shunning them, and for hitting them. He hated everything about her. His family were banned from the house and Maggie refused to have any staff come down from the estate, so there was nobody to protect Emily, except him, and he was out working most of the time trying to make ends meet. Once so in love and now reduced to this – fighting and arguing and striking out at their daughter. *What the hell was wrong with her?*

A tear trickled down his face. *How long can this go on?* He didn't know the answer. It hurt Emily to see him cry, it hurt more than the physical pain she was enduring. He was intense, angry, yet deeply wounded.

"You need to go to the hospital." He wiped his eyes with his shirt sleeve. "I'm going to call an ambulance."

Emily held on, terrified. "No," she whispered, "she'll get angry again."

Maggie had locked herself in her study, but when she heard the ambulance, all hell would break loose. And the neighbours – Emily didn't want everybody to know what went on in their house, she didn't want them to point and stare. They lived in a quiet street, the big house at the end of the cul-de-sac. The ambulance would come screaming down the road and screech to a halt outside, alerting them all that something terrible had happened here.

"She's not going to get away with this Sweetheart. She can beat me up as well and then everybody will know what an abusive person she is! She won't be able to do anything, not right now. You need medical attention straight away; an ambulance will get you to the hospital much faster than I could in rush hour." He left her while he made the call. Emily pulled herself into a sitting position and leant back feeling every punch, kick, slap that had hit her just a few moments earlier. He was talking quietly on the phone. "Yes, 56 Cardwell Avenue, I think my daughter's cracked some ribs. Please hurry. Thanks."

He came back and was just starting to help Emily into her jacket when they heard a noise behind them. They both turned to see Maggie standing in the doorway, a smirk spread across her lips.

"And where do you think you're going?"

James was seething. "You've broken her ribs!" He spoke through clenched teeth and his fists were curling into tight balls.

Emily sat watching, paralysed with fear. *No more fighting, please no more fighting.*

"She should have bought me the right cigarettes!" Maggie was enjoying this.

"You made her buy cigarettes?" He was incredulous. "She's thirteen years old for Christ sake!"

She ignored him and reached for the bottle of Scotch on the bar.

"You haven't answered my question," she said quietly, pouring herself a large glass.

"I've called an ambulance." He was attempting to control the situation, but his voice wavered.

She choked on her drink, "You what?"

"I've called an ambulance," he repeated, "so don't try anything."

At first she was shocked, and then her face went blank. He had surprised her; she hadn't been expecting him to take matters into his own hands. Ambulances were always the last resort, when things had gone too far. Maggie didn't feel this had gone too far. What was going on? Why was it so out of control?

She spluttered and then coughed loudly taking another sip of her drink to steady herself.

There was silence as she swallowed slowly, never taking her eyes off them. Time appeared to be standing still and yet the clock ticked loudly on the wall, registering the seconds, registering the minutes.

She tried to remember what had happened, but it was all too hazy. Why hadn't the situation been contained?

Finally she spoke, her voice composed even if her mind was not, "Well I'll keep out of your way. I wouldn't want to spoil your fun."

James lunged at her with the intention of striking her down, but she found her reflexes in time.

"I don't think so!" she said, ducking out of the way and grabbing his flailing arm.

"You!" he shouted, "You've hurt our daughter and you don't care! How can you be so cruel?"

She backed off and walked towards the hallway. They watched her go but she couldn't resist turning and sneering, "Don't think I'll forget this just like that, oh no. You'll pay for setting me up. You'll pay for sure!" It was directed at James, hateful words with intent.

Emily held onto her father but he didn't answer and wasn't going to. They both knew they couldn't change the cycle of events. They listened to her stomp up the stairs and then they heard the siren wail in the distance.

"Not long now," he said finishing with her jacket, "We'll soon get you sorted out." He hugged her being careful not to squeeze too hard.

The ambulance pulled up outside the house and it wasn't long before Emily was strapped to a stretcher and in the back of it. To her shock a crowd had already formed around the vehicle. She tried to look around but she was fastened in tight. Her eyes drifted upwards back towards the house and she saw Maggie standing in the bedroom window, watching, the same smirk still distorting her face.

*

It was getting late and the nurses were moving around the ward making the patients comfortable for the night. My father was dozing sitting in the chair next to me. I would have to wake him in a minute so he could go home. I didn't want him to leave me, but he wasn't allowed to stay in the hospital overnight.

"Daddy," I whispered, nudging him, "Daddy, you've got to get home."

He opened his eyes and rubbed them. "What's the time?" he asked, yawning.

I checked the clock on the wall above my head. "Time for you to get going."

"Oh ok." I watched him get up, stretch and slip on his jacket. He bent down to give me a kiss on the forehead. "I wish I could stay sweetheart."

"Are you worried about tonight?" I could sense his fear already; we felt each other's pain in a way nobody else could possibly understand.

"I'll be fine, with any luck she's probably gone out and that means I'll be able to lock myself in the spare bedroom. She won't touch me, not tonight anyway. You just rest and concentrate on getting yourself better, your dad can take care of himself." He laughed quietly but it was tinged with sadness. Who was he kidding? Her hateful, bitter words were still fresh in our minds. *Don't think I'll forget this just like that, oh no. You'll pay for setting me up. You'll pay for sure!* She meant it all right, she always had the last word and she always made sure she kept her evil promises. She would be there waiting to strike as soon as he walked through the door, she would be ready.

"Just be careful," I warned, suddenly feeling very tired.

He squeezed my hand, not saying anything. One by one the lights were going out and we were almost in total darkness.

And then he was gone, vanishing into the shadows. And we were both alone; neither of us could save the other.

I closed my eyes, feeling the painkillers kicking in and the aching in my ribs subsiding. But another pain was quickly taking its place and I fell into a restless sleep dreaming about the monster that tormented our souls day after day, night after night.

*

James went to put the key in the lock and found that the door was already ajar.

Did I not close it properly after rushing out to the ambulance with Emily? he thought to himself, trying to wind back the hours and remember, *No, surely I wouldn't have left it unlocked and open, would I?* He walked cautiously into the house the pounding of his heart drowning out any initial noise, and the questions kept coming. Was she waiting for him as she had predicted? He tried to control his heavy breathing but he knew she was there, the radio was playing in the living room and the light was on. Should he make a dash for upstairs or was this just to lure him into a false sense of security? The kitchen was in darkness as he turned and shut the door behind him as quietly as he could. He fumbled for the light switch and suddenly felt a sharp object smack him between the shoulder blades.

He fell to the floor simultaneously and lay on his front trying to refocus, there was a satisfactory laugh from somewhere in the room and he turned over straining to catch a glimpse of her positioning in the shadows. Then, as if to disadvantage him further, she flicked on the light switch and he was momentarily blinded, shading his eyes only to meet her cold, hard glare staring back at him. He noticed the block of uneven wood in her gloved hands and began to edge backwards. This was already way out of control.

"I warned you James," she whispered quietly, "I warned you what would happen." She began to approach him.

"You don't have to be like this," he answered fiercely, scrabbling to get back to his feet but maintaining eye contact, "I was looking out for our daughter, you know *our* daughter. The one you're supposed to be a Mother to, the one you *hurt!*" The words were said in anguish. Even if she was going to attack, he was going to make sure he told her exactly what he thought of her.

She lunged towards him ready to strike again. "I don't have a daughter!" she screamed, raising the wood and catching him on the side of his head. He had managed to stand up but now staggered back into the corner, blood starting to trickle out from the wound she had just caused. "I never had a daughter!" The wood smashed against his head again and he crumpled into a heap.

"I hate what you have become," he murmured, lying semi-consciously sprawled across the floor. She stood over him, towering like an angry giant whose only object was revenge.

"I would finish you off you bastard but then I would be left with just *her*, the pathetic wretch that I hate so much. It's your fault she's here. Do you hear me? It's your fault. You have cursed me, made me a laughing stock in front of everybody who once respected me. And for that you must pay, you must pay every day for the rest of your life. Nobody does what you have done to me and gets away with it. Nobody! Do you hear me?" She kicked him several times in the stomach and he scrunched up even more coughing and spluttering, his head swimming in the pool of blood that was now forming on the tiles. *How had it come to this?*

"Oh how the mighty have fallen." She almost choked on her own laughter, seeing him wriggle and squirm in pain. "These are the moments I cherish."

"You bitch!" he said, getting up onto his knees and spitting out blood. "You'll get your time; everybody gets their time one way or another." Their eyes met.

She didn't answer but threw the block of wood at him. He ducked and it crashed against the fridge splintering into a million pieces all over the floor. He coughed again and fell forwards.

He watched her walk away and, as she reached the door, she turned for one last look. "My time will never come James," she whispered, "because there are too many people on my side. You just remember that, you just remember."

*

I didn't answer him straight away. We were arguing. This was typical of both of us, each worrying about the other and never showing how bad we really felt. But one of us had to back down and in this case it would be me, I could tell my father didn't want to draw too much attention to himself. That would mean explanations and he didn't have any except for the truth - and the truth would only cause more heartache.

He had stopped by to see me on his way to work. I was able to go home later today and he had promised to pick me up. Only one broken rib, but plenty of bruises. He told the Doctor and Nurses I had fallen off my horse.

"You're just as strong as me Em," he said, but there was no hope in his voice. We both knew only too well that even with our combined determination we would still have difficulty in standing up to her. I noticed the sadness in his eyes and squeezed his hand. I thought about all the times we'd been in this situation before and everything we had gone through, and yet she was still winning. Neither of us liked to admit defeat, but maybe that was all we had left.

I remembered the last time this had happened. They were fighting, my father was trying to protect me but she broke his arm. It must have been when the new dining room chandelier got delivered...I signed for it and then she came home and opened the box and it was all smashed up. She started on me and he tried to intervene but she went crazy with him. It was so vivid in my mind...the glass flying everywhere...the violence...and the madness. Sometimes the abuse was easy to forget, but sometimes it wasn't. I had managed to get away and run into the kitchen where I dialled 999; I remembered my father's cries as she twisted his arm round and round even though it was already broken, and her distorted face shrieking with laughter and satisfaction seeing the pain and horror on his. I remembered being surprisingly calm as I shut the kitchen door and phoned for an ambulance, all I could think of was getting him safe away from her and ending this malicious attack. The Operator had asked me lots of questions and I lied convincingly and told them to hurry because it was an emergency, and then I put the phone down and the door opened. I stood there wondering if I would still be alive by the time we heard the siren roaring down our street. She faced me; her eyes wild, her fists clenched into tight balls. I waited for her to make a move, but she didn't, she just carried on staring and it was almost as if she was looking straight through me.

"Did you call for an ambulance?" she had asked gruffly.

"Yes," I had answered.

She shifted her position in the doorway and seemed distracted from what was going on around her. She wasn't looking at me now, she brushed past me as if I didn't exist and clambered up onto a bar stool pouring herself a Brandy.

And that's where I had left her as I made my way into the living room, wondering what I would find. My father was still whimpering, tears stained his eyes and his face was creased up in pain. I helped him into an armchair and wiped his face, but he didn't respond, he seemed to be in deep shock. He was barely conscious when they lifted him onto the stretcher and took him to the hospital. I had travelled with him, reconfirming my story, and I had made sure I was there when he woke up so he told exactly the same one. When he was ready to come home, Mother disappeared for a few days without a trace, but when she came back, the cycle started all over again. This was just one incident that I could remember, yet there were plenty more, like the time she punched me so hard in the face, she broke my nose, and the time she force fed me and then wouldn't let me be sick so I ended up rupturing my stomach. Every once in a while, either my father or I would wind up in hospital with some injury that she had inflicted on us, yet there was nothing to stop her. She was indestructible.

CHAPTER 5

James was sipping his tea, allowing the guilt to ebb and flow through his body so he could deal with it bit by bit. Laura was taking care of the clients whilst he took a break. He'd never got the bigger art gallery out in the country. When Maggie came back to him after he thought it was all over between them, and told him she was pregnant, nothing else had seemed to matter. Laura had stuck by them, but she was never quite the same towards Maggie after what she'd put James through. It had been five dreadful weeks living through the heart wrenching pain of every single second, and Laura had been the one trying to pick up the pieces for her younger brother. Often absent off gallivanting in his teenage years, she was now a solid part of his life. Their parents hadn't exactly approved of the match with Maggie, but they were happy for their son. The Press had loved it and lapped it up - and she had let them. It was the perfect opportunity to re-launch Maggie Dalton. She was getting on with her life, showing the world she didn't care after that fatal night thirteen years ago. But that had been in the beginning after the wedding and the fanfare, the exclusive dinner dates and parties, the jet setting and the fun. When Lucia and Mrs Peters had been allowed to nurse little Emily so James and Maggie could socialise. Before all of the rumours started and things had gradually got more and more out of control. Before Maggie lost it for the very first time and things had never been the same again. Maggie contained the situation by moving out of her father's estate into a quiet residential area in the town next to James's studio, and keeping everyone from the big house.

There had been no negotiation, no talking it through. She'd snapped one day and this was the net result. Now, he was estranged from his parents and only Laura continued to be a part of his life. He knew they were angry with him for allowing the abuse to go on, for not being a big enough man to walk away. That made him feel worse. But still he stayed. Deep down he was hoping Maggie would change, that whatever was plaguing her would stop and she would once again be the woman he fell in love with. A part of him didn't want to give up. But Emily was lying in hospital beaten and battered,

and it wasn't the first time and surely wouldn't be the last. And he had a deep gash to the head, which wasn't the first time and certainly wouldn't be the last.
Where did he draw the line?
Was it here?

*

They sat across the table from each other. He was drumming his fingers impatiently on the table; she was taking long draws on her cigarette. Neither spoke. He was tapping each finger on his left hand individually, except he only had his thumb and two others to tap with. A part of him regretted upsetting her all those years ago. In hindsight it hadn't been a wise move to make the threat. Intemperance came at a price. She'd blown off two of his fingers. Well, she hadn't. She never got her hands dirty. One of the others had tracked him down and done it for her. Luckily it wasn't his killing hand. That would have been a bitch. The stubby leftovers served as a reminder who was in charge, and don't ever cross the line again. He was ok with that. There were other ways to get revenge. Quieter, simpler methods, like bribery. However loyal she thought her team were; they always appreciated a subtle backhander when he took the odd shipment without her knowledge. But she needn't know. His reputation with the others kept him safe. Loose cannon. Reckless. Crazy fool. That sort of thing. He shrugged it off. This was his way of life, his game. Nobody was about to take his place and play instead.
"You want to make this move or what?" He broke the silence.
She said nothing. He wasn't going to rush her. He knew if he fucked with her again, it was game over, so she was content to make him sweat. She did it often enough. And anyway, he got off on it. He was an over energised, uncontrollable pawn on her chessboard. But she could still manoeuvre and coerce him towards her ultimate goal, with a little extra effort. She knew he wasn't completely loyal, but she was satisfied enough to overlook his extracurricular activities because he was close to something she desperately wanted. And now it was finally in her sights. Not just the one thing she'd hunted all those years ago - but the whole damn package had fallen

at her feet. It was too good an opportunity to miss. And once she had her hands on it, only then would it be time for the curtain call.

She finished her cigarette and stubbed it out slowly, purposely making him wait. "Keep putting the pressure on, tipping off the right people and doing anything else you deem necessary."

"But we have a sitting target!"

"I know, but I want to do a little more damage first. I want to take it apart piece by piece." She smirked.

"Chew it up and spit it out." He understood perfectly.

*

Maggie was sitting in her study reading the morning papers, the events of last night already a million miles away. He had cleaned up the kitchen and left relatively early probably to see the little brat in hospital, maybe even get himself sorted out. Either way she didn't care, as long as they weren't around under her feet bothering her. She turned the page and her hand flew to her mouth when she saw the headlines in the business section. She hadn't quite made the front page but this was just as damning. Underneath the big letters *Dalton PLC -A Sinking Ship?* there was a photo of her purposely looking concerned taken last week when she'd visited her yacht to check over the recent refurbishment work. In truth, she *had* been looking concerned because the work was taking far too long and she needed a holiday, but the Media was a nightmare for using your weakest, most insignificant moment to make their biggest point. She carried on reading barely able to, but forcing herself. *Rumours are circulating that Margaret Dalton, owner of the Investment Corporation Dalton PLC, is in serious financial difficulty.* That was enough! She pushed the paper away quickly. She couldn't read anymore. She dropped her head into her hands and thought back over the last few months. Something was going on and she couldn't put her finger on it. Ok, there had been a few deals gone pear shaped recently but it couldn't all be down to bad luck, could it? It wasn't quite catastrophic yet, there was still some money in the pot keeping them afloat, but they really had to square away some new deals pretty soon to get themselves back in business again. *Damage limitation.* God, if only they could rewind back to the good old days. Those heady days in her early twenties when her career had really taken off, and then how it had steamrolled from there peaking five years later when she gained a record number of new clients in less than six months, soaring their profit into the millions. Her segregation from the rest of the Directors had been her secret weapon. On her own, without distraction, that was when she was at her best. No interference from anyone, no guidelines or rules to follow, or people watching over her shoulder. She could do what the hell she liked and had got pretty good at it. She'd left Thomas in charge up at the estate and abandoned Mrs Peters and Lucia so they couldn't fuss or be involved in her day-to-day affairs. They still tried of course, but everything was done on her terms and that meant they didn't stand a chance. She pounded her head with her fists. What was happening to her business? Three months ago, the Press had been linking Maggie with unsavoury characters and, as much as she tried to deny it, Thomas knew she was associating with the likes of Robert Hilton. But she had argued they needed to branch out. What was the point of sticking to the same clientele when they were failing you? Then two weeks ago rumours started to circulate about alcohol abuse. How did they know she liked a drink or two? Were the Paparazzi hiding in her garden? And now there was *this*. Financial worries. She screwed up the paper in disgust and threw it on the floor. What the hell was going on? Was somebody deliberately trying to sabotage everything she had worked so hard for?

Her mobile bleeped, interrupting her thoughts. She turned her attention to the message on her phone. It was from one of her prospective clients. He was cancelling their 10 o'clock meeting due to illness. She had been looking forward to doing business with him, hoping to get a valuable contract signed away. The disappointment was evident on her face.

"Bugger you then," she snapped.

She reached into her top drawer and pulled out the bottle of Brandy. Pouring herself a glass, she got up from her desk and walked to the big bay window. She looked out over the garden. It was beautifully kept by her daughter and husband, but she wasn't interested. She scanned for any Paparazzi, her paranoia reaching new heights. In a silent gesture to whoever was out there, if indeed there was anybody out there, she raised her glass. *Cheers you bastards!* And then downed the drink in one.

*

My eyes were closed, but I couldn't sleep. I was thinking too much and the dread of going home later was overwhelming me. Being here was just a temporary escape, and then it would start up again. It never went away. *She* never went away.

"Look who's here to see you Emily, it's your mum." The Nurse interrupted my thoughts and my eyes snapped open. I tried to smile, but inside I had frozen over. This was bad news.

"She says she's here to take you home."

I carried on staring, my mouth gaping. I couldn't believe she was doing this.

"But Daddy was going to..." I trailed off as I caught my mother's warning glare and fell silent. She could reduce me to a trembling wreck with that look, as she had done countless times before.

"Well, I'm here now Emily and we're going to go home. You're going to go straight to bed like a good girl as I've been told you need plenty of rest." She was looking straight through me as she spoke, her eyes were glazed over and she was slurring on her words. My mother was drunk! How did she even get here in one piece? Couldn't the Nurse see what I was seeing?

"Come on, I'll help you out." The Nurse, oblivious, closed the curtains around my bed and began to assist me with my clothes and trainers, whilst my mother stood and watched. I couldn't speak. Any second now she was going to snap into life and start dominating the situation. Would she pull herself together in time?

"There you go. Well, it was nice meeting you Emily." She finished tying my laces for me and stood up facing my mother. "So, if you'd just like to make a further appointment at the reception, I think that's..."

"Oh no, I'm sure she'll be all right now. Thanks ever so much for your help, but we really must be going." Suddenly my mother came out of her drunken trance and was taking control. She ushered me out of the curtained off area and shoved me in the direction of the visitor reception. Her pace quickened as she realised the Nurse was hot on her heels.

"But you can't leave without making a follow up appointment Mrs Bridges. Emily will need to come back for a check up. The women in reception will be more than happy to help."

"Ok ok, we'll do it when we get there," my mother muttered, waving the Nurse away. She was annoyed and flustered treating the Nurse as if she were a yapping dog, constantly pestering her. She carried on walking, dragging me down the corridor and I was getting out of breath.

Finally, the Nurse stopped trying to keep up with us and backed off. Turning to assist some other visitors, her attention was already focused elsewhere. I wanted to turn around and cry for help, but she'd done all she had to do and now it was time for me to deal with the consequences. I was just another patient, been and gone.

Mother didn't stop at the reception, she walked straight past and out through the doors, still with me in tow. I watched the doors swing shut behind me. I watched another opportunity missed. And then we were alone. Me and her. Her and me. One on one, at war with each other – except there could only be one winner.

She was rough with me after that and locating her sports car; she opened the passenger side and shoved me in. She got into the driver's seat and revved up the engine. Then she turned on me and yanked my seatbelt into place, deliberately hurting my ribs. I cried out but fell silent when I caught her eye. It was the warning stare again: shut up, or die.

We drove in silence until just before reaching the street that turned off into our road. I knew she had something to say. She kept smirking to herself harbouring some private joke.

"Follow up appointments? Ha! They'd have a job!" She slurred on her words and lit a cigarette, one hand on the steering wheel, one hand on the lighter. I looked over at the speed counter and saw she was going way too fast. I noticed the empty bottle of Brandy at my feet. This wasn't good; she was drunk, totally unfocused and speeding. If only a police car would pull out behind us and put her behind bars where she belonged, but oh no, they were never there when you needed them.

"I threatened your father last night." She exhaled loudly.

I said nothing.

"I said you wouldn't get away with this and I meant it! Your father's had his punishment, but yours is still due. Might as well get on with it this afternoon, I have nothing better to do!" This was why she'd brought me home, so she could finish what she'd started. She wasn't even looking at me, just talking and staring straight ahead, seemingly fixed on what was in front of her but with glazed eyes and a motionless expression. She appeared distant and detached, yet her words were real and raw. I could feel the anger in them and I was terrified. In her present state of mind she was capable of anything.

We pulled into the driveway and I undid my seatbelt and got out. She did the same stamping out her fag end on the concrete. We walked down to the door like any other mother and daughter, except in this case she wanted to beat the shit out of me and my heart was pounding so loudly in my ears I couldn't hear anything else.

I wanted to somehow, someway pre-empt her next move, but I didn't know what she had in store for me. It was impossible to tell. She was crazed.

As soon as we were inside she dragged me upstairs to her study. I tried to fight her off but I was suddenly feeling very tired and drowsy from the painkillers. I was no match for her. How did she always seem to know when I was at my most vulnerable?

We were there. She locked the door and poured a Scotch for herself, drank it and poured another. Forcing me into a chair she rammed the drink down my throat, it burnt my chest and I spluttered feeling sick and frightened.

"I'd drink another child; you're going to need it after I've finished with you."

She made me drink another two shots and then had one more herself. She was so drunk her hand shook violently when she poured and she was unsteady on her feet.

She lit another cigarette but it took ages to do it. She could hardly hold the lighter. A sneer spread across her face. I knew something bad was going to happen, something out of control. It was written all over her face.

Little Child

My head was swaying from the alcohol and I was glad I was sitting down. She finished her second drink and then poured one more. This time she dropped a tablet into it and it fizzed and foamed at the edges. Before I knew what was happening, the liquid was being poured down my throat and my cheeks were burning up. I tried to struggle, but she was too strong. She slapped me hard across the face and I lost focus.

"Drink this! Drink it!" She shoved the glass hard into my face, the last lingering drops of liquid rolling down my chin. That's all I could feel. I was paralysed from the neck down. My whole body numb.

My eyes were blurring, my head spinning. Her angry words faded out. I was no longer able to fight for what I knew I couldn't win.

She had drugged me.

*

Had it been hours, or days? My head swam. It felt heavy on my shoulders. I was laying face down on the floor. Why was I lying on the floor? I couldn't sort through the mess in my mind. Everything was a jumble. Somewhere I heard a door click open and I struggled to get up so I could see who it was. Someone was in the room with me. Who was it? Why was I here? Why were *they* here? A boot kicked me over onto my side. I groaned loudly. What had happened? Why couldn't I remember anything?

No one was speaking. I tried to stand but my legs gave way and I slumped down, my back hitting a cabinet. I half expected to be pulled up again, but nothing happened. Someone bent down to my level and slapped me hard three times across the face. I didn't have the energy to protest. I just let them get on with it.

I blinked over and over and let my eyes gradually come back into focus. She was staring at me. My mother.

She got up and left the room, reappearing a moment later with a glass of water. I pushed her hand away unsure, but she made me drink it and I was grateful for the liquid. I wanted to ask her what she'd done with me, but I was too afraid of what she would say.

I looked blankly around the room. We were still in her study.

She sat down in her leather chair, her eyes fixed intently on my every move.

"I want some shopping when you're ready," she said gruffly.

I found myself nodding my head wondering just where I was going to get my strength from and how I was supposed to make my way there and carry it all back. I felt weak to the knees and hopelessly groggy.

"You can't stay in here. You'll have to move yourself." She spoke again this time very softly so that I could barely hear her. When I didn't acknowledge her straight away, she spoke louder. "I said you can't stay in here. You'll have to move yourself!" I could tell she was getting impatient with me.

I found my feet and grabbed hold of the cabinet to steady myself. I stood swaying for a moment longer, and then began to walk towards the door. Every step was an effort.

"The list is on the dining room table and you better get everything on there!"

I turned in the doorway and met her stare, her eyes piercing right through my soul. I didn't say a word, but nodded again and carried on out of the room. She slammed the door shut behind me and I heard the key click in the lock. Whatever had happened in there was going to remain a mystery.

I shivered and suddenly felt sick to my stomach. I stumbled down the stairs and managed to reach the kitchen sink just in time, slumping over and letting my body convulse as I retched uncontrollably. I stayed there for a few minutes and then cleaned myself up, trying to pull my thoughts together.

*

I had done the shopping for my mother and was on my way home, grateful that everything she wanted had been there, yet weary because I was hurting and unbelievably tired. I wondered what my mother was doing now locked away in her study with her drink and her craziness. I half expected there'd be an ambulance outside the house when I got back and a police woman would come up to me and say 'Are you Emily Dalton?' and I would reply, 'No, I'm Emily Bridges but Mrs. Dalton is my mother.' And then she'd break the news to me very gently that my mother was dead from suspected alcohol poisoning and they were taking her body away. In truth, I wouldn't know whether to laugh or cry. A part of me would have died with her, but another part of me would have been set free.

I was so engrossed in my illusions that I never saw the little boy on the skateboard heading straight for me until it was too late and he had knocked one of my bags to the ground. There was a crack and I immediately bent down to see what damage there was, as he carried on down the street not even realising what he'd done or stopping to say sorry. My heart leapt into my mouth when I saw the egg yoke oozing out of the carton and into the bottom of the carrier bag. I felt panic stricken. I really didn't know what to do. I had no money left and if I went back home without the eggs my mother would go ballistic and beat me again. Oh god, why did this happen to me? I should have been paying more attention to where I was going. Oh god...oh god...she's going to kill me! She is definitely going to kill me! It was like the bottom had fallen out of my world. All I could see was her angry face, insulting words and then the physical abuse. I felt the tears stinging my eyes and I quickly wiped them away.

A woman walked past me as I began gathering up the mess on the pavement.

"Are you ok?" she asked, momentarily stopping as a good will gesture.

"Yes, everything's fine. Thanks." I finished what I was doing and stood up. The woman shrugged her shoulders and carried on walking leaving me alone in the street. I couldn't believe this was happening to me. I wanted to be sick. What was I going to do? I started to walk home again. The bags cutting into my fingers and scraping against my legs, but I didn't care. I was running through options a million miles a minute, trying to come up with something. As I came up to the end of my road, dreading to walk down to the big house at the end where my mother would be waiting, there was only one thing I could think of. It was a last ditch attempt to save myself. I would go to Mrs Cash and see if she could help me. Ali had said her mum always had Tuesday afternoons off as she didn't have any lessons. Maybe she would be there and would lend me some eggs. I could just say I forgot them and ran out of money. Oh god, please god, please make Mrs Cash be at home. I started to run, panic rising again within me. At that moment I didn't even care if the twins would be home from school and would see me in this mess. One problem at a time.

My whole body was hurting so much by the time I arrived at their house. I was out of breath and the pain in my ribs was unbearable. Desperation overcoming me, I reached for the bell and when it rang and no one answered straight away, I knocked and knocked and knocked as loud as I could on the door, praying that she'd be home.

The door opened just as I was about to give up hope and Mrs Cash appeared.

"Oh thank god." I almost shouted with relief. I felt so weak and my legs were almost giving way as I tumbled into the hallway.

"Emily, hi, I wasn't expecting to see you! Your father phoned this morning and said you fell from your horse. How are you? Emily, are you ok? What's wrong?"

I dropped the shopping bags and held onto her for dear life, trembling and terrified. I couldn't speak.

"Emily what's going on?" She wasn't letting go of me. I closed my eyes and tried to quiet down. Now I was here, it was going to be ok. I didn't want to let go either.

"Emily?" She continued to hold me. It felt so good to be hugged. There was rational creeping back into my mind, and a calmness flooding my senses.

"I just did some shopping for my mother, but I broke the eggs on the way home and I was wondering if you could replace them as I've ran out of money and…"

"Emily, it's ok, it's ok! Slow down. Come in here. Let me look at you. You look so tired. Shouldn't you be resting up?"

I collapsed in her arms. She helped me into the living room and I sunk gratefully into the sofa. I closed my eyes and lay back. I was so tired.

"Emily," she said softly, "Emily, are you going to tell me what's going on? You shouldn't be out doing shopping, not in your condition, and certainly not after your fall."

She was referring to my long-term illness. I opened my eyes and saw her looking straight back at me, her concern evident. I said nothing. Complication after complication rendered me dumb. All I had to say were those magic words *my mother is hitting me*. I knew that would explain everything. Answer all the questions. But I couldn't do it. It didn't feel that simple.

What if she didn't believe me? What if she thought I was a liar?

Then it wouldn't be over.

It would be just beginning.

I forced myself to sit up, realising that I had to get this over and done with before my mother suspected something was wrong. As much as I wanted to stay in the comfort of my teacher's home, I couldn't, and that fact brought me back to reality with a bang. I stood up, my legs almost buckling with the weight, and I took a moment to collect myself, before saying, "I actually just wondered if you had any eggs you could lend me? I know it's an odd request but..."

"Emily, I don't understand why you aren't resting up? What does your father have to say about all of this?"

God, she was persistent and it was making me very anxious.

"I really have to get back Miss. I really have to. I promised I wouldn't be long." I tried to hide my desperation, but the trembling in my voice gave me away.

She sighed deeply, "Yes, I have some eggs. Here, follow me."

We went into the kitchen and she filled a whole new carton and put it into my bag.

"Are you sure you don't need all of those?" I asked, a wave of relief washing over me.

"No, you take them. I have plenty."

"Thanks, I really appreciate it." *You have no idea just how much I really do appreciate it.*

"Now, are you going to tell me why you aren't resting?" She tried one last time, turning to face me, the same look of compassion fixed intently on her face.

We stared at each other for a minute. What did she know? Did she suspect something already? She was waiting patiently for my answer, but I still couldn't say what I wanted to say. She knew something. I could tell she knew something. It was in her eyes. A sadness. Or was I looking in the mirror seeing a reflection of myself? I shifted uneasily, still silent, trying hard to think of a believable excuse, and then as if by a miracle, I heard the phone ringing.

Mrs Cash snapped into life. "I just need to get that. You wait right here and I'll be back in a second. Ok?"

Relieved, I nodded with no intention of staying. As soon as she disappeared, I hurried to the hallway to let myself out. As

I passed the living room I could hear her talking and I hesitated at the door in two minds as to whether I should confide in the one person I trusted almost as much as my own father.

But what was the use?

There were too many walls boxing me in.

I was too afraid.

I just wanted to be like everyone else. Telling them my secret would only show up my weaknesses and my vulnerability. I didn't want to let them in. I didn't want them to know. My mother would kill me if she ever found out and then I wouldn't have any hope at all.

*

When Beth Cash returned to the kitchen she found Emily had gone, but in her heart she hadn't really expected to see her still standing there. She knew something was wrong, terribly wrong. One day falling from a horse, the next out shopping for your mother. That wasn't right. Surely she should have been resting? No wonder Emily had been fraught. Her thoughts were interrupted when her two children barged through the door and into the kitchen shouting their heads off. Immediately she gave them her full attention.

"Mum! Mum! You're never going to believe this?" Jason reached her first and tugged on her arm.

"Mum! Mum! Was Em just here?" Ali asked, panting for breath only seconds behind her brother.

"Yes, she was. Why? What's happened? Is she ok?" Their mother looked distressed and they couldn't understand why.

"Everything's fine." Jason replied, falling quiet so his sister could explain.

"We saw Em leaving Mum. She was walking quickly down the street carrying some shopping. We called out to her but she carried on going and wouldn't stop, so we chased after her and she said she never heard us. But the odd thing was she looked distant and didn't want to talk about anything."

"And isn't she supposed to be in bed Mum after her fall yesterday? I tried to ask her but she wouldn't say." They both stopped talking and waited for Beth to give them a reasonable explanation, an explanation to make it all right again.

"We don't understand what's going on. Why would she ignore us?" She noticed the dejection on their faces.

"She broke some eggs on the way home from shopping and came round here and I replaced them for her. She seemed very frightened, but I don't know why. I asked her why she wasn't resting and taking it easy after yesterday's fall, but she wouldn't give me a direct answer. I can't give you any more answers until I find some out for myself. I think Emily is very sick and she doesn't want us to know how much so we don't have to worry about her all the time." Beth hated lying to her children. She was starting to suspect the long-term illness didn't really exist.

"But we are worrying about her!" Ali chirped up.

"Yes, all the time!" Jason added.

"I know, but unless Emily confides in us, there isn't really a lot we can do. We can only support her and tell her how well she's doing. We can't do anymore than that. I'm sorry." She reached out and gave them both a hug.

"Can you let us know Mum, I mean if you do find out anything? We are her friends after all and Ben is always asking me and I don't know what I'm supposed to say to him."

"Ben? Looks like Emily has a secret admirer!" She joked, trying to make them laugh, but they didn't respond. She bent down and lifted their chins with her hands. "Look, we've done all we can for Emily. It's up to her now. Don't blame yourself for her behaviour."

"Promise you'll talk to her sometime?" Ali said quietly.

"I promise. I will do my best." She hugged them tighter trying to believe that she really could make a difference and find out what was going on in Emily Bridges's life.

*

I let myself into the house and shut the door behind me. Leaning against it I closed my eyes, so relieved to be home. Ali and Jason had seen me coming out of their house and, as if on cue, they'd caught up with me and tried to make conversation. I thought about how unbelievably rude I'd been. I was disgusted with myself for doing it. These were my friends and my behaviour was inexcusable. It was difficult to apologise after the words had come out. They had backed off saying goodbye and then everything had gone silent and I carried on walking home. If only I could have turned the clock back and started the afternoon all over again. I would have done just about everything differently apart from the shop stocking all the items I needed. But they were so forgiving, that was the worst part. If I went to school tomorrow it would be like nothing had happened. I was hoping they wouldn't tell their mum about it and yet I knew they would. It made me feel even worse.

"I see you're home!" I opened my eyes and saw my mother standing in the doorway.

I looked away and began to unpack the shopping. Thankfully she wasn't drinking anymore, but was still far from sober.

"Did you get everything?"

"Yes."

"Good." I thought the conversation was over, but she continued to stand there and watch me like a hawk.

I finished what I was doing and pretended to be occupied with stacking tins in the cupboard. Finally, she turned and went into the living room giving me some breathing space. She turned on the stereo and collapsed into the leather sofa, her eyes closed, her body slightly swaying to the music. It was classical.

I looked up at the clock and remembered I had to call my father to let him know I wasn't at the hospital and so not to bother picking me up. We could go into explanations later, but I didn't want him to get any angrier than he already would be once he found out she had interfered with his arrangements. I decided to make the call upstairs, that way she wouldn't overhear and we could talk in private. It was a risk but she seemed totally engrossed in her music. I climbed the stairs as quietly as possible and pushed the door shut behind me. If she came up I was sure I would hear her. We had phones in every room of the house. I dialled his mobile number and waited for him to pick up.

There was a few seconds of ringing; then a click and he came on the line.

"Hello, James Bridges speaking."

I was just about to joke with him saying he needed to get call screening sorted out when the door burst open. I turned around and gasped holding the receiver up to defend myself, knowing it was my mother but unsure as to what I should do. I almost decided to throw it at her head to make a distraction, but she was too quick.

"Hello, hello, is anybody there?" I could hear my father on the other end and before I knew it, she had lunged forward and snatched it out of my hand, throwing it across the room where it hit the floor and went dead.

"What do you think you're doing?" she shouted at me, as I cowered under her. "Making secret phone calls to *him*?"

I didn't answer. I was too busy worrying about what my father was going to think when he turned up at the hospital and I wasn't there. He would know in a matter of seconds when we had checked out and who had brought me home. If he had caught on to who had called him and then put two and two together as to why the phone went dead, he would be hysterical now and there was nothing he could do to stop her. Again I had upset her and again I would be punished. This was all too familiar.

"You haven't answered me!" she spat, grabbing me by the scruff of the neck and dragging me out of the room and across the landing. We grappled with each other all the way down the stairs and all of a sudden the music seemed to be much louder than before, splitting my head in half.

"I can't believe you disobeyed me yet again! After everything that has happened this afternoon, I would've thought you'd have learnt by now! This can't go on you! This can't go on!" She was yelling at me raising her voice above the music so I had no choice but to listen to her. I began to cry, my body shaking with each sob. I couldn't take another beating. I was giving up. She had hurt me too much and I was past caring. Too weak to fight, too weak to even try and protest my innocence. She would always see me as guilty. I couldn't win when she had her heart set on being abusive.

She pushed me into the living room and I fell to the floor smacking my head against the armchair. Sprawled across the carpet, I was now totally exposed to this monster that I called my mother. The mother who didn't love me, but who I could never betray. If she hit me again, I never felt it. My mind went blank. The music faded out her words. I was floating beyond this world and into a safe haven, whilst she was burning in a fiery hell. If only. If only that were true. I saw her standing over me. I saw the fists pummel into me. I saw her mouth open

and close. I saw everything. It was real. It was all so terribly real.
And suddenly the scene I was living grinded to a halt. I never saw her leave. I never heard her last words.
She was gone and I was alone. Physically hurting. Emotionally numb. Mentally bewildered.
It was over.

I lay in the evening shadows, confused and distressed, wondering if I was alive, wondering if I was dead, Bizet's Carmen coming to a dramatic climax in the background.

CHAPTER 6

"And I think everybody should live in harmony with each other, where if you make a mistake, you are not punished, or if you try to achieve something and you don't quite make it, you are not ridiculed for your lack of knowledge or ability. A world where nobody is angry, nobody is bitter and nobody is hurt. Yes, that is my ideal world."

I finished speaking and made my way shyly back to my desk. The room burst into applause and I felt the embarrassed glow creeping up my neck to my cheeks.

"That was excellent Emily, absolutely brilliant! I'm really glad you made it here today to perform. I think you deserve a commendation. Remind me at the end of the lesson, ok?"

I nodded to my English teacher who beamed down on me like an angel from heaven.

"Thank you Mrs Cash," I replied, feeling a warm glow spread through my body that no one but me could possibly understand.

"That was really something," she said, more to herself than to the rest of the class, and I wondered if she knew the concealed message behind the words I had so carefully prepared and spoken.

"Now, does anybody else want to volunteer to do their talk, or will I have to nominate someone?"

A few hands went up, but she ignored them. She was searching for Ollie, a boy in my class who never did his homework (or so I was told) and was often absent from school even more times than me.

"How about you Ollie? Let's hear your ideal world."

To everyone's surprise, he didn't protest, but stood up proudly and made his way to the front of the room.

"Haven't you got any notes Ollie?" Mrs Cash asked.

"I don't need them Miss, it's all up here." He pointed to his head, as the rest of the class started to comment. She held up her hand signalling silence.

"Ok, let's hear it then. I can be reasonable if you can give me your best."

Ollie nodded slowly and then began.

"My ideal world would be one full of robots, where we just lie in bed all day and manipulate their movements with digital remote controls…"

At the end of the lesson, Jason, Ali and Ben came over to congratulate me. We were taking it in turns to talk to the class about our ideal world and none of them had had to do theirs yet.

"You were so cool about the whole thing!" Ali said smiling.

"Mum was so impressed!" Jason chipped in.

"Well done Em!" Ben grinned; I could tell he was proud of me and that made me happy inside all over again. I really liked him. I often watched him from my bedroom window up at the stables with his mother at the weekends. Part of our garden backed onto the stables. They rode together frequently, and sometimes his father would join them when he wasn't on emergency call at the Vets he worked at. Ben and his parents loved animals. I teased him about going to live on a farm, but I secretly hoped he wouldn't move away.

"Oh, it was nothing." I tried to shrug it off, but my modesty wouldn't stop their praise for one moment. I had come back to school today after having the first half of the week off recovering from my *accident* and they were all being so supportive. Everything was still sore but I was doing ok and besides, I hadn't wanted to miss this lesson.

"Are we still on for next week?" Ali asked expectantly, putting on her ruck sack.

I looked up from my bag and my hand went straight to my mouth.

"You've forgotten what we arranged, haven't you?" Jason laughed. "I knew you would!"

"No…no…well…yes actually I did forget but only because of everything going on, you know," I said quickly, trying to brush it off.

"So, is it still ok?" Ali persisted.

"Yes…should be…I guess. I don't know what we're having for dinner though. I haven't checked with my mum or anything."

"Well ask her tonight and let us know, then we can get working on some ideas for this History project straight away."

"We eat anything," Jason added.

"By the sounds of things, you'll get whatever's going!" Ben grinned at me. "No offence or anything Em." He wasn't in our project group but he was still interested in what we were doing, probably so he could pinch our ideas and use them instead.

"None taken." I returned his grin and turned back to Ali. "I can't, not tonight. She's away at a conference." I was fumbling around for excuses and lying to my friends. I felt so bad.

"Well, you could always come to ours?" she suggested.

"I'm sure it will be fine," I said hurriedly, trying desperately to convince myself. There was no way my mother would allow me out of the house to go to my friends.

"Talk about disorganised!" Jason said, attempting to wind me up.

Ben and Ali chuckled. They knew what was coming.

"Look here Mr Cash, there's lots about you that I could say. How about the fact that you conveniently forgot your speech today and I heard on the grapevine that you did the wrong homework for Science yesterday, and there's more I'm sure of it!" I teased; glad we were getting sidetracked.

Jason was just about to object when Mrs Cash interrupted.

"Do you want me to ring your mum Emily? If you won't get a chance to speak to her tonight, I'll do it during the day tomorrow. I wouldn't want the twins turning up unannounced."

I hesitated. "I don't think it will be a problem, and we have plenty of time yet." It was only Thursday.

"No, I really don't mind Emily. I want your mum to know how well you're doing at the moment anyway and I need to know whether she will be able to attend the next parent's evening with tutors since she missed the last one."

I nodded dumbly. She took it to mean that I was giving her the go-ahead.

"That's settled then. I'll call her tomorrow. When's the best time?"

"Lunchtime," I heard myself saying, "She usually pops home for a quick bite to eat in between client visits."

"Great! We're sorted." Ali looked pleased, I knew how much this project meant to her. History was her favourite subject and she wanted to make a good impression with our teacher.

"Hey! Come on! Don't you have fifth period to go to? I still need to talk to Emily, so come on, get yourselves upstairs."

My heart started to pound. I was always afraid of these moments; afraid if I spilt the beans I would be called a liar.

"Shouldn't I go too Miss?" I asked, trying to excuse myself, and edged towards the door with the others.

"Come here Emily. It's ok. I just want to talk. I can write you a note, don't worry." She came over and closed the door on my lifeline, my friends, and my escape. I hesitated as I saw Tom wave and mouth the words *see you in a minute,* and I watched them disappear around the corner with a growing sense of desperation. Mrs Cash, aware of my discomfort, led me to her desk and motioned for me to sit down.

"You were brilliant today Emily." She looked straight at me and I met her gaze and nodded my appreciation.

"You don't seem yourself. Are you feeling ok?" The gaze of admiration turned to one of concern.

I nodded again, unable to speak, scared if I opened my mouth I would say too much, or not enough, or worst of all be condemned for the words I so badly needed to communicate.

Was she going to talk about the broken egg incident?

"Actually Emily I kept you behind because I wanted to talk about your progress. I really feel that you are so far ahead compared to the rest of the class in terms of grammar, language, reading ability, writing ability that I was thinking maybe once a month, you could sit in on a Year 8 lesson and then do a little project for me. Would you like that?"

I was so taken aback by this that at first I didn't quite know what to say.

"I like my class Miss, I like you and I like the lesson just the way it is. I don't want to be singled out."

She reached for my hand, but I immediately pulled away.

"Are you afraid?" It was an odd question, one that I couldn't ever answer directly because of the fear I felt inside.

"I don't know," I replied, shaking my head. At least I had been half honest in my answer. That wasn't so bad.

"You can talk to me Emily. If there's anything, anything at all that worries you, frightens you, or distresses you. I'm always here, if you need me."

I nodded. Did she really know what she would be taking on if I ever had the courage to open up my heart to her?

"Do you want to talk now?"

Little Child

This time I shook my head firmly, but tinged with that unyielding promise I had made myself swear to, was the awful feeling of utter hopelessness.

Can she sense my fear?

"Ok...well...just remember what I said. I'm here if you ever do need to talk."

I got up and walked towards the door. It was an offer I knew I would never accept.

I reached for the handle.

"Oh, don't forget your certificate." She came over and put the commendation in my hand. "You deserved this today."

We stood facing each other for what seemed like forever, a million conflicting thoughts and feelings bombarding the walls of my head.

I turned to leave, but she placed a hand on my shoulder, it was almost as heavy as my heart.

"Think about what I said Emily. You could be free if you let yourself, and those projects would be worthwhile, I think you would enjoy them."

Although she didn't know it, I was hanging onto her every word.

"Thanks," I mumbled, managing a small smile before heading towards the stairs for my next lesson.

*

Emily didn't hear the deep sigh that followed, or see the sad eyes that watched her as she walked away.

*

I scrubbed the kitchen floor trying to get the last stubborn dirty marks off the tiles. I had rushed straight home declining the tempting offer to go round Ali and Jason's for tea and then a movie. I really wanted to make up for my rudeness of late, but now was not the right time. Sometimes I wondered if there ever would be a *right* time. As usual they had been ok about it saying I was welcome anytime. Cleaning the house always seemed to be my top priority. Ali and Jason didn't clean their homes, and neither did Ben. Their parents took care of that while they were allowed to grow up and be free. It was frustrating and yet there really wasn't anything I could do about it.

If I rebelled against my mother, the only other option was to get beaten twice as hard and twice as much.

And I didn't want that.

Not now.

Not ever.

I thought about what Mrs Cash had said and immediately the pain of knowing that it could never happen cut me to the core. Fear and despair crippled me. My dreams were always shattered by my mother and what she did.

No, I could not be liberated even if I wanted to.

My mother told my teachers that I had a long-term illness that prevented me from going to school every day. I don't know what this illness was supposed to be but we never got any visits from education welfare officers or social workers. Maybe she told them about the panic attacks as well, but I bet she never mentioned the real reasons behind why I suffered the way I did. She was a very good liar. Maybe one day I would fully understand her perception of reality because it wasn't how I saw real life.

Was I insane?

Yet another worry that frequently played across my mind.

One day I'd expose her. I'd tell the Media everything, everything about my life of hell and injustice. I knew she'd get her time; we all got our time one way or another. If there was a God and he was up there watching down on me, He would help me.

I heard the key in the lock and looked up to see my mother tumble through the door, drunk again, no doubt from a late lunch with a male client who was bowled over with her charm and had offered to keep her in liquor throughout the meal. It wouldn't have surprised me. She was still giggling stupidly to herself.

"This better be an improvement!" she chuckled, as she stamped the mud on her heels all over the clean tiles, "Whoops! Didn't realise they were so dirty!"

I stared in horror at the fresh mess where I had just polished; I couldn't believe she would be so cruel. I opened my mouth to protest and then clamped it shut again. What was the point? As soon as she had disappeared into the living room, I quickly cleared the mud up and threw it into the bin. Then I set about re-polishing the dirty tiles, disgusted with her, disgusted with myself. Why wasn't I strong enough to tell her to do it herself? Why did I care what she did? All I had to do was stand up to her and tell her exactly what I thought of her, and then we'd be even.

But...her heart was too cold and my heart was too vulnerable. One of us would have to back down. And it would always be me.

She was a monster, destroying my soul. She *was* my recurrent nightmare. There was nothing I could do to stop her haunting me over and over again.

I suddenly remembered the commendation on the kitchen counter. I had left it there so I wouldn't forget to show my father when he came home from work. I had to hide it before she saw it and ripped it up.

I got up quickly and was just about to slip the small piece of paper between some cook books, when she came up behind me and yanked my hair, spinning me round so I had to look her straight in the face.

"I said this better be an improvement!" she growled angrily. I fell to my knees and started to shake, knowing exactly what was coming next. Her mood swings were uncontrollable. One minute she'd be laughing in her drunken stupor and the next, she'd be full of abuse.

I stammered some words, an incoherent jumble, but it was enough of an acknowledgement for her.

"Good. For a moment there I thought you were ignoring me and you know how much I hate that!" She started to inspect the floor; I cringed as I watched her eyes dart backwards and forwards sweeping the kitchen tiles like windscreen wipers on a car.

When she finally spoke, the hatred tingled in her voice, "You lazy little girl! You haven't touched it have you? It still looks exactly as I left it. How dare you – you..." She grabbed me by the wrist and pulled me up sharp so I stood level with her, then without warning, she slammed me into the side of the cooker. The impact left me breathless and I slumped over tears stinging my eyes. Another blow in quick succession caught me between the ribs.

"Mother I did clean it! I swear I did..." I screamed, "Can't you see? Please don't hit me, please don't..."

She wasn't listening. "Don't lie to me child, or you'll get one of these and one of these!" She repeatedly hit me as she said this, the words falling into rhythm with her fists. I lay still unable to defend myself.

There was silence and I heard her catch her breath. Something must have caught her attention and my heart sank. I knew exactly what it was. I watched her walk over to where the commendation was. I watched her pick it up and read it. I held my breath, hoping, praying she wouldn't do what I knew deep down she would do. Then I watched in horror as she destroyed my achievement, tearing it up bit by bit.

She took away everything that was good in my life and replaced it with a living hell.

"You went to school did you?" She was standing over me now, holding the pieces in her hand, "No wonder this place looks neglected, you haven't been here!" Her voice rose again and she kicked me simultaneously. One by one the tiny shreds showered down around me like the tears that were running down my own face.

"You pathetic little girl," she whispered maliciously as she walked away.

*

"Are you alright Mags? You look like shit." Sean walked into her office. It was a rare appearance for her and he wondered why she was here. She looked wretched, bloodshot eyes and blotchy skin, like she hadn't slept for days. Her hair was dishevelled and her normally pristine suit was creased all over.

"Leave me alone," she said, scowling at him.

"When did you last sleep?"

"Go away!"

He noticed the open pill pot on her desk and the half empty brandy bottle at her feet. There was no glass. She was swigging from the bottle. How many pills had she taken?

94

"Mags, I told you go easy on these." He walked over and picked up the pot, checking its contents. Then he scooped up the loose pills and pocketed the container.

"What the hell!" she retorted.

"Ok...well, I won't tell if you don't." He winked at her and she glowered at him.

"Get out and leave me alone prick."

She bent down to reach for the bottle. Sean grabbed it from her.

"You've got to pull yourself together Mags."

She pushed her chair back and swung for him, but he was too quick. Before she knew it, he was pinning her arms behind her back and marching her to the bathroom.

"You're going to clean up Mags. I'm not letting you out of here until you do it. If Tom comes by and sees you like this, he'll have a fit. Rush you straight off to the nearest doctor. You want that do you? You want to be locked up and have them throw away the key? I don't know why you came into the office, but it wasn't a good idea."

"Piss off!" She struggled with him but he wrestled her down to the bathroom floor and slapped her hard across the face. She stopped fighting and for a moment he thought she was going to pass out. She stared up at him blankly. God, he wanted her. He'd wanted her all these years, but so far she'd managed to elude him. That only made him want it more. He could take her right here and now on this floor. There wouldn't be much resistance. But no, not yet. He wanted her to know exactly what he was doing to her. He wanted her to feel that special something too.

He pulled her to her feet and shoved her hard into the sink.

"Clean up Mags," he ordered.

She did as she was told. Sean stood over her watching.

"Do you have a spare suit?"

She nodded, feeling better for splashing her face. She dried off and combed through her hair.

"Where is it?"

She pointed to the adjoining door on the other side of the room.

"Go get it and change out of that."

She glared at him, "Piss off Sean. I'm fine just as I am." She held onto the basin rim to stop herself from swaying. The headaches were getting worse.

"Do it!" he warned. What was his problem? She stomped into the next room and pulled her suit from the closet. When she walked back into the bathroom, he'd shut the door and was sitting on the edge of the Jacuzzi.

"You've got to be kidding me!" she exclaimed.

He smirked at her, "I'm not going anywhere. You've denied me every other pleasure with you, but you won't deny me this. Get changed. Remember, I'm doing this because I care."

She shook her head in disbelief, but didn't dare argue. She was no match for him. He would hurt her, she was sure of it. He was already destroying her, giving her pills and she was so desperate, she took them without a second thought. She hated him more and more with each passing day. How had all this started? First ordinary, harmless sedatives. Now something much, much stronger that screwed with her mind, but made her feel so good.

It was a long slippery downward slope from then on in.

She was addicted.

When she finished struggling out of one suit into another, he led her back into her office and pushed her down in the leather chair.

"Now do some work and don't fuck around again Mags." He dangled the pill pot in front of her face, teasing her, "No more of these until you shape up."

She was so angry with him but she couldn't move from the chair. The alcohol and pills were kicking in again. Round two, or was it three? She couldn't pull herself together. She needed those pills. Sean took one last look around the room, and then left, making sure to take the brandy bottle with him.

She lay back and closed her eyes. *Fuck them all.*

*

When Sean got back to his office, he disposed of the bottle and pill container and picked up the phone.

"Hi Sean." Thomas answered the phone.

"Maggie needs to take a break Tom. She's not so good."

"How do you know?"

Little Child

"She's come in today, but it wasn't a wise move."

"She's here today? In her office?"

"Yes."

"Does she need a doctor?"

Sean was quick to reply, "No, no doctor."

Thomas persisted, "If she's not well Sean, she should see a doctor."

"She doesn't need a doctor Tom! She's just over worked. She needs a break. Keep her up at the house for a few days and keep an eye on her. Maybe move her to the yacht after that if she's still not pulled it together." He knew Maggie. He knew she wouldn't rat him out. She needed to dry out for a little while. And then he'd start it all over again.

Things are going to get a whole lot rougher before they get any smoother.

He didn't wait for Thomas to reply before putting the phone down.

*

I had another lesson with my Tutor today and I didn't want to miss it. Mrs Cash taught us for English and we also had Personal and Social development tutor group sessions with her. Three periods today were being dedicated to PSD.

My father and I talked for a long time last night about school – Mrs Cash's offer, parent's evening, and the twins coming to work on our History project next week. I was looking forward to that, but I was dreading it at the same time. There were always sacrifices to be made. One moment's respite meant another moment's beating.

My father promised he would try to make it to my next Parent's evening. Last time when he'd suggested going, she went wild and he hadn't been in any fit state to attend. Consequently, she'd been unnerved and had cancelled. I hoped this time it would be different. I wanted my father to be proud of my achievements. Maybe she would allow him to go. Maybe. If she couldn't keep up the act herself, she might as well have the next best thing – for someone to be present whose interest in her child was 100 percent genuine.

The house was looking tidy, that's why I was taking my chances, but God help me this afternoon when I came home.

I could already anticipate her reaction because from my Tutor's phone call she would know I had again been to school for the second day running. I seemed to live a life of chances. Everything rested on the type of mood my mother was in. It didn't stop the harsh words, they would come whatever the weather, but it did balance out the beatings.

I hoped for a little luck to be with me later today.

*

I was feeling odd. We were discussing the effects of alcohol and drugs. It was too close to me. I didn't want to be here. Why hadn't I stayed at home? There was a

conflict raging on inside of me. Should I speak up? I could pretend I was talking about a relative, not necessarily my mother. Maybe Mrs Cash would eventually connect.

But did I want her to connect?

Could I stand the heat of an interrogation afterwards?

All the questions, the endless questions, and all the sympathy in the world yet it couldn't change my situation. It couldn't make any difference. Things would get worse. People would stare, 'that's the girl' they would say pointing me out from the crowd. And I would become an outcast. They might not believe me. The problem would only get worse.

My pulse rate quickened. My head hurt with all the decisions. I wanted to scream and shout and make these people aware of my living hell.

But can they understand?

Do they have the capacity to help me?

I'm a coward, too scared to face the truth.

I pretend I'm the same as everyone else.

I pretend I'm normal.

But I'm not.

It was becoming too much.

Stop the thoughts. Erase the desire to confront my pain. Lock it away deep inside. Eventually it may stop tormenting me. Eventually.

Mrs Cash wouldn't understand. I didn't want her to pity me. I just wanted to be normal like every other person in my class. Was that too much to ask?

What were they talking about now? Alcohol abuse and what it did to our bodies. My mother should be here. She should be listening to this. She was drowning in brandy and whisky, and she was taking my father and me with her.

My thoughts were spiralling out of control. I felt the beads of sweat build up on my forehead and I was getting hot, so very hot. I tried to scream but nothing came out. The pressure in my rib cage was increasing. My lungs were closing in on me. I couldn't breathe. What was happening to me? Was she here? Was she strangling me?

"Miss!" I whispered, my voice barely audible, "Miss please help me!" I was clutching the sides of my desk with both hands, but I couldn't stop my body from heaving. I felt dizzy. The classroom started to spin and it wouldn't stop going round and round and round, faster and faster. I saw Mrs Cash coming towards me. She was running. I heard someone screaming – was it me? Ben was suddenly right in front of me, holding my hands, and Ali too. She was saying something over and over again. I couldn't hear what it was. Mrs Cash was holding my head. She was looking into my eyes. I couldn't fight her. I couldn't get away.

She wouldn't let go of my face.

They were all talking. There was too much talking. I wanted to be alone. I wanted silence. All this noise it was hurting my ears. I started to cry, my body shaking with each sob. I closed my eyes and prayed.

I felt myself sinking and I wasn't struggling anymore. It seemed as if everything was collapsing around me.

And then it was over.

I lost consciousness.

*

Sean went to the safe in Maggie's room, fiddled around with the dial until he got all the clicks and pulled out the pile of Contracts she'd been working on over the last couple of months. Now she was out of the way, he felt safe to look at them. Earlier he'd hacked into her computer and transferred funds. He'd taken bits from each of the private company accounts and spread it around in the new accounts he'd recently set up. It was the beginning of something beautiful, or the penultimate finish, whichever way you liked to look at it. He smiled to himself. Life was so damn sweet, and getting sweeter and sweeter by the second.

Sean had almost been caught when Thomas walked in. He'd dashed into the bathroom and waited. Thomas was just checking around and hadn't taken long, but it was enough to give Sean the jitters to decide to come back later to tamper with the Contracts. Now, here he was once again logging into Maggie's computer and copying the files onto his pen drive. While they transferred, he shredded the paper copies. *Won't be needing them*. He was getting off on this adrenaline rush. Any moment now someone could walk in and bust him. When danger was staring him in the face, that was what made it all the more exhilarating.

The files finished copying and he took out the drive and shut down the computer. Striding back across the room, he shut the safe door and reset the dial, locking it.

He leant against the wall catching his breath, looking smug and feeling exceptionally satisfied.

Carpe fucking Diem.

And that's what he was doing.

Good old Horace knew what he was talking about. *Carpe diem quam minimum credula postero.*

*

"She wouldn't focus Grace. I was trying to get her to focus. Her eyes were wild and she wouldn't calm down. What was happening?" Beth was standing over Emily.

"She's had a panic attack, but everything's going to be alright, I promise. Don't worry Beth. I know you and the kids must have had quite a shock, but it's all over now. Emily is going to pull through this."

"I just don't know – oh god, look, she's opening her eyes!"

Emily couldn't remember anything. She blinked several times trying to see where she was but the shadows behind her eyelids wouldn't come into focus.

One of the voices sounded familiar. She let out a strangled, frustrated cry and tried again to concentrate on her surroundings.

"Do we have to keep her restrained Grace? Can't we take them off now?"

Nurse Macy shook her head. "Best to keep them on just in case she starts lashing out again."

"Miss? Is that you?" Emily whispered, finding her voice.

"Oh, thank god! Yes it's me Emily. I'm so glad you're ok!" She clasped her hands and peered down anxiously.

"Where am I?"

"Ssshhh, don't try to talk. You need to rest. You're going to be just fine, I promise."

Emily tried to hold on to consciousness, but she felt herself drifting off again.

*

"I was really scared Emily. Don't ever do that to me again."

I was sitting up now talking to Mrs Cash sipping a cup of tea. I was feeling more like myself.

"We should call your parents; let them know what's happened. Do you get them on a regular basis?" She was looking at me carefully.

I knew I couldn't lie, she would know straight away, but what else was I supposed to do? This was what I feared, questions with no straightforward answers, questions that would reveal my darkest secrets. It was always something I worried about. I'd tried to go over in my mind what I'd do if it did happen whilst I was at school, but how can you be prepared if you're not in control? How can you rehearse something when in the cold light of day you lose all sense of reason and your mind and body refuse to work together?

I guess I did have a long-term illness — my mother's abuse. I sighed deeply.

"Emily, are they regular?" she repeated.

Immediately my fear set in. "No!" I said quickly, my heart starting to beat faster; it was pounding loudly in my ears. I tried to calm myself down. I had just got over one panic attack; I didn't want another one in quick succession. That would mean the hospital. More people involved. A visit from my mother...

Stop it! Stop thinking and start dealing with what is, not what might be.

"Emily, are you alright?" Mrs Cash interrupted my unsettled state of mind. I looked at her dumbly.

"Emily! Talk to me! What's the matter?" She held my face again to re-establish eye contact.

This is what I needed and I forced myself to smile.

"Emily, I'm very worried about you. I should call your parents right now." She reached for the phone on the wall above my head, but I immediately pushed her hand back. "No!" My answer was quick.

She might suspect something is wrong. She might sense my anxiety. Cover yourself Emily. Cover yourself!

"I mean…no…I'm fine…really…thanks."

"I'm not so sure you are." She had been taken by surprise; it was her turn to fall silent.

"I'll be back on my feet in a minute, ready for fourth period." I was trying desperately to fill in the gaps, trying to be cheerful, "It was just a one off. I actually haven't had one for ages. It happens when I'm a little stressed out, that's all."

Please believe me. Please.

She was still staring; the worried expression on her face wasn't going to go away. "Ali, Ben and Jason, they were all scared just like me. We didn't know what was going on. Was it the discussion? Did something upset you?"

Was she probing for a reason, or was it just concern? I couldn't tell. She would soon know everything if she carried on like this.

"No…no…it was nothing like that." I managed another fake smile and tried to stop my voice from wavering. I finished my tea and put my cup to one side. It was then that I remembered her promise to phone my mother.

Oh god. Please no.

As always my Tutor was one step ahead of me.

"Emily, look at me. I couldn't get hold of your mother."

The relief almost knocked me out. I closed my eyes.

"I called her at lunchtime but she wasn't at home. Fortunate really. You don't want her to find out, do you."

My eyes snapped open. How did she know so much? She was reading my thoughts like they were written down in front of her.

She didn't wait for me to answer.

"There was no conference last night either was there." Again it was a statement, not a question. She wasn't asking me, she was telling me.

"I guess it got cancelled...I can't really remember," I replied defensively.

"Are you afraid Emily?"

Afraid. Yes. I'm afraid. Afraid of my mother. Afraid of where this conversation is going. Where it's going to end up.

I'm afraid of anything and everything.

"But...I don't understand...I mean...why...how do you..." I couldn't say what I wanted to say. I was too stunned.

She sighed deeply, "Emily, you don't have to hide things from me. I know what's going on. You think adults are stupid, that they go around in their own little world, but they don't, not all of them. I'm different. I'm there for the twins, but it's not like that for you is it?"

I looked away. This was it. This was where my new life began if I let it.

But no, I was fooling myself. My life would only end if I opened my mouth and expressed my deepest fears. No one could ever take on my tormenter. My mother was too dominant in my thoughts to allow me to confess everything. She would kill me and then I wouldn't have any hope. I couldn't sacrifice it; I couldn't sacrifice the hope that one day I would be strong enough and old enough to sort out my own problems. At this moment it wasn't the right time. I would wait. I could wait. There was still time.

"I don't know what you mean," I said, unable to resume eye contact.

"Oh I think you do," she replied, gently lifting my chin so I had to look her in the eyes. We stared at each other for a long while. I could hear distant chatter, kids just like me sharing a laugh, having fun, being ordinary.

I finally pulled away; maybe I was just destined for a bad time.

"You think I can't see the bruises Emily? Do you think I would believe you if you said you'd fallen down the stairs or you'd fallen off your horse? There are people you can talk to in confidence, people like me who care about you. They can help you work out your difficulties. They can make you feel good about yourself and help you to understand your pain.

And I know you are hurting Emily. I can see it in your eyes. You don't have to carry this burden alone."

I didn't know what to say. I thought I had always hidden it so well. She knew too much and yet I hadn't said a word.

"You don't have to bottle everything up either," she added, waiting patiently for a response, trying to prompt me to confide in her. But I couldn't do it. There were too many complications. Everyway I turned, I hit a brick wall. It was just no use. "If not for your own sake, for your friend's sakes…Ali…Jason…and Ben, he cares about you a lot…they all think a great deal of you. Don't ever forget that. They don't like to see you unhappy. They ask me questions and I can't answer them. They're your friends Emily; they're going to stick by you whatever happens, even though they don't understand what's going on. I thought you should know that, they wanted you to know that." She reached for my hand. "Please Emily, please help yourself. It doesn't have to be this way."

I couldn't speak for a long time. Was it really as simple as being vocal about it all?

"I don't have a choice," I replied quietly, "It's all or nothing. There isn't any middle ground."

She seemed relieved that I had broken my silence at last. "Tell me about it Emily. I want to know what troubles you so much."

I couldn't handle this. I got up suddenly, "I can't do this right now. I'm sorry. I just can't do it."

She got up too, "It's ok Emily, it's ok. Don't worry." Her voice was soothing, "I'm here if you need me. I'm always right here if you need me."

I began to cry. I couldn't stop those blasted tears from falling. She came towards me and held me tightly, and this time I didn't try to pull away.

"That's it, let it go," she murmured, "Everything's going to be alright Emily. We're going to work this out I promise."

I didn't answer, but buried my head further into her caring embrace.

CHAPTER 7

Thomas looked at the pill in his hand and weaved it between his fingers. He didn't know Maggie was taking any medication. He made a mental note to pass the pill to Alex and get it checked out. She was becoming more and more distant and elusive. What was wrong with her? It wasn't good for the immaculate image of the company, but then, she'd always been a little on the wild side. Unpredictable. Uncontrollable. Doing what the hell she liked and letting others pick up the pieces around her. That was what was happening now. Bad Press and lots of it. Thomas frowned, thinking back to the papers he'd been reading this morning. He needed to rein this current batch of stories in. Maybe do a press conference? Yes, that should settle things down. He could shake Maggie sometimes. She was too impulsive and erratic...but...in a way that was what made her so great. A smile replaced the frown on his face. Her father challenged boundaries with finesse and grace, but Maggie had taken it to another level in her heyday. She had nerve. The nerve to push the client that little bit further without them even knowing. He wanted to get the best out of her; he knew she had it in her to rise again to those heady days. If she was ill, he must know what was wrong. She had stayed up at the house all weekend. She hadn't wanted to see anybody during that time. Mrs Peters and Lucia had been keeping an eye on her and had reported a fever, but Maggie was refusing a doctor. Thomas despaired of her. She pushed him to his tolerable limits. He had finally agreed to let her leave last night. Johnny, her driver and bodyguard, not that she used one much these days, took her home.

*

I walked into the living room and gasped. She wasn't supposed to be here. She'd been gone for the entire week and I really had started to believe she'd taken a holiday. I noticed the bottle of Scotch on the coffee table and my eyes rested on the already half empty glass in her hand. She was watching TV. She never watched TV. She turned to face me and stood up.

"I'm practicing to be a proper Mum!" she retorted, "I've been expecting you, wondered where you were. Just having a few whiskies before your friends arrive. Trying to make a good impression, but the drink calls me." She started to giggle and fell back into the chair. I watched in disgust. She was never sober these days. I was beginning to think the glass in her hand was actually attached in some way. The drink did call her - too often for my liking.

But this wasn't her usual behaviour. Laughing and my Mother - the two did not go hand in hand. I could sense there would be a change of mood in a minute, so I decided to make the most of it while it lasted and crossed the room to go upstairs. I chanced a look back at her and saw her still smirking to herself. She took another swig from her glass and lent over to refill. I carried on climbing the stairs before she noticed I was no longer in the room.

I dumped my bag at the foot of my bed and then switched on my stereo while I took off my school uniform, changed into my casual clothes and redid my hair tying it back into a ponytail so it wouldn't be hanging in my face when I cooked the dinner. Alanis Morrisette's 'Jagged Little Pill' album was in there and immediately 'Ironic' started up. I loved this song; it always made me feel so free and able to take on the world. With this song I could be and do anything I wanted, it was all so reachable. The whole album inspired me. There were mellow songs and angry songs and the combination suited me just fine. I wanted to turn the volume right up so I could drown out my Mother but she would get mad if she heard it thumping on the floorboards. I'd already been there, done that and it hadn't ended pretty. I thought she'd gone out for the morning so I'd turned it up really loud, but then she came home early. She'd smashed up my stereo and threatened to drop me out of the window as well. It had been terrifying. Luckily the phone had rang which forced her to calm down, but afterwards I got a long lecture about how if the neighbours heard the noise, she'd be reported to the authorities for keeping me home – and she warned me that neither of us wanted that — she'd be exposed and I'd be beaten for betraying her...

The song ended and I switched the player back to stand by. Shutting my bedroom door quietly behind me, I went back down to start preparing for the twins. As expected I met my Mother in the hallway and I knew she had been waiting for me. Her disposition had altered itself dramatically and I wondered if she had heard the music and become agitated.

"You've been scheming behind my back again, haven't you!" She came towards me and I shrank back looking around for protection, but there wasn't any. I'd left myself wide open for attack. She had caught me arriving home from school and she was seething; coming home and finding me not in the house would have provoked her enough, but then there was also the issue of having friends around for dinner, something that was forbidden. The worst part was that she'd had time to think it over, time to work herself into a frenzy and even more time to plan her punishment.

Oh god, what had I done?

"Answer me!" she demanded, slapping me hard across the face. My hand went straight to my cheek and I felt it burn.

"No! I haven't! I tried to stop it happening!" There was another slap and this time I lost my balance.

"That's what going to school does to you," she warned, "You asked for this. You provoked me. I come back to this house after a break and the phone rings. It's your teacher. But then, you already knew that didn't you because she's been trying to get hold of me for nearly a week. I had to lie because of you. I had to tell your stupid teacher that I thought you were an excellent pupil. You made me lie and say I was proud of you! How dare you! How dare you waste my time! Get up! Get up you lazy child! "She grabbed my hair and hauled me up. My knees almost buckled, but I stood my ground.

"Mother please, it's not what you think. Please stop!" I had been lying to Mrs Cash all week, telling her my Mother was out and about seeing a lot of clients and that's probably why she was never there when she phoned. I really thought she would still be away tonight when I had the twins round, so I wasn't concerned. Mrs Cash hadn't told me she'd finally spoken to her.

"You disobeyed me and went to school. I said you weren't to go to school. School is a waste of time just like you are a waste of time. Now I have to entertain some stupid children doing a history project because you couldn't obey me." She punched me in the stomach and I sank to the floor.

"This isn't over yet, I can promise you that!" she snapped, "Now get up and clean this place until it's spotless. Then I want the dinner made and it better be good!" I was pulled to my feet again and dragged to the spare cupboard. She pushed me against the door telling me to get on with it while she went upstairs to take a shower and wash her hair.

I waited until I could hear the water running, then I leaned back against the door to catch my breath. I was ok, just, but no doubt there were already more bruises. Mrs Cash's words echoed in my ears. *You think I can't see the bruises Emily? Do you think I would believe you if you said you'd fallen down the stairs or you'd fallen off your horse?* I tried to block them from my mind.

There was nothing she could do. There was nothing anyone could do…

I was grilling the fish when she appeared again out of the blue and grabbed the spatula from my hand to take over my place in the kitchen.

"You can get out of the way now. I better look like this was my idea." She didn't turn to face me; she was too busy concentrating on the salmon fillets in the pan trying to figure out how to cook them without overdoing it. "Go and sort out the dining room table. Make yourself scarce in here otherwise you'll give the wrong impression. I don't want you hanging around."

"Yes," I murmured, leaving her to it. *Hypocrite.*

I set five places and arranged some flowers in the centre of the table. Mother had already chosen a bottle of Australian Chardonnay for her and my father to drink and the wine glasses were sat upside down on the table waiting to be placed. I made sure that Ali and I would sit together down one side; Jason would be on the other side, with my parents sitting at either end. I didn't want to be anywhere near Mother tonight, in fact the further away the better, so I put Ali next to her and I put myself closest to my father. I went back into the kitchen to find some more glasses and some fruit juice.

"I can't believe what you've done." I turned as my mother spoke. I knew what this was. The guilt tripping and threats that promised what would happen once we were alone again. "You do pick your time to invite people around. I wanted to work on a client profile tonight and now I've got three little brats to contend with, not just one!"

I could tell she was getting frustrated, not just with the cooking, but also with the whole situation. "If you ever spring this upon me again, I swear I'll strangle you." I gulped. Was she going to have one last gripe before Ali and Jason arrived? "I can't even drink a glass of Scotch tonight thanks to you!" She carried on talking, but never once turning to face me. She was trying to relieve her frustration without hitting me and it was proving very challenging for her. I watched her free hand twitch and curl into a fist as she reached for the control turning the cooker down so the fish could simmer. She took a deep breath and I walked back into the dining room placing the glasses and fruit juice on the table. She followed me and stood watching for a second.

"I meant everything I've said to you tonight." I looked up meeting her piercing stare. "If you say one thing out of turn to your friends, I swear I'll beat the shit out of you once they're gone. And don't think I won't be listening; I'll be listening to every word you say, and watching your every movement like a hawk. If you betray me, I *will* kill you. Do you understand? Do you?" She was getting agitated and I backed away into the kitchen. She came after me. Her hands were shaking uncontrollably and she was reaching for my neck.

"Mother please," I whispered, "not here...not now..."

Her hands were getting closer. We were now in the middle of the kitchen and she was blocking the doorway so I had nowhere to run.

"I can't believe you child! Going to school. Disobeying me. All of the goddamn time! And now look where we are. Having friends to tea. Well let me tell you something. I don't do *having friends to tea*! I've never allowed it before and I won't be allowing it again! I'll tie you to your bed, lock the door and throw away the key, anything to stop you disobeying me! And these aren't just any old children, are they? Oh no nono! No! They're your Tutor's children, coming here to spy on me! I have to play *Mum* because of you. I have to pretend I love you and that disgusts me so much I want to throw up. You make me angry. You make me hurt you because you can't do as you're told. You rebel against me all the time. You try and fight me and you know I don't like it." Her voice was rising and her hands were closing in around my neck.

"Mother, don't..." I managed to whisper. This was it. This was where my life ended. This was where the nightmare ended. I couldn't breathe. Her hands were getting tighter, closing off my airways...

Suddenly there was a noise outside the door, the lock clicked and my father, Ali and Jason toppled into the room chatting and laughing, totally oblivious to what was happening inside. Mother released her grip and threw her arms around me, hugging me to death. *Death*. It had almost been upon me...

"I'm sure everything will be fine Emily," she started to say, "yes I'm sure it will." She quickly backed off leaving the impression that she had been comforting me about something, and gave me one final warning glare that spoke volumes. I caught my father's eye and he gave me a questioning look, which I returned with a shrug. He was most probably wondering when she got back. I could explain later.

"Hi Em!" Ali and Jason greeted me in unison.

I took a deep breath and thanked god Ali and Jason had turned up when they did. They would never know how much they had saved my life just then. The thought of what could have happened literally seconds earlier...

Mother busied herself with serving up, and as I glanced up at my father again, I caught another searching look from him. He bent down and kissed me gently on the forehead.

"Shall we go through into the living room?" I offered quickly, and led the way, "Make yourselves at home." I was still shaking from my near miss just seconds earlier, but desperately hoped I wasn't making it obvious in any way. The last thing I wanted to do was draw unnecessary attention to myself, especially with Mother watching my every move, waiting for me to slip up so she could pounce.

"Can I dump these somewhere Em?" Ali asked, as they followed me into the next room. She had brought all her History books over so we had plenty of research material. I noticed Jason wasn't carrying anything; he sure was hopeless when it came to homework and school projects - even if his Mum was a teacher.

"Yes, no problem." I took them from her and put them on the side table making sure I was careful not to upset any of my mother's precious ornaments.

"You have a great place Mr Bridges," Jason remarked, as he wandered around taking everything in.

"Jase don't be so rude!" Ali scolded jokingly and we all burst out laughing. It was amusing listening to Ali telling him off.

"Well, we try and keep up with the neighbours, you know how it is!" My father had followed us into the living room and I could tell he was really enjoying this larking around. It was plain to see all three of them had hit it off straight away, and that put a smile on my face.

We fell into mindless conversation then and were all having a great time laughing and chatting. It was the happiest I had seen my father for a long time, despite the circumstances, and I could tell he felt the same way about me.

"So Em, are you really ok now?" Ali asked suddenly and the joke I had been sharing with Jason came to an abrupt end as I looked up sharply and met her concerned eyes.

Before I could answer, my father was right there one step ahead of me, "Ok after what?" he quizzed, a puzzled expression on his face. I hesitated and was just about to reply when Jason chipped in.

"Well when we arrived you seemed upset about something Em and then the panic attack last week..."

I cut him off, "Sure, everything's fine." I stood up trying to think of a distraction, "Look, who wants a drink?" But my father wasn't going to let me off the hook that easily. "No, wait a second...sit down Em...what panic attack is this?"

"Sorry Em," Ali murmured apologetically and I noticed her looking over at Jason who shrugged his shoulders.

Then, as if on cue, Mother came into the dining room serving up the dinner and I froze, unable to speak as I heard her say, "Did somebody mention panic attacks?" Now it was my father's turn to patch things up; I hadn't wanted him to find out and we both hadn't wanted her to find out, but that was Ali and Jason for you. Always showing concern at the wrong time!

Ali butted in before either of us could answer. She probably felt she had to explain because of dropping me in it with my father just moments earlier.

"Em had one at school last week and it shook us up a bit. We were very worried about her."

"And when we came in Em seemed upset and we wondered if she was ok." Jason added, putting his arm around my shoulders.

I could see Mother putting two and two together, composing herself and working out what her artificial 'Motherly' reaction should be to the news she had just received. My father and I waited in silence, watching her mulling it over in her mind.

Would she let the curtain of pretence slip?

I let out a short exasperated sigh, but nobody was looking at me. They were waiting for my mother to say something.

"Yes that's right I was comforting her when you came in," she paused, adding to the effect that she really did care about my welfare, "Emily's illness isn't easy," she turned to face me for a split second and then quickly turned back to Ali, "Please don't worry yourselves. I've been taking good care of her."

She feigned a smile as I nodded in agreement, even though she was lying. She hadn't been around since Friday. She'd disappeared all weekend. And now here she was saying she'd been looking after me. It made me feel sick just thinking about how easily she could fool people. She was lying through her teeth, but it sounded so convincing. She hadn't even known about the attack. I hadn't even told my father yet. I dared to look over to him and he mouthed the words "We need to talk". I could see he was very agitated, but it was going to have to wait.

"But we can't help worrying," Jason persisted, "The other day we saw Em shopping and only the day before that she'd cracked some ribs. Did you know she went shopping?" He still had his arm draped across my shoulders. "We just care that's all," he said, giving me a friendly squeeze.

"Will you stop telling tales! It was only one rib." I pulled away from him trying to make light of the situation. "Did your Mum put you up to this Spanish Inquisition by any chance?" As soon as the words were out of my mouth, I immediately regretted saying them. Mother looked up at me sharply, her icy glare piercing through me. My hands flew to my mouth. Oh God, what had I said? This was exactly what she thought and now I had only gone and confirmed her suspicions without intending to. She would think I was in on it to catch her out.

That I had set this up on purpose. I dropped my head, ashamed. I could sense my father was a nervous wreck standing behind me.

"Emily did you really go shopping straight after I brought you back from the hospital?" she asked me, faking her concern when really all she wanted to do was beat me to death, "You promised me you wouldn't. You promised me you'd stay in bed and rest." Her voice grated my ears. The words were meaningless.

"We don't want to get Em into any trouble," Ali spoke up hastily, "As Jason said, it's just that we worry a lot about her, and so does Mum."

"Well, Emily is lucky to have such good friends and a Tutor who cares so much about her," Mother replied through clenched teeth, keeping herself occupied so she didn't have to lash out at me for supposedly lying to her, "but you really mustn't concern yourselves because she really is in very safe hands here with James and I watching over her. We take care of her every need."

I was feeling sick with all this undue attention and, even though Mother appeared to be handling it extremely well and saying all the right things, I knew deep down her blood was boiling over and I dreaded to think the punishments she was conjuring up in her mind for me when Ali and Jason returned home.

"Right that's enough! For the last time, I'm fine. Let's eat dinner shall we." I laughed, but my voice trembled. All the questions were exhausting me and I was rapidly falling to pieces.

Mother acted as if she hadn't heard me and began preoccupying herself with seating everyone, and when she got to me, she stopped and let out a long sigh.

"I don't know Emily. I can't let you out of my sight for one minute before you're overdoing it again. What am I going to do with you?" And then she moved to her seat and sat down and I closed my eyes in a silent prayer wondering just how I was supposed to make it through the rest of the evening and come out the other end still sane.

"This is a delicious dinner Mrs Bridges. How did you know we love salmon?"

We were halfway through the meal and so far everything was going to plan. To my relief my health was no longer the topic of conversation and everyone seemed to be getting along just fine.

Every time one of the twins referred to her as Mrs Bridges, she gave my father an evil stare, but always quickly replaced by a smile to the twins.

"Ali, you're lying to me!" my mother joked, "Salmon isn't really your favourite. You're just trying to make me feel better."

My father nudged my leg with his own under the table and I frowned. This dinner was my creation not hers and I couldn't help feeling some resentment.

"No seriously, it is Mrs Bridges!" Jason said adamantly.

Another stare, another quick turnaround into a smile.

"Well maybe I got just a teenie weenie tip off from somewhere then," she laughed and waved her arm in my direction.

This time it was my turn to nudge my father. She'd already had three glasses of Chardonnay and the fizz was going to her head. Ali and Jason were laughing at another joke of hers. They seemed besotted with her and a twinge of something niggled the back of my mind. Was it jealousy? Apprehension? Guilt?

She might say something in a minute that would cause this whole happy scene to blow up in our faces. It was like sitting on the edge of a time bomb knowing that it could explode at any moment but not being able to control the situation or do anything to prevent it from happening. It was like watching the sand in an egg timer gradually run out, or having a ball of string tumbling from your grasp.

"We *are* going to talk later on," my father whispered, as he reached across me for the butter, "You have a lot of explaining to do."

They were still laughing loudly down the other end of the table.

"If we survive this!" I dared to murmur back.

"No, whatever happens, you *will* be telling me exactly what's been going on." I could see that he was tense and wasn't going to leave it until he knew what had happened at school. I nodded as I put the butter back for him trying to decide just how I was supposed to tone the panic attack right down. After rushing home realising Mother had brought me back from the hospital early, he'd found me sprawled across the living room floor semi-conscious in a worse condition than when he had left me that morning. I told him she'd drugged me and beat me and then made me go shopping a couple of hours later barely able to breathe, let alone walk and carry heavy bags. And then there had been the broken eggs, the hurried phone call where we had got cut off, and then finally the dragging down the stairs and subsequent abuse that probably would have killed me if she hadn't stopped when she did. A shiver went down my spine as I remembered all too clearly the hell she had put me through that day, and to recount it all to my father had almost been unbearable. Now I was having panic attacks again and it was way too much to deal with.

"So what does your father do?" I heard my mother asking and my mind span back to the present.

Jason finished his last potato and put his fork to one side.

"Well he's a Lawyer," he said proudly.

"But he doesn't live with us," Ali added, taking a sip of her juice.

"The only reason they split up was because Dad works away from home a lot on really big cases so Mum was never seeing him. It was a mutual agreement and we still get to see him nearly every weekend when he's around, don't we Al."

"Yes, and they're still friends."

I smiled across at her. "That's good. It's great they're on speaking terms."

Everyone fell silent. Jason and Ali finished their dinner, Mother kept herself calm with yet another glass of wine and my father and I exchanged relieved glances. So far she was keeping herself in check and not flaring up at anything unexpectedly. But for those of us sitting around the table who knew her well, she was like a volcano waiting to erupt – and we sat on tenterhooks waiting for it to happen.

"So what sort of cases does your father work on?" Mother asked quietly, putting down her glass and leaning back in her chair.

"Mainly big criminal cases," Jason said proudly.

I watched my mother's eyebrow raise an inch and an apprehensive expression crossed her face.

"So…he's a good guy then?" she probed, fixing a smile on her face but disguising the suspicion in her voice. I noticed the tension in her body language.

"Yes, definitely. I don't think he's ever had to represent any guilty parties before. He always defends the good guys," Ali answered.

Mother looked thoughtful for a second.

"But that could change one day you know. One day he might have to represent the bad guys because his career might depend on it. Then how would you feel?"

Ali and Jason looked at her surprised.

"Do you think so?" Jason asked.

Mother shrugged her shoulders and stared straight at me with a nasty twinkle in her eye, "Well you just never know, do you?" I tried to analyse what she was implying, but the moment was over before I could begin to.

"I don't think so," Ali butted in defensively, "He wouldn't do it. He's established in the business so he could easily refuse. I can't see how representing someone he knew was guilty would enhance his career. I think it would do exactly the opposite!"

Mother took a long swig from her glass and leant forward cupping her chin in her hands and resting her elbows on the table.

"Ah, but you've forgotten one small point Ali," she said wisely.

"And what's that?"

"Well…what would happen if the good guys your father was representing were really the bad guys?" Mother looked smug as she said it.

"How do you mean?" Jason was intrigued, but Ali was getting annoyed. I was waiting for my father to step in, but he was sitting quietly at the other end of the table pretending to be engrossed in finishing his dinner, although I knew from experience he was listening and taking in every word, thinking how he could end the conversation peacefully before it got out of hand.

"That could never happen," Ali replied quickly.

"But how do you know? Sometimes right and wrong can easily get distorted. Your father might not find out until the last minute and then what?" She seemed to be enjoying winding them up because she knew that interrogating them innocently like this was tearing me and my father up. It was a foretaste of what was to come once Ali and Jason had gone home. She was warning us. Threatening us.

They stared blankly back at her, unsure what to say next. I was too scared to speak up and my father was still deep in thought. She had a wry smile on her face.

"Mags, can you get the dessert?" my father broke the silence, forcing a smile on his face as he spoke.

I watched Mother's expression turn to resentment as she looked over at him, she hesitated for a fraction of a second, then got up steadying herself with one hand on the table and the other on the back of the chair.

"Yes, of course I will. Chocolate gateaux…I'm sure you'll love it!" She averted her eyes and in an instant became the charming motherly figure once more. Jason and Ali both laughed seeming to forget the conversation they had been having only moments before, and gave me a thumbs-up. I watched my mother closely as she put all her concentration into making it into the kitchen without keeling over.

My father had already turned his attention to smoothing everything over and was now talking animatedly about football.

I breathed a sigh of relief and waited for Mother to come back to the table with the dessert. It was obvious only to me that she had just sacrificed a great deal in that split second, and I would surely pay for it later. My heart sank as I looked from one twin to the other. They had a prefect life with a prefect mum and right now they were giggling at one of my father's jokes completely oblivious to the politics going on around them. If only. Those two magical words again. Sometimes I wondered whether it would just be better to be dead. No more suffering. No more sadness. No more pain and hurt and grief. Maybe there was something better waiting for me on the other side. Maybe.

I would come close to finding out once we were alone again. There was no mistaking that.

*

"History must be my worse subject!" Jason groaned loudly, as he pushed a book aside and put the lid on his pen.

Ali looked at me and we grinned at each other. He had barely contributed to our project at all, choosing instead to watch England play a home game Friendly with my father. It wasn't exactly my favourite lesson either but I thought I'd better look interested just to keep Ali happy. She was really into it.

"When are we ever going to need this stuff anyway?" Jason continued, looking over Ali's shoulder unimpressed at her double spread on Oliver Cromwell, "Charles was an idiot to upset the people. That's about the long and short of it. How are we supposed to do a ten minute presentation on that?"

My father, who was still sitting in the living room, now watching a comedy, gave a stifled laugh, and then turned to face us.

"I can see his point girls," he said, "I've never needed to know about Cromwell and Charles." He got up and stood under the arch separating the two rooms, as Ali tutted at him.

"A Historian might have something to say about that!" she replied curtly.

"And it could come in handy for pub quizzes," I joined in supporting Ali, even though he was trying to make me laugh by pulling faces behind her back.

"Well, I'll have to leave you to your debate because I'm off to bed," he turned and switched the TV off throwing down the control on the sofa, "Night all. Em, don't forget to lock up."

"Thanks for having us Mr Bridges." Jason said, coming over and shaking his hand.

"Not a problem, you're welcome anytime." I raised an eyebrow at this but he disappeared into the hallway without noticing, and a moment later we heard him climbing the stairs. I knew it was quite late but there was no doubt that Mother would still be busy working on her client profile. Sometimes she didn't sleep at all, although this was becoming rarer and rarer due to all the drinking she did. She often passed out by 8 o'clock every evening, a bottle of whiskey or brandy nearby and an empty glass in her hand.

She had been charming all the way through dessert as we helped ourselves to chocolate gateaux, something I was hardly ever allowed to eat because she had a fear I'd become fat. There were no more tense moments, or unexpected questions, she just kept eating and drinking and making pleasant conversation enthralling Ali and Jason with her tales of being at the top and how she'd got so successful. Ali, in particular, was taking in her every word. She had big plans to be as good as her own father.

After dinner she'd left us to wash up whilst she excused herself and disappeared into her study, but not before remarking how wonderful it was to have the twins over. She was tipsy from the wine, but had passed it off because of her buoyant mood. I knew however, that when I saw her next she wouldn't be so amiable. Her mood would be transformed into something far uglier and far sinister then I had ever experienced before. Once she locked herself away, that was it, she'd be left with only her thoughts and her drink. And all she needed was time, a little time to plot her punishments.

"I guess that's me finished then Em," Ali said, putting down her pen and ignoring the fact that Jason had already packed up his things for her to put away, "So we should be ready for the presentation on Monday."

She gave a wary look at her twin as I said, "Jason do you know what you have to do?"

"Yeh, I'll make it up as I go along," he replied.

Ali sighed, "Have it your own way then, but don't go blaming me when Mum looks at your end of term History mark and freaks out! Remember, you can't go riding on mine and Em's back for this one. We get marked for our individual preparation and contribution to the project."

"Ok, ok, I get the picture. I've got a paragraph or two." Jason seemed completely unperturbed by all the fuss.

"Jason, that's not enough, you'll..." Ali began, but I interrupted her not wanting a noisy row right beneath my mother's study.

"Hey, come on you two, hadn't you better be getting home?" I glanced anxiously upwards, but couldn't hear any movement. I turned to face Ali and was just helping her pack up her bag when I heard movement on the stairs.

"Where are you, you little wretch?" I heard my mother's voice as she came into the living room. Jason was in the kitchen getting a drink of water, but Ali had frozen beside me midway in buckling up her bag.

She saw us and stopped suddenly her mouth working. I could tell she was trying to compose herself, trying to pretend she hadn't been drinking the bottle of Scotch she probably kept in the top drawer of her desk.

"Mother!" I exclaimed.

But she wasn't looking at me. Her eyes rested uncomfortably on Ali as it dawned on her what she'd just done.

"Ali, dear, I thought you had gone home." She tried to smile and keep her voice steady, but I could tell she was very drunk. And if I could tell, surely Ali could too.

"No, we were just leaving actually." Ali quickly finished with her bag and backed away into the kitchen, clearly very distressed. I met my mother's threatening glare as she remained standing in the middle of the living room, almost frozen in time.

That was it. The last straw. The volcano had just erupted.

I dashed into the kitchen to find Ali whispering frantically to Jason. He saw me first and pulled way from his sister, forcing a grin on his face.

"Well, thanks for having us Em."

"And we'll see you soon." Ali couldn't look me in the eye, but she gave me a quick hug before hurrying out the door. I looked up at Jason. He didn't make any move to follow her.

There was an awkward silence, then, "Em, Mum's just round the corner if you need her."

I nodded, not really knowing what to say.

"We'll call round tomorrow if you want."

I struggled to find my voice, "Maybe," I whispered.

He came towards me and gave me a tight hug, then vanished into the night.

CHAPTER 8

For James, this was the last straw. He looked down at his daughter and felt tears stinging his eyes. She had fallen into a restless sleep, twisting and turning and crying out. Maggie had beaten her to within an inch of her life last night and James had been powerless to do anything. Locked in his bedroom, he could only sit and listen to the screaming and shouting downstairs and know that something terrible was happening. He had debated calling the police but was afraid to do it. He was kicking himself now. *He should have done it.* Having her friends for supper had been too much of a sacrifice for Emily. Now it was James' turn to right the wrongs and make some sacrifices himself. He had to get Emily out of here. There was no other option. Maggie didn't live in the real world. She was out of control.

*

Beth Cash knew something was wrong as she watched her children sitting in silence barely touching their breakfast. Usually on a Saturday morning they would be fighting over the TV control and arguing about what cartoons they should watch, but today nothing of the sort was happening. They were both very quiet.

She finished making her cup of tea and came over and sat down at the table looking from one to the other.

"Ok, which one of you is going to tell me what's going on?" she asked, sipping her tea.

Jason looked up at his mum, but neither twin said anything.

"Ok, let's try again," Beth sighed, "Does this have anything to do with your visit to Emily's house last night?"

Ali finally met her mum's concerned eyes, "Yes, it does," she replied nodding.

"You want to tell me? I've never seen the pair of you looking so troubled."

"Mum," Ali said in a very small voice, "I think Mrs. Bridges was drunk last night. She came downstairs as we were leaving and said something nasty and Emily looked terrified."

For a moment Beth didn't say anything. How was she supposed to explain what she was thinking to her thirteen year old children who had never witnessed any type of violence in their lives before?

"Maybe we should go and see Emily. Would that put your minds at rest?"

"Mum, do you think she got hurt last night?" Jason asked quickly, ignoring his mum's question with one of his own.

"Is this what's bothering you so much?"

Ali and Jason both nodded.

"I can't answer that," she said putting down her tea and moving round to give them a cuddle, "and we can't go around making accusations either. Ok?"

They nodded again, and Ali wiped a tear from her eye.

"Please leave it to me. I'll talk to Emily and try and find out what's going on. I'll also see…" But Jason had cut her off.

"Mum, Em won't tell you the truth, she'll lie! I know she will!"

"Listen to me. Both of you. You cannot go around saying these things!" She pulled them tighter into her embrace. "This is complicated stuff, personal stuff that could affect Emily for the rest of her life. I know it's hard but you've got to leave it to me. You've got to trust me. I've never let you down before and I won't this time. You need to be there for Emily, that's the most important thing right now, whatever's going on in her life. Do you understand me?"

"Oh mum," Ali said starting to cry, as she buried her head into her mum's shoulder. Beth looked at Jason who shrugged and stared back helplessly.

It crossed her mind briefly as she tried to comfort her children that they were far too young to be dealing with this. Far too young.

The telephone started to ring, breaking the silence. She got up from the table disentangling herself from the twins, and leaned over the breakfast bar to grab the phone.

"Hello, Beth Cash."

Ali and Jason watched their mum and tried to figure out who was on the other end. They didn't have to wait long.

"Oh, hi Mr Bridges. Yes they got back fine thank you. Oh, is she alright? No…no…I don't think that will be a problem. Ok. Are you sure she's alright? I'll see what I can do. You don't mind if the twins come as well do you? That's great. I'll let them know. See you in about ten minutes. No, no, it's no trouble honestly. Ok, ok, bye." She hung up the phone and turned to face them.

"Don't ask me any questions, just get your coats and be ready to leave in two minutes. We're going round to see Emily whilst her dad pops out for a few hours. She's not very well and he didn't want to leave her on her own."

"But where's her m…" Ali began, but Beth interrupted.

"Get your coats and no questions!" she scolded, pushing them in the direction of the hallway. When they were out of sight she put her head in her hands and leant heavily on the bar. This was going to be harder than she imagined. Children's feelings were so easily susceptible to vulnerability, and she didn't want her own dragged into this. But it was too late, and that was a hard realisation for her to take on board and deal with. She needed to speak to her husband. He would know what to do. He was always so level headed.

*

When they got to the house James was in a state, but he was trying to put on a brave face and stay calm when he greeted them.

"I didn't know what to do. Her mother left early for work and when I went up to see her she wasn't with it at all. I'm terribly sorry to bother you with all this, but as your children are friends of Emily's, I thought I'd ask. I do have to go out for a few hours on business. I wouldn't normally do this but it's quite important that I go." He feigned a small smile, which looked more like a grimace Beth thought.

"It's ok. Where's Emily? Is she still upstairs in bed?"

"Yes…here…let me show you." He led the way through the kitchen and into the hallway. Ali and Jason made to follow their mum up the stairs, but she turned quickly and said, "I think it would be best if we don't bombard Emily all at once. Why don't you two stay downstairs and watch TV."

They looked at her and opened their mouths to protest, but then shut them again when they saw the knowing look on her face, and reluctantly made their way into the living room where they'd been entertained only the night before.

Beth followed James across the big landing, down another smaller landing and into one of the bedrooms. Emily was propped up on a pile of cushions murmuring to herself and dozing restlessly. She had a black eye and a cut lip and even though Beth tried to reason with herself that Emily could have tripped into something, her mind wouldn't let her. She had not looked like she'd been beaten up the previous day at school.

"She must have tripped into something," James said almost immediately.

Beth couldn't help noticing the hopefulness in his voice. Was he trying to believe his own words?

"Maybe," she replied, going across to the bed and sitting down on one side, "Does she have a temperature?" She raised her hand and gently felt Emily's forehead. "No, I didn't think so."

James looked at her helplessly. Was he doing the right thing involving other people? Beth saw that he looked terrible himself. Dark patches under his eyes as if he hadn't slept for days, or was extremely worried about something.

She cleared her throat trying to break the uneasy silence between them.

"You go and do whatever you have to do and I'll look after Emily until you get back." He nodded appreciatively. "Is there any chance that Mrs Bridges will be home later today?"

"No...she's out all day and not contactable," he lied. He actually didn't know whether she would be back this morning or this afternoon, and he certainly had no idea whether she had her mobile with her. She had left the house very early leaving James to wake up and face the mess she'd left behind and the mess she'd made of their daughter. It was horrific. He felt tears sting his eyes again as the memory came flooding back. His emotions were still raw and burnt a hole through his heart. He quickly pulled himself together and turned away to wipe his eyes on the back of his sleeve.

He reached for the door and said over his shoulder, "So I'll just tell the twins to make themselves at home shall I?"

"Yes, if you wouldn't mind. I don't think they should see Emily like this." She met his eyes and he almost trusted her enough to tell her everything, but the moment was gone just as quickly as it had come, and the thought of what lay ahead of him today was much more pressing. He was doing it for Emily and soon it would all be finalised and he would be able to tell her. She would be so happy, he was certain of that. He wouldn't have taken such a huge risk in getting her teacher involved if this wasn't as important as it was. He had to do this. Freedom and Emily's safety were so close, he could almost reach out and touch it.

He closed the door quietly behind him leaving Beth Cash to attend to his daughter.

*

I sensed somebody was in the room with me but I didn't know who it was or why. A replay of last night kept running through my mind disturbing me every time I drifted into a restless sleep – my mother ripping into me with a fresh wave of venom. Incredibly drunk, seething with rage and shaking violently. Beating after beating hitting me at full force. Accusations that I had invited my friends to dinner so they could check up on her and report back to their mum, my Tutor. Allegations that I had betrayed her yet again because their father was a lawyer. And then when the shouting was over, she was walking away, and I was collapsed face down on the floor unable to move, unable to talk...

*

Emily was screaming and crying out and Beth didn't know what to do. She didn't want the twins to hear this or see Emily thrashing about. She held her tight and rocked her back to sleep, but it wasn't peaceful sleep. Emily was fighting her and when she stopped that and Beth laid her back down, she was tossing and turning and mumbling things. Beth tried to catch the words but it wasn't coherent. Beth knew she was in too deep now to walk away. Whatever demons Emily was harbouring, they needed to be released otherwise the poor child would break down. That was what had happened to her best friend back when they were teenagers and Beth still felt guilt for ignoring all the signs. It twinged in her gut bringing back painful, suppressed memories. Beth scrunched up her face trying to block it out. This was all so familiar. Now her friend was dead. Suicide. And Beth was not about to make the same mistake again.

*

"There you go." He came into the living room and gave me my glass of squash, then perched on the arm of the sofa. I took a sip and put my drink to one side waiting for him to speak. It was Sunday morning and I was awake but I couldn't say a day in bed had given me much peace, or rest. I knew Mrs Cash had been looking after me and I knew it was because my father was up to something. He told me I'd had a terrible 36 hours, but on my request he'd carried me downstairs and tucked me in on the sofa with my duvet and several DVDs. Now I wanted him to tell me why he'd taken such a big risk.

He sighed deeply. "This is getting way out of control. Your mother is way out of control. Before long she's going to kill one of us."

I knew what he was saying was true, but I said nothing.

"Yesterday I was looking at cottages, sweetheart, out in the sticks, that's why I needed Mrs Cash to look after you. It's always been my dream and now we're going to make it happen. Aunty Laura is going to an auction next week, on my behalf, to bid on one particular property I really took a shine to yesterday. Fingers crossed we'll get it." He beamed down on me. Behind the smile I saw relief mixed with elation in his eyes.

So this is it!

I grinned back at him, but what I felt inside was much, much more. Finally we were going to get out of here! *Finally!*

If I had the energy, I would've been running up and down the house screaming with delight by now. This was surely what winning the lottery must feel like. I wanted to shout my joy from the rooftops.

"I don't know what to say."

"Are you happy?"

I looked at him for a long moment, "More than words can say!"

"I'm sorry I left it so long to do this sweetheart. I don't know why I didn't act sooner."

I said nothing.

"I can't explain why. I hope you aren't angry with me."

I was feeling so many different emotions, but anger wasn't one of them.

Little Child

I reached for his hand and squeezed it.

"You're doing something now and that's what counts."

*

There was a knock on the door; I got up to answer it. It was early Monday evening. I'd been to school, done the History presentation – we'd all got top marks, even Jason – and I'd been home for a few hours relaxing in front of the TV. Mother was locked away working in her study and my father was in the kitchen repairing some tiles.

"Hi Ali!"

"Hi Em. We were such a team today! Just thought I'd see if you wanted to come to ours for dinner. Like a celebratory supper!"

Before I could answer, both my parents appeared in the hallway.

"Hi Ali," they said together, jostling for position.

"Hello," Ali replied, not noticing what they were doing and turning her attention back to me, "So...are you up for it Em? We could get a movie out and order in pizza. Mum says it's ok."

I opened my mouth to answer, but my mother got there first.

"Emily, you have chores to do. I want your bedroom cleaned," she said sternly.

I flinched almost as if she were hitting me instead of talking to me.

"No, Mags, Emily's room is clean enough. She deserves a night off," my father objected, giving her a look that spoke volumes. She gave one back that said *don't mess with me,* but he continued.

"No, Em, you go and have a good time. Your room can wait another day. We'll see you later. Don't be late." He was standing his ground. Mother opened her mouth to speak, but he hauled her back down the hallway and into the kitchen before she could say anything further. I heard the door slam and we were alone again.

"Ok, you're on!" I grabbed my jacket from the coat rack and put it on. I stepped outside and as I went to shut the door, I hesitated for a fraction of a second, thinking about my father and worrying she might do something to him whilst I was away. Ali tugged on my arm.

"Come on. It's cold out here!"

I forced a grin on my face and followed her down the path hoping my father would be ok and not daring to look back.

*

"Mum, thanks for letting Em come round tonight." Ali sat down at the table.

Beth looked up from her magazine, "That's ok sweetheart, anytime."

Jason wandered into the kitchen and opened the fridge for a coke.

"No, Jason! No more coke. You've had enough tonight. Go and clean your teeth and get ready for bed."

"But mum…"

Beth looked at him across the breakfast bar, "Don't argue. Come on."

He shut the door and stomped off, grumbling to himself. Beth laughed and went back to her magazine.

"Mum, there is something else…" Ali waited for her to look up again.

"What's that?" She was only half listening.

"When I asked Em over her mum was quite abrupt with her saying she had to do chores first."

Beth raised her head sharply. "Maybe she just had a bad day." She tried to brush it off, but knew there was some truth to what her daughter was saying. She couldn't help remembering the conversation she'd had with Ben's mum who lived a few doors down from the Bridges's big house. Jayne Hartford had been joking about the Bridges's wealth and were they that stingy they couldn't afford a housekeeper? She'd mentioned how often she saw Emily in the garden hanging up washing; in fact she said every morning, when she mucked out their horses in the stables that backed on to the north wing of the Bridges's garden, the washing line was always burdened down with bedding or clothes. She'd even said she'd spied Emily busy at it during the week when she was coming in from her impromptu hacks, but Beth had refused to believe that Emily was being kept at home to do housework. Until now. Maybe there was some truth to what Jayne was saying. Everything was such a mess. She was trying to put the pieces of the jigsaw together to try and find out what was going on in Emily's life, yet there were too many loose ends.

"I wouldn't worry about it Ali," she said soothingly, "Now go and get yourself ready for bed."

*

She lowered her face to mine.

"You are the limit!" she said breathlessly, "If I wasn't so sober, I'd beat you to death!"

She'd knocked my father around after I'd gone but a late client meeting meant she wasn't drinking, then and now. We'd both been spared this one time. *Thank you God.*

I backed away, but she kept advancing. "You're not supposed to think for yourself. It's dangerous when *you* think. Now get out of my sight before I beat you again and again until you've learnt your lesson! Get out! Get out!" She raised her fists but for once in my life luck was on my side again and I ducked under her and ran out of the room and upstairs. I could hear Dad close behind me.

I turned quickly, "Go away Dad! Go away!" I was crying. He tried to get near me but I fought him off. We struggled. Exhausted I crumpled into a heap outside my bedroom door and he sat down beside me and reached out to hold me. I shook my head warily; one cuddle wasn't going to change anything.

*

We were a couple of days away from the auction and the tension was almost too much to bear. My father was walking around in a daze and I was so excited beyond belief. Trying to hide my feelings from my mother was proving harder than I imagined. Every time she had a go at me, I had to bite my tongue from telling her about our secret plan to escape away from here, and more importantly, away from her. I wanted her to know her time was almost up. I kept praying it was going to work out ok. *It had to.*

I was in the kitchen wondering what to cook for dinner when she appeared in the doorway, interrupting my thoughts. I looked up as I felt her presence in the room. Immediately I was full of fear, terrified and so helpless. Surely she wasn't planning on more abuse? A sneer spread across her evil face when she read the horror on my own.

"Where's my dinner?" she demanded quietly, threateningly.

"I was just going to do it."

She looked wild, and then it dawned on me why she was looking so smug.

"Where's Daddy? What have you done with him?" My voice shook uncontrollably. I already knew the answer.

"You and your precious father should never ever forget who comes first in this house. Let this be a lesson to you girl." She was coming towards me.

"What have you done? Where is my daddy? Where is he?" I was pleading now, crying, on the verge of hysteria. Had she found out about the cottage? "What have you done to him?" Fresh tears flowed as she grabbed my arm and dragged me off the stool. "What have you done to him?" I screamed repeatedly before she clamped a hand over my mouth and forced me to walk.

"You'll see sweet daughter. You'll see," she mocked, whispering in my ear.

She pushed me along the hallway and into the living room. There lay my father, blood smeared across his face from a head wound. I tried to struggle but she jabbed my ribs and I crumpled to the floor, unable to crawl towards my father to help him. Oh god, why hadn't I seen this coming? Why hadn't I heard her beating him up?

"We can't save each other," he murmured, watching me fall. Both on a par. Both helpless.

"That's right, you can't!" my mother laughed cruelly, "I'm here to teach you a lesson, to teach both of you a lesson." She pushed me over onto my stomach and I felt my hands being bound together. "Wouldn't want you to spoil the fun now would I sweet daughter." Her voice rebounded around my bead. I was still dizzy from the fall and I felt like I couldn't breathe.

"I can't..." I began to say, but she clamped my mouth again and pushed me in a sitting position.

"Shut up or I'll kill you first." I heard the words yet they didn't register. I sat still, waiting, not bearing to look.

She went over to my father and yanked his hair, pulling him to his knees.

"I hate you," she said, spitting the words into his face. He didn't react. I don't think he had the strength. The expression on his face showed all the pain he'd ever feel tonight.

"Never ever put this pathetic child ahead of me again, or I swear I'll kill you. Do you hear me? I come first in this house. This is my house and you'll do exactly what I want!" She was angry. Drunk. Out of her mind. She had never been this bad before, making me watch the abuse attack on my father, usually I was spared. Maybe this was a foretaste of something far worse. My head swan with all these ideas. Nothing made sense. Nothing fit together.

She had hit him across the chest. He was sprawled on the carpet. Then she went wild, losing control completely, her fists were just flashes of pink flesh hitting my father repeatedly.

"Stop it!" I was screaming without realising, "Please stop hurting him!" I couldn't bear it. I tried to move but couldn't. Paralysed by fear. I carried on screaming, but she wasn't listening. Her own words were far louder, far angrier, far more abusive. Just like when she beat me.

"I hate you!" she was shouting over and over again. My head felt like it was going to explode. I prayed my silent prayer this time for my father. God had to be listening. I can't remember if I finished it because by this time I was floating into a state of unconsciousness. The shouting and screaming were receding to the back of my mind. The fists were slowing down. The pleading was fading away.

That was all I remembered, then I passed out.

*

I woke up in a daze, recalling nothing until I realised I was still bound, still in the living room, still hurting from the abuse. It came flooding back then as if a cloud had cleared to show the bright sunshine beneath it, although the events of last night were nowhere near as brilliant as bright sunshine. It hurt to think. I didn't want to feel anything. Was it really morning? Questions swam around in my head, unanswered. Where was my mother? Was my father alive? When did it all end? I didn't know if was supposed to feel desperate or calm. The numbness was spreading around my body, protecting me from the pain.

Someone had unsecured the knots in the rope, or had they just worked themselves loose? I didn't know which, but was relieved when my hands were free and I could get the life back into them.

I looked around the room and realised I was the only one there when I didn't see my father lying on the floor where he'd been last night. I wondered where he was. Surely he hadn't gone to work, not like that? Maybe Aunty Laura was helping him right now. Maybe she was fixing him up. He must have been bad because he hadn't moved me.

I didn't know what to do. The clock on the wall held my attention momentarily whilst it chimed on the hour, but what hour? I strained to see and couldn't believe it was midday already. Usually I would be up early cleaning and polishing, after having been dragged out of bed by my mother. I wondered where she was, what she was scheming for her next attack, and why she hadn't ordered me to do anything this morning. Maybe she was out. I really hoped she was out.

I tried to get up using anything I could reach to help me. I had a quick image of walking into school like this to fulfil my dream of exposing my mother, but it left me as soon as I realised I'd never make it to the back door, let alone the school.

*

She didn't know whether he would be home, but she decided to try his private residence anyway. He was a new acquaintance, her age, slightly younger perhaps. She wasn't sure. She had been seeing him for a few months and he did for the time being like her other male friends, of which she had many. His wealth had originally attracted her, and still did to a certain extent, but he was also a great lover on the rare occasions when he was sober. She could only take him in small doses because he overpowered her in ways she didn't know how to cope with. He thrilled her, pushed her, and inspired her, yet his motives were not where his heart was. He was obsessive, strong willed, a womaniser and delightfully charming all in one go, and these vices and virtues added together made her feel unsteady. She wasn't sure if it was because she could never predict his next move, as he was so spontaneous, or whether it was because he was always right regardless of how much you tried to refute him. She needed him now though. She needed the strength of his character to absorb her and make them one and the same. *He better be there.*

The doorbell echoed through the empty hall. She had driven up the long driveway slowly, searching for any clues that might testify to him being home.

There were none, so when he came to the door, she was as surprised at seeing him as he was at seeing her.

"I wasn't expecting you today," he said calmly, the initial reaction fading quickly. He was never surprised or shocked for long, "I thought it might have been one of the others." He knew she slept around.

"Where's the butler?" she asked, her surprise still evident. She had been expecting him to appear first to escort her inside.

"Oh, it's Jack's day off," he said absently. Then, discarding the subject suddenly as if it were simply trash, he said softly, "You look gorgeous." and his eyes fell over her body; firm breasts, slim waist, perfect hips, curves in all the right places. He reached for her hand and pulled her roughly through the doorway. The door slammed shut behind her as he led her into the living room with its contemporary, minimalistic image splashed throughout. "Sit down," he ordered, and she obeyed almost as if he were her master. She sunk gratefully into the leather chesterfield that had had its identity and authenticity ripped from it, so it to now looked as if it actually belonged amongst the other contemporary pieces. He challenged everything, even his furniture and décor. But it fitted in perfectly with the rest of the room.

When I enter this place, I am just like this chesterfield, she thought to herself; *my identity is stripped from me so that I fit in with his life. His game. The game I dared to play.*

"Drink?" He was pouring himself one.

"No thank you," she replied.

"Do I detect the slight hint of a hangover in that *No thank you*?" She saw him smile to himself.

Smug bastard.

"Actually, I've been unwell, so I'm trying to cut back. I'm not getting any younger."

"When have you ever worried about drinking and your health as a combined subject?" There was a touch of scorn in his voice. One way or another be was going to make her have a drink. After all, he had her in the palm of his hand and she knew and understood that perfectly. It was part of their relationship, to keep it in balance, almost as if it were a term laid down before he even agreed to see her, or be involved with her. A silent term that they both played to.

"Ok, just a small Scotch." She was flustered. He was controlling her, bullying her. She knew it was coming, but it was always difficult for her to accept.

"That's what I like to hear. I knew your resistance was pretty low this morning." He poured her a large Scotch. She didn't argue. It was a game he played to win her over, to make her his, so he had the power to do exactly what he wanted with her whether it be sexual or otherwise. They were lovers but they were also enemies. They played each other, tested each other. Neither trusted one another, yet they allowed themselves to be drawn in so they could explore each other's characters intimately. It was all just a game, but a very dangerous one.

She sipped at her drink, letting it go to her head so she didn't have to be responsible for what followed, if it did follow.

He sat down opposite her, glass in hand already half empty, looking pleased with himself. He always won these rounds of persuasion.

"Have you anything planned for today?" She didn't want him to be asking all of the questions.

"Not really. You?"

"No."

They were silent; she sipped her Scotch tentatively while he swigged his Brandy as if it were water. He got up to refill his glass.

"Steady," she said, watching him. He was easily intoxicated when he drank so fast. "Another one won't do any harm." He finished pouring and came up behind her. He stroked her hair then let his hand slip down the side of her cheek, down her neck and over her breast, where it stopped. He leaned over, "I want you," he whispered in her ear. His hand didn't move while he took another gulp.

She was flattered but also not in the mood, the drink wasn't particularly working and she did have a slight headache. She had come for his company, yet all he wanted was sex. There was no use trying to talk him out of it, he always had his own way and she didn't want to argue. The points were building up on his side whilst her table still had zero written across it. The power be exercised over her and his obsession with her body made her a perfect candidate for putty in his hand that he could squish and mould to his liking. She couldn't fight it even though she wanted to. She was helpless and he knew it, so he was easily able to take advantage of her mental, emotional and sexual state. Mind games were his speciality and this was one person even she couldn't beat.

"You really shouldn't do that," she said slyly, getting up and putting her glass on the side cabinet. If she was to play his game and try to win, she had to at least make some effort to lay down a few ground rules herself.

The one advantage she had over him was that she was loaning him money to finance his latest enterprise. It was not usually the style of business she conducted. But exceptions could be made when there was something she wanted in return.

He said nothing and took another swig from his glass.

"Your money is my money darling. We both know that."

She wasn't impressed with his logic, even though she knew he was right.

"You can run with me or you can sink into deprivation, I really don't care which."

She stared at him. "That doesn't mean you can just demand sex. I came to discuss business with you, but if you'd rather not then..." He cut her off, slamming down his drink. Her frankness about their current situation had thrown him off balance, but only for a second.

"We have little ground rules that we both agreed on right from the beginning; you finance me and I'll share my profits. But you still owe me something otherwise why would I ever have decided to do business with you? You and I both know that I don't really need your money, I would just have to wait a bit longer, that's all. I could handle that."

She was trapped in his obscure reasoning and she knew it. She had to back down, but she could always play for time if she could just get him to sit down and discuss their venture. He had three pleasures in his life; money, drink and sex. The drink and the sex always went hand in hand, whilst the money side of things always came out on top. When the pound signs were ringing and he could see himself making money and lots of it, then that became his sole focus. And here was her chance. He had put

his glass to one side and was getting out some papers from the small desk in the corner.

"You want to talk about this venture," she asked cautiously.

"If we have to." He came over and sat down opposite her, handing her the papers. "Read these. I need some signatures."

She had finally managed to distract him. He was now assuredly focused on business. She had reached her safety net and he had fallen into it easily. She breathed a sigh of relief but he took it to mean her impatience with having to look through so much.

"You suggested it," he said, slightly confused.

She was glad it had been misconstrued. "I know," she replied, "Get me a drink."

He got up. "Scotch?"

"That'll be fine." She carried on reading the top sheet. "Do you have a pen handy?" He finished pouring her drink, placed it on the table and opened the drawer in his desk to get a pen. "Here you go." He brought it over and she took it from him without looking up.

"You seem engrossed, you don't have to read it all. I'll show you where to sign." She didn't respond. Something had caught her eye. Something wasn't quite right.

"This is not the amount we agreed on," she said calmly, but unable to hide the hint of suspicion in her voice.

He laughed harshly, "If I remember rightly, we did agree on that figure."

She looked at him then. "I was drunk. I rang your secretary up the next day and left a message with her to let you know I'd halved the amount, that I was only joking when I said a quarter of a mil. You had the opportunity to get back to me and you never did, so I assumed we were agreed on the matter. You knew I was drunk. It was a party and we were having a good time, that's all. I never meant it. I'm not signing anything until it gets changed."

"Darling, you know I get unpleasant when people argue with me." He spoke quietly. It was a warning for her not to push her luck.

"I've told you, I'm not signing it." She could sense he was getting angry, and that he was threatening her. *Time to make a hasty exit.*

He got up and loosened his tie, then went over to the drinks cabinet and poured himself yet another brandy, which he promptly drank straight down.

"Sign it!" he said fiercely, once he was through.

She put the pile of papers and pen on the table and got up to leave.

"I can't, not until it's been changed."

He ignored her. "Where do you think you're going!" It wasn't a question.

"I'm leaving. I've got another date." She had wanted it to come out boldly, but her voice wavered.

"You're not going anywhere." He came towards her and forced her back down onto the chesterfield. "I don't like to hurt you, but sometimes you really push your luck darling."

She knew he was tipsy, maybe too tipsy, and wasn't going to let her go until she'd signed the legal papers requesting the amount she had said she was investing into his new business.

"Maybe we can talk about this later, when you've calmed down a bit," she suggested. He bent down so that he was level with her.

"The papers get signed today before you leave." It wasn't an option.

"I'm withdrawing then!" she said defiantly, "You said yourself that you didn't really need my money." Her sudden confidence sparked an angry reaction.

"But you still owe me darling," he sneered, slapping her across the face. She tried to get up, but he held her down. She knew exactly what he meant.

"If we can't sort this out by talking then we'll sort it out in our special way right now." He grabbed her and pulled her up into a standing position. He started to fumble with the buttons down her blouse.

"You're drunk and repulsive!" she cried out, trying to struggle from his clutch.

"Don't deny it! This is exactly what you came for anyway," he retaliated, "You can't resist me."

It was no use; he already had her blouse off and was swiftly moving onto the clasp on her bra. He was much stronger than her and the worst part was - he was right - she did need him badly. He'd hit the nail on the head when he'd remarked her resistance was pretty low this morning.

He finished with her bra and half dragged her; half led her towards the bedroom. By the time they got there, she had no fight left in her. He finished ripping off her clothes and forced her down onto the bed.

A day later, a transaction for £250,000.00 was made to Robert Hilton's account.

CHAPTER 9

It was going to be a good day today. Whatever trials and tribulations lay before me, I was ready for them. Nothing my mother would do to me today could shake of this wonderful feeling of peace and happiness I was starting to feel within me because there, right there, at the end of the tunnel was light - and it was almost touchable. My god, it was almost touchable! How I rejoiced to say those words. This was it, our salvation at last. A few more days, that was all, and then my mother could go to hell.

My father had asked Aunty Laura to go to the auction for him. I don't think he'd intended to go - too risky - and besides, he was still in a bad way from the other evening. He'd told me to act normal around my mother in case she got suspicious, but this was going to be tough considering I was on the verge of screaming out loud with triumph, excitement, elation.

I can face you today mother. I can face anything today.

*

There was a bidding war going on and Laura was losing her bottle. She was fighting it out with two other buyers and she was almost reaching James' financial limit. She couldn't fathom why anybody would be going after this cottage. She thought it would be a done deal and she'd have it in the bag by now. Yes it was unique, a barn conversion, but the property was a shambles needing so much work. James had purposely chosen it. Cheap and cheerful, but most importantly - out of the way. Not quite the country property he had envisaged all those years ago. Laura cringed at the thought of them living there, but this was what James wanted and if she let him down, she would never be able to look him in the eye again. Not after what she promised him yesterday morning when he came to her distressed, a broken man, cuts and bruises all over his face, hands and body. She knew what went on. She didn't condone it, but she saw the trap her brother and niece were ensnared in. Maggie Dalton was a tempestuous, calculating, unstable, dangerous woman who had friends in all the right places. If James and Emily ever bought shame upon her, they would most probably pay with their lives. Maybe it wasn't as crazy as that, but Laura felt nauseous whenever she thought of the damage Maggie had already done to them - and what she was still capable of. Her abuse was an unknown quantity.

"The bid is in the room for property 146 at sixty two thousand pounds."

This was all so completely unexpected. Laura held her breath, waiting for one of the others to bid again.

"Going once."

It had been fast bidding between the three of them since the start at £40,000.00 Laura had a limit of £65,000.00 but she and James had both thought that it wouldn't go any higher than £50,000.00 max. How wrong they were!

"Going twice."

She didn't dare look across the room at the two other buyers. She wanted to avoid being recognised and avoid eye contact. Maybe they knew who she was and they were sabotaging James's plan to escape with Emily.

She waited for the hammer to fall. *Finally* the cottage would be hers and she could get out of here... but then she caught something in the corner of her eye and her heart sank.

"Is that a bid for sixty two and a half thousand pounds?"

One of the buyers must have nodded because the auctioneer repeated the price and looked her way, waiting for her counter bid, then he looked at the third buyer and waited.

The bidding rocketed again and Laura concentrated with all of her energy. She didn't have much money left to play with, so every bid counted. The other two were showing no sign of letting up though. Perched on the edge of her chair, she was giving herself away. The two men could see how desperate she was becoming. This was her first auction and it showed. They knew she had a limit and it was fast approaching. She knew she wasn't being cool and calm like she should be but it was all too much. She raised her hand at £65,000.00 knowing this was it. Knowing she couldn't go any higher. The man she'd stolen the bid from smirked. *Such an amateur.* If this lady wanted it so badly, she should have waited until *Going twice* at least, maybe even waited until the auctioneer was preparing to strike his hammer. Now he was going to do that to her. Make her feel like she almost had it, then snatch it away again. Unlike her, he didn't have a ceiling price. He was fighting with the third bidder and he *would* gazump him.

"The bid stands at sixty five thousand pounds. Going once...going twice..." The auctioneer raised his hammer. Laura couldn't breathe. Was she finally going to get lucky?

No.

One of the others raised his hand. For a fraction of a second she thought she'd won, and the relief ebbed into her body. But then she saw his hand move, it registered like slow motion, and she felt the disappointment and frustration suddenly consume her. It was overwhelming.

"We have a bid for sixty five and a half thousand pounds." He looked in her direction again.

A hush fell over the room. The silence engulfed Laura. The audience was enjoying this, but she wasn't. Her heart was beating loudly in her ears. Surely they could all hear it.

She shook her head slowly. The auctioneer raised an eyebrow as if to say *You're giving up now? After all that?* Laura shook her head again signalling she was bailing out. Her head fell forwards onto her chest as she slumped in her seat. She had failed. So had the other bidder. He had bailed out too. The hammer had fallen. Neither of them had the cottage. She dared to steal a glance in his direction and wondered whether his loss was greater than hers. Probably not. *Definitely not!* He was already flicking forward through the catalogue choosing his next option. But he did look disappointed, and when she dared to stare a moment longer than was wise, she even noticed he was fumbling through the book rather than taking his time. Was it desperation? Had he let someone down too? She was intrigued but didn't want to blow her cover, so looked away quickly. The urgency of her own situation taking over her thoughts again. That's what James should have had – a second, third, even fourth alternative. He'd only given her the one chance. Now she was going to walk away empty-handed. There could be only one winner.

*

It took a while for the news to sink in and then Maggie felt the blood rush to her head and the white-hot surge of anger flood her body. She threw the phone across the room and picked up her glass. Taking a long drink, she allowed herself to feel every bit of the rage until it penetrated her very core. She wanted to hurt somebody and she wanted to hurt them bad. She slammed the glass down and refilled. Storming down the landing, she flung open Emily's door. Emily screamed and backed into a corner, her half open blouse almost catching on the chest of drawers. She saw the glass in her mother's hand and her heart leapt into her mouth. This was going to be a real test of her strength and courage. Maggie looked awful. Wild. She lunged at her daughter but Emily dived for the safety of her bed and hid under the covers trembling.

"Get out of there!" she ordered.

Emily cowered under the covers wishing her mother would go away. She felt the tears rising and tried to stop them. It was a battle between her and the monster that stood over her, and a battle between her and the tears she couldn't fight back.

If only it was just the tears she had to contend with.

"I said get out of there!" She ripped the clothes from Emily, exposing her. Raising her fist, Emily shrank back to avoid contact, but she caught her full across the face. Her head swam, as she lay motionless across the bed.

"You lazy little bitch!" she shouted, dragging her off the bed by her hair. Emily fell to the floor struggling with consciousness. Maggie leant over and slapped her face.

"You will pay for your idleness! You think just because I turn my back you can do nothing!"

Emily lay in a huddled ball at her feet. She watched Maggie's arm go up and at first she thought she was going to strike her again, but the resounding smash against the wall made her realise she had thrown her glass across the room. There was silence for a full minute. Emily counted the seconds in her head…waiting for the next hit. It came eventually, but never too soon.

"You think you don't have to do what I say? You think you can do what you want? Is that it? Is that it? Well you can't! You can't! This is my house and you'll do exactly as I say!"

Emily heard the words, she felt the hatred, and her heart ached. She couldn't stop what followed. It was relentless, blow after blow, without let up.

Little Child

She cried out to stop her mother, over and over she begged her, but she wouldn't listen. She *never* listened. Maggie's voice overpowered hers like her fists overpowered hers. Emily was helpless. She couldn't do anything other than just try to stay alive, just try to keep breathing. And all the while one thought was haunting her; that this monster who hated her so much was actually her mother who she was supposed to love and who was supposed to love her. How could two people so closely connected, be so different? Why did her mother hurt her so? What had she done wrong? When would it stop?

She prayed silently, willing her mother to end her ranting, end the violent threats, and the terrible abuse. But it wasn't working. God wasn't on her side. There was nobody to save her. If this was hell, she couldn't see it getting much worse. Was she still alive? Had she floated beyond this world, the scary world that carried the monster that tortured her soul?

She felt nothing but an overwhelming sense of loneliness deep inside. Everything else was numb. The loneliness consumed her.

Take me away, she prayed.

Maggie was now pulling her across the bedroom towards the door.

"Now you'll see what happens when you don't do as you're told!"

Emily semiconsciously heard the words. Something was about to happen. Something crazy. She couldn't connect the sentence together and a trickle of blood down the side of her face only served to distract her further.

She tried to plead again, "Mother, what are you doing?" Reaching for the banister she dragged herself into a standing position. She couldn't let this happen. Whatever crazy thing was going to happen, she couldn't let it.

Maggie reached the door and pushed her out onto the landing.

"Shut up! Shut up child! I always said you would pay for your wickedness one day."

Emily was standing at the top of the stairs, barely breathing, her whole body racked with pain, but the pain she felt in her heart was much much worse.

"Please don't do this," she whispered, beginning to cry again, "Please don't do it."

Was she going to push her?

She closed her eyes.

Maggie caught her breath and said nothing for a long time. She was trying to segregate her anger, understand it, rationalise it, but the fury she felt blinded her senses. This was nothing to do with Emily. This was to do with not getting what she wanted.

But it *was* all her fault.

No it *wasn't*.

Yes it *was*.

Yes. Yes. Yes.

It *was* everything to do with her daughter.

She had taken her down, piece by piece, getting in the way of Maggie's ambitions. Cumbersome. A distraction. Maggie had been forced to take her eye off the ball. And now when she was trying to rectify it, sort the mess out, Emily was getting in the way again.

Damn child.

Damn, damn child.

This time Emily wasn't counting the seconds or minutes. She just waited...and waited...and waited...

The silence was heavy. Emily's mind went blank. Was her mother still there?

Nothing happened.

Her legs began to give way. Any longer and she would be a heap on the floor.

Finally, unable to stand, she slumped down on her knees, fully expecting to be pulled back up again.

But still there was no movement from Maggie.

It was then that she heard the weeping.

She opened her eyes, turned around slowly and leaned heavily against the wall to avoid tumbling down the stairs. Her mother was on her knees, her head in her hands, and she was crying.

But they weren't tears of shame.

Emily watched the splashes trickle over her almost perfect cheekbones, yet she couldn't find it in her heart to comfort her.

Little Child

*

James took one look at Laura and knew it was game over. She shook her head slowly to confirm it. Tears welled in their eyes as they embraced. How was he going to tell his little angel they hadn't got the cottage? His heart sank, reaching a new depth of hopelessness.

Despair was strangling him.

He couldn't tell her.

The news was too much to bear. How would she be able to take it?

Why was God punishing them?

*

She didn't know whether she wanted to visit him tonight. He had promised her dinner at her favourite restaurant, but if she was going to see him, she wanted to stay in and ask his advice on something that was bothering her.

She instinctively drove towards his house, although she hadn't yet made up her mind what she was going to do.

She picked up her mobile and dialled his number, steering with one hand. It rang and rang, and she was just going to hang up when she heard his deep voice on the other end. The lines were familiar...his usual business manner.

"Hello? Thomas Anderson speaking." She would have died for his voice.

"This isn't business darling." She spoke softly. Sensual.

"Hello Maggie. I was expecting your call. Are we dining out tonight, or have you changed your mind?" He spoke with his usual pleasantness. It never failed to arouse her. Always cordial. Always gracious.

"I need your advice." She knew he would approve. He was her mentor, the person she would seek out when she needed help. It was rare, but when it happened, Thomas relished the moments for as long as they lasted. That's how their relationship was. There was never much physical pleasure derived from their meetings. They used words to stir the emotions. The rest was left to the imagination. In her opinion it worked just as well. It left him in a state of wanting more, but unable to have more. She, on the other hand, simply loved the power. She seemed to be exercising so little these days that this felt good, real good. She didn't feel cheap with him, as she did with most of the others. He listened with interest to anything she had to say even if he didn't agree with her. He had spent too many years patiently moulding her to throw it all away over one slight disagreement. If they fell out, as they so often did, she always came back.

She would always come back.

"We'll talk when you get here." He knew better than to ask her now.

"I'll be at the gates in a minute," she said quietly.

"See you then." He hung up.

She carried on driving, feeling better than she had all day. The events of this morning already seemed a lifetime away, and she was grateful. She hadn't cried for a very long time, and she hadn't cried in front of anyone *forever*. Crying took her back to her childhood. The bad part she blocked out. She mustn't cry again. There was also the small issue of Robert Hilton. She still couldn't justify giving him so much money. If Thomas ever found out, he would go ballistic. She was going to settle her score with Robert one of these days. She knew she had bitten off more than she could chew. He had hired her someone for the auction as promised, but what a waste of space he'd turned out to be! Had Robert done it on purpose? Was he playing mind games again? In any case, she would get even with him - and then dump him. She didn't want men like Robert around for too long. He was a liability.

She stopped at the gates to check in with security. They opened mechanically before her as the car neared them. She drove through carefully and began the long, winding ascent up the gravel driveway. There were trees everywhere and as she passed them, she wondered how many gardeners tended to the estate these days. Maybe that would be the topic of conversation tonight. *Each to his own*. She laughed out loud and it felt good.

She reached the house and got out of the car. It was such a beautiful house. Her house…but no longer her home. People moved on. She *had* moved on. She stood admiring it all the while reflecting on the good times she'd had here both with her father, and without. Now Thomas was running the estate and had taken up residence in the east wing. She had never cared for the east wing. He was welcome to it.

He was waiting for her at the door, leaning against one of the marble pillars with his arms folded across his chest. He waved as she walked up to him.

"Shall we go in?"

She smiled and followed him into the hallway. He led her through to the living room and motioned for her to sit down. She did. There was no threat here. His presence made her feel very comfortable.

"Drink?" he asked.

"Yes, I'd love one. Thanks."

"The usual?"

She nodded and kicked off her shoes so she could stretch out on the chaise.

"It's been a long day," she said, settling herself back into a comfy position, "I just want to relax and chat…if that's ok with you."

He finished pouring her Scotch and brought it over.

"Yes. I'd like that very much." He hadn't seen her since he'd kept her at the house on Sean's recommendation, and then she hadn't been in the best of spirits. "So, what's bothering you?"

She noticed he didn't have a drink and ignored his question to ask, "Aren't you having one?"

"No. Not right now." He looked expectantly at her, waiting.

She shrugged, "There's something I want that I can't have." She looked like a spoilt child who'd just been slighted.

"And what's that?" Thomas was used to this scene. It happened all the time with Maggie.

"I want to enjoy what I have left Tom. I don't want to be dealing with tedious business affairs for the rest of my life. I want to get out now while I still can."

Thomas wondered whether the recent bad press was starting to get to her. He'd always believed she was tougher than that. When someone tried to kill her at the age of twenty-one, instead of running scared, she had done just the opposite. The incident had been the catalyst propelling her to instant fame and recognition. It had been a remarkable turn of events. *Ah, the good old hey days*, he mused. And touch wood nothing like that had happened since. There were constant rumblings, but nothing ever coming to fruition.

"Fair enough," he said, also thinking how ironical she could be sometimes. How could taking all the prospective clients to bed possibly be tedious? It wasn't what he would class as strenuous work. Well, not much. He laughed to himself.

"What's so funny?" Maggie demanded, annoyed she hadn't been included in his private joke.

"Nothing darling." He changed tact, "So what have you decided to do?"

"Well, I was thinking about having a place somewhere quieter, away from the town life, even away from the neighbourhood, where I could escape when things get a bit too much."

He didn't want to start questioning her motives, that could come later, but he didn't like the sound of this. He still needed her on the team. She was already all bar a recluse and it was becoming increasingly difficult for him and Alex to handle and arrange all the various meetings, appointments, schedules, conferences and deals without her. She still needed to have an input in the day-to-day running of the business. This was her father's company after all. And it was good for the company image to have her show her face every now and then. Keeping up appearances was important.

"And is there a place you're interested in?" He knew the answer already. There was a place, but she couldn't have it. More dubious deals to be done. *And I'll get roped into it somehow,* he thought to himself.

"There is," she paused, searching for the right words, "but I need your help."

Silence. He had been right.

"Will you help me?" She didn't like it when he went quiet on her.

"It depends." He looked thoughtful.

"On what?" She was getting impatient with him.

"On what I have to do."

"There's a cottage that I want. I sent someone to auction today but the damn fool failed miserably and we didn't get it."

"I'm sorry to hear that." Thomas was humouring her.

"We were outbid, and so was someone else, so I know it's in demand. But *I* want it!" The spoilt child look again.

"What happened to your bidder?"

"Well he obviously lost his nerve stupid fool!"

"No, I mean what happened to him afterwards when he broke the news to you?"

"I fired him!"

Thomas grinned. Exactly the answer he was expecting.

"Ah Mags, you can be so harsh."

She looked at him. "Don't patronise me Tom. He's no good to me now. So...where was I...can you do a little digging? Maybe throw some bribes around? If that doesn't work, do what you have to do. But I want it, and I want it as soon as possible. Can you do that for me?"

"I don't know. If it's just been bought then that makes things a lot more complicated, especially if the new people have already moved in. Why this property? Isn't there anywhere else you like?"

"No!" She was resolute, uncompromising.

He sighed, backing down, "All right. All right. I'll give it a go. But don't expect miracles. And I'm doing this on one condition."

She pulled a face, "What's that?"

"You have to let me know where it is."

She smiled, and jumped up giving him a hug.

"You won't regret it darling! Do you want the details now, or later?"

"Do you know who's bought it?"

"No...I was leaving that bit for you to find out."

"Well, you better give them to me then if you have them."

She sat back down and pulled out the property sheets from her handbag.

"Here you go."

He took them from her and did a quick scan through.

"Seems to be all there."

"But do you like it?" She was excited he'd agreed to help her. She was confident it would soon be all hers. She took a long drink from her glass.

"It's ok. Definitely not your usual taste." He tried to hide his sarcasm. To him it looked at utter shambles. A far cry from anything he would ever set foot in.

"Wait until I finish renovating it! And don't forget, it is private remember."

"Oh, of course. It's perfect then, if it's intended for that purpose."

She didn't notice his indifference, "One other thing Tom."

He looked up, "You know the rule darling. Only one favour per meeting."

"Please keep this to yourself…ok? Deal?"

He smiled, "I'd already gathered I wasn't to say anything to anyone…"

She looked relieved, "Thanks."

Was the pressure getting to her? Thomas wondered, *What was going on in her personal life?*

She paused, "We don't need to shake hands do we?" She was joking with him. Handshaking was always his formal practice when clinching a deal. He was known countrywide for his very particular handshake.

He got up and extended his arm to her, "No, but I would like to take you out to dinner now. Will you join me?"

"That would be lovely." She finished her drink and put down the empty glass. Linking his arm, he led her outside to his Jag. There were other cars, but he loved the Jag the most. She loved the car's plush interior. Her own car, a Porsche, was just as luxurious.

He opened the passenger door and she slid into the leather seat with ease. He walked around to his side but didn't get in. She heard the ring of his mobile and shifted in her seat to see what was going on. He had answered but the expression on his face was gradually becoming more and more displeased. She wondered who it was and what they wanted. *Anything to spoil our evening,* she thought sullenly, *that's the problem with business – it never goes away. Always deals to clinch. Always clients to see. Always people to fight with, bargain with and lunch with. Always someone who wanted to speak to you and always something that had to be done yesterday…very, very tiresome…*

She was getting annoyed. What was keeping him?

He finally ended the call and opened the door to get in. She noticed he was ruffled.

"What's wrong?" She was impatient to know who it was and what they wanted.

"That was Sean. He's putting pressure on me to discuss the business. He wants to meet us with a proposition."

"Who the hell does he think he is?" she demanded, unimpressed, "Some jumped up little shit that I've never liked. Can't we sack him?"

"Don't be stupid Maggie. I can't afford to lose his expertise and you know it! And it doesn't work like that. We're teetering on trouble and I'm obliged to hear him out," he fired back. He was more obliged than she knew.

She was beginning to see the picture and it wasn't a very nice one. Sean calling the shots? No way!

"You do realise what could happen to me if all this gets aired to the Public?"

"I know what the consequences are, thank you!" Now he was becoming angry at her and her selfish attitude. Me meme, that's all it was to her. "But what do you expect me to do? Boycott him? That could turn the Board against us and then we're really in at the deep end."

"Sort it out Tom! Sort it out before my name gets dragged under," she paused, catching her breath, "Do whatever it takes. Get nasty. I don't care. Just clear this mess up before it gets out of hand. I don't trust him!"

They were both silent. She was thinking how this could affect her reputation. He was pondering his dilemma.

"We should meet him," he spoke softly, interrupting her thoughts.

She stared at him coldly. "You have a choice. Make your decision and act on it. I'll call you in the morning."

"But what about dinner?" He was frustrated. He couldn't work her out at all.

"I've changed my mind." She got out of the car and walked over to her own. He saw her hesitate before getting in and revving the engine. Then she drove down towards the gates. The security scanner read her number plate and they opened automatically before her. She carried on driving, leaving a cloud of dust hanging in the air behind her.

He watched her leave, the disappointment rising, whilst she headed for the nearest bar.

Damn you Maggie Dalton.

*

The transaction had failed. Robert Hilton wasn't impressed as he put the phone down and settled back in his office chair. But despite this, he smiled to himself. So she wanted to play dirty did she? Well, now she owed him big time. She was feisty all right and a lot to handle. Definitely the real deal. He would hold onto her. Keep her close. The smile grew bigger. Yes, he would certainly keep her close.

CHAPTER 10

My heart skipped a beat. Something was wrong. It was written all over my father's face. He came home looking upset and angry and wouldn't talk to me about anything until my mother had gone out for the evening. He cooked me dinner in silence, we ate in silence; my father sparingly while he brooded, me hungrily because I wanted to get it out of the way so he would talk to me.

But the silence continued while we washed up; me drying, my father washing.

Whatever it was, it was getting to him pretty bad. His face was troubled and he was totally absorbed in thought.

"We need to talk," he said finally, as he lifted me level with the shelf so I could put the last clean plate away.

I nodded and followed him back into the dining room. He gestured for me to sit down opposite him.

"Has she hurt you again?" He knew the answer already. There were visible cuts on my face and I had bruises on my arms and legs where I'd been pushed and shoved around this morning.

"Yes," I whispered.

He didn't say anything but reached for my hand and squeezed it.

"What is it Daddy? Tell me what's wrong?" I wanted to know so desperately so we could share it and he wouldn't have to carry this burden alone.

"It's the cottage..." he faltered, unable to look at me. His face was tortured.

"What is it? Can we fix it?"

A laugh escaped from his lips. "The innocence of youth," he murmured, lifting his head to stare at me. I met his gaze and saw the unbelievable sadness in his eyes. He had once told me that the eyes were the window to the soul. I didn't know what he'd meant at the time, but now I could see how true that expression was.

"We didn't get it Sweetheart." He dropped his head again.

I felt the air rushing out of my lungs and my whole body went into shock. I tried to focus on feeling something, anything, but couldn't. The numbness I was so used to was taking over again, protecting me somehow.

Was I really surprised by this news?

I think I'd been expecting it.

Nothing this good could ever have happened to my father and me.

It wasn't meant to be.

It never was.

We didn't get it Sweetheart.

I let the words sink in…

We didn't get it Sweetheart.

I saw the light at the end of the tunnel slowly go out. I saw our hope of freedom being wrenched from our grasp. The dream was suddenly slipping away.

I choked back the tears, but one escaped and rolled down over my cheek. I watched it drop onto my hand and run down my finger.

"So we have to stay here for a bit longer?" My throat was so constricted, and my voice so small, I had to force the question out.

He looked up and nodded.

"But they'll be other properties right? We do have alternatives?"

He didn't answer for a long while.

"This cottage was unique and perfect for us in every way. Properties like this don't come along very often especially at such a good price." He leant back and folded his arms across his chest. "Plus everything has to be undercover and undercover takes twice as long. But I'll keep looking Sweetheart. I promise you I will."

He tried to smile to reassure me, but I sensed his despair. He got up and came over to me. His big, strong arms closed around me and I felt safe in his warm, tender embrace.

"Just a while longer and soon we'll be safe… I promise Sweetheart. Everything is going to be all right… I promise." He spoke gently, holding me close.

The words made me feel a little better, but didn't completely soothe me. I huddled into his arms further trying to rid my mind of future beatings.

"I hope so," I whispered, my voice barely audible, "I hope so."

He held me tighter as if protecting me from the monster we both feared.

She couldn't have been back until late last night because when I awoke the next morning, I was safely tucked up in bed and my father was snoring softly on the sofa bed at the other end of the room. He only occasionally slept in my room when he felt the need to protect me. The rest of the time he slept in one of the spare bedrooms.

He must have felt that need last night.

*

Maggie dialled his number slowly. She knew she was petulant and had acted irrationally last night, and she feared the reaction she might get from him this morning. But she wasn't about to make excuses for her behaviour.

"Maggie?"

"Tom?"

"I was expecting your call sooner." He was huffy, and seemed to be in a hurry to get somewhere fast.

She opened her mouth to begin a tirade and then quickly decided against it. Now was not the time to argue.

"Tom, about last night…"

He cut her off, "Maggie, there's no time for this. I'm going into a meeting with the Board right now. I'm meeting Sean afterwards. You better be there." He hung up before she could say anything further. He was really angry with her. This was not a good start. She needed to keep him sweet so he'd help her with the cottage escape. *Damn damn damn!*

For not the first time in her life, she wished she could turn the clock back.

*

Sean was leading the discussion and neither Thomas nor Alex felt comfortable with this. Thomas was supposed to be the one chairing the crisis meeting, yet Sean was taking over, and worse still; the other Directors in the room seemed to be listening to him.

Whatever was going on was puzzling both of them.

"Look at this Tom. Maggie's estate is in serious financial difficulty. Here, take a look at these." Sean shoved the most recent bank statements in Thomas' direction and his jaw dropped open when he saw the worrying figures.

"I don't get it!" he exclaimed, "Why didn't I know about this sooner?"

"You've been busy keeping the Press at bay. We understand. But now it's time to take action. We can't continue like this." He shoved more papers at Thomas, as the other Directors murmured their agreement.

Alex didn't get it either. He was just as perplexed as Thomas. He took the statements from Thomas and studied them carefully. Something was bothering him, but he couldn't quite put his finger on it. He knew Thomas would want a thorough analysis. He didn't trust Sean.

Thomas addressed the Accountant on the Board, "Are these figures a hundred and ten percent correct?" Like Alex, he too felt uneasy. He hadn't taken his eye off the ball so why were Sean and the others making him feel as if he had. Ok, he had been doing a lot of worrying about Maggie recently. Smoothing things over. Covering for her. Standing in for her even. But he was still on top of his game. He was used to juggling many different things, after all, he'd been taught from the best, Maggie's father, the late Richard Dalton. It was second nature to him.

The Accountant nodded. Sean had briefed him prior to the meeting and warned him to watch carefully what he said. The figures had been manipulated to cover the money Sean was embezzling for his little business on the side.

Thomas shook his head. This couldn't be right. *It couldn't!* Something as serious as this would *not* have slipped passed him. He was a businessman, meticulous in everything he did. Mistakes like this just didn't happen in his world. Every company account could not be bordering on the red as these statements were suggesting.

"We have twenty four hours to come up with a solution for the bank, then it's game over Tom. I'm sorry."

"Twenty four hours!"

Sean shrugged. "That's what they told Karl. Right Karl?"

The Accountant nodded again.

Thomas looked from one to the other in disbelief.

"I think that concludes our business today gentleman. We'll meet again tomorrow, same time. Hopefully we'll have a plan by then." He winked in their direction. Neither Thomas or Alex noticed.

People started shuffling paper and rising from their seats heading back to their offices. Sean held back. Thomas remained seated, as did Alex.

"What's going on Sean? I don't believe these figures." Thomas turned to him and his eyes narrowed in suspicion.

Sean smiled. "You're a clever man Tom. Not much slips passed you does it? But this has."

"Cut the bullshit Sean. What's going on?"

Before Sean could reply, Maggie came storming in.

"How bad is it?" she asked, sitting down quickly, "Are we really in trouble or are you messing around?" She'd got the low down from her secretary that things were not looking good, but like Thomas and Alex, she couldn't fathom it. She knew things hadn't been happening for them lately – bad publicity scaring the clients off – but honestly, no money coming in *at all*...she refused to believe that!

"Pretty awful Mags." Alex handed her some of the statements so she could see for herself.

"So what are we going to do about it?" She looked directly at Sean.

"I can offer you a way out."

The three of them stared at him. What was he talking about now?

"I already said cut the bullshit. Tell us what's really going on!" Thomas demanded again. Sean was winding him up. He was tackling his usual cool demeanour.

"Ok, here's the thing. I've got a sideline business going and it's proving quite profitable. You want in?"

Nobody said anything.

"It'll see you safely out of the water...and a bit more..."

Silence.

"I don't see you have any other choice...I'll happily cut you in."

"What is it?" Thomas' suspicion was growing. He had a feeling he wasn't going to like the answer, and he was right.

"Cocaine, my friend. The purest kind."

Thomas' face fell, as did Alex's and Maggie's.

Cocaine!

He was incensed at Sean's audacity. "You seem to forget that we're not a drug smuggling business. We have a reputation and an image to uphold. We are an investment company. The biggest and the best in the country. How can you expect us to lower ourselves to this? I should fire you right now!"

Sean laughed. "Fire me! Oh dear Tom, you really don't have your finger on the pulse with this one."

"What? What do you mean?"

"You don't have a choice…" Sean was enjoying drawing this out. Playing them. Manipulating them. He couldn't wait for the penny to drop and see the look on their faces when they realised.

"You're talking nonsense. You can't bribe us," Alex said, but Thomas was one step ahead and Sean saw the realisation dawning on him.

"Take your time boys and girls," he smirked.

Any minute now…

Maggie got there first. She groaned loudly and got up from the table, but she suddenly felt very sick and her legs buckled underneath her, forcing her to sit back down again. It was all making sense – the pills Sean had been feeding her, her addiction and nightmares, and prior to that the sedatives that knocked her out every time she went anywhere with him, the fact she could never remember all the events of the night before. Because he didn't want her to…until now! Dominic Clayton came into her mind. *God, Clayton! He'd been the very first one all those years ago.* Sean had been doing this since then? Influencing all of the client meetings he'd ever set up and reaping the rewards? Was Robert Hilton one of *those*? She couldn't believe it. He'd been coercing her into his little scheme and she hadn't even suspected a thing. *Jesus Christ.*

"*Clayton*," she whispered.

Thomas was only seconds behind her. He turned on her then, furious. "You knew! You knew about all of this!" He was accusing her. Pointing the finger. She backed away.

Sean watched in amusement. This was better than the big screen.

"Shit." Alex slumped forwards onto the table, his head in his hands.

"No! No! I swear Tom. I never knew this was going on!"

"You bitch! You bitch! You knew. You were party to it. How could you Maggie? How could you? What was it huh? A secret backhander from him -" he jabbed a finger in Sean's direction, "to get exactly what you wanted? All that bull shit you fed me last night about it being too much and all the time you had it all figured out. You were going to use the funds from *this*, this disgusting revenue to finance your little plan!"

Maggie tried to quiet him, but he wouldn't stop. She didn't want him to mention the cottage, she didn't want anyone to know, but she needn't have worried because Sean wasn't listening. He was patiently waiting for the right moment to cut in with his second of three little revelations.

Alex still had his head in his hands in disbelief.

"I swear Tom. I swear to you I never knew anything about it!" He had hold of her and was shaking her. Right at that moment he wanted to kill her. He wanted to hurt her really bad. How could she? How could she do this to him? How could she do this to her father?

"Cool down Tom." Sean pulled him off Maggie and shoved him back down into his seat. He was shaking with rage and almost clobbered Sean around the head, but he ducked just in time. "You've got it all wrong about Mags."

He waited for their absolute attention before continuing. He wasn't going to admit to using and abusing Maggie. That could wait. Besides, once they knew the whole truth, they were going to have to agree to the use and abuse to get themselves out of trouble. They wouldn't have a choice then.

"I've been stealing your money to finance my little venture." He spoke slowly letting the news sink in.

There was a moment's silence, then, "No…no way. I don't believe it!" Thomas uttered. He felt sick to the stomach.

"It's true Tom. I'm your man. Guilty as charged."

"Then I *should* fire you right here and now!" He went for him again and this time he brought him down. They wrestled around on the floor hurling obscenities at each other and throwing punches. Maggie looked on, bewildered, but didn't dare try to separate them.

"That's enough!" Alex shouted above the din dragging Thomas away from Sean. They were both bloody. Sean staggered to a chair nursing a cut lip. Maggie gingerly leant over and wiped Thomas' nose where Sean had smacked him one.

Men! They were impossible. Always wanting to fight each other and beat each other up to prove their point.

Sean was laughing hysterically now.

"What's so funny?" Thomas hissed, pushing Maggie's hand away and attending to his bloody nose himself.

"You still don't fucking get it!"

"Don't get what? What's he talking about?" Thomas made to start on him again, but Alex held him down.

"The crux of the whole thing!"

Sean could barely speak, he was laughing so hard. Every fibre in Thomas' body wanted to give him a good hiding.

Maggie thought Sean was deranged and it was making her nervous. He was playing with them like pawns on a chessboard and there was absolutely nothing they could do to stop him. She had never felt so powerless in all of her life. And it frightened her.

"The crux? The crux? What the hell is he talking about?" Thomas looked around wildly at Maggie and Alex. This was not making sense. Nothing was making sense. He dabbed at his nose some more. Maggie shrugged. She couldn't speak.

"What are you talking about Sean?" Alex was unperturbed. He wanted to get to the bottom of all this.

Sean was still laughing. Thomas was getting pissed off. He threw down his bloody tissue, got up and grabbed hold of Sean and shook him hard. Sean carried on laughing.

"What-are-you-talking-about?" He said the words slowly, spelling it out. He was rapidly losing his rag with this idiot. Nobody had *ever* got under his skin more.

"They're all on my side."

"They? They? Who's they?" Thomas was so angry he could no longer think straight. Maggie didn't get it either. This time it was Alex who realised what Sean was talking about.

"You've got all of them? All of them? Into your thing? Your drug smuggling caper?" He couldn't believe it.

Thomas let go of Sean and backed off. He'd heard Alex and the pieces were suddenly clicking into place. Sean had got them all in on it. Segregated himself and Alex to make them vulnerable. Stuck them in a situation they couldn't get out of.

Maggie gasped, catching up, "This is entrapment you bastard!"

Sean stopped laughing and became serious for a moment. "It's taken me thirteen long years to get them all on board, but now we're finally here. Converted one and all." He looked triumphant. Smug. Conceited.

Carpe diem. It definitely didn't get much better than this.

Thomas's face went grey. He swore under his breath.

Maggie wanted a piece of him now but she was rooted to her chair. This was getting worse and worse by the second. Sean had them all tied up like kippers. It was blow after blow after blow coming at them like an AK-47.

It really was game over.

"What do you want Sean? Why are you doing this?" Thomas could see no obvious way out. He needed to calm right down. He looked across at Alex and nodded. Together they sat down at the table. "Sit down Sean. Let's talk about this."

Sean pulled up a chair.

"What do you want?" Thomas repeated.

"I want to cut the three of you in."

"That's it?"

"That's it."

"What for?"

"To save the company."

Thomas clenched his fists. "Spare me the bull shit."

Sean said nothing.

Thomas slammed his fists down on the table.

"Spare-me-the-bull-shit!"

"You do this for me. The company gets a much-needed cash injection. I walk away."

"You're lying."

"That's all I want."

"You're-lying!"

Alex decided to intervene and change tact. "If we do this for you, what happens next?"

"I told you. I'll resign."

"No you won't. You're angling for a deal. So come right out with it and stop messing us around."

"There's no deal. This is all I want. To have you on board with the others."

"So you can set us up? Is that it?"

Sean said nothing.

"What's the catch? I know there's a catch." He was trying even Alex's patience now.

"Ok, you've beat it out of me. I confess." He held up his hands. "I need the show of unity for this particular supplier. They need to see you on board." He was lying, but how were they to know. Again, the truth could come later once they were in too deep to back out.

Alex felt he'd pushed it as far as he could. "Can you give us a minute?" He gestured towards the door. Sean rose and walked out. He shut the door quietly behind him. From experience, he knew this wouldn't take long.

"This isn't sitting right." Thomas spoke first. "I don't like it."

"Hang on." Alex signalled for them to stop talking. He went from one chair to the next feeling underneath for bugs. Next he went under the table and did the same thing. Finally he felt around the telephone, and then sat back down.

"From now on, we trust no one. Ok?"

Inside Maggie was raging. How could she have been so stupid to let this happen to her father's business?

"We don't have a choice Tom, he's got us right where he wants us. We've been fools not to see it coming, but maybe there's still time to reverse this whole damn charade. Get the others back on side. We could play along with it for now and bide our time. Keep him and the others sweet. This much I do know, Sean's a loner. He acts only for himself. He's probably going to stitch the rest of them up, just like he's stitched us up. Then he'll be gone."

"Yes, with my company!" Maggie's voice was shrill.

"Maybe…maybe not. We say yes, bide our time, watch things take shape, find out what he's really after…and then make our move. Are we agreed?"

Thomas shook his head. This was bad news. All of his instincts were telling him *no*, but like Alex said, what choice did they have?

"Ok," he said finally, "Mags?"

"Fuck him," she snorted.

"Is that a *yes*?"

She nodded. "Call the son of a bitch back in then."

Alex went to get him. They both re-entered the room together.

"We'll go with it." Thomas kept a straight face as he spoke.

"Ok. We have a deal." Sean clapped his hands together. "Good."

"So what's next?"

"We talk tomorrow."

"And that's it? We say yes and you fob us off for another day?" Thomas could feel the fury rising again.

"What you going to do Tom? Call Security? We talk tomorrow and that's final. I'm calling the shots now and you better fall in line."

Thomas went for him, but Alex and Maggie held him down. Sean smirked and walked out of the room, not turning back. He had a phone call to make. Several in fact.

Then he would celebrate. By god, he was going to celebrate.

*

I felt deflated and empty. All day I'd been working my way through the chores, not even thinking about what I was doing. I was like a robot. Programmed to make all the beds, wash the clothes, scrub the floor, hang things up to dry, vacuum, polish. I just kept going. A sub conscious voice telling me not to stop because then I would have time to think. And worry. And despair. That it wasn't ever going to be over. We were never going to get out of here. The walls were going to close in on us and crush us...

No no no! Stop it Emily! I beat my fists against my head. *Don't think.*

I was polishing the wooden furniture, making sure there were no smears, when she came through to watch me. I dreaded this moment. It was almost as bad as being beaten. The silence. The roving eyes staring, searching, piercing into my back and scolding me like two hot irons. Any mark, however small, would be spotted immediately and that would mean trouble. I was so scared, so frightened that sometimes I wondered if the punishment was almost a justification because at least then it was over for another day and I could hide away out of her dreaded path. Bruises and cuts could heal with time, but harsh words that were intended to wound would always come back to haunt me.

This afternoon I had really worked hard on the dining table surface, but I knew my efforts wouldn't be viewed as good enough. Nothing was ever good enough for my mother. I could scrub and polish all day and all night and she would still find something to disparage.

She had been watching for some time when she walked over and began inspecting more closely. My throat closed up as I carried on working.

"You are hopeless child. If I didn't know better, I would do it myself!" The words were cruel and sunk deep into my heart. No matter how hard I tried, I couldn't shake her criticisms from my mind. I couldn't just ignore them. They were personal insults directed deliberately at me, and the hatred was so intense that it stung.

I wanted to shout in her face, *Why don't you then?*

She was rubbing her finger across the surface, making smudges. I stopped what I was doing and watched in horror, as the marks got bigger and bigger.

"You've used too much again. You always use too much! Why won't you ever learn?" She was getting annoyed now, so I carried on wiping. I was too wise to retort back. The best thing was to keep quiet and carry on being busy.

I never saw her move towards me until I felt her strong grip on my chin so I was suddenly staring into those cold steel eyes. I held my breath, fearing the worst.

"You never answered my question." She was accusing me of petulance.

I said nothing. I tried to work myself loose from her grasp but she held on more tightly, crushing my jaw.

"Why won't you ever learn?" she repeated.

I remained dumb, sure that it was the best thing to do. We stared at each other for a long time. I didn't dare look away. She was in an odd mood. Not angry. Not crazed. Not even drunk. Just odd. Off key. Maybe something had happened at the office this morning. She had dashed out of the house like she was on fire, not even stopping to beat me, or give orders for the day. A chill went down my spine and I visibly shivered. She didn't seem to notice. I was facing my nightmare and I had no chance of survival.

Finally, she spoke very softly. "You're pathetic, you know that. Absolutely, god damn pathetic. I'm embarrassed to call you mine. You are a disgrace."

I never answered back but was relieved when she let go. I turned away, ashamed of my tears. She viewed crying as a weakness and I didn't want her to see that she'd crushed my spirit. It would only give her fuel to gloat. I picked up my cloth and started to work again, trying to fight the tears that so often fell these days.

She was still watching and her hand slid back towards the smudges that she herself had created just moments before. "This isn't good enough."

When I didn't reply, she started to inspect the chairs. "Neither are these!"

She walked over to the drinks cabinet and poured herself a large brandy. I looked up momentarily and met her gaze.

"Yes?" she said questioningly, taking a very big swig from her glass. I shrugged my shoulders and kept my head down. I didn't want another confrontation as to how early she should start drinking.

She read my thoughts and replied, "Anyway, it's good for you. Maybe you should try it sometime!"

I wasn't sure whether the drink was making her sarcastic, or whether she really did mean it. Either way, I had promised myself that I would never touch it. I didn't want to be like my mother in any way, shape or form, and that one thing I was certain of.

She took another gulp and refilled her glass. I knew what she was doing and I began to be afraid. Everything was a million times worse when she was belittling with the aid of her drink.

Her finger ran across the cabinet's top and in the sunlight I saw the tiny dust particles stir and float around in the air before settling back down again.

"This is disgraceful!" The irritation rose slightly in her voice. Another swig. Another refill.

"And this bookcase too, covered in dirt!" she scorned, mocking me, "Oh, but don't tell me. You haven't had a chance to dust it yet either!"

I watched her out of the corner of my eye, going from one object to the next, voicing her criticism and then gulping down her brandy as if it were simply water, each time coming back to refill her glass before carrying on with her diatribe of my uselessness.

I wanted to scream that she wasn't being fair, that I was trying my hardest to make everything look as clean as she expected it. I wanted to explain. I wanted to reason. I wanted to do *anything* but stand and watch and listen to her going on and on and on about how pathetic I was, how worthless I was.

Where was the justice? Where were the patience, the love, and the compassion?

Couldn't she see that I was trying so hard to make it right? Didn't she realise the pain she was causing me?

My heart bled.

Where was the fairness in my life?

*

They were still stunned by the news but they couldn't let this get the better of them. It mustn't cloud their judgement for today's meeting.

What were they getting themselves into? Thomas was still far from happy to buy into Sean's deal. Maybe they should consider taking him out. *No!* What was he thinking? That was not the way he operated. He couldn't lower himself to *that*. Not again.

Sean was running through the plan quickly mainly for their benefit. The shipment was coming in tomorrow evening. After an exam, it would be loaded up and sold on quickly. They were making deliveries and drops that same night. Sean already had the buyers lined up but they were expecting prompt service, so nobody could mess around and nothing could go wrong. *Talk about a tight turn around,* Thomas thought. But everybody else around the table seemed to be already up to speed.

He made one last ditch attempt to reason with Sean and the rest of the Directors. "What happens if something goes wrong? Our reputations are at stake here and the reputation of the company!"

"Trust me Tom. I've never let you down before, have I? And besides, relax. This is my business now. I've perfected it into an art form. I know what I'm doing."

Thomas was far from reassured, as were Maggie and Alex. Sean gave him a knowing look that only Thomas understood in its entirety. He swallowed slowly and deliberately, wanting to look away but not able to. Sean was referring to *that time*. In that one, single moment, Thomas regretted ever asking him. But it was too late. *Thirteen years too late.*
He owed him.

*

Another urgent meeting. Maggie was sick of urgent meetings. Thomas was hell-bent on finding out when the other Directors had sold themselves to Sean. Maggie couldn't see what difference it made. They had cheated on her father, and on *her*, and that was all she needed to know. Betrayal and abandonment. As soon as this was over, she would sack them all. There was no loyalty anymore on either side. Let Sean screw them. It would be nothing short of what they'd deserve.
So we have twenty-four hours to sabotage this deal? Maggie's hollow laugh echoed around the four walls of her study. *No chance.*
Unless we just blow the whole goddamn lot up?
She stopped laughing and sat up straight. It was a crazy idea…but it could work…
Could it?
They didn't have very many options left. Maybe now was the time for quick, decisive action. She could make a few phone calls. She knew the right people. Then they would be saved. No more deal. No more shipment. No more drugs to taint her name. If they were with Sean, he wouldn't suspect them.
Hell, he must have loads of enemies anyway!
The more she thought about it, the more she thought it could work. Then she would be able to get Thomas to refocus on her cottage escape. It was taking a back seat at the moment and she was far from happy with this. It was just as important to her.
Yes, it *was* going to work.
We'll blow it up.
All she had to do now was convince him and Alex…

*

"I'm going to have to tell her Alex." Thomas was staring straight ahead, glass in hand.

Alex noticed how distracted his friend looked and he was worried. He needed Thomas to have his wits about him especially with what was coming up. They had discussed a few ideas relating to Sean's entrapment and they were waiting for Maggie to arrive so they could talk it through with her. They needed her buy-in before proceeding.

He didn't answer Thomas.

"I owe Sean. He hasn't said it in as many words, but that look he gave me this morning spoke volumes."

Alex let out a deep sigh. "Whatever you chose, I'll stick by your decision. You know that."

"I don't know how she's going to react. All these years of knowing her and I still can't predict what she'll do."

"She should be pleased."

"She should," Thomas agreed, "She doesn't exactly have fond memories but..." he faltered, taking a drink from his glass, "you just never know with Mags."

Alex didn't say anything. He knew all too well about Maggie's volatility.

"I shouldn't have messed with it Alex. I realise that now."

"You did what you thought was best."

"It still doesn't make it right."

"There's no room for regrets Tom." Alex was warning him. He could see the path Thomas wanted to take him down. "You can't change what's happened."

"I wish I could." He finished his drink.

Alex rose from his seat and took the glass from Thomas' hand.

"There's no point in this," he spoke quietly, watching his friend. He placed the glass back on the side cabinet. "You've got to pull yourself together."

There was no resistance from Thomas. He looked at him absently. He was living and breathing Sean Hamilton and Alex could see in his face how much this had all taken its toll.

"I'm not going to do this with you Tom."

Silence.

"You need to keep a clear head if we're to follow this through."

Finally, Thomas nodded slowly. He loosened his tie and sat back.

"I won't tell her yet. It's not the right time. We'll do this and then I'll tell her."

Alex smiled. This was more like the Thomas he knew. Decisive. He hid his relief well. "That's settled then," he replied.

"So, are we ready?"

"Yes."

"Well let's get this part over and done with and see what Maggie thinks. There's a lot to do."

CHAPTER 11

Maggie scanned the business pages looking for a particular name. Every morning for the last week she had been doing the same thing. She was looking for that punk's name. He was scum. She shivered uncontrollably. Powerful scum though.

It still made her squirm to think about it, her whole reputation at stake balancing in the shadows of one man's resentment – and ego.

He would stop at nothing. She was sure of that now.

He had put a gun to her head for Christ sakes! Pulled the trigger! Thank god it had been a blank. But he had still pulled the trigger! On her!

It had happened to her before, a long time ago, gun to the head, but this time it was somebody she knew, somebody she was working with.

Not just a total stranger.

Sean had almost killed her! He had *wanted* to kill her.

He had pulled the trigger!

Jesus Christ.

He knew about the explosives. How did he know about the explosives?

Someone must have ratted us out. Must have been a big pay off, or a big threat.

If only, she thought to herself.

If only!

If only she could turn the clock back to that day when they made the decision to act. It had all gone so wrong, so terribly wrong. The plan had been perfect...flawless...and yet, here she was gingerly looking through the paper worried about what she might read as each page turned. If If If...she could keep on saying that word for the rest of her life, but it didn't change the situation and it wouldn't change her downfall – *if* it came.

Why does everything I stand for hang on one word? she pondered, *Why me?*

There was still hope of rescuing this, but only if they succeeded in taking more risks, and you couldn't always guarantee anything, not in this game.

Little Child

She finished her coffee and poured herself another, her hangover still persistently lingering. Her thoughts were not on business today but on trying to put the next stage of their plan into action. There were to be no negotiations, that only gave Sean more options to play with, and they didn't want him to have the monopoly over them. He already had enough of that. This had got real dirty now and it was far too dangerous.

Her head ached and all her nerves were jangling. She desperately needed to speak to Thomas, but he was angry with her yet again and had temporarily cut her off. Alex was taking messages.

She sighed, deeply unsure of her next move and agitated with her predicament, and reached into her top drawer, the faithful bottle once again coming to her rescue.

*

My father and I knew she was fraught and that something was going on. All week she had been acting peculiar, more so than usual. Hardly noticing us and locking herself in her study for hours and hours on end. This wasn't normal behaviour. I wanted to know what was happening. We needed to be prepared. I was going to school everyday and she wasn't even batting an eyelid! She was preoccupied with something and my instincts told me it wasn't something good. And there would be a backlash. I could be sure of that. She was going to erupt – and when she did, all hell would break loose.

No question.

*

Her study was littered with discarded newspaper clippings. Empty liquor bottles surrounded her. She felt like she was slowly going insane. One pile of clippings charted her success and achievements; another pile was for the scandals. In her many drunken stupors over the last week she had put these together to see which one contained the most. It had seemed such a good idea at the time. There had always been the odd scandal relating to Maggie over the years, yet nothing they couldn't put a lid on and squash. But the last few months had been hell on earth. Vicious rumours cracking her open bit by bit. Some of it true. Most of it not. Who was responsible for this? Was it Sean and Sean alone? She was gradually being exposed and the clients and the public were not liking what they saw.

Most careers peaked and troughed naturally, but hers had climaxed prematurely and now was spiralling uncontrollably downwards.

Sean was sabotaging everything she'd worked so hard for!

Her father would be so disappointed.

She caught her breath. *Her father.* How she missed him.

She shook with rage and slumped forwards onto the desk. Her emotions were out of control. One minute pain, the next fury beyond words.

She beat the desk with her fists, and then she beat her head. She needed to clear up this mess once and for all. Not just in her study, but in her mind and in her life as well. Sean needed to be stopped and there was only one way left now.

Pull it together Maggie. Sort it out once and for all.

*

She listened to the message on her voicemail and then replayed it. She was sitting at a bar. She had drunk her house dry so, after attempting to clear up her study, she'd treated herself to a large Scotch in a pub she knew out of the way. It was nice and quiet. Peaceful. She needed the fresh air and the open spaces. Being cooped up alone for days on end had driven her crazy. Most of the time she'd been too drunk to care, but in those rare sober moments, she had felt terrible. She could sense all was not as it should be by the way Thomas had spoken. So he was still angry with her. There wasn't a lot she could do about that, but her own reaction to his urgent request to meet her later this evening was troubling her. Why? Because this was it? Crunch time? Time to face up to the reality of the situation? Face up to the mess they were in?

She downed the Scotch and ordered another.

A part of her didn't want to face up to anything. She just wanted her cottage. In a way, Thomas's silence had been her saviour. It had bought her time. But now there was no time left.

Little Child

It was zero hour.

She nursed her glass. Alcohol continued to be a soother for her whenever she felt a growing resentment things were not going her way.

The prospect of having a hide-away to indulge in her own secret pleasures was reassuring her through the confusion, but the thought that it may be slipping from her grasp scared her beyond belief.

No news was good news, she supposed.

But the mounting tension was almost too much to bear. She couldn't escape from that.

She tried to prepare herself for the mind field that lay ahead. She would remain adamant that killing off Sean was the only way to go. They wouldn't like it. They never did. She wanted to put a stop to this business right here, right now. She couldn't live in the knowledge that Sean could destroy everything, even her. And one thing was certain; she had to convince Thomas of her desire to acquire the cottage in any way possible - and as soon as possible. Nothing was allowed to get in the way, and if it did, well, he was going to have to be ruthless. It would do him good to get nasty for once in his life. A change was as good as a rest. Sometimes enough was enough.

*

She hadn't been back all day, which wasn't unusual considering her "activities." This was the first time she had been out for over a week, but I was relieved to see her following normal protocol again. I wondered who was falling victim to her right now and how far she had gone to win them over. I shuddered to think. She was capable of anything and everything. She was without scruples despite her portrayal in the Media. Although, even that was failing her recently.

She brought some of them home sometimes, introducing them as friends of her father. My father got angry with her, but what could he do? He couldn't exactly stop her. She'd only hurt him. I knew he was trying to protect me from her erratic, crazy lifestyle and the charming, sleazy men on her arm. They didn't hide their affection for her, even in front of us. They too were without scruples. But the worse part of all this charade was the fact that she made out I was her only beloved daughter whom she cherished. And they believed every word! Couldn't they see by the state of me that I so obviously wasn't? She made sure I was dressed up though, just so I did look presentable, and sometimes she'd cover the bruises with foundation. She always did my make up and hair, but it was never done nicely. I always came out looking like a scarecrow, or something worse. I may have the latest designer dress on, but every single time I had to re-do my face and hair. Her hand was never steady to do a good enough job.

*

She drove to his house, knowing what to expect but not knowing how she was going to persuade him to carry her request through. He usually took it upon himself to help her in any way he could whenever she asked him for a favour, yet lately he seemed to be falling at the first hurdle and not picking himself back up again. Where was his determination? They hadn't spoken of their previous argument and subsequent parting on bad terms, and she hoped it wouldn't interfere this evening. She wanted to put this business of Sean to bed for a while and concentrate on the cottage. There was work to do and nothing should get in the way of that. She already knew Thomas would think differently.

Security cleared her through and the gates opened up for her as she drove towards them. Then she began the long ascent up towards house. The drive was usually a beautiful one, but the cracks of their financial situation were beginning to show. Sean was holding all of the remaining money and there was little left to keep the gardens in shape. Thomas had reduced the number of gardeners and maintenance staff by half. The thought of losing staff brought a knot to her stomach. Many of them had lived on the estate for years. She tried desperately to visualise how it should have looked but there were too many ugly sights clouding the picture. She suddenly felt spent. For so long now she had been furious with Sean and the rest of them, letting the rage consume her and eat into her. Now she couldn't feel anything except a tiredness like she'd never known before. She mustn't cry. She really had to fight back the tears.

The house came into view, the sun setting just below the roof. It was perfection. A far cry from the rest of the estate. Thomas was using his money to keep it in tact. He loved it just as much as Maggie and would rather die than let it fall into disrepair. She knew he would look after it for as long as he could. He was also keeping on the house staff - Lucia, Mrs Peters, the other maids, Cook and his butler. *Thank god.* Maggie couldn't bear the thought of anything changing. That was probably why she felt so at ease whenever she visited Thomas, despite their frequent arguments and spats. This was her childhood home where she had played with her father. Everything was so familiar and so safe. She had truly adored her father...

She shook her head to clear the thoughts. It was no use remembering when you could never have it back, and besides she needed to be on the ball tonight. It was going to be a tough meeting with Thomas.

He was there in his usual spot, leaning against the pillar, half shrouded in shadow from the roof of the porch. His arms folded across his chest. Waiting for her. She could even predict his first words. Those same words in the same husky voice, *I've been expecting you.* But would it be different tonight? Was he still angry with her?

She couldn't read him to tell.

He smiled as she got out of her car and walked over to him. Maybe all *was* forgiven? Or was he playing games? She was wary. He bent down to kiss her lightly on the cheek, then turned and led her up the steps, down the hall and into the living room.

"Take a seat. Would you like a drink?" The usual formalities. Always the way he did things.

"Please. Make it a large one." She perched on the each of the chaise and thought about how to broach the subject of the cottage.

He was one step ahead of her.

"There you go." He handed her the glass. "I know you want to talk about the cottage Maggie but whether you like it or not, we have a situation here. This just got serious."

She said nothing.

"How have you been?" He could tell she was fraught even though she was doing her best to hide it from him.

She shrugged. "Ok. As well as can be expected considering that awful fuck up."

He daren't mention about the gun to her head. It had been terrifying even for him, and Alex too.

"Sean is clever," was all he could manage in reply.

They both brooded for a moment, each lost in their own thoughts. It had been a nasty experience. Sean had been out of his mind when he realised their plan to blow up the whole shipment. He'd salvaged the deal because that was his job, and it had all gone off as planned for him and the rest of the Directors. But Sean had moved the goalposts, making them pay for their disloyalty. He now had them even more trapped than before and was manipulating them like puppets. Pulling their strings. He had control of them, the business, everything. It was a hopeless situation.

Maggie wanted to say what she really felt, but it would have to wait. She didn't have the strength to go into it now. The cottage was more important.

"There must be a way out of all this," Thomas said absently, "I just haven't found it yet."

"Tom?" she bought him back to her, "Do we have to talk about this now? We should wait for Alex's input. He may be able to do something..." She tailed off aware he was staring at her. Was he still angry? Was he going to shout? He was so hard to read tonight.

How to bring Sean Hamilton down had been dominating his every waking hour to the point that now he was barely sleeping. It was keeping him alive though. Keeping him teetering on the edge of reason. He had never felt more alive in his life. He *would* get his revenge one way or another.

He checked himself, pushing any rash thoughts to the back of his mind. "Yes, we'll sit tight and wait it out," he agreed.

It was time to change the subject. "Now, about your cottage. There are complications." He was aware he needed a different focus, something he knew he would be able to solve with time to keep the craziness of their situation at bay, but he would never admit this to Maggie.

Despite herself, Maggie had noticed the dark patches around his eyes. Realised his fuse may be short, that he could kick her out at any moment and resume the silence between them. But she had to press on regardless. This was important to her.

"Tell me," she said quietly, trying to contain her eagerness.

"This is a private sell and the buyer is proving to be very elusive."

"And?" This information was nothing new to her. She hid the annoyance in her voice.

"I've heard bits and pieces on the grapevine, rumour mostly, but some of it makes sense. This could be someone we know."

"How close?"

"Pretty close."

"Too close for comfort?"

"Yes."

"So?"

"So what?"

"So, what are you going to do about it Tom?" Maggie was getting irritated.

"Maggie, do you not understand what I'm saying? This could be dangerous. We have a lot of enemies at the moment! In light of what's going on, you should be keeping a very low profile."

She growled at him in frustration.

"Have you forgotten the fucking disaster of a week ago? We have to be careful Maggie! If they, whoever *they* are, know what you're planning, they could be planning something too."

"Thomas!" she cried, leaping off the chaise, "The situation with Sean can't be the be all and end all. It can't affect *this*!"

"Maggie, listen to me." He grabbed her by the shoulders. "Something's are not meant to be!" As soon as the words were out of his mouth, he regretted saying them.

She pushed him away roughly. He staggered back. "You promised you'd help me Tom! And you will! Until this cottage is mine. Do you hear me? Until the cottage is mine!"

He had to calm her down before she got out of hand. The spoilt child had returned. Uncontrollable. Demanding. Thoughtless. Sometimes he could slap her.

"All right! I didn't mean what I said. We just need to put our heads together and have a rethink. A rethink about how best to approach this."

She nodded her approval, sitting back down. "That's more like the Thomas I know!"

"Don't push it," he warned, getting up to refill his glass. "Another?" he offered, wondering if he should or not. He may end up doing something he might regret later.

"Yes, thanks."

He poured slowly, mulling everything over in his mind. There was a core piece to this jigsaw puzzle – the mess with Sean and the cottage - but he just couldn't put his finger on it yet.

"They paid for the property with cash. I know that much." He brought over the fresh drinks and sat down opposite her.

"Well, that's our first clue." She couldn't hide the relief in her voice, and Thomas noticed. "If we can hack into our accounts, we can check out whether it's any of..."

Thomas cut her off, "No way Mags! We're in enough trouble."

"But..." she began to protest.

"Listen, Sean has shut us out of the system and he's probably closed down a lot of the accounts already. The bank was asking too many questions. We're being watched and we can't enter the office without one of his escorts. There is no way we'd ever pull this off. You must understand!"

"We'll go direct to our bank manager!"

"He's most probably being watched as well."

"Ok, so we'll send someone for us, or disguise ourselves!" She looked pleased with herself.

"I will not let you do this Maggie. I don't approve!" He shook his head, very unhappy with her proposal. It was on the verge of being hysterical. Maggie was resilient, but was that blinding her common sense? It made him wonder.

"You think of another idea then. I'm open to suggestion! But you know as well as I do that this will be the only option we end up with." She took a long drink from her glass, almost as if she were already celebrating. Thomas also took a long drink, but for very different reasons.

"We'll soon have this figured out," she said triumphantly, "Cheers!"

Was she living on her own little planet? Thomas just about ready to flip.

"What if we get caught Mags? What then? And what happens if it all blows up in our face again? Did that thought ever cross your mind? We know about Sean, but how many other people are there in the web? How many other people want revenge? For all we know, Sean could just be the start of our problems!" He spoke harshly, trying to reason with her. She seemed oblivious to the hell he was going through. Her priorities were all wrong. Didn't she care about her father's business?

She stared at him for a long time. Icy blue eyes pierced him, showing no mercy.

"Nothing is impossible if you want it that badly Tom. Nobody else is out to get me. Nobody else hates me. *You* are complicating things with your paranoia! And besides, no one but you and me know about the cottage, so stop over reacting for Christ sake!"

"But you don't know that for sure, do you?" He was desperate now, pleading with her to reconsider.

"There are no absolutes in this life Tom, but if we don't try, we'll never know!" He was disturbing her. What was wrong with him?

"You're pushing it too far! You're out of your depth!"

"What's the matter with you? What are you talking about Tom?" He shrugged his shoulders helplessly. It was clear she wasn't going to listen to him. "See, you can't answer me. That in itself proves you're crazy!"

"I am not crazy! Have you forgotten everything? What about thirteen years ago?"

"They never tried again! This is incredulous that we're even having this conversation."

Thomas was beginning to tire. She was hard to reason with, hard to fight with, and even harder to keep his temper with. He loved her dearly, yet she always seemed to toss him off, like she didn't need his protection, and this made him more distressed than angry.

"I won't be sucked into your paranoia Tom! Anyone would think you're hiding something from me?"

Thomas didn't answer straight away.

For a fraction of a second, she was suspicious. Then momentarily alarmed. Finally, her expression became questioning.

"Well?" she demanded impatiently.

"I'm not hiding anything Mags." He let out an exasperated sigh, but she didn't hear him.

"Good!" she replied, "Now we can toast since the way forward is settled at last."

She got up to refill her glass, then turned to face him.

"Are you joining me in this little celebration or not?"

He raised his glass and they chinked against each other.

"Cheers," he said, without smiling and without enthusiasm.

"Cheers!" she responded, with a slight twinkle in her eye.

Things were going her way and that was good news.

*

Mother was having someone to dinner tonight. We didn't know who but I had a pretty good idea – another one of her so-called business associates no doubt.

This evening was going to be difficult especially after the day I was about to go through. My mother couldn't have guests to the house if it wasn't completely spotless. I hadn't heard anything else all morning. There had been no beatings because she was in high spirits, but the work was plenty and she wouldn't shut up about how important this client was to her. I felt every bit of her nervous tension.

My father had taken a few days off work to concentrate on securing us a new place to live, but it wasn't going very well. He needed to raise more money. He promised to be home early to help me prepare the dinner so I wouldn't have to cope on my own. He hadn't mentioned where he was going because my mother had been close by. I could guess though – to the bank and his solicitors. I was certain all would be revealed later on when she would be too drunk to care.

I started to vacuum downstairs making sure to keep out of her way. I knew she was upstairs in her study at the moment. I would have loved to put my ear against the door and listen to her numerous telephone conversations, but if she ever came out and saw me…

My mind wandered as I worked. The cottage was constantly there, just out of reach. I wanted to be there. I wanted to be anywhere but here. I needed to be free to see and breathe and think for myself without this unbearable weight on my shoulders. It was so oppressive. I longed for a normal life and I missed my friends terribly. When I wasn't with them, I was thinking about the next best time. For a moment, I thought of taking off for school to see them, but abandoning the house now when we were having company tonight…she would almost certainly kill me. Besides, if I could escape her anger by doing exactly what she wanted, then I would without hesitation.

It's better to be spared by doing what you're told, than being scared because you haven't.

Where did that come from? I must have heard it somewhere and it'd stayed with me.

It couldn't be more true.

I wanted my mother to love me and to take notice of the hard work I did for her. To praise me, instead of constantly criticising.

The cottage came floating back into my mind; an idealistic picture I'd conjured up from my imagination. I longed to see whether it would be really all that my heart desired…

I finished the vacuuming and was halfway through polishing the wooden furniture when she made an appearance in the dining room arch. I cringed, ready for the onslaught of how useless I was - but it never came. All she said was, "I'm going out. When I come back I expect this house to look immaculate!" and turned on her heel and left. It was a relief to hear the door slam shut behind her. Now I was able to work in peace and take breaks, without the fear of being caught.

I went upstairs feeling I was due a rest. I sat down on the edge of my bed and reached inside my top drawer for my special notepad that my father had bought me. I only ever wrote down my thoughts and feelings in this book and sometimes they turned into little somethings. I amused myself for a while, flipping through the pages. Ripping out a page, I picked up the biro on the side cabinet and stared at the clean white page in front of me. I wasn't thinking about anything in particular, I just felt a need to write *something*. Anything. It didn't matter what. I began scribbling but I had no idea of what the outcome would be. That was part of the fun…

I guess I was thinking of my mother. There was no escaping that she dominated my every waking hour whether I wanted her to, or not. A severed connection…

I am two different people.

This sentence pleased me. It was a start in the right direction. I carried on, feeling suddenly inspired.

The person at school who is all smiles, all laughs, all up-for-anything…

But what did I really feel deep down? Loneliness? Despair?

The person inside who feels lonely. Disconnected from past friends, present situations, future dreams and aspirations…

How true this was. I always seemed to be taking one step forward but two steps back. Never making any progress.

My pen continued to write, my thoughts continuing to flow…

What did I really want out of life? Why couldn't I ever seem to achieve this?

I want to be the best that I can be, but sometimes even the best isn't quite good enough…

I reread that line and scribbled out *isn't quite good enough*. It didn't fit somehow…

but sometimes even the best seems to fall short of the mark of perfection…

I liked it better. Now, how to end…

The mirror shows two faces. The mirror tells no lies.

There. All finished. A new poem to add to my collection of many.

I was chuffed as I read through the whole piece. Sometimes I really did surprise myself. But something was missing…a title…

I read it again, searching for some hidden clue. It was the last line that provided me with the final satisfaction.

Mirror Image.

Perfect.

Suddenly the phone rang, disturbing my thoughts. I scrambled off the bed and ran out onto the landing wondering who it could be. My father? My friends? One of my mother's associates?

Should I answer?

I didn't give myself a moment longer to think about the possibilities. I picked it up as soon as I reached it.

"Hello?" I said cautiously.

A cheery voice answered me, "Good morning. I'd like to speak to Maggie Dalton please," before I could reply, "But she did say to leave a message if she wasn't home…I wasn't expecting anyone else to answer. I'm sorry."

Was my mother trying to catch me out? Was this some kind of trick?

I hesitated, wondering whether to tell him who I was. Deciding against it, I asked, "Well, can I take a message?"

"Sorry, who am I speaking to?"

The bombshell. Now I didn't have a choice.

"I'm her daughter."

"Oh! Shouldn't you be at school young lady?"

"No…not today," I said quietly. I hated awkward questions. They got you in too deep before you even realised it.

"Oh," he said again, "not feeling too good? Maggie says you do very well at school. She says you're the best pupil in the class. She's very proud of you."

The words hit me like a brick. *What?* I was completely lost for words. I almost dropped the receiver with shock.

"Hello? Hello? Are you still there?"

I managed a small *Yes.*

"What's your favourite subject?"

"English."

"Well wouldn't you know? I'm in the writing business! Publishing. Maybe tonight you can show me some of your work. How about it?"

Now I knew who I was speaking to – one of my mother's rather younger clients, but he seemed all right. Maybe dinner tonight would be interesting after all.

"Yes, I'd really like that Mr…" I faltered, realising he hadn't even introduced himself yet.

Recognising his mistake, he spoke up straight away. "Oh, I am sorry! How rude of me Miss Dalton, not even introducing myself. I promise my manners will be much better tonight. You will be joining us, won't you? Your mother speaks so highly of you that I'm dying to meet you."

I was flattered, but you could say under false pretences.

"Yes, I will be at dinner Mr…" I stopped in mid sentence again, not so much because I still didn't know his name, but because I nearly said, *yes, and I'll be cooking it as well.* Luckily I checked myself just in time.

"Mr Louis. Michael Louis," he said, prompting me, "I look forward to meeting you Miss Dalton." Funny how they always assumed I'd taken my mother's name. "I was phoning to let

Maggie know that I may be a little late. She said to call if there were any problems."

"I'll let her know for you Mr Louis," I replied, wondering at the same time just exactly how I was going to do that.

"I do sincerely hope you feel better tonight, and remember to have some writing to enthral me with. Ok?"

I laughed, "Yes, I will do. Thanks for calling. Goodbye now."

My head was spinning with questions and I barely heard him reply until I realised the phone was dead and he had rung off.

I didn't go back into my bedroom but went downstairs instead. Is this what my mother told all of her clients? And did she really mean it? Surely not! Her vicious actions spoke far louder than any words of praise heard second hand ever could. I was bewildered. I wished my father was here so I could tell him all about this conversation. The worrying thing was – we had gotten on over the phone wonderfully. How was my mother going to like *that*?

The simple answer was that she wasn't.

I would have to be very careful tonight. If Mr Louis showed me too much attention, she would become jealous and show herself, and us, up. I could just picture it now. She would try to act like it wasn't bothering her, like she didn't really care, but she would slowly be boiling over. Eventually she'd explode, blowing the little idyllic story she'd created – the one where I was supposed to be central to her life - right out of the window. We would all feel really stupid and embarrassed; she would have exposed her true character, lost the deal, and the minute Mr Louis walked out the door, my father and I would be in for the biggest beating of our lives. That was the extreme scenario. It had never happened before, but we'd been close a few times.

No. It definitely couldn't happen tonight.

*

"It's been so perfect! Everything falling into place like it was meant to be." Kaiser was jubilantly walking around the room, sloshing champagne everywhere and recounting his tale over and over again. She could see he was getting ahead of himself, but the hardest part was yet to come.

"I need you to be focused," she interrupted him, lighting up a cigarette.

"What's wrong with a little celebration?"

She disproved of celebrating before the final event. In her experience, it was a sign that the pressure was becoming too much. They needed to release pent up energy too early. He should be more controlled. Save himself for the showdown. Letting go too soon could mean mistakes at the most crucial point. She wasn't happy. He could not mess this up for her when they were so close now.

He continued his drunken march and chatter, not waiting for an answer. The champagne was spilling all over her antique furniture and her patience was wearing thin. She signalled to the men on the door.

"Take his gun and lock him up for the night. Bring him to me in the morning once the hangover's cleared. He's no good to me like this. And have some one clear up this mess."

They grabbed Kaiser by the arms and hauled him out of the room. He tried to fight them off, but he was too far gone. She sat for a moment puffing methodically on her cigarette until it burned low. Then she too got up and walked out of the room.

It was almost time.

CHAPTER 12

James walked into the solicitors and approached the receptionist. He had purposely chosen a reputable outfit in London because things could get messy with Maggie over Emily and their finances. The tube had been a nightmare, but it was worth it. She would have the very best team to fight him should she go after him for kidnap, and he needed to match her. But money was tight and this would drain his resources. He'd paid a visit to the bank earlier this morning and they were still considering his request for a loan. He had a meeting with the bank manager later next week. He was already praying it would go ok. Maggie detested Emily, but having a daughter was good for her image. He knew she pretended to everyone domestic life suited her. Over the years, any cracks to show otherwise were quickly sealed over by her people. That's why James had had such a hard time convincing his family she was beating them because everything they read indicated bliss. Now, it was all on its head – he had stayed too long and they couldn't understand why.

"Can I help you Sir?" the receptionist asked immediately. There was the usual smile stuck across her face, fixed, ready to shine as if on call, all day, everyday.

Did they ever stop smiling? Did they ever realise that when they were angry or upset, they could frown or pout? Or, was the smile a disguise, or even a permanent fixed contract, part of the job; five days a week, every week, with a half day on Saturdays, every Saturday? He chuckled to himself. The receptionist looked baffled before repeating, "Can I help you Sir?" with more emphasis on the Sir this time round.

He noticed the smile straining to stay fixed on her face. Was she going to break protocol and frown?

He hid another chuckle. "Yes. I have an appointment with Mr Cartwright."

"And your name please *Sir*?"

"Mr Bridges. James Bridges."

He watched her work on the computer for a moment.

"Ok. Please take a seat and Mr Cartwright will be with you soon."

He sat down on the pristine leather sofa and picked up a magazine pretending to read. There were a couple of other people waiting with him. They looked very official with their dark suits.

It wasn't long before he was called in. He stood up, brushed himself down and followed the receptionist up the wide staircase to the offices on the next floor...

Just a little over an hour later, he reappeared, feeling slightly better than when he went in. Everything had been discussed, laid bare, and it was now in the hands of the experts. It had felt awkward, at first, trusting somebody outside of his unit. He was so paranoid about Maggie ever finding out he'd talked, but it needed to be done if this was what he really wanted for his and Emily's safe future. So he'd put his concerns aside and confessed all, every single little detail. They needed to know what was going on if they were to have any chance of fighting Maggie and her powerful entourage – and of winning the case. Now they were working on building a rock solid defence for him. Preparing early to catch the other team off guard.

The only thing worrying him now was the bill. He glanced down at the piece of paper in his hands and gulped. This would wipe him out for a while until he secured the loan. *If he managed to secure the loan.*

He must, otherwise god help him.

*

She came home and went straight into her study. She had been to see Robert and finally he had promised to dig around for her, although she hadn't mentioned exactly what it was for and she hadn't told him about the nasty business with Sean. That must stay under wraps, at least for the time being. He'd given her a list of names, likely suspects with dirt soiling their clean cut image, people who had something to hide who may want *out*. She'd been trying to persuade him for a while now, but as always it was a case of what was in it for him. He had been intrigued, probing hard for information, but she had remained silent and officiated a bribe instead. He'd fallen for it, just as she knew he would. Mention a six-figure number and he'd do anything. Seven figures and it was a piece of cake. It was so easy to work the charm on Robert when money was in the equation. And no contract had been drawn up or signed so, as far as she was concerned, once he'd helped her that was it. There wasn't going to be any follow up payment this time - it still grated on her that he'd forced a quarter of a mil out of her bank account - but even before he realised she hadn't kept her side of the bargain, she would be safely tucked away and he would never know where to find her.

Perfect.

Sadness kept creeping up on her. Her emotions were way out of sync. Five minutes ago she'd felt elated, but now, as she sat at her desk and caught sight of the broadsheet left open from earlier this morning, she was feeling upset. Blinking back tears she shoved the newspaper away. Was this a sign of future troubles about to befall her? She shivered and dismissed the thought before it had time to take root. Uneasiness replaced the sadness. She tried to shrug it off, but it lingered. A drink was in order, a large one. She opened the top drawer of her desk and pulled out a fresh bottle of brandy. Meeting Robert whilst sober had almost torn her to shreds.

There was no glass to hand so she swigged from the bottle. The burning liquid rippled down her throat and left her feeling warm inside. Her peace of mind gradually returned as she drank. That was more like it. The absence of a glass reminded her how little crystal she had left. She must stop smashing it up, and she must order some more immediately! She smiled. She had always enjoyed throwing glasses. It was crazy, but it proved she wasn't afraid of losing something dear to her to get something much, much better. Reckless. That was Maggie Dalton. Always had been, and always would be. She dialled through to her secretary at the office. Sean had allowed hers and Alex's and Thomas' to remain in place but they each had to report to him every evening. He was keeping tabs on everything they did. Well this would give him something to write down in his little notebook! *Maggie ordered more crystal glasses today.* She laughed as she put down the receiver, and took another swig from the bottle. *Screw you Sean Hamilton!* There would be no violence tonight though. She couldn't look a fool in front of Michael.

Little Child

She was due to meet Thomas in a minute to see if there was any news on the cottage and if he had managed to pick up any new leads. She had made up her mind about something. If she saw any reluctance from him today, she was taking matters into her own hands. She needed to move her plan along. He probably wouldn't be grateful for the information she'd extracted out of Robert. She was in for another lecture on her safety being paramount and keeping a low profile. These names were her last card. In giving them to Thomas she would be showing him she was truly determined to get what she wanted - and she *would* go to any lengths to do it. If she knew him like she thought she did, he would work harder because he would be too concerned for her not too. She took one last swig and pushed her chair back. Now she was ready to see him with her fresh ammunition. She replaced the bottle of brandy back in her drawer. Grabbing her bag she stuffed the names inside and dashed out locking the door as she went.

Her daughter was laying a new tablecloth on the dining room table when she came back downstairs.

"Any messages?" she asked gruffly.

"Mr Louis called," Emily replied, keeping her voice steady, "He said he might be a little late tonight."

"Oh!" Emily could tell her mother wanted to know more, "Did you talk long?"

"No...we didn't," she lied, sensing her anxiety.

"Good." Maggie was relieved, but didn't show it.

And with that she left, banging the door shut behind her.

*

Beth Cash was thinking about Emily. She hadn't seen her at school for a couple of days. This wasn't unusual. Emily was often absent for days on end, according to her records because of a long-term illness. There were no details in her file. Why was that? Beth couldn't help being suspicious, especially now that she knew, or at least had certain insights to judge the situation with. She knew her mother was a powerful force in the community. No public appearances or charitable works for a very long time, but continuing to ride on her father's good name. And mostly the Public were buying it...but there were hints she could be trouble...the odd story cropping up...always explained away quickly, but still, they were there... Her husband had dug around for her, made a few inquiries. Beth was paying more attention to the news, reading everything she could find on Maggie Dalton. She was trying to put the pieces together.

Right now she was obliged to make a phone call to Emily's parents. Neither of them had returned the parent's evening slip even though her mother had fervently expressed her desire to attend.

She didn't want to make the call. She had been staring at the phone for an hour or more in between marking assignments. She didn't want to intrude on this private affair, but deep down she knew she had to. She couldn't turn her back this time. There was too much at stake. Witnessing the emptiness in Emily's eyes had been unbearable. She imagined the pain in her heart was much, much worse. Killing her even. She was deeply afraid for Emily; afraid she might reach the fateful conclusion that she would be better off dead.

Yet rightly or wrongly something was holding Beth back. She had reservations she couldn't work through. Was she trying to protect her children? Was she trying to protect herself? She didn't know what the reason was, but it was there, plain as day. A knawing feeling in the pit of her stomach.

She picked up the receiver and dialled Emily's home number. She had to get this part over and done with. Maybe it would pave the way to figure out what to do next.

She hoped so. She really did.

*

"Any news for me?" Maggie settled herself comfortably on the chaise with a Scotch in her hand. She was determined to get some progress out of Thomas.

"On what? The situation with Sean – which you should be concerned about – or your runaway plans?"

Maggie gave him a look that spoke volumes and didn't answer. She watched him pace up and down in front of her, and sipped calmly from her glass.

"Actually there is, and don't look so surprised! I am trying my best to help you even though the thing with Sean should be taking precedent!" He was agitated, debating whether to tell her or not. It would only give her hope and fuel her enthusiasm beyond bounds, which he didn't want. In fact, he didn't even want her to have a secret hideaway and despite what he'd just said, he wasn't interested at all. He'd made a decision. Maggie was not going to runaway from the Sean problem. It was just as much her problem as it was Alex's and his. Why should she leave them to do all the dirty work? It was her responsibility to stay and fight as well – and Thomas was going to make damn sure she did.

"Well? Come on then, tell me! I don't want to be kept in suspense forever Tom." She was already getting excited and had moved to the edge of her seat giving him her full attention.

He took a deep breath. "We may be able to fix a meeting with our bank manager. Find out when the accounts were rifled and by whom, and see if there's a link."

Maggie shook her head in frustration. "No *maybes* Tom. It has to be done! This isn't moving fast enough. *You're* not moving fast enough."

Thomas was about ready to explode. She was pushing all of his buttons and he was rapidly losing his patience with her. What did he have to do to spell it out to her? Her father's company had been sabotaged and she didn't care! He couldn't comprehend it. He couldn't comprehend her.

"I want to know who's bought it and I want to start right here, with our Board!" She was adamant. She wasn't going to budge. Thomas could clearly see nothing else mattered to her. He was speechless with it all.

She finished her drink and reached into her bag. Looking thoughtful, she handed him the piece of paper listing potential names from outside the firm.

"Check these out as well will you."

He snatched it from her. Through clenched teeth he said, "I told you not to get involved. Don't you ever take any notice of me?"

"You're-not-working-fast-enough," she repeated angrily.

He didn't even make an effort to look at the paper in his hand but tossed it aside, equally upset, as his mobile began to ring. He picked it up to take the call.

"Hello. Thomas Anderson speaking." He looked over at her. She made a move to signal that she was leaving. He turned his back on her. It was an instant dismissal. She'd really tried him today.

"Hi Alex. No, Maggie was just here. She's been snooping around herself, which I don't like. Robert is probably helping her. She says I'm not moving fast enough. You want to meet up? When? For lunch? Sure, I can do that. Do you think we'll be followed? I suppose it won't matter. What? Confront Mags? Yes, good idea. We'll pile on the pressure. Ok, what time? Two? That should be fine. So you'll call her now? No, she left here before I answered your call. She won't suspect. She's got a bad case of single vision at the moment. Ok, you do that and I'll see you there. Ok...ok... bye." He put his phone in his pocket and smiled to himself. A two-pronged attack was always going to be better than one.

Maggie needed containing and it was time to get even.

Noticing the paper he'd thrown aside moments earlier, he picked it up and glanced at it out of curiosity. There were some familiar names but none that stood out as suspects. He stuffed it in his pocket, making a mental note to show it to Alex later on.

*

Her phone told her she had five missed calls. It was Alex's number. The fact he'd tried to call her several times usually meant whatever he needed to speak to her about was pretty urgent. He rarely called her direct, usually mediating through Thomas. She'd called him back and they'd arranged to meet for a late lunch at one of his favourite restaurants. He had made a specific point of asking her to put all calls on hold. He didn't want any interruptions. That meant no mobile left on, no meetings to rush off to, and no clients to go and see urgently. Whatever Alex wanted was definitely one of those 'drop everything you're doing' affairs, so she made her way to The Masquerade to find out exactly what all the commotion was about.

*

Little Child

Alex Coombes was thirty-one and used to being in the background. He didn't advocate all of his business advancements, but instead took the quieter approach and just got on with it. He was very good friends with Thomas and between them they tried to keep Maggie on the straight and narrow. Sure they liked their pleasures in life, but looking after Maggie and her father's company, which they'd invested so much, time, energy and money into, was always the number one priority.

Lately, Thomas had been worrying him. Going against the grain and acting out of character. He knew it was Maggie's doing. She was pushing him in ways they hadn't ever dealt with before. She wasn't capable of running the show - yet that's exactly what she *was* doing.

How had they got into this mess?

First Sean.

Now Maggie.

Both out of control, but in very different ways. Both calling the shots and creating huge waves within the Investment Company. It was a disaster. A sinking ship. Alex understood how Thomas must have been feeling. He was, after all, the closest to Maggie's father, Richard. Thomas had been his protégé.

They were anxious about Maggie's safety, even more so than thirteen years ago - because this was something else – and it hadn't happened yet. Alex shared Thomas' feelings that they were building up to something. Something big. Something that would change all of their lives forever. The Sean revelations were just the start of it. There was more to come, they were sure.

It would certainly be a tough meeting with her. No one told Maggie Dalton how to run her business affairs. Luckily, Alex was always ready for a challenge.

But then, so was Maggie.

He was sitting in the far corner, almost hidden from view, when she walked into the restaurant. A waiter was on her arm immediately directing her to the table. She knew Alex had tipped him to do this and it annoyed her. She was perfectly capable of finding the table. She didn't show her disapproval but sat down opposite him in the chair offered by the waiter. He gave them both a wine list and menu, and promptly left.

"Good to see you Maggie."

"Likewise."

"Would you like some wine?"

She nodded, then, coming straight to the point, "What did you want to discuss?"

He didn't answer but signalled for the waiter and ordered a bottle of red. When the waiter had disappeared again, Maggie repeated, "Well? What is it?"

He looked at her intently. "You Maggie. You and all your crazy, hair brain ideas."

She shook her head in bewilderment, not knowing what to say. This had come right out of the blue for her. What was so wrong with pursuing something you really wanted?

"I don't understand," she stammered.

They were interrupted as the waiter came back with the wine. To Maggie, he seemed deliberately to be polishing their glasses and pouring the wine slowly, when all she wanted to do was get some explanation from Alex for his outright comment. Finally the waiter finished and they ordered lunch. Her heart wasn't in it, but Alex appeared to be quite enjoying himself. And he was. He'd got her where he wanted her with no effort at all. It must be some sort of a miracle.

"I don't understand Alex." She was trying to get his attention, not even realising he'd ordered for three instead of just two. He finished talking to the waiter and turned to face her, aware she wasn't expecting anyone else to join them.

"Sorry about that. Had to make sure everything was in order." And then, as if on cue, Thomas walked through the door and locating them, he quickly came over.

"Ah, here he is!" Alex announced, watching with amusement as Maggie scrambled round to see whom he was talking about. She wasn't impressed when she realised she'd been set up, and stood up clutching her handbag, her surprise evident.

"What the...!" she began to say, but Alex already had a firm grip on her arm and Thomas, reaching her at the same time, forced her back down into her seat. He then took his seat on the side of her closest to the exit so she was sandwiched in and couldn't try and escape. He poured himself a glass of wine while Alex sat bemused watching Maggie as she looked from one to the other dumbly. She was trying desperately to think of her next move or how she could get out of the restaurant without the boys realising she was giving them the slip, but it was impossible.

"Now Maggie, we want some answers." Thomas spoke firmly. "We don't want to harm you in any way. We aren't here to blackmail you or do anything of that nature. We come in peace, as friends, who are very troubled over your recent behaviour."

Alex agreed, making no shame of the fact he was very grateful Thomas had turned up when he did. He had tipped Maggie off balance and Thomas' arrival had been perfectly timed.

"I've been set up," she murmured, more to herself than to them. Even though they hadn't specifically admitted the reason for both of them being here was because in a pair they could handle her better, she was aware of it already and consequently felt extremely helpless. The only ray of hope came from her ability to manipulate conversations to her advantage. Maybe if she denied all, they would let her go without too much quizzing.

"Ok...so what do you want boys? This is very clever," she waved in their direction, "this whole thing, setting me up...but I really don't have a clue what you're talking about."

"Don't play games Maggie," Thomas warned. He looked over at Alex and they exchanged glances. They had a deal they would force it out of her if they had to, but she wasn't leaving here until she admitted she *was* worried about her father's business. They couldn't believe she wasn't. This was going to be about patience and asking the right questions. Questions that would strike a chord with her deep inside that sensitive place she kept so well hidden from everyone, including herself. Thomas remembered the conversation he'd had with her the day after she was shot at. He'd managed to break her down then, and he *would* do it again.

"Why are you acting as if you don't care Maggie?"

"Don't care about what?"

"Your father's business."

A hush fell across the table. Maggie sipped nervously from her glass. Thomas and Alex didn't take their eyes off her.

It was a long while before anyone spoke again. Their starters came and went. Maggie hardly ate a thing whilst the men tucked in heartily. They had all the time in the world, but Maggie knew her time had just run out.

"I do care," she said quietly, once their plates had been cleared away.

This was music to their ears, but they didn't let on.

"So…why do you act as if you don't?" It was another probing question. Would she be able to cope? Thomas had long since known she was as fragile as a butterfly inside. He didn't force her there often, but she had been unbelievably selfish since they'd found out about Sean, and he felt a trip to visit her demons was in order. She would have to confront them sooner or later.

"Protection," she said simply. It was no use arguing with them. They had hold of something and they weren't going to let it go until she confessed all. She felt sick to her stomach. She badly needed more alcohol to make it through this. Being stripped bare terrified her.

"You have to face this Maggie. You have to take it seriously," Alex continued.

Hanging her head in shame, she said nothing. They were making her feel minute. They were making her feel like her mother used to. New mysterious emotions were rising within her. She tried to suppress them.

"You're a part of it whether you like it or not," Thomas reasoned.

Still she said nothing.

"From now on Maggie, full co-operation…ok?"

She nodded weakly.

"When do you see Michael Louis?"

Her head snapped up. "You know about that?"

"Yes."

"How?"

"Don't ask absurd questions. It's my business to know."

She sighed, "Tonight. We're having dinner tonight."

"Good. He's important to us. He knows the right sort of people for our next big deal. We get him on side, we get the backing and then we can tackle Sean head on. Make sure you pull out all the stops. He has to be impressed tonight."

"I know Tom!" Maggie was pulling back, reviving herself after that earlier episode. This was what she was good at. This was her metier. How dare Thomas tell her what she must do!

He held up his hands in defence. "Ok...ok...you know the score, but you know you haven't had your eye on the ball, so I thought a little prompting was necessary..."

She wanted to slap him.

"Piss off!" she hissed. This whole charade was beginning to wear thin. She was not going to go out like this, being talked down to and brow beaten. She was better than this. She was the boss!

She sat up straight, shoulders back, rising to her full height.

"The cottage is still important to me."

Thomas was ready for her comeback. "I know. You help me, I'll help you."

"So that's the way it's going to be?"

"From now on, yes."

"But if Robert helps me first..." She tailed off, waiting for him to bite the bait. It was all about manipulation.

The two men looked at each other. Alex took a sip from his glass while Thomas sat forwards in his chair.

"Now that's what we're worried about Maggie, your acquaintance with Robert. You know as well as we do how controlling he is. You've told me yourself that he forces you into bed just so you'll pay what you owe, even though you don't actually owe anything. You stay away from him. Dealing occasionally with people like Robert Hilton is one thing, but dancing with the devil is another!"

She was aghast at Thomas' revelations of her personal life in public. "Thomas!" she said, trying not to raise her voice and at the same time looking around wildly, "Just because you're jealous, doesn't mean you have to insult me!"

"And why would I be jealous?" he hissed back, painfully aware of the imaginary knife she'd just stuck in his back. He walked into that one all right and now he was going to have to walk right out again, unless of course she apologised, but what were the chances of that?

She didn't know why or how, but as soon as she'd said it, she regretted it. Instead of answering his question she decided to attempt the gentler approach. Maybe it would butter them up and she could slip away. If there wasn't any need for confrontation, why allow for it to creep in?

"I'm sorry Tom," she whispered, looking sheepish, "That was very rude of me."

He took her hand and squeezed it under the table, playing along.

"And I didn't mean to be so ignorant Maggie," he paused, knowing she wouldn't like the next part, "but that still doesn't let you off the hook!"

She pulled her hand away in disgust. No amount of flattery and remorse was going to break these two down. She thought about trying another tactic and was just about to speak when the waiter brought their main course to the table and being men, they tucked in again, seeming to ignore her for the time being.

"I'm really not hungry," she remarked, pushing her plate away and rising quickly. Thomas was on the ball though and sat her back down.

"None of that now Maggie, and you will eat your lunch." He arranged the plate in front of her and handed her a fork. She snatched it off of him and began to pick at the food, wondering if she would ever get out of the restaurant alive.

"Give it up Maggie. We aren't letting you go until you tell us what's going on with Robert," Alex said, as if reading her thoughts.

"He's bad news, and definitely not our kind of clientele," Thomas added.

"Our kind of clientele!" Maggie was outraged, "You mean the clientele who have deserted us?"

Thomas looked up sharply. "They haven't deserted us!"

Maggie folded her arms across her chest defensively. "So where are they then, all these faithful clients?" she demanded.

"I'm not doing this with you Maggie."

"And you're conveniently veering off the subject," Alex interjected.

She frowned at him. "I've told you everything, I swear. I'm only bribing Robert to help me and he doesn't know what for. He doesn't even know about Sean. Please boys, I do have a dinner to prepare - and a very important one at that."

"Nice try Maggie, but we know there's more to it than that. What are you buttering him up for? How can you be sure he isn't in league with Sean and the rest of them? What have we always said – keep your friends close, and your enemies closer."

"But that's exactly what I'm doing!" Maggie was getting exasperated with the pair of them.

"No you're not! You've only got one thing in mind and you're not considering the bigger picture. You're not watching your back."

"That's what you're both here for!"

"You've got to watch your own. You walk around, no Johnny, no driver…what do you think this is? A game?"

She rolled her eyes. *Here we go again, more lectures.*

"Listen. I really don't think Robert is involved with Sean. Robert will help me with the cottage, and there's nothing else on the agenda." She was fibbing a tiny bit. There was a plan forming in her mind for something else, but that's all it was at the moment – a half-baked idea. It required a lot more thought before she did anything cohesive with it.

"So you don't know anything other than what you've told us?" Thomas was persistent. He took a long drink from his glass.

"No, I swear. If I knew anything else I would tell you. I promise I would." They could see she was being sincere. As usual they should have guessed her purposes were wholly selfish. Nothing ever changed with Maggie. She was a spoilt child at heart through and through.

"Ok…case closed for the time being." He held up his hand, surrendering.

Maggie started to breathe easier. She was glad the interrogation was over.

Thomas looked over at Alex. They may have saved her before she went too far this time, but who was to know what was just around the corner.

Once they had finished eating and Maggie had excused herself and left, Thomas took out the now rather crumpled piece of paper and handed it to Alex.

"What do you think of these?"

Alex took the paper and stared at it, thinking hard. "What are these? Names that Maggie got hold of?"

"Yes. People who are currently floundering in the Public Eye who may be interested in purchasing a hide away."

"Oh…I really don't know why it has to be this property for Mags." He gave it back and Thomas slipped it into his inside jacket pocket.

"No, neither do I. I'll keep it just in case." Thomas poured some more wine for himself. "Do you have any plans for the weekend?"

Alex shook his head. "Just watching our back."

"Hmmmm," Thomas agreed, draining his glass.

"You seem to be drinking more these days Tom."

"That's what comes of trying to keep Maggie in hand for as long as I've had to. She can be hell sometimes. This Sean business doesn't help either. I swear I'm getting grey hairs."

They both laughed, as Thomas got up to leave.

"We'll meet up Monday."

"Ok."

Alex watched Thomas disappear through the door and sighing heavily, he too refilled his glass and promptly downed the contents.

"Would you like to order some more wine Sir?"

Alex looked up; unaware the waiter was at his side, pen and paper at the ready, poised for action. He focused on the empty bottle for a moment, and then replied, "No…no more red. Just a double brandy if you don't mind."

CHAPTER 13

The day had dragged. An endless round of washing, polishing and cleaning. I couldn't wait for my father to get home. He'd phoned to say he was running late. An important buyer had just turned up at the gallery and it was an opportunity he didn't want to miss. I understood. We desperately needed the money.

When he got back we would have to start preparing the meal for tonight before my mother arrived home. I didn't know what to make, she hadn't offered any guidance, and flicking through the cookbooks had proved a waste of time as nothing had caught my eye. Her cookbooks were all fancy stuff you'd probably never ever make for yourself, let alone actually eat. I wondered whether she was making the situation difficult on purpose. Not telling us what she wanted meant she could later fault, not only the meal, but the choice as well. For the millionth time I asked myself why she didn't bring in staff to prepare these dinner parties for her. Why did she always leave it to us? There was plenty of staff up at the estate to do all this for her – and they'd most probably make a much better job of it. If she was looking for appearances and elegance and perfection, she was looking in the wrong place. It wasn't *us*. It wasn't my father and me at all.

God, how was this evening going to turn out? My father would have to watch his wife humiliate herself over and over just so she could feel good about what she was doing.

One thing I had decided was to keep the dinner simple. There wouldn't be much eating. My father and I would want to be anywhere but in the same room, and she and Michael would be too busy flirting with each other to care.

Maybe my father would have some good news to cheer me up, even if it was just to say he'd started the legal stuff.

The cottage was there again in my mind. I'd lost sight of it for a while, or tried to block it out because it was too painful. I didn't know which. I knew now I had to keep my hope alive. I didn't want the prospect of freedom to distance itself again. Patience was all we needed, and a little luck.

I heard the door click. My father was home at last. I ran into the kitchen and straight into his arms. He gave me a big hug and then pulled away, taking off his coat.

"What's wrong?"

"Nothing Sweetheart. Just remembered what night it is, that's all." He smiled and came over to pick me up. "So you want to hear what happened to me today?" He carried me into the living room and we sat down on the sofa.

"Is it good news, bad news, or a bit of both?"

"The last one," he teased, drawing it out.

I rolled my eyes. "Ok, so what happened?" I pretended to sound really impatient, all the time watching the expression on his face for clues.

"No loan yet, hopefully next week, but I have started legal proceedings."

I nodded. "How did it go just now?"

"With that buyer?"

"Yes."

"He bought a couple of expensive pieces and is considering one more for his collection."

"So that's good right?"

"It certainly is. It all helps at the end of the day."

"So why aren't you more happy?"

"I am, Sweetheart!"

"Don't lie to me Daddy."

We looked at each other for a moment. He wanted to tell me something, but at the same time he didn't.

"Tell me," I murmured, moving closer to him.

"I know there are problems ahead Sweetheart. I can sense it with your mother."

"I know…I can sense it too."

"You can?"

"Sure…she's not being consistent. Sometimes drinking, sometimes not. Spending a week in her study and then spending no time at all at home. Little things like that."

"So living with you're mother's temperament is getting to you too?"

"She's edgy, more so than usual. Almost hyper in a weird kind of way."

My father agreed with me, "I know."

We both fell silent for a spell, cuddling each other.

"It's important to me that you understand I am trying my best to get us away from here. I won't fail you I promise. Do you believe me? You have to tell me how you really feel Emily… I hate seeing you suffer… Can you do that? Can you tell me?"

I wasn't used to all these questions from my father. I felt like our roles had been strangely reversed – me the carer, him the cared for. I was now supposed to be the one in control. I pulled away and stood up.

"Of course… I know what you're trying to do and I know you're trying hard to do it, but please don't question how I feel. We should have faith in each other not start doubting the other's capabilities." I needed to be honest with him. This was making me uncomfortable. I smiled at him, but behind the smile I was afraid. I wanted him to stay resolute to do the right thing and yet, seeing him imploring for my favour and my respect for his decisions was heartbreaking. We had to be strong for each other. It just wouldn't work if it was all one way. For the first time, I saw a weakness in my father, but I wasn't angry with him because of it. I think more than anything else it was a reminder that in our individual moments of hardship, even the ones we love most of all can't save us. It was a very sobering thought.

"You're an old head on young shoulders."

I came out of my private contemplating. "What?"

"I said you're very wise for your age."

I shrugged. I'd had to grow up fast with my mother around.

He got up and lifted me onto his shoulders. Changing the subject, he asked, "Hadn't we better start dinner? What are we cooking? Any ideas?"

I laughed as he took me into the kitchen. It always felt so good to laugh. It eased the tension and pressure I carried around with me. These were the moments I truly enjoyed; when my father and I could just be normal, doing ordinary things like everybody else I watched around me. The serious stuff had been forgotten for the time being and it was now the way it should be – fun, jokes, and my father attempting to be like one of the chefs on television.

"I am really stuck for ideas," I confessed, as he put me back down and began to flick through the cookbook I'd already scanned for inspiration.

"No luck in here?" he asked.

"We could do a prawn cocktail starter, lasagne for main, and there's gateaux in the freezer for dessert. That's simple enough."

My father shut the book and placed it back on the shelf, "Great idea!"

It was a tried and tested formula. We'd used it before a few times. I just hoped it was going to be ok for tonight. Mother hadn't said Michael was a vegetarian.

I tool the gateaux out of the freezer and placed in on a dessert stand. It could sit there and defrost and would hopefully reach room temperature by the time we came to eat it. I wanted to tuck in now. It looked so delicious.

"Now where are the pasta sheets and have we got a Bolognaise sauce? I know there's mince in the fridge. Do we have parmigiano reggiano?" My father was already enthusiastically getting to work on the main course, so I started the prawn cocktails.

Once the lasagne was in the oven, he searched in the rack for another red wine to compliment dinner, as he'd used up the opened one for the sauce *and* helped himself to a glass. There were numerous varieties but he finally made a selection. He also opened a bottle of white. Whilst I put the finishing touches to the prawn cocktails and placed them in the fridge, my father proceeded to set the table, organise subtle lighting and prepare some flowers as the centrepiece to the arrangement. I surveyed his work and nodded my approval. Then I re-joined him in the dining room to give it one last going over. I polished the cutlery and re-laid it and he dusted and hovered starting first in the dining room where we would be spending most of our time, and then branching out into the living room where drinks would be served afterwards while my father and I washed up. Business discussions would soon move to my mother's study and then and only then, would we be able to breathe a sign of relief. I stopped the thoughts there, not allowing my mind to wander any further. There were more important things to worry about, like what were we going to wear. That was a point – what *were* we going to wear? It hadn't even crossed my mind…until now…

I didn't have to worry for long as this time it was my mother's turn to walk in and inspect our hard work. Neither of us heard the door click announcing her arrival, so we were completely caught unawares.

We waited silently as she surveyed the room in her usual imposing manner. Would she pick on something and fault it? I didn't dare take my eyes off of her to catch my father's expression.

Finally, she shook her head, "More light James. The rest will do."

It could have been much worse.

She turned to face us and I flinched. My father was immediately at my side. She seemed amused by our sudden protective reactions.

"I was only going to ask what was for dinner?"

"Lasagne."

"And the Starter?"

"Prawn Cocktail."

"Show me."

He led the way into the kitchen. I followed them. We stood there like two naughty school children as she again inspected our efforts. Her presence was overpowering. I felt so intimidated. How could she be my mother when I felt like this whenever she was close to me?

"Hmmm, not bad," she remarked.

Next came the choice of wines. She was pleased.

"Let's hope your dress sense is as good as your selection of wine," she said to him. That was the closest we would get to a compliment tonight.

She walked back into the living room and poured herself a small Scotch. We watched as she downed it all in one go. My father hurried to fix the lighting.

"Is that better?" he asked her.

"Yes. Now go and get dressed."

He motioned for me to follow, but she lunged at us and knocked him off balance so that he slumped in the doorway. I backed towards him to help him up, but she was much too quick and dragged me by the hair to her side.

"Get up!" she ordered. My father obeyed and got to his feet, "I'll be dressing Emily tonight. Never assume anything with me. You know that." She smirked. He nodded and began up the stairs. If this was supposed to be a lesson in leadership skills, I didn't want it.

She released me and shoved me into the nearest chair. I had to watch her drink two more shots before she pulled me upstairs to get ready for tonight. I didn't know what she had in mind, but one thing was certain, I wouldn't come out of this looking my best.

We heard my father fumbling about in his bedroom as Mother opened the door to hers and pushed me roughly into the room. She ordered me to sit quietly on the bed and wait. Walking over to the huge walk in wardrobe that was her pride and joy, she started to casually look through her collection of dresses. They were beautiful. There were vintage, contemporary and chic styles to suit any occasion. And this was only a small selection. A lot of her stuff was still up at the estate gathering dust.

I wondered what she was doing. We were both the same size but she was taller than me. Most of her dresses would be way too long. After what seemed like ages, she pulled out one of them and admired it for a moment before turning around to face me.

"Put this on," she said gruffly. I took the dress from her whilst she went over to her dressing table and began rummaging around in the top drawer, pulling out some of her make up.

I held the red garment up to me in front of her full-length mirror and it looked about the right length. She must have hired it or borrowed it for tonight. Either way, it was actually very flattering. It cut quite low at the bust and had an asymmetric hemline. I liked it. I really did like it. I changed out of my jeans and cashmere jumper and slipped it over my head letting it fall across my body. It was gorgeous. I was already falling in love with the flower detail running down one side.

She turned around just as I finished and came towards me surveying the dress with critical eyes.

"You better not spill anything on this tonight," she said, her eyes still roving, her tone quiet, "I borrowed it from a client whose daughter is more worthy of such clothes."

I felt the tears well up in my eyes as her words crushed the joy I'd just been feeling. For that one single moment, I'd stupidly thought she'd wanted me to look beautiful so she could be proud of me. I felt an idiot. I could hope and pray and wish that she would love me, but that's all it ever was – a hope, a prayer or a wish.

She turned me around and started searching for visible bruises. This was a usual practice. One I hated. She grabbed me by the arm, pinching the skin as I was forced onto the stool facing her dressing table mirror. I winced with the pain and almost knocked over a bottle of foundation. I thought she hadn't noticed, but the sharp sting across my face told me in no uncertain terms she had.

"You clumsy girl!" she cried, slapping me again, "Just sit there and don't move or you'll get another one of these." This time the third slap was much harder and made my eyes water, but I didn't dare raise my hand to wipe them.

She tipped the foundation onto some cotton wool and began her cover up process on my arms and neck.

"Now for your make up," she announced, and started to apply the foundation to my face. Once she was through, she sat on the edge of the bed and poured herself a drink. She held the glass up to me.

"Cheers," she said absently, and then downed it and poured another.

I watched her, speechless. A hundred different emotions flooding through me. I allowed myself to feel each of them. Anger was first. Anger was always first. I wanted to rip the bottle from her hand and smash up the glass into tiny pieces and then stick those pieces into her. But I was rooted to my chair and my legs didn't want to work. This was my mother and I knew her behaviour like the back of my hand, but sometimes she bordered on eccentric. What was she doing now? Should I carry on making up my face alone, or was she going to do it herself? I couldn't ask her. Asking a question, or even speaking in the subdued silence was daunting. She tied my tongue every time – and she didn't even know it. Or maybe she did. Had she forgotten I was there? Was all the booze soaking away her brain? I sat very still in the gathering shadows. Soon we would be in total darkness. Should I turn on the lights? She poured herself a third shot and took some pills with it. I didn't even want to know what they were. Would they calm her, or would they do the opposite?

She snapped into life and flipped on the lights. Drawing the curtains she still seemed to be in her own little world. She stood stroking the curtains, murmuring to herself. I couldn't hear what she was saying.

I glanced up at the clock. Time was rushing by. Soon Michael would be here. I hesitated before saying quietly, "Mother?"

She span round. "What?" She stared at me with glassy eyes as if I was intruding on her personal space.

I thought she might hit me so I looked up at the clock again and back to her, hoping she'd get the hint. I didn't speak.

"Face the mirror," she ordered, coming across the room.

Usually she would try her best to apply the make up professionally even though on most occasions her hand was shaking violently, but this evening there was a gleam in her eye. It was something new. Something wicked. It was ominous. It made me feel terrified. I knew she was going to do something awful and I couldn't stop her. I watched in horror as she applied more foundation. Had she forgotten she'd already put some on, or was this being done purposely? And I nearly screamed out loud when I caught sight of the bright red lipstick lying harmlessly on the bed. I scrunched up my eyes so I wouldn't have to see the foundation streaking down my cheeks as she carelessly rubbed it in, but a sudden pull on my hair warned me to open them.

"Keep watching," she whispered in my ear, looking back at me in the mirror threateningly, "because you're going to look real pretty once I'm done."

A chill went down my spine. So this was it. Making me watch her apply the clown like mask. Destroying my true beauty. It was a double humiliation…a double punishment…and she was enjoying every second of it. This was the catch; the dress would be perfect, my hair would be perfect, but my face would be hidden under the mess she'd purposely created.

"This is the base to my ugly conception," she taunted, holding up the bottle of foundation triumphantly.

Had she forgotten what evening it was? Had she forgotten Michael was coming to dinner? One of her most important clients! How was this going to help her achieve what she was so desperately wanted to achieve? How was making me look like *this* going to help anybody?

What was the point Mother? What was the point?

I clenched my fists into tight balls. I wanted to punch her away, but beneath the surge in anger, I was scared. Always scared. I tried not to focus on my ruined face as she flicked the lid off the lipstick and smeared it across my lips, holding my chin still and forcing my mouth to open slightly. I didn't fight. What was the use? She was far stronger, far quicker even in her erratic drunken state, and would most probably beat me if I chanced anything.

I would sort it out once she'd finished. Yes. I would sort it out. There would be time. *Just sit still and be patient. There will be time once she's done.*

I was shaking all over. The eye shadow was next. A dark pink colour that completely clashed with my lipstick and my dress. I screwed up my eyes; grateful I didn't have to watch this part. My face was an utter mess and I dreaded opening them again.

They remained shut as she applied the mascara. I could feel the heavy blobs burdening my lashes, and once or twice she must have gone overboard because she viciously rubbed the excess that had splashed onto my cheekbones.

Finally the blusher. I was going to look like an embarrassed panda. She just slapped it on and left it. There was no toning process.

I couldn't believe what I saw even though I knew it was coming. I looked absolutely awful and desperately wished the ground would open up and swallow me.

"Like it sweet child?" she asked, hovering over me and taking in my shocked reaction with glee. I said nothing, watching the gleam in her eye grow as she picked up her comb and started to brush my hair, tugging roughly at the knots and nearly pulling me off balance. She decided to lecture as she worked, while I tried to focus on anything but being in this room. It was impossible though. The stark face that stared back at me, covered in the most terrifying array of make up, was a chilling reminder of the living hell I was being dragged through seemingly for her pleasure and enjoyment.

"There is a saying children should be seen and not heard. You will be living by that principle tonight."

She continued to comb.

"You must be perfect in every way; polite, well spoken, courteous. I don't think I need to tell you what the punishment will be if I find you not measuring up to these standards."

I hadn't been listening, but a sharp jerk of my head as she fussed with my hair brought me back to attention.

I focused on the twist she was tightening to pin up neatly on the top of my head, but my hair was so thin, strands kept falling loose. I could see her getting agitated. Boy, I couldn't keep up with her moods tonight.

She carried on with her instructions.

"You will not speak a word unless you are spoken to and even then your replies must be brief, or you will make me very angry. I've told Mr Louis a few untruths regarding our relationship and you will play along with this fake scenario. If you don't, there will be trouble afterwards. You've been warned."

Like I didn't already know...

There was another yank on my hair as she added the finishing touches. She clipped back the loose pieces and then dismissed me. Reaching for the bottle of Scotch, she poured herself yet another shot, but this time she only sipped at it. Maybe all the excitement of tonight was catching up with her. I waited, unsure what to do. Was I supposed to leave the room now? She perched on the edge of the bed and lit a cigarette.

"You need to tidy up your face."

I rose from the stool and walked passed her towards the door.

"Michael thinks I love you." The words were spoken callously. She inhaled deeply.

I kept walking and said nothing.

She started to laugh. "You look awful child! Absolutely bloody awful!"

I turned quickly to face her and met her stare. She took another puff. My heart started to pound. Those icy, steel eyes were no match for me. They pierced my soul and ripped at my heart. But I was angry, so very angry. I took a step towards her.

"Michael thinks you're good at school." Now she was getting hysterical. Her hollow laugh echoed around the room, making me dizzy. I had to get out of here before either she, or I, lost it completely.

"He thinks my world revolves around you." She was almost choking on her own frenzy, the cigarette burned dangerously low, but all I could do was stand there and watch in horror. A conflict was raging inside of me. I didn't want to help her. I wanted to hurt her bad. I wanted to shut her up for good.

"He thinks all these crazy things I just made up to impress him!" She finished her shot of whisky and threw the glass to the floor. It didn't smash but bounced on the thick plush carpet. I backed towards the door again watching her stub the cigarette out.

Then she hauled herself up and came towards me. I waited, head bowed, praying she wouldn't strike me. When she spoke, her voice was composed, back to its normal insensitive manner. She was scaring me with her random, quick fire mood swings. I could sense she was like a time bomb, but she was playing with it. Delaying the explosion. Tampering with the connections inside her head. Why was she doing this to herself? Why was she doing it to *me*?

"Leave the room. I have to get ready." That was my cue and I couldn't get out of there quick enough. Her display had been frightening.

Once I was on the other side of the door, I leant against it allowing myself some time to calm down. A huge sigh of relief escaped my lips. I was grateful I didn't have to watch her preen herself to perfection and drink herself to destruction.

I wondered how my father was getting on and went downstairs to find him. Maybe he could help take some of this awful makeup off.

I found him in the kitchen checking on the lasagne. He took one look at me and dropped everything.

"You look stunning Sweetheart!" he exclaimed.

I felt my cheeks start to burn with embarrassment, but there was no way he was going to see that under all this makeup.

"Really?"

"Well, apart from what she's done to your face, yes you do." He came over and hugged me. "What has she done to your face?"

I shook my head. "She's racing through the mood swings tonight. I know this is going to be difficult. *She's* going to be difficult." I didn't tell him about the phone call with Michael Louis earlier, or the cruel confessions she'd just come out with. He was used to her extreme behaviour as much as I was. I didn't want him to worry.

"So how do you think I look?"

I laughed. He was so down to earth and calm in the most precarious of situations, and that gave me a warm glow inside. Something to hold on to, to get me through this nightmare.

I examined him for some time, using the same scrutiny we were so accustomed to with my mother.

It was his turn to laugh. "I feel like it's one of *her* inspections!"

"Never mind that. You look fine. The tux is great! Now, can you give me a hand?"

He looked at me questioningly, "With what?"

"My makeup of course!" I replied, going over to the sink, "I have to take all of this off and start over."

"Ok…" He took a cloth and started to wipe off the mascara blobs that had hardened on my cheeks. Damn mascara! I could never get it off myself. I ran upstairs and scrubbed my face. Then I set about re-doing it all. My toned down version looked much better than the clown face. Taking one last look and satisfied with the improvement, I ran back downstairs into the kitchen to get my father's approval.

"What do you think now?" I asked.

"Perfect. Subtle. Much, much better." He smiled, and I laughed.

Suddenly the doorbell chimed through the hall and she came floating down the stairs. I was dying to see what she looked like, but he held me back and we waited patiently in the living room for their appearance.

We heard greetings and kisses being exchanged, and then they walked into the room.

*

The dinner was going well. We were finishing the pasta and dessert was looming. Only one more course, a little bit more conversation, and then my father and I could escape. Actually, my first impressions of Michael Louis had been pretty spot on. He seemed to be quite a nice man. He didn't drape himself all over my mother and he hadn't smelt of whisky when he greeted me and kissed me on both cheeks, saying how pleased he was to finally meet me after everything he'd heard. Mother had given me one of those piercing glares: *shut up or die*, so I'd just smiled and nodded, trying to show and hide my appreciation all at the same time.

She was watching her drinking tonight making one glass of wine last the entire meal and refusing a top up from Michael. She was attempting to flirt with him, sometimes embarrassingly so, although if he knew, he never let on, preferring to keep the conversation flowing rushing through topics at break neck speed. He was early thirties, blonde hair, blue eyes... I could see how my mother could fancy him. Not that she deserved him mind. He was absolutely charming and adorable and no sleaziness in sight. It made a refreshing change.

Well travelled, he'd finally decided to put his experiences down on paper and cracked into the freelance travel writing market. I was impressed, but why Mother had business with him was a mystery. I sincerely hoped she wasn't out to corrupt him. He was so much better than her and all the others I'd had to meet over the years. He had principles and self respect for a start. How I wished I were meeting him under nicer circumstances. I could sit and listen to his stories for days. Momentarily he was lifting me out of the horrible existence I was part of, reconfirming that there was a bigger world out there and I should hang in, keep going, and one day soon I might get the chance to see and do the things he was describing to me. My father could tell I was enthralled. He kept looking over and smiling, visibly appreciative this man had something to offer me rather than the usual sleaze my mother introduced us to.

Noticing everyone was almost finished; he got up and started to clear away the plates. It was then that Michael turned to me suddenly.

"Emily I've just remembered you were going to show me some of your writing. How about it? I'd love to see your work. Now don't go all shy on me...you did promise!"

He was teasing me, but my mother was displeased, no longer the centre of attention, and I could see my father was equally surprised as he sat back down in his chair.

"What's this?" she said sharply, "Emily, you never mentioned it." She tried not to look bothered, but I was able to read her like a book. I said nothing, annoyed with myself for not remembering our telephone conversation earlier and trying to pre-empt this somehow.

"I...I..." Stammering, I wasn't really sure what to say.

Michael came to my rescue. "Well I know English is Emily's favourite subject because she told me so, and then she promised to show me some of her writing." He winked at me, oblivious to the atmosphere building around the table.

I returned his smile, but didn't dare say a word.

"Michael, we have dessert and I really need you to look over those papers for me afterwards. Emily can show you her writing anytime." Mother was getting agitated, although she was trying her best to hide it behind a smile fixed across her face. I watched her fiddle with her napkin, scrunching it up and then smoothing it out. Scrunch. Smooth. Scrunch. Smooth.

Michael waved away her concerns.

"Come on Mags, lighten up! You know I'm not one for missing an opportunity to experience someone else's perceptions. Remember what I was telling you about Wuthering Heights?"

She didn't answer. She was probably trying to recall what he had told her. She didn't even read books. This was a classic example of another one of her *get acquainted with what the client likes and pretend I'm an expert too* scenarios.

My father cut in, putting himself on the line.

"Off you go then Em. Better not keep Mr Louis waiting!"

Mother snapped back to life as I rose from the table, once again resuming her pretence of devoted mother and wife.

"Yes...yes...of course you must show Michael, Emily. He is our guest after all." She gave me a fleeting glance, and turned her attention back to Michael. "I guess the papers can wait." She smiled, patting his arm and lifting her glass for another sip of wine.

"I'll serve up the dessert then," my father said rising. The relief was evident on his face.

I left the room and ran up stairs two at a time. That had been close. Too close. I ran to my bedroom and flung open the door, diving into my bottom drawer to see what I could find. Something innocent that wouldn't upset my mother, although she was already mad at me for taking Michael's focus away from her. God, what was I going to show him? He couldn't see my latest poem. I stood up straight, thinking frantically. *My latest poem! Where was it?* I couldn't remember what I'd done with it. Had I left it on the bed? Had she come in and seen it? Panic hit me. But if she had it now I'd surely be dead. Ok, so maybe it was still in this room, somewhere. I tossed it to the back of my mind. I was getting distracted. I could look for it later. I definitely couldn't worry about it now. Finding something to entertain Michael with was far more important and I mustn't keep them waiting. I quickly sifted through my various poems and picked one about the colour yellow and one I'd written on my favourite female singer Alanis Morrisette, and desperately hoped they'd be sufficient...

As it turned out, Michael enjoyed them both and we ended up having a long discussion about Alanis over dessert.

"Too much scary feminist passion in that woman! You don't seem the type Emily," he joked.

Mother had tried to join in as best she could, but had no idea who we were talking about and this increased her frustration. She broke her resolve and drank the rest of the bottle during that short time. I gave my father a quick glance, warning him, and he wound up the conversation. Then we both excused ourselves to wash up, leaving Mother to her precious Michael. Whatever those papers were, she seemed pretty keen to get him to look through them. I tried to question my father, but he told me to leave well alone.

"Look Sweetheart...it's probably best if you turn a blind eye and don't get involved. I know you like Michael, he seems a decent chap, but once she gets hold of him, that'll be it. You can't save him."

I didn't quite know what he meant by that last comment. I wasn't trying to save anyone. Or maybe I was. Maybe I did want to protect him. I knew more about her than he did and I didn't want her to get her claws into him and corrupt him.

But my father was right. Michael was a grown man, able to handle himself. And it was none of my business.

He finished what he was doing and turned to face me as I put away the last glass in the cabinet.

"One day Sweetheart you'll find a man just like Michael and he'll sweep you off your feet and make all your dreams come true."

I smiled, secretly blushing under my makeup.

"And you know what? You would've deserved it. You would've deserved every second of it. And you know something else?" he paused, resting his hands on my shoulders and squeezing them gently, looking me straight in the eye, "When this happens your mother won't be able to do anything to stop it from happening. She won't be able to interfere. She won't be able to take it away from you. Because you'll be free Sweetheart, completely free to enjoy what life has to offer you. I really believe that…I really do…"
I blushed again, hoping beyond hope he was right.

CHAPTER 14

It was Monday morning and Thomas was blasting Maggie over the phone. Dinner with Michael Louis had gone well. The investment deal was wrapped up. But they'd quickly discovered it wasn't enough to get them out of trouble, even with his links to the Media. Michael was helping them keep the Press on side at a very favourable rate, yet Thomas knew it was only a matter of time.

Someone would slip up.

They always did.

"Nothing in the morning papers today, but how long can this go on? Sean is hassling me, threatening to go public. When will you realise how serious this is and start taking responsibility for your actions? And even if you can't do that, at least have a decent Plan B so we aren't left hanging our dirty laundry out to dry. Your stupid cottage idea! I can see what it's all about now – so you can put this behind you and disappear. Well it won't work Maggie. It won't! They'll hunt you down, they'll find you and then God knows what they'll do to you. Sean wants you under his thumb. You're the face of your father's company. Without you, the business is nothing! I'm coming to see you at 11, no excuses…"

Seething, he slammed down the phone. Maggie could sense his rage was reaching boiling point. She didn't want him to come to the house, but she realised she had little choice. At least Emily had gone to school. For once, that was a blessing in disguise.

Maybe he'll calm down once he knows there is a Plan B, she thought hopefully, sipping her coffee and desperately trying to unscramble her thoughts into something cohesive with which she could face Thomas. She closed the broadsheet and sighed heavily. He was right, they had played nearly all their cards - but he was wrong about the cottage. She had wanted it even before all this business kicked off with Sean. How dare he imply such things! She promised herself she'd fight him on that one.

*

217

It felt like his last chance to reach out to Maggie and make her aware of how serious a situation they were in. He was going to tell her about her mother and how he owed Sean. He didn't know how she would react. He didn't expect any sympathy for the anguish he had carried around inside of him for too long now. Maggie was selfish through and through, only ever looking after number one. How different she was to her father. Thomas had tried his hardest to prove to himself, and to those around him, that Maggie was as good as her father, if not better – and he had succeeded. But, as for being as great as her father in character and spirit, she would never be that. Her temperament was all her mother's. She wasn't kind, generous or loyal. She hadn't become a charity heroine in the local community. She hadn't triumphed in that way. In the beginning, she'd honoured her promise to the Media and given them everything they wanted. But she'd retreated too fast soon after her marriage and pregnancy, a time when the Paparazzi were especially eager to report events to the Public. They didn't even know her daughter at all. And Thomas felt they'd been denied that right. Maggie had never understood how high profile she was and how that brought about certain responsibilities. She should have shared her child with the people. She owed them after all the support and encouragement they'd given her father over the years. He had given himself to them, investing and improving the small businesses and communities around him. Helping people. Being one of them. People respected Maggie, but they didn't like her. Not like the way they had loved her father. She wasn't one of them. She simply refused to give up any of her time for them.

*

They were arguing again. They could both see this was how it was going to be from now on. Clashing and fighting; each trying to subdue the other, and attempting to beat one another into submission.

"I knew it was a bad idea to get involved with one of your stupid schemes. I'm always left to clear up the trail of crap you leave behind!"

She grabbed his arm, a sudden surge of rage building up inside of her.

"This isn't my fault Thomas!"

"You made everything worse!"

"I can't help who I am!"

"What are you talking about?"

"I can't help being who I am."

Thomas was indignant. He came over and seized her by the shoulders.

"You don't help yourself though do you? And you don't help us, Alex and me?"

"I only asked you to assist me, not to give me all the hassle under the sun!"

"Your priorities are all wrong Maggie! You can't look after yourself and you know it, so stop goddamn pretending. I only got involved in the first place because of my promise to your father and because of what happened when you turned twenty-one. Don't you understand?"

She shook herself free from his grasp. "You have played that line with me so much over the last few weeks that I'm sick of it. Do you hear me? I'm sick of it! Richard Dalton's daughter...people out to get me...blah blah blah... I've heard it all before and I'm telling you I can't help what I am!"

"You never take responsibility for who you are. That's the problem!"

She couldn't answer him so turned away, frustrated and angry.

Thomas knew he'd struck a chord and decided to capitalise on it.

"It's time to stop playing games Maggie," he said quietly.

She swung round, her face contorted.

"Stop playing games?" she hissed, "You're the one playing games! Your evasiveness...your defensive attitude whenever we talk about what's going on...your hesitation...your unwillingness... This isn't the Thomas I know and begrudgingly admire, the Thomas I learnt everything from when I was younger. Are you really sure you don't know more than you're letting on? I tell you what I think shall I? I think you're hiding something from me, and I'll tell you something else. If you don't come clean with me, you can forget that I ever knew you and you can start looking for a new place to live right now!"

How did she do it? How did she know he was keeping something back? And how did she manage to flatter him - and then crush him - all in one go?

He looked over and met her cold eyes, not knowing what to say to counter her uncanny acuity. He thought about how evil she could be sometimes and whether a friendship under false pretences and on her terms was really worth it. He tried to calm himself before answering, but couldn't. She had unnerved him. Suddenly he felt a need to hurt her, to bring her back to the more pressing matters confronting them.

"There you go again, avoiding the real issues! Me evasive? Take a long, hard look at yourself Maggie. You're the one being defensive and unwilling, not me!"

She began to answer, but his phone started to ring. He picked it up from Maggie's desk, in a way grateful it had interrupted their argument. Maybe it would dispel some of the hostility and tension mounting in the room.

He pointed an accusing finger at her. "Don't you dare move. We'll carry this on in a minute. I haven't finished with you yet."

He got up and walked to her window as she began to protest. How dare he speak to her as if she were a child! He held up his hand to silence her and she sat down heavily in her chair, rejected and fuming.

"Hello? Thomas speaking."

Even if it was a private call, she knew he wouldn't leave the room. He didn't trust her to stay put, so she just waited to see who it was.

"Hi Alex. No, I'm with Maggie at her house. More news? Sean's called? He couldn't get hold of me? What did he want? Oh...well...he can wait. Yes...I'm about to tell her. Are you coming? Ok...ok...see you in ten."

He threw his mobile back onto the desk, but didn't move from the window.

Maggie let the silence settle in the room before asking quietly, "Why is Alex coming here?"

He said nothing.

"Why Thomas? What's going on?"

Still he said nothing.

She sighed loudly. "I have to go out shortly."

"You'll stay put until you've heard what I have to say." He didn't turn around, but continued to stare into the garden.

She tilted her head to one side. "So you were hiding something from me?"

It took him a while to answer. "Yes...I was..."

"Well, I want to know!" she demanded, "I want to know now! Don't hide it from me any longer; just give it to me straight. I want to know what the hell is going on...all of it...everything!"

He turned to look at her, his heart heavy. There were no other options now. She had to know the whole truth.

*

Alex had joined them in Maggie's study. Thomas was pacing up and down. Maggie was sat at her desk waiting for one of them to speak. Alex had taken one of the guest armchairs.

"Well?" Maggie demanded for the umpteenth time, "Are you going to tell me or not?"

Thomas had stalled until Alex arrived, but Alex knew he was still stalling. He didn't want to tell Maggie and Alex understood why. Maggie was unpredictable. How would she take the news? There was also the concern that she would see weakness in her protectors and act out, leaving them both high and dry, or making the situation much worse.

"I owe Sean." Thomas continued to pace the room.

"Don't be stupid Tom. How?"

"I owe Sean," he repeated, "that's why I haven't been able to fight him like I wanted to fight him when this all kicked off. He has me dancing in the palm of his hand Maggie."

"No," she said, laughing nervously and looking over at Alex for confirmation. He nodded silently back at her. "I don't understand Tom. What do you mean? How can you owe him? Is he working for someone you know? Is he working for my mother?" She gasped. That terrifying thought had only just dawned on her.

"He killed your mother..."

Maggie's jaw dropped open. Their eyes locked across the room.

"And I sent him to do it thirteen years ago..."

Maggie shook her head in disbelief. So her mother was dead? All of these years she had been left wondering. Was she?

Wasn't she? She didn't know how or what she was supposed to feel. Anger because Thomas had lied to her? Relief because she was free from her mother's evil?

Thomas pulled out a cigar and lit it. His hands shook and it took him several attempts. He took long draws and moved back to the window. Smoke swirled around him.

Alex rose from his chair and poured each of them a large brandy.

"Here," he said, handing out the glasses, "I think we could all use one of these."

He sat back down. Everyone sipped gratefully at their drinks, lost in their own thoughts.

Finally, Maggie spoke. "Tell me everything Tom. I need to know everything."

"Is it necessary? What's done is done, Maggie."

Alex cut in before Maggie could start arguing. "Tom, she has a right to know."

Thomas span around. "Don't you think I feel bad enough about all of this without going over all the tiny, dirty details again and again and again? How many years has this haunted my every waking hour? You! You of all people should understand how I feel Alex!"

Alex remained calm. He always did. "She still has a right to know."

Thomas turned away puffing loudly on his cigar. He knew Alex was right. He knew he owed it to Maggie to explain why he did what he did back then.

"We thought it might have been your mother who hired someone to shoot you at your father's charity ball. It was the obvious choice."

"So to stop her from doing it again…" Maggie tailed off.

"Yes."

"But why Sean, Tom? He's always been a loose cannon! I don't know what my father ever saw in him."

"We knew he was the only one close enough to us who would do it and keep his mouth shut. He had it good on the Board, coming from nowhere and getting to be a Director soon after. He wouldn't throw all of that away. Sean was never stupid."

"But how did you know he could shoot?"

"Because of his credentials."

"What credentials?" Maggie began to ask, then it dawned on her, "Oh yes...coming from the police force."

"That's another reason why we never got heavy with Sean over this business. We didn't fancy being shot, or having you shot at."

Maggie had to ask the obvious question, "But...what if it wasn't my mother?"

"Well, no-one has ever tried again, have they?"

Silence engulfed the room. Thomas and Alex were both grateful Maggie was being rational about their decision. They finished their drinks in peace and Thomas stubbed out his cigar, but little did they know that Maggie's mind was still racing. Her Plan B had seemed the only way out, and now it really *was* the only way out. Suddenly as plain as day it was obvious to her what they must do to end all of this once and for all. And how could either of them object after their latest revelation!

She spoke softly as she looked from Thomas to Alex and back again, "As I see it, there's only one thing left to do."

"And what's that?" Thomas was only half listening. More relieved than anything that he'd finally told Maggie the truth, nothing else seemed to matter for the moment.

"We hire a hit to take out Sean."

*

Thomas had let Maggie talk him into the never-ending whirlpool of deceit and corruption - and now *murder* - and he was sorely regretting it. It should never have played out like this. They should've stayed calm. Waited it out like Alex had first suggested. No rash decisions or actions. Now what were they left with? Nothing, but the worst of the worst. Sean had stripped them bare and forced them into the deepest, darkest corners. Thomas was agreeing to some random plan more crazy than the first. Why was Maggie doing this to him? Why was she pushing him down these extreme paths? And why was he letting her? He should have been working hard to salvage any scraps left lying at their feet, but instead he felt more and more compelled to go along with her idea. Taking Sean out was the only solution. The last thing he wanted was fresh blood on his hands, but like Maggie, he was beginning to believe there was no other way.

*

"So...will you arrange it?" Maggie had gone straight from her meeting with Thomas and Alex to see Robert. Best to get it over and done with, she'd told them. No stalling. And certainly no time allowed to change their minds. Robert was the one person she believed would do this for her. Not connected to her father's business in any way, he posed no threat if the pay off was high enough. Theoretically they would be eating into their reserve capital that Sean didn't yet know about, but it would be worth it to get rid of him for good.

"In my mind this is a priceless act, but for you Maggie, I'll do it for this." He punched some numbers into the calculator on his desk and held it up for her to see. She looked at the seven-figures and smiled.

"That won't be a problem."

"Half now, half once the job is completed."

She nodded.

"Oh...and this is my reward." He held up the calculator again.

She frowned, looking at a fresh, higher seven-figure number.

"What do you mean?"

"I hire someone to do it and I pay them well to keep their mouth shut, but I also want to be paid to keep my mouth shut. I don't work for nothing, after all."

Realisation dawned on her. Two pay outs for one hit. She hadn't even considered it.

The boys were going to have a fit. "I'll have to consult my other..."

"Maggie!" he interrupted her, "Don't mess around with me! Either you want this, or you don't."

She hesitated, knowing she could lose his interest as quickly as she'd gained it. Money was always his incentive. *Promise the earth,* she reminded herself, *it's not like he's ever going to see a penny of it anyway.*

"Ok," she said slowly, looking straight at him, "You have a deal."

He smiled. "All of this up front."

She didn't bite, but held his stare with her own. *Bluff Maggie, bluff.* Swallowing hard, she replied, "Ok."

His grin grew wider. He came over and they shook hands.

"When will it be done?" she asked.

"I'll call you. Just make sure I have the first payments by end of play tomorrow, or…" He crouched down in front of her so his face was level with hers. Gripping her shoulder with one hand and holding her chin with the other, he finished, "Or I'll get very unpleasant."

Maggie remained very still. On the outside she was as hard as nails, but inside her heart fluttered uncontrollably. It took everything she had not to tremble. She knew she was gambling with her life.

"No tricks Maggie…not this time…" He stroked the back of his finger down her cheek.

So this was it. There was no turning back now.

The deed was as good as done.

*

Robert dialled the number carefully. This was an important call. It would cost him a lot if he made any mistakes. He wanted everything to run smoothly from the beginning. He wanted to set a precedent for the operation.

"Hello?" came the reply from the other end of the telephone.

"Kaiser please."

"This is Kaiser speaking."

"I have a target for you. Are you available?"

There was a pause. This wasn't great timing for Kaiser…but a job was a job. And it meant thrill and money, neither of which he could resist.

"If it's something I can do within say the next couple of days, then yes…"

"It is."

"Ok…let's meet."

*

Maggie reread the poem in front of her.

The mirror shows two faces. The mirror tells no lies.

Her hands began to shake and she almost dropped the paper. Clinging to it with one hand, she wiped her other sweaty palm on her trousers.

Where had it come from?

She'd noticed it lying innocently in the hallway.

She'd picked it up.

Then, it had just been a piece of paper.

Harmless.

But now, it was something else.

Something menacing.

What it contained was a message.

A message that was eating into her paranoia again.

Stunned and light headed she stumbled towards her study, desperately needing to sit down and have a drink. She didn't make it as far as the door. She collapsed in a heap outside and the paper fell from her grasp. She clawed at the carpet, but her body was immobilised by fear. Frightening images flashed before her eyes. Terrible memories she'd suppressed for so long. This was her penance for all the bad things she'd done. And now she'd succumb to the ultimate deed. To take another's life. The devil was coming to drag her away, torture her soul and lock her up in a fiery hell forever. There she would face her mother. She was waiting for her…

She screamed and held her head, rocking back and forth. Trying to shake away the nightmarish thoughts.

Finally, she stopped thrashing and lay still for a while. She allowed the emotion to flood her body. Finding some strength from somewhere she hauled herself up and crashed into the room, slamming the door shut behind her and locking and bolting it. Breathing heavily she reached for her chair and fell into it. She didn't have anything left to be able to pick up the bottle and pour. But she had to if she wanted to do this. She had to dig into her reserve if she wanted to fight back. And she would fight back. She would!

She was going to fight them all.

*

Sean put his phone back in his shirt pocket and watched Maggie leave the house and stagger to her car. He already knew where she was going. It was inevitable. He would follow at a safe distance and intervene when the time was right. He wanted to see what happened. He wanted to see how much bottle she had left, how much spirit. Suppression could only work for so long and then you exploded. Acted out. Became irrational. Did stupid things believing them to be the best way forward. She was cracking. He could see it. There was no need for any more pills, not just now. She had fallen right into the palm of his hand. She was about to make the biggest mistake of her life. She was about to make a public fool of herself. And Sean was ready for her.

And so were the Press.

They would be there because he'd tipped them off. She would come out of the bank to a frenzied media hungry audience. Cameras flashing. People in her face. Pushing and shoving for a story. It would make the situation worse. She'd struggle and fight, maybe even punch a reporter to the ground. It would be a side to Maggie Dalton no one had ever seen before, but one they'd probably always suspected since the rumours began. Then Sean would be there, coming to her rescue. He would drag Maggie to Thomas and Alex and demand more from them. They were still holding back capital and information and he didn't like that. He would use Maggie as he'd always used her – as a weapon against herself and those who protected her. He would insist containment, or threats far sinister. Yet once again, he was already two, three, four steps ahead. Whatever the outcome of this, whatever they did and however they reacted, the final blow would still be the same. The last move on the chessboard. The last hand he would deal. It was the game. It was destiny.

*

James came out of the bank and immediately noticed the commotion opposite. He didn't know for sure, but he had a gut feeling this was all about Maggie. Paparazzi rarely came to the small town of Fleet and she was the biggest personality they had. What had she done now? He didn't want to stop to find out. He and Emily would be a part of the backlash and that was enough. He'd secured the loan and couldn't wait to get home to tell his daughter the good news. The plan to runaway was back on! Now he just needed to find another secluded property. His mind wandered briefly to the original cottage, which had seemed perfect in every way...but then again, maybe not... Why would a place like that attract so much attention to the point of a bidding war? Thinking about it now, James really was suspicious. Had Maggie been involved? And who was the third buyer? Thank god he had sent Laura in disguise.

His mobile rang as he made a dash to the car park. Fishing it out of his top pocket he answered, "Hello?"

"James, it's me. Have you seen the breaking headlines? Your wife is splashed all over the evening news!"

"She's what?"

"Where are you?"

"In Fleet, about to drive home."

"Anywhere near her bank?"

"Yes, I just came out of mine opposite," then it dawned on him. So he had been right about Maggie! "You mean there's been an incident?"

"Yes, there's been an incident all right! She's been letting off steam at her bank manager and staff in front of the public. Even a mention of alcohol..."

"No surprise there. Have the police been called? Should I go back?"

"Definitely not! No, no police. She was lucky this time. Someone came to her rescue and spoke for her while they bundled her into a car."

"So...what is this all about?"

"I didn't want to say anything before, but you must have seen the rumours James..." The detective tailed off.

"Hell, there's been a lot of rumours lately, but then she's always been surrounded by scandal! I thought this was just more of the same."

"James, for Maggie to show herself up in public means something's going on. In all these years, she's never made a mistake like this. Maybe she's being blackmailed. Maybe she's in trouble, financial or otherwise."

"I'm not going there. You can't expect me to go *there*!" James was aghast. Maggie was somebody he no longer knew. He couldn't start playing the doting husband again, not after everything that had gone on.

"I'm not asking you to do anything James, but I am suggesting there could be trouble brewing. If you're going...now's the time to do it. I'm giving you a warning. We can hit her when she's down and it will make our job a lot easier when the case goes to court."

"Have you been talking to my solicitor?"

"Yes."

There was a pause, and then James spoke, "Well, thank god I've secured the loan then."

*

Nobody expected the evening's headlines. Not even Michael Louis with all of his contacts could stem the tide of retribution for Maggie. Any news travels fast, but salacious news of the most powerful woman in the community was always going to be greedily snapped up by the Paparazzi and commuters making their way home for the day. A picture of Maggie grappling with a reporter had made the front page, and it could have been a lot worse – for her – if Sean hadn't stepped in, calmed her down and made a statement on her behalf, whilst Johnny ushered her frantically into the waiting limousine. She had gone to the bank to try and find out what was going on with their accounts and to make the necessary transfers for Robert, but as Sean predicted, she had quickly lost her temper in front of staff and customers alike and the result had been what Thomas and Alex and thousands of other people were reading now. On his way to see them, Sean had waited, and picked up one of the first copies of the evening paper as it hit the newsstands. This is what he'd thrust into Thomas' hand when he was greeted at the door of the estate...

And this was where his next negotiations would start...

Maggie was dazed, sitting quietly in the corner, and Sean was eagerly anticipating their reaction to his little scandal set up. *Such power!*

"She's becoming a liability, our Mags."

Thomas looked up, anger flashing through his eyes.

"You did this!" he accused, shaking the paper at Sean.

"Precisely! Because you've been lying to me." He came straight to the point.

"What are you talking about now?" Thomas snapped.

"Maggie was transferring funds."

"So?"

"So, why didn't I know about these accounts?"

"We were saving them for a rainy day!" Alex retorted.

"Ha! Not wise my friends, not wise."

Inside, Thomas was kicking himself hard. Maggie had taken it upon herself to push her cottage plan forward just as she'd threatened she would, and she'd talked him into organising the hit on Sean herself. This mess was getting worse and worse. *She'd* made it worse. Sean always seemed to be one step ahead of them whichever way they turned. Did he know about the hit? How were they going to fund it now if Sean knew about the separate accounts? Those same questions were concerning Alex and Maggie, but for the time being, they would have to wait to ask each other. Making a trip to the Bank had not been a smart move on Maggie's part. Not for the first time he was asking himself why hadn't he seen this coming? And why hadn't he stepped in and stopped her, reasoned with her, deterred her? Maggie certainly *was* becoming a liability, not just to Sean, but to Alex and him as well.

"I want to talk to you." Sean pointed at Thomas.

"Anything you have to say can be said to all of us."

"I don't think you have much bargaining power right now."

Thomas looked across at Alex.

"I'll take Maggie downstairs." Alex didn't wait for Thomas to protest. He helped Maggie up and walked with her out of the room.

"Give us ten minutes," Thomas called after them.

Sean smirked. "You're very confident."

"I don't expect this will take long." He folded the paper and put it down on the table.

"I'll hurt Mags if you play any more games with me."

"You wouldn't dare."

Sean shrugged. "You know better than to test me Tom."

"You hurt Maggie and we'll hurt you." Thomas knew Sean was bluffing. He couldn't hurt Maggie without putting the company's reputation at stake. Even what he'd done today had been a huge gamble. Bad Press meant bad business. Surely Sean wasn't that crazy...

"What I did today will be nothing in comparison."

"You're a fool Sean!" Thomas wanted to throttle the man right here and now.

Sean didn't answer as he walked out of the room. For the moment, a threat was enough. After all, it really didn't matter. The outcome would still be the same.

*

"We're screwed thanks to you! You certainly took your cottage to another level – once again putting your interests ahead of your father's esteemed business! I can imagine he's turning in his grave. Just what did you think interrogating Mr Jefferson was going to do for us, or for you? And as for transferring money so openly...! What was so wrong with using a telephone?" Alex and Maggie had rejoined Thomas and he was shouting at Maggie. She was in a state of shock with what had happened, parts of her feeling an utter fool and parts of her still shaking with anger. She'd walked into a trap and she hadn't seen it coming. Her sharpness was whack, her senses completely destroyed. The visit to the Bank had seemed so right. She couldn't explain that feeling to anyone, and why should she anyway? Nothing was making sense. She felt she was playing out a story for someone, but the plot wasn't in her control.

"Do you think Sean knows?" Alex dared to throw the question out there.

"About the hit?"

Maggie struggled to speak. "He doesn't know. I didn't tell anybody why I was transferring funds. Sean assumed it was because we were running low, which we are."

"But he knows about the ten million?"

"Only half of it."

"How can you be sure of that Maggie?" Alex asked.

"That's all I told him."

"But what if he *pressed* our Bank Manager for the truth?"

"Mr Jefferson can handle himself. He knows people."

"So...your whole argument rests on the fact our Bank Manager can protect his interests...and we're supposed to be reassured with that?" Thomas was incredulous.

Maggie snapped to life. She didn't like being taken for a complete fool. Ok, she'd messed up pretty bad this afternoon, but not everything was lost.

"That other account, the special one, is not mentioned on any of my paperwork at the office. I've gone to great lengths to hide the documents, even from you. To protect you both!"

"Ha!"

"Let her finish Tom."

"They're not at the bank, in my home or even here in the estate. Mr Jefferson doesn't even know. I've moved the account to Switzerland. I did it some time ago. I never told you because it didn't matter, until now. Robert wants three and a half million for himself and one and a half for the hit. I knew the two accounts out of the three had enough to cover us."

"So it just means you'll now have to wire money from Switzerland?"

"Yes, and I better get on to it right away." She had no intention of paying out but she had to set up the transactions to look like there was some activity. "Robert wants most of the money by the end of tomorrow. The funds won't clear in time and I still don't know where I'm wiring the money. Sean has made everything twice as complicated. Damn him!"

"But it's not a train smash..."

"Not the train smash you were expecting, no."

Thomas looked up to the heavens and uttered a silent prayer. He didn't care who was listening.

*

Sean waited in the shadows of the estate rehearsing the plan in his mind over and over. He couldn't mess this one up, and he wouldn't. It was fool proof. Nobody was around and all was quiet, so when Maggie came out of the house first, as he knew she would, he grabbed her from behind and forced her to the ground. Quickly tying her hands together and shoving some cloth into her mouth, he hauled her to her feet and stuck the gun into the back of her head.

"Make any noise and this goes off. Understand?" he hissed in her ear.

She nodded slowly, unsure of her captor, dazed and confused by the sudden attack, but resenting his hot breath on her face. Either way, whatever she did now, she was a dead woman, or as good as... Because when Robert discovered she hadn't paid him up front again, as agreed, he would surely turn the hit to her.

She was shoved forwards.

"Now walk, and don't turn around."

CHAPTER 15

I had seen the evening news - my mother plastered all over it. I'd been clued to the screen for an hour or more watching the coverage and not quite believing my eyes. I looked up at my father as he came into the room.

"I told you something was going on."

He nodded. "We have to get out."

"Now?" I almost jumped out of my chair with excitement.

"I've been talking to Charles."

"Charles the detective."

"Yes, Charles the detective. He's given me a warning. You should go and pack your bag and hide it where you don't think your mother will find it. While you're doing that, I'm going to make some phone calls. I have to spend the next few days solidly looking at properties."

"When she comes home, it's going to be hell."

"I know." He reached for my hand. "So we have to be ready to walk away. Otherwise we'll get trapped again, and this time it might be too late. If we don't do it now, I fear we never will."

I saw the desperation in his eyes, but a faint glimmer of hope stirred within me.

"Go pack your bag," he urged.

"And go find our new home before she comes back." I smiled, kissing him on the forehead, before running up the stairs two at a time.

But she never did come back to the house that night, or the next night, or the night after that.

Mother had disappeared.

*

Sean drove fast through the night deeper and deeper into the countryside. He was taking Maggie somewhere she knew very well. She lay on the back seat bound and gagged, and now blindfolded also. When he bundled her into the car she had tried to turn to see who her captor was, so he had taken away that liberty from her. Desperately uncomfortable with pins and needles in all of her limbs, fighting against her bonds was proving fruitless. She had turned her attention to trying to focus on where he could be taking her. Picturing the route in her mind, she mentally stacked every left turn, every right turn and every roundabout. The way her body pitched against the seat helped decipher which was which. But now they were just driving straight. Was it motorway? No, it couldn't be. There were too many bumps and potholes. The car jolted and bounced. She could tell they were doing some speed. Were they being pursued? Momentarily she was hopeful and struggled again to loosen the ropes cutting into her hands.

"Keep still," he shouted at her.

She kicked out wishing she knew where his head was. Several seconds of thrashing about were soon brought to a stop when she heard him shout again and the gun clicked in her ear. Defeated, she whimpered into her gag suddenly feeling very tired. She needed to keep some reserves for when they got to wherever they were going. It was obvious she was being taken to someone; otherwise she would have been killed outright.

What did they want with her?

She was thrown from the seat as the car took a sharp right and lurched down a steep track. The only road she knew that did this was the one leading down to her cottage, well, the cottage she'd had snatched from her at auction.

It couldn't be, could it?

Was this the successful bidder seeking revenge?

Was she being set up?

Expectation was killing her. She wasn't used to being monopolised so brutally. And so helplessly.

She tried to spit out the gag and strained against the blindfold adjusting her eyes to the dark material, which unfortunately was too dark to see anything through.

She let out another strangled, frustrated cry as the car slowed significantly, rolled forwards a little bit more, and then came to a shuddering halt. The next thing she knew she was being dragged out of the car, made to stand on her shaky legs and marched over gravel much the same as on the driveway of her cottage.

"Know where you are?" Sean hissed in her ear.

She had stopped and was once again straining against the blindfold.

"Home at last Maggie." The gun dug into the nape of her neck and she stumbled. He caught her and she carried on walking, putting one foot in front of the other, unsure of her step and every now and then faltering.

She knew that voice but the energy was draining out of her and she badly needed a drink and a smoke. Her cravings immobilised her thought processes from going any further.

She staggered up the steps and Sean unlocked the door. Flipping switches as he walked, he grabbed her arm and led her along the hallway. Opening another door, he took her down some steep stairs, she assumed into a cellar, and then moved her towards a chair where he pushed her down and tied more rope around her body and legs fastening them in place. Ripping off her blindfold, she blinked over and over to adjust her eyes to the harsh lighting in the sparsely furnished room. She knew this room. In fact, she knew the whole place. The layout was etched into her brain, as were all the minutest of details – every light switch, every creaky floorboard, every doorknob. This *was* her cottage! And Sean was standing in front of her, hands on hips, looking immensely pleased with himself.

She fought against the rope when her eyes rested on him and she cried out into the cloth wedged in her mouth. The muffled noise faded into the silence, barely making any impact. Sean watched her. He was laughing quietly. This was feeling really good, seeing Maggie struggle and fight, helpless and truly his at last. His prize. His ticket to bigger and better things. She could thrash about all she liked but he wasn't about to let her out of his sight. Not now. Not when he was so close to handing her over and getting his reward.

"Like I said Mags. Home at last."

Every inch of her mind and body was cursing him. She looked at him through hostile eyes as he paced around the room, swinging the gun idly by his side, occasionally pulling on the trigger and stopping to watch her reaction. But she wasn't going to be intimidated by him. He could go to hell!

"I'm going to keep you here until your friends decide they want to talk. The longer they leave it, the more I torture you. Understand?"

She didn't react, so he came towards her and smacked her across the face with his gun. Her head reeled back as he spat in her face.

"Do-you-understand?"

She nodded weakly.

He left the room and was only gone for a few minutes before he came back with a jug of water and a glass. He poured the water and came over to her again. Placing the glass on the floor and tearing the cloth out of her mouth gingerly so as she wouldn't bite him, he then reached into his jacket pocket and pulled out a pot of pills all too familiar to Maggie.

"Remember these?" He jangled the pot in her face. Unscrewing the cap, he took a couple out and jammed them into her mouth before she could turn her head away.

He reached for the glass and pushed it roughly to her lips. She had no choice but to swallow.

Drained of energy and emotion, the water tasted good. He let her finish the whole glass, screwed the cap back on and took both pot and glass back to the table.

She knew the pills would soon kick in. Oh god. He really was going to fuck her up.

"Can I have a smoke?" It was a stupid question but she didn't know what else to do. Right now, the thought of a cigarette burning on her lips was heaven.

He sneered at her. "I suspect our Mags also wants a *proper* drink. Well, she's going to have to wait. I'm pretty tired after all that's gone on today." He turned away looking for another piece of cloth.

"You're leaving me here like this?" She was horrified. She badly needed to sleep. How was she going to sleep tied to a chair?

"Oh don't worry," he said casually, "These pills are even stronger. Your dreams, or should I say nightmares, will probably keep you awake all night. Sleep will be out of the question."

"You bastard!" she shouted, and would've said more if he hadn't gagged her again.

He listened to her strangled cries, enjoying the thought of torturing her mind until she barely knew who she was.

"Sweet dreams," he jeered, before turning on her and walking back up the steps. The door banged loudly behind him and

Maggie was left alone in the darkness, knowing her nightmare was only just beginning.

*

Thomas held his head in his hands and groaned loudly.

"Kidnap you say?"

"It's possible. Neither Sean or Maggie have been seen for three days."

"Is that significant?"

"It is…now Robert Hilton's asking questions…"

Thomas took longer to piece the puzzle together than Alex, but he eventually came to the same conclusion.

"And if Maggie's with Sean…"

"She could be in danger, yes."

"Can we stop the hit?"

"I don't think so, no…"

"Can we try?"

"I don't have enough resource Tom. All the team are working on locating Maggie and Sean. We don't have time to change tactics now. I'm sorry." He pushed his chair back. "You should get some sleep."

Thomas didn't answer. He was trying to decide their next move. Should they sit it out and wait? Should he and Alex start searching, making their own inquiries? The clock was ticking. Maggie often disappeared, but Sean disappearing as well… It was too much of a coincidence.

"I'll drop by later this afternoon with an update."

"And in the meantime?"

"You should get some sleep."

Alex was just walking out the door, when Thomas remembered something.

"Did you ever find out about those pills Mags was taking?"

Alex stopped in his tracks and turned back to his friend. "I know they went away for analysis. Let me chase it up and come back to you."

"Do that. It could be the key we're looking for in all this."

*

"I'm not having a go at you James, but it isn't just about getting away from Maggie. You're not considering the bigger picture at all!"

Laura was sipping her coffee across the table from him. They were at the art studio taking a break while their assistant worked beneath them, liaising with suppliers and sweet-talking clients. Laura never set foot in their family home. In her mind, if she kept away from James and Emily, she hoped Maggie might forget she existed. Foolish thinking really, but she clung to it all the same. She didn't want to hamper her brother and niece any more than they already were. Some things needed to be said today though. She could see James floundering, getting frustrated and letting the tiniest details irritate him so he stopped making progress. And she knew time was running out because she too had seen the press coverage over the last few days after that appalling incident at the bank in the high street in broad daylight. Maggie had done herself no favours there, and it had been a hideous display of her true nature and character. Laura wanted to rejoice that finally the World was seeing the real Maggie Dalton, but it was a double-edged sword. If Maggie was indeed cracking up as the papers suggested, this would mean only bad things for James and Emily.

James drank his coffee and said nothing. Laura was right, but he couldn't bring himself to say it. Problems, considerations and obstacles were not his friends lately.

"You're going to have to go to the Police at some point."

Still he said nothing.

"You'll need to go into a protection plan until the case is over. She'll stop at nothing James, to get Emily back. You know that. She doesn't love her, but Emily is her outlet for all the drinking and violence. Maggie can't function without Emily being there, without her being around," she paused, "And have you thought about Emily's schooling?"

"I'll teach her at home."

"She may not want that James. She has friends at her school and she has that tutor you were telling me about. She has a support system there that you can't simply take away from her. It isn't fair to Emily. Who are you really doing this for hmmm? Yourself to make *you* feel better? Is it just about you?

Or are you truly doing it for your daughter? Do you have her best intentions at heart?"

James didn't react straight away, he never did. Laura wished that sometimes he would. She wanted him to get angry and passionate about something he really cared for and felt strongly for. What was the use otherwise? He might as well just give up.

Years of abuse were telling. Had Maggie browbeaten him so much he could no longer think rationally?

"First we run. Then we make choices. I can't do this any other way sis. I can't."

Laura suddenly felt immense compassion for her younger brother. She rose from her chair and knelt down beside him. Hesitating at first, she slid her arms around him. He tipped his head into her shoulder and she hugged him tighter. It was hard for all of them, but she knew it was especially hard for James.

Expectation weighed heavily, and she certainly knew all about that. Packing up her bag and booking round the world tickets to escape her over bearing parents had been her outlet for finding her way in this World. It was hardly in the same league to James's dilemma, but at least she could understand some of what he was going through, however small and insignificant it felt.

*

Thomas answered his phone as he put down his brandy and turned away from the desk to look out of the window. He had one of the best views of the beautiful gardens and it brought some tranquillity to him now.

But only for a minute.

"Hello?"

Alex didn't waste any time in getting to the point. "Tom, those pills are a mix of antipsychotics – geodon and seroquel – with ecstasy and a hint of cocaine for good measure.

"Christ!" Thomas's brain was working quickly. "I didn't know Maggie was on medication, certainly not neuroleptics. And the drugs…"

"The doctor told me if the patient is mentally unstable enough to be on multiple antipsychotics, they shouldn't be messing around with mind altering drugs. You can imagine the results."

"If she was prescribed any pills, she should have told us. It's in her contract to tell us!"

"Tom, don't jump the gun. What if she's being forced to take them? She wouldn't take ecstasy willingly. That's not Maggie's style."

But Thomas already had his own ideas about this latest eye-opener.

"She's sampling the merchandise! She's got her hand in with Sean and she's working with him against the company. She's going to bring the whole lot down so she can disappear for good. That's it Alex...that's it! That's what the cottage is all about. All that bullshit she gave us about taking Sean out...! She'd already planned it with him."

Alex wasn't so sure. This didn't sound plausible. Maggie was many things, but she wasn't a drug user.

"Don't rush into anything," he warned, "This is all supposition...your supposition."

"So...you don't think I'm right?" Thomas stood up, challenging Alex down the phone. "Well I do! It suddenly all makes perfect sense. It explains why she was never concerned about the company folding, why she continued to push her cottage plan, and why she took the hit out herself!"

"So why is Robert chasing up his payment? Why did Maggie even make contact with him?"

"Because she wanted to get her own back. He uses and abuses her. She said so herself. She wanted to hurt him where she knew she could – in his wallet. She had no intention of paying him."

Alex didn't respond.

"I know I'm right Alex, I know I am." Thomas was adamant, pacing up and down with the bit between his teeth like an impatient horse waiting for the Grand National to start. He was on to something and he wasn't about to let it go. "Where did she say that cottage was? Dorset somewhere? I bet that's where she's shacked up right now...her and Sean...together...plotting their next move. Their base to hide their illegal business deals and her sex scandals!"

Alex sighed heavily down the phone. "But why would she have told us about the cottage? That part certainly doesn't make sense."

"Damn it man! I don't have all the answers, do I? We need to go to that cottage and we need to go right away. I want it out with the pair of them! You better organise some back up."

But there was no need because as soon as Thomas put the phone down, he and Alex both received a text message from Sean summoning them to the property, which had caused them so much grief over the last few weeks. Thomas rang the number back to check it out, and it was then that he learned Maggie had been taken hostage and Sean was torturing her with the very same drugs.

Was it a trap?

They didn't know for sure, but they were about to find out.

*

"I've told them the truth, but they don't believe me. I think *they* think you're working with me." Sean smirked. He was sitting on a chair opposite Maggie and puffing on his cigarette. Letting the smoke swirl around so her cravings worsened. In just a few days she was already looking unrecognisable. Her hair dishevelled, her clothes torn, cuts and bruises all over her body where Sean had handled her roughly. He had whipped her and beaten her into submission, and finally he had been allowed to take her with all the lust and force and power he'd restrained for so long. Now she hardly knew what he was doing to her. She hardly knew where or who she was. Her mind was too far-gone. She was hallucinating and mumbling and crying and screaming for release from the demons inside her head. Sean was enjoying every single second of this. Taking Maggie Dalton apart piece by piece had always been his ultimate fantasy. And now he was going to stop the pills and leave her for a while. Stand back and witness what might happen. Cold turkey was a beautiful thing when it wasn't happening to you.

*

The car pulled up outside the Dalton estate and after being frisked and searched for weapons and phones and anything else deemed a threat to this operation, Thomas and Alex were shoved into the back seat. They were being escorted to the cottage by some of Sean's consortium. It wasn't ideal, but Alex had back up on stand by. No phone meant no communication, so he'd given them a time for tomorrow. If no word came through by that time, they were to raid the building and bring out Maggie safely, then come back for Thomas and Alex.

It was a slow drive, done purposely to create apprehension. Sean's men were in no hurry. As long as they brought the pair to him before nightfall, they would be paid. In between, they could do what they liked with their victims.

Intimidation, scaremongering, a few knocks here and there. It was all part of the fun.

Alex looked across at Thomas. He was staring straight ahead, concentrating. Alex knew his friend was worried for Maggie's safety even after everything she'd put them through recently.

He was calm. It was what he liked to call *shit or bust time*. His primary responsibilities were Thomas and Maggie, and he knew what he had to do.

The car snaked along the country roads and he wondered how much longer. They had never driven to view this place so he had no idea exactly where it was and how long it took to drive there. He wished they had made a trip. It would have come in handy knowing the layout, knowing any hidden rooms or details, and knowing what furniture and utensils were already in the house. He could have made a better job of briefing his men, but there hadn't been time. He just had to keep everyone talking. As long as they talked, there wouldn't be any shooting or casualties. It would buy him time. Valuable time.

Thomas stared straight ahead, wondering how they'd got into this foolish position. He replayed every single detail over and over in his mind, yet again trying to piece the gigantic puzzle together. There was Sean and the Board working against them for years, building up a client portfolio big enough to finance the drug smuggling. Gradually, step-by-step, they were taking over Dalton PLC. And maybe they wanted Maggie to remain the face of the company. That meant they had no further need of him or Alex as soon as they wrangled every last detail out of them regarding her father's business. Sean knew they were withholding important information. He probably suspected, rightly, that they had other money stashed away. He'd already ambushed Maggie's visit to the Bank. How did he know to do that? And why were the Media so quick to respond? Was Maggie actually in on all of this? Why would she want bad press now? Was it a ploy to throw them both off? The antipsychotics medication came into his mind. Alex didn't agree with him, but to Thomas it seemed a compelling case for sedition on her part. However, he was also disgusted with himself. What had he done to salvage what little standing they had left within Dalton PLC? Plan A had been a monumental fuck up, and Plan B looked set to be just as reckless. Maggie had to be protecting hers and Sean's interests. Yes...she had to be. The more Thomas thought about it, the more he came to the same conclusion. Blowing up the shipment should have worked, but Maggie obviously tipped Sean off. And now, here they were, walking head first into another one of her traps. God, when was it ever going to end? He was getting exhausted struggling in the numerous webs of deceit and corruption entangling them.

It had to end soon. One way or another, it had to end soon.

*

Two stops later, the afternoon wearing on into early evening, with Thomas and Alex knocked around and bruised, the car came to a halt outside what must have been the cottage. It was nothing to look at, and when they were jostled inside, looking around, there wasn't much in here to change their initial impression. It was poorly furnished, stripped back to its bare bones. Whoever had bought it, hadn't yet put anything into it. But what it lacked in character, it certainly made up for in location. Secluded and well set back from the road, you wouldn't even know it existed. Thomas had noticed there was no sign to announce the cottage. They simply took one of the many dirt tracks and here they were. Surrounded by dense forest and miles from civilisation. Thomas thought of the back up and hoped they were coming cross-country on foot. At least they had rough co-ordinates to work with.

"Where's the son of a bitch?" he demanded, stepping into the hallway.

"If you mean Mr Hamilton, you'll see him soon enough," one of the men replied.

They were hustled into a room leading off the living room. A long table with an assortment of chairs sat crudely in the middle. A drinks cabinet was to one side and a desk to the other. The pokey window didn't let in much light.

"Make yourselves comfortable."

Thomas and Alex sat down.

Seconds later, Sean, informed of their arrival, came into the room.

"Drink boys? Smoke?" He shut the door behind him, ushering the other men out of the room.

"Where is Maggie?" Thomas was on his feet immediately.

"She's around. She didn't want to see you just yet. Wanted to compose herself, I believe." Sean was lying, playing along with their idea that she might be working with him.

"Where-is-she?"

Sean lit up a cigarette. "You sure you don't want one?"

Thomas went for him, but Sean expertly ducked out of the way and sat down at the table with Alex, training his gun from one to the other.

"You know something Tom, Alex is smart. He's always been smarter than you. He doesn't react, just sits and observes. You're too impulsive Tom. It could cost you one of these days."

"Ok. Ok!" Thomas shoved his fists deep into his trouser pockets. He didn't want Sean to see he was getting to him. He also didn't want the gun to go off unnecessarily.

Sean put the gun back in his belt, sat back in the chair and puffed idly on his smoke. "This is the life. This is most definitely the life."

Alex looked across at Thomas and mouthed for him to keep talking. Thomas knew the deal. He couldn't jeopardise their position without first finding out all the information.

"Are you going to tell us why we're here?"

"I think you know why you're here Tom."

Thomas said nothing. Neither did Alex.

"You haven't told me everything I need to know yet. You're withholding certain details – pass codes, client profiles, that sort of thing. Oh…and there's somebody I'd like you to meet. A long, lost *friend*. But that can wait for the moment. I have business with Maggie first."

"What business? And who is this person?" Thomas was racking his brains as he spoke. "What business do you have with Maggie? Why can't we see her tonight?"

"All in good time Tom, all in good time. Meanwhile, why don't you take a leaf out of Alex's book and relax. He's got the right idea. Help yourself to a drink and cigar. You'll be shown to your quarters shortly where there's a meal waiting for you."

"So you're kidnapping us too?" Alex was bemused.

Sean laughed. "Very funny Mr Coombes, very funny. Enjoy your evening boys. See you tomorrow bright and early." And with that he stubbed out his cigarette on the floor and walked out, leaving them alone in the room.

The henchmen came back to escort them upstairs. As they climbed the wooden steps, their footsteps echoing back down the hallway, they heard a scream. Thomas stiffened and stopped walking. Another scream resounded around their part of the building. Alex swallowed. It was definitely coming from a woman.

"Keep moving." Both men pulled out guns and flipped the safety catches. Thomas opened his mouth to speak, but clamped it shut again. So Maggie *was* being held against her will. It had to be Maggie screaming. Who else could it be? He gave a fleeting glance at Alex. Their worried stares met each other. But they had little choice right now to do anything about it. They weren't armed and there wasn't even anything lying around they could use as weapons. They were just going to have to sit it out and wait to see what tomorrow might bring, as painful and frustrating as that realisation was.

*

Sean looked up to the ceiling, knowing full well Thomas and Alex would be listening to her screams right now as they made their way upstairs. His gaze dropped back to Maggie, strapped and bound tightly to the bed and fighting with every inch of her being to be set free and given another shot. He was weaning her off the drugs. The make shift drip was all but toppling over with her thrashing about. He wanted her to be ready for the big staging tomorrow morning. They wouldn't recognise her. She wouldn't even recognise herself. She was ravaged and starved, rushing from restless sleep headlong into nightmares and back again. Hallucinations filled her mind and made the screaming more intense. She would be putty in his hand once all this was over.

She'd never dare cross him again.

*

It was early morning and they were sitting in the same room as the evening before with Sean. Nobody was speaking. Alex checked his watch. 9:07 am. He had given his men until 10:00 am. Just under an hour to keep things ticking over smoothly. Then, and only then, could they do what the hell they liked.

"Who was screaming Sean? Was it Maggie?" Thomas couldn't wait any longer. He needed to know what he was dealing with.

Sean didn't answer straight away. He was looking forward to the final, ultimate show down. The one he'd been building up to all these years and more recently dreaming, planning and scheming about every single day.

"I'm fucking with her mind Tom, like you're fucking with me. Surprising what one says when one is under pressure."

"You sadistic bastard!" Thomas hissed through clenched teeth, "If you've hurt her..."

"Why would I do that Tom when she's going to sign over Dalton PLC pretty soon."

"Over my dead body!"

"Could well be my friend, could well be..."

Thomas ignored the jibe. His immediate concern was for Maggie. "So how bad is it? Is she hurt?"

"She'll live to fight another day," Sean sneered, "She needed to be brought down a peg or two, that's all."

"You forced those pills on her?"

"That took some time. I thought you were never going to get there!"

"She's not working with you?"

"No, not yet, but I'm pretty sure she will be soon." As he spoke, there was a knock on the door and one of the men came in and whispered something in his ear. "Show her in," he answered. Speaking again to Thomas and Alex, he said, "Boys, there's somebody I'd like you to meet...ah...here she is...right on cue!"

They turned in their seats to see who it was. Both of their jaws dropped open in shock and disbelief as Kite greeted Sean warmly, and joined them at the table.

Checkmate.

CHAPTER 16

"Oh my good god!" Thomas exclaimed.

Alex wanted to punch somebody. This had to be a nightmare. They would surely wake up any second now.

The arrival of Elizabeth Dalton, like a ghost from the grave, had just made the whole goddamn situation twice as ugly and twice as complicated.

Sean clapped his hands. "Drink ma'am?" he asked, as one of the men stepped forward. Sean muttered something to him as he poured himself a large brandy.

"No. I would like a clear head for this..." She turned to Thomas and Alex, "Don't mind if I smoke though, do you?"

They didn't answer and she lit up anyway. Sean rejoined them at the table, enjoying the bewildered expressions on both of their faces. Elizabeth placed the lighter on the table. The word Kite ran down one side. She puffed lazily on her cigarette.

"Well this is all very civilised," she laughed, and her eyes sparkled with excitement and intent. For a moment Thomas saw an older Maggie across the table, beautiful yet devious. Elizabeth had aged well; she had obviously conquered her drinking and cleaned up her act. She had been a frightful mess in the last pictures they had seen of her. He shook his head slowly and deliberately, lost in his thoughts. This well dressed woman sitting before him could not be Elizabeth Dalton. It couldn't be.

"Where's Margaret?"

Shit! Maggie! Thomas and Alex were catapulted back into the present. They had forgotten about Maggie with the jolt of seeing Elizabeth alive and well, after all this time believing she was rotting in hell somewhere.

Shit! Shit! Shit! Maggie...

"On her way," Sean replied, "then we can begin..."

The room fell quiet. Smoke swirled and the fumes of alcohol punctuated the air.

Both Thomas and Alex felt sick to the stomach. By no stretch of the imagination had they bargained on this. Why hadn't they followed up after sending Sean to do their dirty work for them? Why had they trusted him? It was the final, fatal move on the chessboard. Their reluctance to accept, or even acknowledge the terrible deed they'd lowered themselves to, had swallowed them whole. It had blocked out any further involvement.

It was done. They had blood on their hands. And now they must forget it lest it should consume them.

But they didn't have blood on their hands.

She was alive.

And being well looked after...plotting and scheming for the ultimate revenge.

Is that why she was here?

Alex checked his watch. 9:37 am.

*

Maggie was being hauled to her feet and ordered to smarten up. She went into the adjoining bathroom and looked at herself in the mirror. She didn't know who she was anymore. Little sleep and rough handling had left damage all over her face and body, and worse still – her mind.

One of the men threw in some clothes for her. "Hurry up darling. You've got visitors!"

Visitors! She couldn't see visitors looking like this! What were they doing to her?

"Please...leave me alone," she moaned, turning on the tap and splashing her face. Everything she did was slow and deliberate. It would take ages to make herself presentable enough for visitors.

Visitors!

Thomas?

Alex?

The thought of her friends stirred something within her.

Renewed hope?

Maybe, just maybe, she would make it out of here alive...

There was a shower, but she didn't feel she could manage being that length of time under water. Instead she reached for the bar of soap and cloth and began cleaning up and attending to her cuts and bruises. It seemed to take forever and all the while she was trying to remember whether she had committed to anything whilst Sean was tormenting her. She didn't think she had signed anything, but it was all such a blur. The cold water felt good against her skin. It was awakening some of the old Maggie Dalton. Some of that old fiery, survival spirit. But how battered she felt, how dirty! And then another thought played into her mind. Far darker. Had Sean touched her?

Had he...? She couldn't go there. She couldn't let her mind wander to that disgusting possibility. She visibly shivered and scrubbed more vigorously. Looking across at the pile of clothes, she noticed it was one of her suits from the office. Why did she have to look so smart? Who were these visitors?

"Are you done yet?" One of the men banged loudly on the door. "They're waiting for you!"

Who? Who was waiting for her?

She wanted to ask, but was too afraid of being beaten again. These people working for Sean spared no mercy, and neither did he.

*

Outside snipers were assembling on and around the building, using the trees and shrubbery to cover them. Sean obviously hadn't anticipated any sort of rebellion, as there were no henchmen patrolling the grounds. Foolish...very foolish... The Colonel in charge of the operation smiled to himself. In fact, it was almost too good to be true.

Indifference to chance is a vanity in any game. The team knew there were guns inside, but nothing of their calibre. Alex had ordered firepower and lots of it. *He* had anticipated well.

"On my command then," he spoke softly into his microphone. He would fire the first grenade into the outhouses. This would distract most of the people inside. Then they would raid the cottage and take back control.

The Colonel hoisted the gun onto his shoulder and took aim... Inside, Alex checked his watch. He knew the drill. 9:57 am.

*

Maggie straightened up, brushed down her suit and combed her fingers gently through her chestnut hair teasing out the multitude of knots. This was going to have to do, the men outside were getting impatient and she knew she was pushing her luck.

She came slowly out of the bathroom, steadying herself with whatever she could reach in time. Levelling her voice, she said, "I'm ready."

The men flipped their safety catches off. "Follow me," one of them commanded gruffly.

They left the room, Maggie sandwiched between them holding out for the wall to keep herself from toppling over. She badly needed some water. She was so thirsty. They made their way across the landing and down the stairs. Maggie was just putting her last foot down when an almighty explosion threw them all to the ground. Her mind raced and for a moment she was transported back to the charity ball. The same thing had happened then...a loud bang...and being thrown to the floor.

What the heck was going on?

One of the men got up and lunged towards her. She didn't have the strength to resist him as he crashed to her side and pinned her hands behind her back. The other man lay motionless in the hallway. The force of the impact had toppled him from above them, smacking his head on the ground and knocking him out cold. *One down, one to go,* Maggie thought grimly. She pretended to play dead and let her body go limp under his weight. She was banking on the conscious thug to take off and see what all the commotion was about. He lay still for what seemed like forever and then finally pulled himself off of her. Maggie didn't move. She'd noticed the gun lying on the floor. If she could just get to it... He grunted and got to his feet. Believing Maggie to be unconscious like his colleague, he ambled off in the direction of the explosion, dazed and confused, his gun hanging limply from his hand.

When she was sure the coast was clear, she too got up and picked up the gun. Waiting a few more seconds and straining her ears for any noise, she uttered *Forgive me God* and aiming it at the man's head, pulled the trigger. Not daring to look back, she wandered cautiously after her other captor. She knew she couldn't afford to take any prisoners now. She had to shoot to kill.

*

The explosion shattered the silence in the room with a deafening roar.

"What the…!" Sean jumped to his feet and darted out of the room. Elizabeth ran after him. Thomas took one look at Alex and nodded.

"Hey you!" Alex called.

That was all Thomas needed to react. Reaching for the brandy bottle he swung and smashed it down hard on the remaining man's head. The heavy went down like a skittle and Thomas was quick to grab his gun.

"We need to get you one of these!"

"No need…look what Sean left us…" Alex held up the gun lying innocently on the table.

"So what now? They won't have gone far…"

"The outhouses are to our left. We need to get into the barns on the right. I told the Colonel not to touch the barns."

"Do you think there's more men waiting outside?"

"I don't know. I only ever saw three or four and Sean. But we shoot to kill, don't hesitate unless you're compromised. There's already a half dozen snipers trained on the building and the Colonel and one other on the ground. We need to get out of here."

They edged towards the door. Alex went first and swung it open. It creaked on the hinges. There was nobody outside. Alex beckoned to Thomas to follow him. They crept along the dimly lit passageway, training their guns and heading to the back of the cottage. Still, nobody in sight.

"If they're outside, we need to be prepared and above all, stick to the plan. We want to avoid the forest. It'll trip us all up if we find ourselves stuck in there."

Thomas whispered his agreement and continued following Alex. They passed more rooms, but it appeared the house had emptied.

"What about upstairs? What about Maggie?"

"Leave it to the Colonel, Tom. He'll find her. We need to get to the barns before they blow this place to kingdom come."

"You didn't…" Thomas tailed off.

So, there *would* be blood on their hands after today.

"Yes…I did. We do what needs to be done." Alex looked at him gravely. "Now come on. Stay focused."

*

Maggie crept along keeping her gun out in front of her and peering into each room as she passed by. She was making her way to the back of the house, following her other subjugator. She was shaking and breaking out into a cold sweat. She had never fired a gun before, least of all killed somebody. Wiping the liquid from her eyes, she took a moment to steel herself. Sooner or later she was going to come across him and she had to be ready. He would definitely come back for her and his colleague. She heard a noise behind her and span around wildly. Her arms flailed as she kept spinning doing a complete 360, and the gun nearly slipped from her grasp. There was nobody there. She stifled a cry of relief and hurried through the kitchen and out into the yard.

The Colonel saw the man charge at her before she did. He took aim and fired slightly ahead so he would run into the bullet. It hit him just above the ear and he went down immediately. Maggie staggered back and a scream escaped her lips, howling into the mid morning calmness. The Colonel lunged towards her and once again she was falling through the air, hitting the ground with a loud thud.

"Are you ok? Are you hurt?" he kept asking over and over, but she wasn't listening. She still had a hold of her gun and was waving it about dangerously. A sniper up in the trees above them aimed at her. When he saw it was a woman, he stopped to take another look through his binoculars. It was definitely Maggie. He didn't have orders to shoot - but she was attacking the Colonel, her rescuer! He hesitated, and in that fraction of a second, a shot rang out and then the Colonel was kicking and shouting as Maggie ran off still clutching her gun. The sniper took aim again, but she was quickly in amongst the trees making a clean shot nigh on impossible.

"Colonel down! Colonel down!" he shouted into his microphone, "Back up required. I repeat. Back up required. Target running towards outhouses."

He dropped to the ground and helped the Colonel move into cover. Maggie had shot him in the leg.

*

Maggie ran and ran, her body aching and willing her to stop, but her mind pushing her to keep going. What were army personnel doing here? Whose side were they on? Had she just shot the wrong person? She was getting more and more confused, and tiredness and exhaustion were creeping up on her. Had he shot the thug for her, or had someone else?

The outhouses came into view, or what was left of them. The wooden panels were strewn all around and smoke was rising from the centre. It looked like a bomb had gone off in there. She desperately needed to lie down and rest her weary body, but she couldn't stay here. Then she remembered the barns. They would be safe. She had to get to the barns.

She knew her legs were about to give out so she crawled the last few metres to the first of three. It didn't matter that her expensive suit and designer shoes were completely ruined. It didn't matter that she needed water so badly. Reaching for the handle, she pulled herself inside and let the door shut behind her with a quiet thud. Darkness engulfed her. She fell forwards into the dirt and lay there breathing heavily. She didn't feel as if she could move another inch, but at least she was safe. Nobody was going to find her in here.

*

"What is going on?" Elizabeth demanded, "You gave me your word, but from where I'm standing, this is a total screw up! If you've jeopardised my operation…it's over. It's all over!"

He wasn't listening to her. He wanted to know who was messing with him. This was his moment, his glorification, and somebody had stolen it from him. They would pay. They would dearly pay when he got his hands on them. Whoever they were!

Coming back to the room after rushing out, he'd found Thomas and Alex gone and one of his men out stone cold. He'd grabbed another revolver and then they'd found another of his men with a bullet through his brain at the foot of the stairs. A thorough search of the bedrooms revealed Maggie, his prize possession, was also missing.

"Shit!" he groaned, finding his third man down not far from the yard. He kicked him onto his side and took his gun. He couldn't shoot two at the same time after his accident, but in any case, the more ammunition, the better.

Elizabeth had stopped talking. Sean turned to face her.

"Put the gun down," she ordered.

"Oh no," he answered calmly, "We're in this together now, remember. My enemies are your enemies. Think about it but don't take long. We can still do this. I know we can."

She kept the gun pointing at his chest, considering her next move.

"I want Margaret and everything she brings with her."

"And I want Dalton PLC," he paused, daring to go on, "The goal posts haven't changed."

She pulled on the trigger.

"Lower the gun ma'am. You know we can still get what we want out of this."

The trigger inched back.

"You need me and I need you. One doesn't work without the other." Sean spoke calmly, but inside his heart was thumping loudly against his rib cage.

She fired at him. The bullet whistled passed his right ear. He didn't flinch. He knew he was too valuable to her even at this stage of the game.

Nerves of steel.

But Elizabeth Dalton wasn't stupid.

She was just trigger-happy.

*

The Colonel's back up entered the building in close pursuit of one of the targets identified as a heavy. He saw the man at the foot of the stairs and blood seeping into the worn carpet. Putting two and two together he ran upstairs and checked out every room, moving swiftly and quietly. Racing back down, he did the same, making sure he didn't miss anything. When he came to the small room off the living area, he heard muffled noises. The door was ajar. He inched it open and peered inside. A big man was leaning over trying to wake up another man on the floor. His back was turned away from the door. He was urging his colleague to get up, engrossed in his task. Shards of glass littered the room and it smelled strongly of brandy. The soldier fired a neat shot into his head, execution style. He slumped forwards. The soldier strode across the room and fired another shot into the other man's head.

Job done.

Now he must look for the woman.

*

Maggie eased herself into a sitting position as she heard footsteps approaching. Two lots of footsteps. She shoved the gun into her waistband. Oh god, who were they? She desperately needed to run and hide, but her body wouldn't allow it. Immobilised with exhaustion and fear, all she could do was lie there as the door was pushed open in one sweeping motion and two figures entered the barn. She cowered under the sudden burst of light and shaded her eyes to see who it was. Blinking and rubbing, she couldn't adjust her vision quick enough as the voice she now dreaded more than anything spoke loudly, filling the silence with his voice.

"There you are." Sean crouched down in front of her, leering in her face. She started to crawl away from him, clawing at the earth and wishing the ground would swallow her whole. This had to be a nightmare!

"You can run but you can't hide Maggie my dear." He stood in her path. She changed direction, but he kept moving to block her. He looked over at Elizabeth. "Now we wait. I'm sure they'll come for her."

Maggie had forgotten someone else had entered the barn with Sean. She span around, took one look at Elizabeth, and screamed.

"Come now Margaret. That's no way to greet your mother after all this time."

Sean opened his mouth and a cruel, empty laugh escaped his lips, filling Maggie's head and rebounding around its walls. She gasped in stale air and felt her body convulsing with terror and dread.

"I thought you were dead," she whispered, "They told me you were dead."

Her mother looked down on her with disdain. Kicking her in the chest, she smirked and turned away. Maggie was no daughter of hers. She was just another pawn. Another pawn in the great game of corruption and deceit.

Maggie attempted to crawl away as Sean aimed another kick in her direction. His boot grazed her temple and she fell back against the concrete floor.

"You're just my mother's henchman!" she mocked, "That's all!" Sean rewarded her with a backhand to the face. She writhed on the floor, the intense pain momentarily blinding her.

"Hold it right there!" Thomas yelled, crashing into the barn with Alex only seconds behind him. Both men levelled their guns. Sean immediately went for his, and so did Elizabeth. Maggie remained very still, reassured by her own gun digging into her gut, hidden and out of sight.

"It's over Sean. All your men are dead." Thomas didn't know if this was strictly true, but Sean wasn't to know.

"We have back up all around. You won't get out of here alive." Alex added.

Somewhere in the recesses of Maggie's frightened and dazed mind, the words registered slowly to her. *Back up...thank god...* She just wanted it to be over.

"Give us Maggie."

Sean reached down and grabbed a fistful of Maggie's hair, forcing her to her knees.

She groaned loudly, but didn't fight him off. She didn't have any strength left in her to do it.

"I'll put a bullet through her brain," Sean jeered. Elizabeth stiffened. This was not the plan.

"I don't think Elizabeth would like that," Thomas retorted, noting the look on her face. She glared first at him, then back at Sean.

"Well...ok...she's better alive to us than dead...but if the worse comes to the worse..." he purposely stopped in mid sentence, leaving nothing and everything to the imagination. He winked at Elizabeth.

"What do you both want? What is this all about?" Thomas detested their steely determination and evident lack of fear. It was beginning to set off the alarm bells in his head. Having snipers outside meant nothing to these two inhuman beings. *They* would stop at nothing.

"Let's start from the beginning." The hint of a smile danced across Elizabeth's lips. Now she knew the line Sean was taking, she felt more comfortable. She was even beginning to enjoy it. "You sent Sean," she savoured his name, she had never known his real name until now, "to kill me. He is a hit man by profession after all."

Thomas and Alex looked at Sean, their guns still trained. Sean rubbed the back of his head with his revolver and smiled.

"Police force..." Thomas mocked himself. "I should have known!"

"But the good lady here negotiated an irresistible deal and once established, together we took it to another level. Sure it was a rough ride," he smirked, thinking back, "and it took me a while to learn the one and only lesson. Don't ever cross Elizabeth Dalton," he held up his wounded hand, "because she doesn't take prisoners kindly."

Thomas and Alex stared at the crude stubs on his left hand. Maggie raised her head. "That was a boating accident," she murmured. Her mother hadn't really blown off two of his fingers, *had she?*

Elizabeth spoke, breaking the uncertainty hanging in the air, "You know Margaret, when the mood takes me, I can order anything to be done. You know that." And Maggie did know. She had been under her mother's evil hand a long, long time ago. Subjected to vile and degrading acts and beaten to within inches of her life, she knew all too well what her mother was really capable of.

"Kaiser has been at my beck and call ever since," she added smugly, "Amazing what it takes to get you men to submit, isn't it?"

"Kaiser!" They all blurted out at the same time.

"Just a little nickname for my second in command." She turned to Sean and smiled. "A modern day Caesar. Do carry on."

Tightening his grip on Maggie's hair, Sean continued slowly and deliberately, letting each word sink in. He was pissed at them for killing his men. He felt the rage bubbling away within him. How dare they think they could take him down and dominate his moment of glory.

"Robert Hilton phoned me. I was the hit for myself!" His insane shriek leapt around the room. Thomas looked to Alex, Alex looked to Maggie. She couldn't look either of them in the eye. Another screw up. Another irreversible screw up!

"You lot are amateurs!" Sean scorned, "Put your guns down boys. You haven't got it in you to shoot anyone. That's why I had to do your dirty work for you!"

They didn't move a muscle. Silence fell on the room. All eyes were trained on each other. Nobody wanted to make a mistake...

Elizabeth fired first. The bullet ricocheted off the ground in front of Alex and flew dangerously passed him, burying itself in the window, which smashed. Glass flew everywhere covering Alex. He involuntary dropped his gun and Sean quickly kicked it away. Released, Maggie slumped forwards. Thomas's reflexes meant he shot at Elizabeth but missed her by miles. Sean expertly shot the gun from his hand just grazing his bare skin with the bullet.

"Fuck!" Thomas yelled, grabbing his injury, as the gun jumped away from him and banged loudly on the concrete. He and Alex were now back to back with two guns in their faces. Alex attempted to pick the glass from his face. Blood trickled down his neck.

"Don't shoot!" he yelped.

Sean ignored his plea, as he and Elizabeth kept advancing. "You know Tom, we tried to have Maggie shot down at the ripe, pert age of twenty-one, but it didn't quite work out and that poor boy got the bullet instead. Damn shame. I never like it when an innocent gets murdered in cold blood. But...there you go... Oh, and the hit man got it too. Fucking terrible he was. I should have done it myself, but then we wouldn't be where we are today. Isn't hindsight a wonderful thing?"

Thomas stared at Elizabeth. "So it *was* you. All along it *was* you!"

"Stop talking," she hissed.

"I fucked her Tom, I fucked her real good."

Thomas stared at him in disbelief, nursing his hand and shaking his head. "No..." he whispered, "No...!"

"She loved it Tom. She begged me for more!" Sean was taunting him, knowing he couldn't do a thing to him now.

"I didn't Tom, I didn't!" Maggie came to life and sat back up. She really wanted to get onto her feet, but that was too difficult at the moment. The gun was still sticking in her gut, reassuring her. She would use it when she could get to her feet. She would save her friends.

"Shut up bitch!" Sean fired a shot in her direction, warning her not to say another word.

She shrank back, her determination wavering very slightly. Could she trust herself to do this? She would have to be quick. And efficient. There wasn't much energy left inside of her.

"It was easy to manoeuvre Maggie into becoming a liability, and the rest is, as they say, history... She fell right where I wanted her."

Thomas and Alex stared at their captors, minds in overdrive, sorting out the confusion.

"Margaret and Dalton PLC are my property." Elizabeth held her gun to Thomas's temple. "You'll hand over every last detail."

"What do you get out of this Sean?" Thomas dared to ask.

"I get promotion at your expense. You're both fired!" He spat the words in their direction.

Elizabeth inched closer. How she had waited for this moment! Her speech was flawless, rehearsed over and over in her mind until she knew it by heart. "This is what I want to happen - and you will do it - otherwise I turn Margaret over to the gutter press. You'll go quietly of course to save what little reputation you and she have left because there are a few things you should know about Margaret," she paused for impact, "She beats her husband and daughter senseless and she's an alcoholic, so much so they want to ditch her. Do you hear that Margaret? Your own family want to cast you off!" Maggie didn't move as her mother continued with her tirade. "Then what happens Margaret? You would've lost everything. Do you hear me? Everything! How does that make you feel? *How does it make you feel?*"

Maggie reached for the gun tucked into her waistband. She was going to do what she should have done years ago. Nobody was looking at her. Thomas and Alex were taking in this latest exposure, shocked to the core, the pieces of the jigsaw finally slotting into place. Wondering at the same time where that left them. Frantically thinking... scrambling for a way out... Sean and Elizabeth were pressing in, getting impatient, waiting for some kind of acknowledgement. Nobody suspected Maggie had a gun. They were fools, the lot of them. Underestimating Maggie Dalton was a mistake. It had always been a mistake. She took aim, steadying her arm. It was going to be beautiful.

The shot rang out and Elizabeth folded and went down. A second bullet escaped Maggie's gun and Sean reeled back, also hit, but at the same time pulling on his own trigger. The bullet went straight through Thomas's head. Alex screamed and dived for Maggie. The gun fell from her grasp as the scene played out in slow motion before her – first Sean hitting the ground, and then Thomas. Her beloved Thomas. Dead. Gone.

Forever.

Her own screams reached fever pitch as Alex held her down. She struggled against him as more bullets zipped around their heads filling the stuffy air with heavy gunfire. She was twenty-one again and looking into the dead face of Bradley Lewis.

"We're in here! We're in here!" Alex shouted, as he pinned Maggie to the floor, "We're ok! Don't shoot! Don't shoot!" He glanced in Thomas's direction and saw his best friend lying there facing him, eyes wide, blank, expressionless, a trickle of blood edging down his forehead. And he knew he would never forget this moment. It was going to haunt him forever.

*

A walker heard the shooting coming from the valley and started to take pictures from her vantage point on the hill. *Bloody hell, this was exciting!*

Reaching for her mobile, she quickly dialled her boyfriend's number, shaking with adrenaline.

"Get here quick! There's a full blown gun fight going on at the deserted cottage on Ramble Lane!"

"Whereabouts are you?"

"On top the hill… Hurry!"

"Shall I call the Police?"

"I would! And an ambulance! Blimin' heck…" She was thrown to the ground. Still able to shout into her phone, she yelled, "The whole lots just exploded! Don't forget to phone Marcie. She'll want a piece of this for her evening news!"

*

James switched over to the ten o'clock news and watched in horror as the latest story unfolded. Pictures were being shown of the very first property he'd set his sights on burning to the ground. In fact, it was all going up in smoke – the barns, the cottage, the outhouses…

The lot.

It was crystal clear to him then, that Maggie had had a hand in all of this, and had done so right from the beginning.

God, it was a terrifying thought.

Maggie knew.

But, for how long?

And where was she? Was she waiting to ambush them?

Oh my god. A lump caught in his throat and he nearly choked on it.

He had to get Emily out of here and safely hidden away before she returned to them, otherwise they would surely be dead.

CHAPTER 17

Maggie threw the earth onto the coffin as the father said the prayers at the graveside burial. She stood there for a moment, head bent, trying not to think about life without her friend, and then wiping a tear from her eye, she took her place back at Alex's side. She had been the last to pay her respects. He slid his arm around her and held her close. United in grief. His other arm was locked around his wife and his two children stood in front of them holding hands, finishing the picture of a family racked with sadness. They had been very fond of their Uncle Tom. Across the grave, Thomas's wife and only son, Thomas Jnr held each other tightly, both quietly sobbing. Maggie's heart bled for them. They could never know the real truth.

It was only a small crowd in black; just close friends and immediate family. Alex had insisted they keep it low key. Very low key. Not even any Media present. He had made a short statement confirming the suicide of Thomas Anderson, Vice Chairman of Dalton PLC and requested privacy during this traumatic and difficult time. The Colonel's back up had dragged Thomas's body from the barn before blowing the whole site to kingdom come. All evidence of the incident had to be destroyed. He had paid off a private doctor to validate that Thomas took his own life in his office up at the estate. Then he'd had the tough job of telling Erica and her son. He soothed them and told them they didn't have to worry about a thing because he and Amy would take care of them, but all the while his mind was in turmoil. How could he lie to Erica like this? How could he lie to his own wife and children? Every night he got on his knees and prayed for forgiveness.

Thomas would never have taken his own life, ever.

Maggie had not been available for comment because she was still too hysterical. Her drinking had worsened and it was taking all of Alex's nerve to keep her on side. He kept her sedated and under a doctor most of the time because not even the thought of Sean and her mother now decorating the countryside with their ashes, and re-electing a new Board of Directors could ease the pain she felt within her. In between shots, when she was fully awake and aware of her surroundings, she confessed to Alex that she wished it had been her to die. Alex desperately hoped she wouldn't make a scene today. He had taken a big risk letting her out so soon after the tragedy. He was keeping her very close and not letting her out of his sight. At any moment she could go off on one, shattering his whole damn cover. Long term he still didn't know what he was going to do with her. Maybe send her away for an indefinite period of time, so he could focus on the business and get it back on track. There was a lot to be done after Sean had been through the place. The real investment trade had been freefalling for at least a month and they were losing more money than they were putting back in. Sean and the bogus Directors had really done some damage…

The service was over and Maggie was first to embrace Erica. She wondered how much or how little Erica knew of her husband's business life for he never talked about his family. Did she know of the affairs? In the beginning they had all socialised as couples - her and James, Thomas and Erica, Alex and Amy – but that hadn't lasted because they soon found themselves pregnant. Then Maggie wanted to disappear off the Socialite scene. She knew Erica and Amy were close and their families still holidayed together. She hoped they could find comfort in each other now. She was too pained to be of any use to anyone, and she didn't want the awkward questions. What could she possibly tell them, if it couldn't be the truth? Drawing back, she let Amy take her place with Erica. Alex tugged her arm.

"Are you ok?" he asked carefully.

She looked deep into his eyes and he struggled to hold her stare. "How can you do this Alex? How can you lie to them all like this?"

He pulled her further away from the gathering, so they couldn't be overheard. "Because we have to Maggie. We don't have a choice. Do you think I feel comfortable lying to the people I love more than anything. It's a sacrifice Maggie…a sacrifice we have to make for Tom."

She laughed then, a sad, empty sound that hung in the air, finally fading away into nothingness. "*We* sacrificed Tom! He always looked after us and this is how we repay him."

"Don't start Maggie, not here." Alex ran his hand through his hair nervously.

"I can't live with myself."

"Well you have to!" He seized her by the shoulders. "You have to Maggie."

She shook her head. "I can't."

*

Beth Cash finished making the drinks and took a moment to observe her husband playing happily with their children. They were taking their annual Easter break in the South of France together. Renting an exclusive villa inside a seven-acre private hilltop estate near Saint Tropez and Gassin, it was another beautiful day stretching out for them to enjoy, and the views towards Pampelonne took her breath away. It had been a wonderful holiday thus far.

She came back outside onto the patio and sat down next to him as Ali and Jason grabbed their drinks and ran off to resume their game of tennis on the courts.

Dan reached for his glass of wine. "You're looking very pensive," he remarked.

"Oh…I was just thinking…"

"About the kids?"

"Yes, about the kids," she smiled at him.

"So…what's bothering you now?"

She took a sip from her glass. "Do you ever wonder if this is a healthy atmosphere for them?"

"You mean you and me…here…together…with the kids? Like a family, even though we're separated?"

"Yes."

"I don't think they would want it any other way Beth."

"But…" she hesitated, "what about us?"

"What about us?" he repeated.

"Is it a healthy atmosphere for *us*? Shouldn't we be moving on with our lives?"

He looked at her. "I can't let you go," he said simply.

Her sudden intake of breath gave away her true emotions. "Don't say things like that Dan. *You* left us remember. *We* haven't gone anywhere."

"Don't hide behind the kids," he teased.

"Don't avoid the issue," she fired back, laughing.

They were quiet for a spell. Then, leaning over she kissed him lightly on the cheek.

"*I haven't gone anywhere.*" Getting up, she walked back towards the kitchen, her skirt dancing in the cool Mediterranean breeze.

He hesitated for a moment, reliving the sensation of her lips graze his skin. He touched the spot where she'd kissed him, and closed his eyes. Snapping them open seconds later, he drained his glass and stood up, following her into the villa.

*

I was listless. Ali and Jason weren't even around to spend time with because they were on holiday with their parents. No sign of Mother now for a whole week. Would she come back today? Unless on holiday herself, she'd never stayed away for longer than a week. I wondered where she was and what was going on. I'd barely touched the housework, enjoying the reprieve and the Easter holidays, and really only thinking of our escape. It surely had to be soon…it had to be…

My father and I were on tenterhooks, and he had been even more uptight all morning. I didn't know why, but I didn't dare ask him. He was out viewing another property right now, and I was anxiously waiting for him to come home to know if finally he had found somewhere for us to run away to. I was also trying to pluck up enough courage to find out if everything was all right. When he was jittery, it usually meant trouble. And it usually meant my mother. Maybe he knew where she was and it was bad news and he was waiting for the right moment to tell me.

Come on Daddy! Come home! I want to know what's going on!

I walked around the house, flicking the television, radio, CD player on and off, trying to distract myself, but without much luck. Hours dragged by until when I least expected it, I heard the door click, and finally he was home.

*

James knew he had all but a price on his head. Maggie would stop at nothing now. When she returned, she would unleash her full fury on James and Emily. So they had to make a break for it, but the clock was ticking...and little by little they were running out of time...

He had decided to tell Emily about the very first cottage going up in smoke. Was it a wise decision? He didn't know for sure, but she was not a child anymore and had witnessed and dealt with far worse. If he couldn't share it all with her, what was the point? She needed to know every single detail so if he didn't make it, she would have the knowledge and determination to go on without him. He already feared the worse. Yet another thing he didn't know for certain. It was just a feeling he had and it was nagging away at him. Making him alert and fearful. Maybe a bad case of paranoia, but then again, maybe not.

Maggie was unpredictable, tempestuous and impulsive. He couldn't read her even if he wanted to.

There were a lot of things to consider besides getting Emily out of there. He was aware of that. Laura needn't have made him feel worse by pointing it out. He should be thinking about a police protection plan and court injunctions and schooling, but they seemed to create chaos and conflict within him. Surely his main priority was to get Emily safe, and always had been? And if they ever got to a civilised custody battle, Maggie would be bound and determined and put up a hard fight. And it would be dirty. Who would testify to the abuse? Who would dare stand up against her in court? He didn't want either Emily or Laura to do it, but he knew they would have to. And so would he.

She would have a good solicitor. The best in the country. And the jury would be got at before they even heard any of the details of the case. They would all be corrupt; there was no doubt in James's mind.

He visibly shivered. In many ways her reign of terror was above the law. She would manipulate, intimidate and use and abuse anyone who stood in her way. She was out of control. They didn't stand a chance and in his heart, James knew it, but because of Emily, he had to keep fighting. *He had to.*

*

"She's going crazy again Mr Coombes. We have to restrain her!" Mrs Peters was trying to grab Maggie's flailing arms, whilst Lucia attempted to sit on her legs. Alex had been urgently summoned to Maggie's quarters to bring some order to the commotion he saw before him. He immediately intervened and grabbed Maggie's arms from the housekeeper, pinning them to her side.

Slightly out of breath, he said, "Give her the shot now Carmen before she has a chance to break free again. Lucia, hold her legs for as long as you can. I don't want a kick in the head!"

Lucia smiled up at Alex. She dearly missed the master of the house, Mr Anderson, but there couldn't have been a better replacement than in Mr Coombes. Even though he hadn't taken steps to move in permanently, he was always there for the staff whenever they needed him. Gentle and kind and never speaking harshly to any of them, he kept control and knew exactly what to do in an emergency, like now. He was a true Godsend after the tragedy that had befallen their household.

Mrs Peters gingerly held the needle above Maggie wondering which arm to sink it into. She quickly picked her right and administered the liquid sedative. Maggie continued to thrash against the mattress for a few seconds, as Alex and Lucia let her go and got up from the bed together, then she lay back, her head falling into the pillows and closed her eyes.

"She's found peace again Mister Coombes," Lucia said, still smiling at him.

"That she has," he remarked, "so if that's all, I better be off." He stooped down to Maggie and brushed her cheek with his lips, and then nodding to Mrs Peters, he left the room.

"Thank you!" she called after him.

Maggie was drowsy, but not totally out as Lucia went into the bathroom to get a bowl of soapy water and a cloth to bathe her with.

Mrs Peters sat down beside Maggie and took her hand. She squeezed it gently reassuring her. This was how it had been for the best part of a week now. Alex had brought Maggie to them and told them how Thomas had taken his life and Maggie had found him. She was to remain in their care under sedation because she was unable to cope with her horrific discovery. Mrs Peters knew there was more to the story and the rumours circulating around the estate only served to fuel the possibilities. She too couldn't believe that Mr Anderson would have killed himself, but she also didn't think Mr Coombes would have murdered his best friend. They were inseparable and it was ludicrous to even contemplate it. Yet, she couldn't help overhearing the gardeners talking amongst themselves. She hadn't been privy to the whole conversation, but according to their version of events, Mr Anderson was already dead when he returned to the estate. They had obviously witnessed his body returning in one of the cars...

Maggie stirred and Mrs Peters shook the thoughts from her mind. She needed to concentrate on the here and now for Maggie's sake, not speculate on what could have happened that fateful night.

"Carmen," Maggie whispered.

Mrs Peters could see it was a great effort for her to speak, so she tried to hush her back to sleep.

"Carmen... Carmen..." Maggie wasn't giving up.

"Hush my dear...hush... You need to rest after that little episode."

"Carmen," Maggie persisted, "listen to me...please listen to me..."

"What is it my dear? What's the matter?"

Maggie fell silent, her eyes closed and Mrs Peters thought she had finally settled. She was just about to say something soothing, when Maggie spoke again, very softly and it was hard for the housekeeper to catch the words.

"Carmen, I've done something terrible..."

Mrs Peters didn't react. She didn't want to know the ins and outs of events leading up to Mr Anderson's death. It wasn't her place to know such things. What had happened had happened, and it had been God's Will. No amount of remorse or confession was going to change that. Maggie was her charge and she Maggie's confidant. She had promised to take care of her, and it was a lifetime's promise meaning nothing Maggie did, however bad, would ever change the situation.

"Help me Carmen...please help me..."

"There, there my dear. It's been a terrible ordeal for you. But you must rest now." She patted Maggie's hand, not wanting her to go on for fear of what she might say.

"Will you help me Carmen? Promise you will help me...I have to make amends as soon as I'm well again...I have to do it...You're the only one I can trust..."

She was getting worked up. Beads of sweat were building on her forehead and for a moment Mrs Peters thought there might be another fight, but Maggie was weak and the sedative was working through her now. She opened her mouth to speak, but no sound came out.

Mrs Peters leaned in close, knowing this wasn't the end of it, but fully aware Maggie may have forgotten all about it when she awoke the next morning. After all, she had been prone to the odd fit of fallacy in the past. This was nothing new.

Nevertheless, she vowed to herself that she wouldn't say a word to anyone, not even to Mr Coombes.

"If you need help, I will be here," she murmured into Maggie's hair, as she kissed her tenderly and sat back down to wait for Lucia. Maggie was many things, but she wasn't a murderer... *was she?*

*

"Maggie we've been over this already! You can't leave here until I feel sure you're going to be ok." Alex was perched on the edge of the sofa in Maggie's private sitting room. He sipped at his Scotch, watching her pacing the room.

"You can't keep me here as a prisoner!" she snapped.

"I can and I will Maggie."

"You can't!" She was getting agitated with him. He was controlling her and she didn't like it. She thought her controlling days were over once she witnessed her mother and that bastard get shot to pieces. She should have been rejoicing now. Free at last... But they weren't over. They were far from over.

Alex didn't trust her to step outside and keep her silence about the events that played out that day. He didn't want to let her go. She was going to quietly go insane, stuck with only Mrs Peters and Lucia and Cook for company. It wasn't right of Alex to make her do this! It wasn't fair of him to hold her prisoner!

"I have to get out! I'll go crazy cooped up here for the rest of my life!" Desperation tinged her words. She held her head in her hands and gripped her hair.

"What? And go back to your husband and daughter who you beat? Go back to your alcohol? What kind of life is that

Maggie, honestly? You need to calm down...then you need rehab. After rehab, you can go on a long holiday until I get everything back on track with the business."

"Rehab!" She spat the words, still clinging to her hair with both hands.

"Yes...rehab, counselling, whatever they call it these days. It isn't a dirty word and you need help. You can't go back to your old existence. I didn't know things had got so bad with you." He spoke quietly, all the while contemplating. He should have kept a closer eye on her. Her life had spiralled into a nightmare. *She* was a total nightmare.

"You can't control me!" she practically shouted in his face, evidently on the verge of another hysterical fit.

"Maggie, listen to me." He put his glass down and came to her, taking her gently by the shoulders. "This isn't about control. This is about getting you back to where you should be, to the Maggie I once knew. Right now, you're like a stranger to me."

Suddenly devoid of energy, she let him embrace her. "Don't you care Alex? Don't you care about any of it? Don't you care we have blood on our hands?" Her head fell onto his shoulder and he felt her body heave as she sobbed.

He chose not to answer, instead concentrating his efforts to comfort her, but little did he know that deep beneath the tears the feisty, unstoppable Maggie was preparing to resurface. She had to get out of here and she would ask her faithful friend and bodyguard Johnny to help her, like he had done so many, many times before.

Maggie Dalton could never be contained! She was a free spirit making her own way in this World. Trusting and relying on no one, and backing and following her instincts. The revelations about her personal life were the last straw. She had to take care of things her way.

*

Over a fortnight without my mother and we were beginning to wonder whether she would ever return. Maybe she *had* taken an impromptu holiday. As time went on it was bothering me less and less, but having the opposite effect on my father. He was working hard on securing the new property he'd found for us and spending the rest of his time with me, making every second count. He said every moment was precious and we should treasure it. I didn't get it, but I went along with him. He'd told me about the very first cottage being blown to bits and like him I was initially frightened and worried, but surely if she was on our trail, wouldn't she be home beating the truth out of us? It was some consolation she wasn't. I was gradually convincing myself the two events were not linked. Every day that went by and she didn't come home; it was easier to convince myself. Finally, my father said we would go tomorrow and not look back, but when tomorrow came, I asked for one more day and he really believed it would be ok…and I did too…

*

So when Maggie returned, they were totally unsuspecting. Her absence had lulled them into a false sense of safety. They thought it wouldn't matter. Just one more day. Just…one…more…day…
But it was going to make all the difference. All the difference in the world.

*

James stepped out into the early May sunshine waiting for Emily to join him. She was round the back of the house, taking one last look at the garden, lingering to touch and smell the flowers she would probably never see again. She looked up to bask in the warm sun and it was only then that her eyes came to rest on her mother, leaning lazily up against the wall only a few feet in front of her. Johnny had dropped Maggie right outside, but she'd told him not to wait. She didn't want any witnesses. She'd made her way quietly to the back of the house to steel herself for what she was about to do. Nursing a bottle of scotch, she hadn't had to wait too long. It appeared she'd come back just in time. One more day and they would have been out of her life forever. It would have been too late to get her revenge. Timing was everything to Maggie. Timing was critical.

Both mother and daughter stood perfectly still staring at each other across the pond. Maggie raised the gun in her hand. "Get in the house. Now!"

Emily's heart leapt into her throat and pounded her ears with its beat. *A gun!*

She did as she was told, making her way slowly and carefully back inside, never taking her eyes off the weapon. The terror and panic it was stirring within her was hypnotic.

"Sit!"

Emily climbed onto a stool at the bar and waited. She didn't know what she was waiting for.

James was getting impatient to be off. He walked around the house but Emily wasn't there. Retracing the steps Emily and Maggie had taken just seconds before, he wandered back inside the house and nearly passed out when he saw Maggie first with the gun, and then Emily cowering on a stool.

"Don't shoot her!" he cried out.

Maggie swung the gun on him.

"There you are!" she hissed, "All of us together at last."

James decided to brave a confrontation. If this was to be his last ever fight with Maggie, he wanted to make it count. He wanted to make sure he gave as good as he got.

Except she had a gun...

That disadvantaged him straight away.

He looked wildly around the room trying to find a weapon for himself. "What do you want with us? You haven't been home in weeks!" He saw a clay statue on the mantelpiece. That would be perfect, if only he could just get to it. He started to edge towards the living room.

The gun followed him. "I'm doing what I should have done a long time ago. Things have been overtaking me recently, and then it came to me in my darkest hour - like a flash of brilliant light - what I must do. Eradicate the problems as they announce themselves, and don't ever look back." She slurred on her words, but her hand was pretty steady for someone so drunk.

"So...we're a problem, is that it?" James wanted to keep her talking for as long as he could. His mind was in overdrive.

Emily sat rooted to her seat, unable to help her father. She registered the conversation playing out before her, but her whole body was immobilised by shock and fear. She couldn't even open her mouth to speak. They'd gone to bed happy and contented and the very next morning woken up to *this*! Her mind too was in a tailspin. This was supposed to be the perfect day. The day when they finally ran away and started a new life for good. No more pain. No more abuse. No more tears... But the ironical twist was, Maggie didn't even have to beat them or shout or threaten anymore. The gun was doing all of the intimidating for her. With a gun she was all-powerful, larger than life and more terrifying than ever. She had the ultimate advantage now. There was absolutely no way out for them.

"No, just you James. You've always been a problem to me."

He stopped moving to stare at her. "What?"

"You're the next problem," she said calmly. The gun was still straight out in front of her. She held it with both hands, concentrating hard.

He didn't reply immediately. He was almost at the statue. Just a few more steps...

"So what about Emily?"

Maggie pondered the question as James inched towards the mantelpiece. In truth she didn't know what she was going to do with Emily once this was over. Keep her as a cleaner and punch bag most probably. That's all her daughter had ever been to her anyway. A weak and pathetic excuse for a human being.

"I'm going to kill you now James. Don't make a scene. I don't want the neighbours to hear."

"You're crazy and insane Maggie!" James's fingers clasped around the statue.

"Maybe, but I think this is for the best." Her finger inched back on the trigger.

"You can't kill my father!" Something snapped inside of Emily as she leapt off the stool and flung herself at her mother. Maybe it was years of belittlement finally coming to a head, or maybe it was one too many bad scenes witnessed. She didn't know, and she didn't have time to rationalise her feelings of pure hatred for this monster she called her mother. Anger ripped through her body and adrenaline pumped into her veins. She was reaching out for Maggie, wanting to strike her down...

At the same time James hurled the statue in Maggie's direction…

But they were both too late.

The bullet had left the gun.

Nobody saw it hit James. He didn't even see it. As the statue crashed around them, Emily dived on the floor to avoid being knocked out by stray pieces. She watched her father fall to the ground and saw Maggie jump out of the way until the chaos settled, then make her way back to her husband. Standing over him, she fired another bullet into his head. Emily couldn't move. Tears erupted from her eyes and she held herself tight rocking backwards and forwards on her knees.

Totally alone, it cut her to the core. The aching and numbness within her tore her to pieces. She beat the floor with her fists feeling all of the pain and anguish her mother had caused them over the years exploding around her. All of the injustice. All of the horror.

And now it had come to this… it was over.

Maggie had betrayed them. Taken from them what wasn't hers to take. Her father was dead. Murdered in cold blood.

He would never again hold her. Never again whisper how much he loved her. Never again kiss her goodnight.

"I love you Daddy! I love you!" she wailed, but he couldn't hear her. He would never hear her again.

*

"You've taken everything from me!" I wept and howled as I kicked and screamed for what little was left of my soul, "You knew I loved him and you took him from me! You took him! So kill me! I want you to kill me now!" I clawed at the table leg as she dragged me out. Rolling me onto my stomach, she stuffed some cloth into my mouth and tied my hands behind my back, but that didn't stop me thrashing about with my legs. She had destroyed me and now I wanted her to finish the job. I wanted to be with my father. I wanted to be safe. I didn't want to be stuck with this monster for the rest of my life.

She pulled me to my feet and ordered me outside, the gun sticking in the small of my back. I stopped fighting and tried to channel my energy into focusing on the feeling the gun was making. If I forced myself back on her and we fell, would her finger tug the trigger and put a bullet in me?

She stopped at the shed and pulled out a shovel. The garden was secluded, stretching out towards the forest. Our neighbours on either side couldn't see in because the house stood on its own at the end of the street. I prayed somebody would be up at the stables, but would they all be out riding now? Time had stopped for me. I no longer wanted to live. She pushed me passed the pond and on towards the trees. Eventually we stopped and she undid my hands and took out my gag. Stepping away, she threw the shovel down at my feet.

"Don't scream," she warned.

"I wouldn't anyway. I want you to kill me like you killed my father." I heard myself retorting as tears started streaming down my face again. The hopelessness was clawing inside me like a knawing pain.

"Start digging child!" she ordered.

"Is this my grave?" I dared to mock, a part of me hoping it was.

"No. It's your fathers."

I stopped in my tracks and the shovel clattered to the floor.

"Go to hell!" I shouted.

"Don't mess with me child! Do as I say!" She raised the gun and I just stood there. This is what I wanted. I wanted to die. She must have seen it in my eyes because she stooped to pick up the shovel and thrust it into my hand.

"I won't give you what you want," she hissed, "I'm not going to make this easy for you."

I held up the shovel. "I won't do it! Not now! Not ever!"

"Dig, or I'll riddle your legs with bullets and make you kneel at your father's graveside until the hole is deep enough. It could be a very long time before the hole gets deep enough and a horrible way to die, bleeding to death. Slow and painful I imagine…" She lit a cigarette. "Your choice."

I glared at her and blinked away my tears. If I was to die, I wanted it to be quick like my father's death. What if I didn't die and she only maimed me? I'd have to live with that for the rest of my life, being pushed around in a wheelchair. The thought was horrific.

"You manipulative bitch!" I hated her. I wanted to hurt her bad, but I wanted her to hurt me more than ever. Why wasn't she beating me? I wanted her to beat me. I needed to feel her anger and rage. I needed it to consume me. I didn't want her to control me like this. So quietly. So serenely.

I shut my eyes and gripped the shovel. I started to dig. I took my despair out on the earth. Sweat poured from my body while she stood calmly, watching, puffing methodically on her cigarette until it burned low, and then lighting another.

"I'm going to get a drink. Don't try anything. I'll find you, maim you and bring you back to dig. You can be sure of that." She was already walking back to the house.

It was a risk, but she knew she had me exactly where she wanted me. Dancing around in the palm of her hand.

I couldn't take this anymore. Tears sprang up again and flowed down my face. I let them fall around what was to be my father's graveside. *Oh god, my father!* Every time I saw his face in my mind, the pain shot through me and crippled my heart. I dropped the shovel and clutched at my chest.

"Mother!"

She turned to face me, the gun still in her hands and the fresh cigarette burning on her lips. We stood there for no time at all and then suddenly, overcome with all of the many emotions bombarding every part of me, I ran at her screaming and shouting, fists raised, looking to make contact... and the gun went off for a third and final time.

And I just knew in that single, precious moment that our lives would never be the same again.

EPILOGUE

"Shit, it hurts Johnny!" Maggie groaned, looking down at the wound in her thigh. They'd tied it up tight, but the blood was seeping through. Johnny was driving fast to the mooring. He'd arranged for a doctor to meet them on the yacht so Maggie could be fixed up. Then they had to get the hell away. That was as far as the planning had got. The gunshot blasting out in the calm of the still, May morning had brought some clarity to Maggie's mind. As the bullet pierced her leg, she'd swung out and knocked Emily to the floor. Her daughter had been out cold and she hadn't stopped to check whether dead or alive. She'd phoned Johnny to pick her up before the alarm was raised. Anybody and everybody would have heard the shot - and she couldn't be linked to it. It would be the ruin of her - and that's not what this plan had been about - it was supposed to signify the beginning...*not the end*...

*

"What happened to you?" Beth murmured for the hundredth time as she gazed at Emily through the window in the private hospital ward. She had been standing there for some time watching, desperately wishing Emily to turn her head and acknowledge the presence of her tutor. But she never did, and Beth's heart was bleeding for her. Every day for the last week she had done this. It was now a part of her daily routine. She wouldn't let Ali, or Jason, or Ben visit, but she was always there, every day, without fail.

Emily was lying perfectly still, on her back and staring straight ahead. She didn't seem aware of the armed police guard that was taking turns keeping watch over her, or know that she was a murder suspect.
She hadn't spoken since being hospitalised and refused to eat or drink. She hadn't even changed her position in the bed. She was like a ghost, her skin translucent and her body fragile. Small, lost and vulnerable, the room engulfed her. There was no fight in her when the nurses fed wires into her body and she was hooked up to a drip. It was almost like she was giving up on life and willing herself to die, and this pained

Beth more than she could bear to dwell on. A doctor and psychiatrist came to see her daily, but so far Emily had not broken her silence and showed no signs of ever doing so. If this went on, they would soon be forced to move her to inpatient psychiatric care.

Beth hadn't known what else to do when she found her hugging the corpse of her dead father, sobbing and delirious. It had been a horrific sight; blood spattered everywhere and the remnants of a struggle. Jayne Hartford had been coming in from a hack when she heard the gun go off. Immediately she was suspicious and phoned the police. They went searching in the nearby woods, and by the time Jayne had phoned Beth, they had already uncovered a makeshift grave on the edge of the Bridges's estate. Beth had rushed over to the big house, found the door open and let herself in. The police weren't far behind. She felt silly afterwards putting her life at risk, but Emily meant so much to her, and she hadn't thought about the danger. Emily was hospitalised in a prison ward straight away, but Beth had insisted she move to a private residential ward instead. She couldn't believe Emily had murdered her father, *she just couldn't*. Dan had pulled the necessary strings and obtained clearance for Emily to move, he was also footing the bill because he knew how much this meant to Beth. He was already working on Emily's case, but there was no way of finding out what had happened to Emily or her father until she chose to speak up. Rumours were circulating that Maggie Dalton was missing. *Had she murdered her husband?* Forensics had been at the house and items had gone to the lab to be tested. The police were still searching for the weapon. There was confusion surrounding the packed up car in the driveway. It looked as if James and Emily had been leaving that morning – but to where? Dan was still working on proving this theory. If he could come up with something concrete, he knew he had a case for Emily. A week ago he had received an anonymous phone call requesting representation for Dalton PLC. He had stalled trying to find out more about it before he committed. There had been no more phone calls after that.

It was a complete mystery to Beth, and the children were impatient to know what was going on with their best friend. Beth couldn't answer their questions. It was assumed she was suffering with posttraumatic stress and that's all she'd been able to tell them. There was an aunty, her father's sister, but so far attempts to contact her had been futile, as had the attempts to contact her paternal grandparents. It seemed to Beth astonishingly that everyone had deserted Emily in her most critical hour, and she couldn't get her head around that at all. Who were these people and how could they do such a thing? Was the family in some kind of trouble and had simply fled the country leaving Emily to fend for herself? Was she such a burden to them that nobody else wanted to take on the responsibility of caring for her?

Beth looked up to the heavens for some inspiration. Nothing made sense. She sighed heavily as she took one last look at Emily and turned to leave. Her mobile started to ring as she walked down the corridor.

"Hello?"

"Beth, it's Dan."

"Hi, I'm just leaving the hospital now."

"Beth, listen to me. I've finally got evidence James was moving out. He bought another property. We've found the paper trail."

"Did you tell them I suspected abuse?"

"Yes. We know he was taking Emily with him. Her stuff was in the car too. And there's something else… Some of the results came back this morning. Maggie Dalton was in the house at the time of the murder."

There was a moment's silence. "So she came back…and saw them leaving…and she…she…she…mur…" Beth couldn't finish the sentence. She was horrified.

"That's what I believe too. The police have issued a warrant for her arrest." He paused. "Let me buy you a drink. I'll be outside the hospital in a sec."

Beth ended the call and put her phone back in her pocket. She slumped against the wall and closed her eyes. *What had Emily witnessed?* It was terrifying and difficult to comprehend. She looked back up towards Emily's ward and for a moment almost ran back there, her mind flooded with foolish ideas of trying to get Emily to talk to her. But it was no use. She knew

Emily would not speak until she had the courage to do so. And that would take time, especially if she had witnessed these terrible events.

Yes, it would almost certainly take time.

Lightning Source UK Ltd.
Milton Keynes UK

176566UK00001B/25/P